Susan E. D. Smith, John Little

The Soldier's friend; being a thrilling narrative of Grandma Smith's

four Years' experience and observations, as Matron

Susan E. D. Smith, John Little

The Soldier's friend; being a thrilling narrative of Grandma Smith's
four Years' experience and observations, as Matron

ISBN/EAN: 9783337018177

Printed in Europe, USA, Canada, Australia, Japan

Cover: Foto ©Andreas Hilbeck / pixelio.de

More available books at **www.hansebooks.com**

THE

SOLDIER'S FRIEND;

BEING A

THRILLING NARRATIVE

OF GRANDMA SMITH'S FOUR YEARS' EXPERIENCE AND
OBSERVATION, AS MATRON, IN THE HOSPITALS
OF THE SOUTH, DURING THE LATE DISAS-
TROUS CONFLICT IN AMERICA.

———

BY MRS. S. E. D. SMITH.

———

REVISED BY REV. JOHN LITTLE,

AND DEDICATED TO

The Rebel Soldiers.

———

MEMPHIS, TENN:
PRINTED BY THE BULLETIN PUBLISHING COMPANY.
1867.

BULLETIN
PUBLISHING COMPANY,
BINDERS,
No. 222 Second street.

DEDICATION.

TO ALL

TRUE PHILANTHROPISTS,

AS WELL AS ALL TRUE

PATRIOTIC LOVERS OF TRUE VALOR;

AND ALL WHO CAN SYMPATHIZE WITH

SUFFERING AND THE DISAPPOINTED,

THIS WORK IS

RESPECTFULLY DEDICATED.

PREFACE.

The following work is unlike anything else ever offered to the public. In all the wars which compose so large a a portion of the History of this world, there was never a book written in such a place as a hospital, and by such a person as an *uneducated*, but Christian Matron.

The authoress, gives, in language which fictitious writers would fain counterfeit, the scenes and incidents connected with warfares which are usually left behind the curtain. Perhaps the world would not so fondly relish the glories of war, if this vail were lifted, so as to exhibit the various phases of human suffering, protracted, or relieved as circumstances may enable or disable the various officers of the hospital.

This book, should it be issued from the press, goes not forth, in a vindictive spirit to advocate a cause that has been forever abandoned, but which, during the services of the author, was thought to be a just one; but the object is to hold a light within the darkest recesses of the soldiers' bloody march down the road of carnage.

Let the reader forget every other feature of the work but the one last mentioned above, and he will pray that there should never be another war.

· PARVUS.

THE SOLDIER'S FRIEND.

CHAPTER I.

The writer was born in Wilson County, Middle Tennessee, July 23, 1817, of parents whose names were Lewis and Sarah Kirby, who emmigrated from Nash County, North Carolina, to Middle Tennessee, at a very early day, when it was almost a howling wilderness, (as my mother has often told me,) there being but here and there a family interspersed. My parents settled on a small piece of land owned by Britton Drake, Esq., first cousin to my father. Their affection and esteem for each other was very great. They derived much pleasure in being near neighbors; however, their almost unalloyed happiness was enjoyed but for a short period of time, ere death, by his unrelenting and obtrusive hand, dashed the cup from their lips and spread darkness and gloom over our once happy circle, and blighted forever the anticipated happiness, those two cousins had hoped the future held in reservation for them and families, by removing forever from our midst my beloved father, leaving my mother with six small children to grope her way through this inhospitable and uncharitable world as best she could.

In the spring of 1818, my eldest brother returned from

A*

a visit to New Orleans, where he had contracted that most dreaded disease of all diseases, the small pox. This was communicated to the entire family—my father proving its first victim—and myself becoming a cripple for life, an afflicted orphan, at a period too young to realize the loss of, doubtless, an affectionate father, and the misfortune of being a cripple. On my brother's arrival, his disease, by the symptoms, was not detected either by the family or the neighbors, until my father consulted a medical book and learned therein, with sad dismay, the true character of the disease. Until then, the neighbors had not ceased to visit him, and tender every attention in their power, but as soon as the disease was determined they became alarmed, and at once ceased to visit him or the family, leaving my mother, alone, the arduous task of nursing the entire family, (seven in number), all of whom soon manifested symptoms of the disease. My father called in two of the most eminent physicians the country could afford; Dr. Samuel Hogg, of Nashville, and Dr. Frazier, of Lebanon, our residence being but six miles from the latter place. Subsequently two good nurses were procured, Uncle Pat (as we were taught to call him) from the Emerald Isle; also, a negro woman belonging to Mr. Martin, living near by, both of whom had had the small pox, who rendered great assistance to my mother at a time of so much need, and when she was laboring under such great distress. Our neighbors, notwithstanding they had ceased to visit us, manifested great kindness in sending us nourishment. They would deposit it at a safe distance from the house, from whence it was brought by the nurses, who also communicated the condition of the family to our kind and anxious neighbors, who were awaiting in the forest hard by. It was a trying time to my dear mother, eight in family, and she alone, scarcely able to render any assistance to the sick. She, fortunately, had it very slight.

My mother, having been deprived of the assistance and
sympathy of our kind neighbors, had alone, to bear up
under the crushing weight of doubt and fear, for the ter-
.mination of the disease.   Father, brothers and myself
remained for many long and anxious days and nights in a
critical situation.

After the death of my father, the neighbors being fearful to approach the house to render assistance in his
burial, that sad duty had to be performed alone by my
mother and the two nurses. Can the reader imagine a
scene more sad and heart-rending, a weak and helpless
woman bearing her own husband's lifeless body to its last
resting place with none but the two nurses affording any
assistance? What added more sadness and gloom to the occasion, my mother was denied the poor privilege of burying
him in the common graveyard, lest the disease might be
spread thereby. She, therefore, was compelled to bury him
in a lonely spot in the silent woods.

Who, but those that have passed through kindred scenes
of affliction, can realize the heart-rending anguish of the
occasion? Pen and language are too inadequate to portray the remotest idea of the reality.   The effects of
those events bore heavily upon my mother, tincturing all
her subsequent joys with a degree of sadness.   Time will
never erase from memory the sad sensation which
would steal through my young heart, while sitting
by my mother's side, listening to the recitals of those trying and sad events. Oft would she clasp me to her bosom
and call me her dear little crippled fatherless babe.

I was petted and caressed by all the members of the
family, especially by my brother, who brought the disease
into the family circle; he ever proved affectionate, and his
actions, at all times, evinced the fact that he felt at heart,
with deep regret, as being the lone cause of my orphanage
and bodily affliction.

I was three years old before I began to walk; and it was not until then, that it was known that I was a cripple.

Since I have become a mother, I can readily imagine a mother's grief at the knowledge of her last babe having to contend with all the trying vicissitudes of this world a cripple. But such was my fate.

When I arrived at the age of maturity, I was constrained to thank God for thus afflicting me. This remark may seem strange to some, but when I assign my reasons for it, they will not wonder at my seeming rashness.

I was lively in my disposition, and generally commanded friends and near and dear associates wherever I might be thrown; many who were gay, and fond of the amusements of those days, such as dancing, etc., etc., which I always admired. Could I have indulged in the so-called innocent amusements, and all the temptations which were set before me, in all probability I would have yielded, and would have been led off to serve sin and the devil, instead of the living God.

But as it was, I had no desire to attend such places, not even as a spectator; my mind, therefore, was directed to better and more lasting pleasures. At a very early age I was led, by the mercy of God, to seek a home where parents and children (who have long been separated, by death, in this world) will meet to part no more, forever; and where those who have endured a life-time's affliction in this sin-smitten world, will have the free use of their limbs, and where they can walk the golden streets of the new Jerusalem.

I therefore thank God for affliction.

Through my affliction I was brought to seek the salvation of my soul.

Should I have retained all the faculties of my body, I might have lived in sin and folly, and have died a wretched sinner.

When it was known that I was lamed by the small-pox, it created quite a sensation among the neighbors, as well as untold grief in the family circles. I elicited great sympathy from all who knew me; my playmates were ready to lend me assistance in our sports and plays.

I felt the affectionate respect shown me, even at an early day, and I still love the names of my mother's kind old neighbors and their children for the kindness manifested towards me.

It was a case of much consultation and minute examination among the physicians of the surrounding country—all trying to divine the cause of the effect of the disease upon me. I yet remember distinctly how fearful I became on seeing any gentleman riding towards our house. I would at once make for the nearest hiding place, and it was not until a promise from my mother of a lump of maple sugar, of which I was very fond, was made, that I could be induced to make my appearance before the doctors.

The doctors seldom left me without placing some little token of affection in my hands, which greatly endeared them to me, notwithstanding my fear of them, growing out of the impression I had imbibed of their intention of amputating my leg; I therefore suffered almost constant fear until I was six years of age, or upwards, when all hopes of bettering my condition was abandoned, and I dismissed to go in peace.

It was an evident fact that I would never enjoy the ineffable pleasure of taking one even step in this life. I now am fully impressed that had the surgeons of those days been as ready to try experiments as the surgeons of the present age, my affliction might have been greatly alleviated.

Yet I murmur not at the doings of God. "He doeth all things well." I meekly bow to His holy will, knowing it is all for the best.

My mother did not live long at the place where my father

died. Soon after that sad event, she leased a place on Cedar
creek, near an "Old Side Baptist" church, or "meeting
house," in which Mr. Willis and Uncle Billy White were
the preachers. During our severe affliction, already detailed, the latter was a friend indeed. The place of bap-
tizing was near my mother's house; and it was there I
I first witnessed an immersion. And here permit
me to relate an incident which occurred at one of those
"baptizings," that was quite amusing at the time it transpired, and caused some criticism. There were several
baptized, and among them some ladies. As one of them
was being raised out of the water, a good old brother who
was sitting at the root of a tree near the bank of the stream,
was heard to exclaim, in a loud tone, "dip her again, Brother
Willis, for all of her head did not go under!" At that
suggestion, Brother Willis dipped her the second time,
which seemed to give full satisfaction to the old brother.
The circumstance is as fresh in my memory as though it
occurred but recently; and perhaps I am not the only one
living who witnessed, and who recollects, that event—yet
but few of the old settlers of that neighborhood are now
living. Time, with its ever mowing scythe, has cut them
down, and they have passed away, and others have taken
their places.

Among my mother's neighbors was Frank Anderson,
father of Paul Anderson, Sr., and grand father of Paul
Anderson, Jr., colonel in the late Confederate army. Our
families were intimate friends and associates. The few
years we lived near them were spent in almost unalloyed
happiness—at least by the juvenile part of the families.

Those were days in which my mind began to dawn and
expand. The recollection of the events are vivid, and seem
but as yesterday, yet I am now classed with those called old.

Col. Paul Anderson, Jr., was the first infant I ever beheld.
I now remember well how I loved Mrs. Anderson's little

black-eyed babe, little dreaming, in a future day, we should be participants in one of the most stupendous wars ever recorded in history; he in the field, and I in the hospital. The memories of those days are pleasant. O days, sweet days of my childhood, how I love thee still!

But time with its stern realities soon cast a gloomy shade over those once happy days. How fondly would I erase from recollection the events of my latter days, especially the last four years of unparalleled carnage, devastation and ruin; also, the present thralldom and oppression that my people have to endure. It is pleasant to brush from memory for a time the recollection of these unpleasant events, and roam in fancy, fields of juvenile days, when with my beloved brothers, and only dear sister, with our fishing tackle in hand, stealing along through the green forest to the banks of the babbling brook, where each one, with heart elated, dashed the baited hook into the limpid stream, expecting soon to lift the shining perch therefrom. With the sweet warblings of the feathered songsters, perched upon the adjacent trees, regaling our ears with their melodies; or, with my brothers, chasing the butterfly through the green meadows, and anon throwing stones at the water moccasins, which were abundant in those days; or, perhaps, from a stream flowing from a large spring of crystal waters, wherein we oft did slake our thirst when we would become weary of our innocent sports.

O, how I love, in fancy, to live over again my tripping along the green path, on a pleasant summer's eve, by the side of my loved and adored mother, to the house of our ever pleasant and kind neighbor, Mr. Paul Anderson—my young heart throbbing with delight at the thought of having a romp and play with little Paul. Yes, I love to be a child again. It gives fresh vigor to the soul, and strength to the wearied mind, and enables us to more successfully battle with the trying events of the present, and to more fully contemplate the joys and happiness held in reservation for those who serve God upon earth, when they have ceased to labor and to suffer in this vale of sorrow, grief and tears, and are transplanted to that heavenly Eden where the redeemed of the Lord shall sing anthems of praises to that God who has redeemed us from the thralldom of sin, and washed us white in his own precious blood.

I hope the reader will not charge me with incredulity, when I affirm a faith in the recognition of friends in the spirit land, that have long been lost to our embrace in this sin-smitten world of ours. For the faith within me, I offer the consoling language of the Apostle, "We shall see as we are seen; and know, also, as we are known." I cultivate the consoling impression, that if in this mortal life we possess the faculty of knowing each other, we will know also in the life which is to come, where our minds will be more vivid, and more capable of comprehension. I was more forcibly impressed with this subject on being thrown among some of my long absent friends, some of whom I had not seen for forty years. O, what sensations of exquisite pleasure and joy pervaded my being upon that occasion. Surely it was akin to heaven.

One of the number that formed that happy group was the veritable Col. Paul Anderson, the once wee little babe I loved so fondly, to whom I have above alluded. I need not tell the reader I gazed upon him with that scrutiny that gave satisfaction to my mind, and filled me with unutterable joy and gratitude. To know that God, who had preserved me through all the trying vicissitudes of my life, permitted me to look once again upon the form of him who had been the idol of my childish heart in the days when I knew no sin, was to me a pleasure indeed. He, however, knew me not, having left his neighborhood ere he was old enough to retain lasting impressions of any one.

Eight summers passed, and my fond and indulgent

mother was claimed by the King of Terrors as his lawful prey, leaving me a crippled orphan at the age when I most stood in need of a mother's counsel and affection. How sadly I felt my bereavement. Yet too young to fully realize the loss of an only parent, I felt, for a time, as though I could not live without my mother. There was no one to fill her place in my lonely heart, or in the family circle. The vacant chair could not be filled. The void thus created in my heart could not be reoccupied.

It was several years after my mother's death before I met with any one who could come near filling her place. My brothers all were very kind to me, and seemed to idolize me, but my oldest brother seemed to manifest special care and affection for me; in fact, he became to me as my all in all. I almost adored him.

My sister, though young, acted nobly, was kind, and loved always to make us comfortable and happy; and through her industry and maternal care my brother was enabled to keep us together. A short time before my mother's death, my brother purchased a home, which was then known as the Bethel place—named after Bethlehem church, near by. At that place mother spent the last two years of her widowed life, breathing her last on the 25th of September, 1826.

Mournfully, her six orphan and beloved children, with a large concourse of friends, followed her to her last resting place. With hearts filled with unutterable grief we saw our last earthly parent and dearest friend consigned to the cold and silent grave by the side of our father, who had slept there for eight years.

The mournful and saddening scene of that day left a lasting and touching impression upon my young and tender heart; but time, with its sad realities, admonished us that we were alone, and that it behooved us to do the best we could for ourselves. At the close of the second summer of our orphanage, we were found making preparations to leave our dear old home, with all the fond ties that clustered around that lovely spot.

My brother having purchased a home in Brownsville, West Tennessee, which was at that time a new part of the State, land being cheap, with other great inducements, we moved to that part of the country. Several of our neighbors had already located there, and many followed soon after—among whom were Peter Rogers, William Moore, William Harding and Esquire Purtle, all of Wilson county.

Soon after our mother's death, my second and third brothers left home in order to learn a trade, preferring it to farming. Again the family circle must be broken, perhaps never to be again united. How sad was that separation! Young as I was, it was almost insufferable to see my two brothers leave the once parental fireside to battle with the cold and indifferent world, and seek a home among strangers. They had been my playmates; and as comforters in part, since my mother's death, deeply I deplored their departure, and that parting has never been erased from my memory. But such is life. The swift wings of time hurry us on from event to event, and from scene to scene, and when we arrive at mature age, we can look back upon the past with wonder and surprise at the many trying and heart rending scenes we have passed through, and yet we live; but God in his infinite wisdom and mercy "tempers the wind to the shorn lamb," and suffers us not to be tempted and tried beyond that which we are able to bear—giving unmistakable evidence that as our days may demand, His strength will ever be.

In February, 1828, my oldest and yougest brothers, with my sister and myself, bade farewell to loved neighbors and home; my native land, the home of my childhood; the graves of my beloved parents and a beloved brother, together with many much esteemed associates and neighbors. We embarked in a flatboat, which my brother had fitted out for the occasion, it being the usual mode of emigrating on water in those early days. We quietly glided down the proud old Cumberland into the Ohio, from thence into the father of waters, the Mississippi, to the mouth of the Hatchie; up its narrow crooked channel we continued our navigation, by means of hooks and poles—rather an odd way of travelling, when contrasted with the magnificent steamers in use at the present time. But the flat and keel boats of those days were made comfortable; in them, families could be pleasantly quartered. A slow way of travelling, it is true, yet the beautiful scenery that everywhere met the eye along the banks of those rivers, at that time, served, in a great degree, to dispel the monotony of slow travelling.

I being young, and naturally fond of the beauties of nature, enjoyed the perilous trip with pleasure, not being aware of the many dangers that hourly surrounded us. I usually took my knitting and repaired to the deck of the boat, where my youngest brother was acting as pilot and steersman. There I would sit for hours knitting and singing, while my eyes would feast upon the beautiful scenery that was constantly presented to the view.

Not unfrequently would landscapes remind us of the dear old spot we had so recently left and we did not forget our brother, whom we so sadly left behind in the city, or village of Nashville. We would often count the years that would elapse before his apprenticeship would expire, and he be free again, and come to our embrace. Four years seemed to us a long time. Oft our hearts would become impatient in contemplating the "tardy movings of the wheels of time." But, every bitter has its sweet, as Æsop has said in one of his fables, which has often cheered my drooping spirits. When sad at the recollection of the absent brother left behind, my heart would become elated in the anticipation of again meeting another fond brother, who had preceded us one year to our new home, anxiously awaiting our arrival.

Hatchie river, at that time, was scarcely navigable even by the boats that then plyed that stream. A steamer had never been known to venture up its narrow confines until February, 1828. On a beautiful day of that month, while efforts were being made to extricate our little craft, which was fast upon a log, and which seemed almost impossible to move, to our great joy and surprise a beautiful little steamer bearing the apellation of Rover, came puffing and darting around a bend of the river. We all were delighted in seeing it, and were proud to know we had the pleasure of seeing the first steamboat that ever plowed the waters of Hatchie river.

Great was the sensation manifested by the inhabitants of Brownsville and vicinity, on its landing. A banquet was prepared in honor of the captain and the ladies that were aboard; a grand reception was also given them by the citizens of Brownsville, which was then but a little village, but now is quite a city. No doubt some of the old inhabitants are yet living, who remember the foregoing incidents. We were four weeks making our way up the narrow stream, and, notwithstanding our pleasure while on the voyage, I was glad when we reached the place of our destination, and was no less delighted at the prospect of living in town, altogether a new feature in my life.

The associations I formed, in the short space of time I lived there, were very pleasant and lasting in memory.

Brownsville at that time afforded a very good school, two hotels, three dry good stores, one tailor shop, three doctors, one blacksmith shop and one grocery, I believe. Major Hiram Bradford and brother kept what was called the Western Hotel and a dry good store, Steel and Patton a dry good store, and Esquire Bray a hotel. Drs. Johnson, Barber and Bruce were our practicing physicians.

I spent two years in that pleasant little village, and truly they were the happiest days of my childhood. After losing my mother, my schoolmates were ever kind to me, and manifested respect for my crippled condition, which greatly endeared them to me.

It is pleasant to forget the trials of riper years, and recur to our school-girl days, when the boys played the beau, and the girls mimicked the belle; when each had their special companion, and all was revelry and happiness upon the "old play ground."

Who, that recollects the happy days of youth, does not feel a desire to be a child again? Is there a person in all christendom who does not refer to school days as the happiest in life—when trouble and care seemed to be a stranger?

We remember our teachers, fondly, who were Mrs. Russel and Alfred Hume; the father of the latter then presided over the Female Institute at Nashville. They were very efficient and careful in their instructions to me, manifesting sympathy for my misfortune—I being quite sensitive to the manifestations of others towards me, therefore, kind treatment was a balm to my heart. And when I thought I discovered an indication of slight, or heard a seeming taunt relative to my condition, it would sting me to the very quick, and cause me to shed many bitter tears.

The reader will pardon me for reverting back beyond the period detailed in the foregoing pages.

In the spring of 1827, my eldest brother said to me—

"Pet"—for by that name he was wont to call me— "do you want to go to school?"

"O, yes, very much, will you send me?" was my response.

"Yes," said he, "but I fear you cannot walk two miles."

"O, yes I can, Tommy, when will you send me?"

"On Monday, if you think you can stand the walk."

Very impatiently I waited for Monday to roll round; it came at last, and with a light step and heart I went to work assisting my sister in fitting me out for the happiest event of my young life. Soon all things were ready, and with my three youngest brothers I was on my march to the Old Academy, situated on or near the road leading from Murfreesboro to Lebanon, in Wilson county.

Almost forgetting my inefficiency in locomotion, I journeyed on, delighted with the forest songsters, and imagining their songs far more sweet and charming that morning than ever before. In fact everything seemed to me to have donned its most charming garb.

At length we came in sight of the Academy, the place where I received my first lessons in school, save what had been given me by Warren Moore, in sabbath school which I had visited a few times at Bethlehem church. I recollect distinctly my first Sabbath school ticket, which read thus: "A good name is better than precious ointment."

I have ever endeavored to profit by the teaching of those scriptural words, striving to maintain a good name and a spotless character in whatever community I may have been thrown, believing them to be the most precious jewels of earthly possessions. Here also, I received my first Sabbath school tracts: "Poor Sarah," and the "Dairyman's Daughter." To the reading of the latter, through the divine assistance of the God of the orphan, I attribute my first awakening to the knowledge of my sinful nature, and that without a change of heart I could not see God in peace.

I thank my Heavenly Father for the blessing of Sabbath schools, with all the religious tracts and periodicals pertaining thereto. Thousands, undoubtedly, with myself, can date the dawning of their salvation or conversion, to those means.

I have kept that precious tract until the present hour as a sacred memento from my Sabbath school teacher. May he receive his reward in Heaven, when God makes up his jewels from earth.

The Academy to which I was going, stood in a grove, hard by the road already alluded to, on a somewhat elevated piece of ground. In front of the house and beyond the road, we had a full view of a large mound or ridge, known in those days as "Hickory ridge."

It was supposed by many that a great battle had been fought on that notable place by the Indians in some past age, judg. from relics discovered We would frequently go up on the ridge and often pick up curiosities, such as skull bones, of human shape, spikes and tomahawks.

I well recollect how my heart would pulsate each morning with delight as we would arrive in sight of the old school house, our old familiar teacher standing in the door to welcome us with a smile within its walls. When the old gentleman would take his seat, and say "books, books," we would scamper to our seats respectfully, and soon all was silent. In a few moments he would again cry "lessons,"when several children would go up, and so on until all the classes had recited. This was his general rule. The first morning I went he called me, and asked me if I knew my A. B. C.'s. I soon convinced him that I did, and could spell "rellish"— that being the first word I ever spelt in school. It being a word in the old Webster spelling book, it is doubtful if any of the same could be found in this latter day of improvement. At the close of my first lesson, my teacher gave me great praise, saying he was going to give me a little classmate, and I must not let him excel me in learning, calling out, "Calvin Moss, here is this little girl you must have for a classmate, learn her her lessons, so she may get even with you, then we will see who will beat." Never will I forget his zeal and assiduity in teaching me my lessons until I got up to him in our book. The first opportunity my little teacher had he informed me that "we children say our lessons in turn—the one who gets here in the morning first reads first, and so on through the day." "Now," says he, "when you get near the school house, and see me, you need not run. I can run for both of us." I appreciated his kindness, and felt very grateful for it. It saved me many a hard race and much mortification of having been beaten. Several families of children would come in sight of each other near the school house, and then such running for the first lesson. It was quite amusing. The contestants were youths from six to eighteen years of age—each endeavoring to get to the door first. How I would strain my eyes to catch a sight of Calvin, my little classmate, who seldom failed to throw up his little sunburnt hands as a signal that I need not run, which always made my heart bound with joy and gladness. Seldom were we behind with our recitations. When "old daddy Mack" (as the scholars used to call the teacher, as a token of their high respect for him,) would call out lessons, two prouder little hearts never approached the recitation seat than Calvin Moss and his humble classmate. We seldom left the seat without receiving a word of commendation and praise from our beloved old teacher.

Callous and obtuse must be the heart that cannot revert back to the days of its early school life without ineffable pleasure, and with joy recount the innumerable innocent sports and plays indulged in. Is there one of my fond old schoolmates yet living that does not recollect with how much pleasure our kind old teacher, while standing in the door, would smile at our amusements and sports? If any of us let drop an apple he would nod his head, signifying that it belonged to him. This was to teach us to be more careful in handling our things. Yet many an apple was let fall on purpose so he might get it—all feeling a great delight in contributing to the pleasure of our teacher, who manifested so much sympathy for his pupils. Sometimes he was enabled to tie up a large cotton handkerchief full of the trophies he would thus gain through the day. Oft did Calvin slip a large white apple into my hand, whispering, "here, Sue, is an apple to let fall to-day." Thus passed my first school-day life. Many may look upon the above minutiæ of detail as superfluous, but hearts as appreciative as mine is of acts and manifestations of kindness and sympathy will not criticise nor condemn; and perhaps all will, ere these pages are finished, see my motive in being so minute in my reminiscences, though imperfect they be.

My unalloyed happiness at that school terminated much sooner than I could have wished, owing to my inability to continue to walk so far. I therefore was compelled to bid farewell to the spot that had become to me so dear, and especially my little classmate. How sad was his adieu to me! He remarked, "you will come back, won't you, when you get rested? I wish I could help you walk, then you could come to school all the time." I often wonder if he yet lives. If so, may angels guard his declining years. How dear is the memory of that kind hearted little boy to his long lost classmate. Nearly a half century has elapsed since those happy events. How apropos to my feelings at that time, are the lines of the immortal Moore:

> " How sad 'mid the sunshine that gladdens the scene
> Comes the thought that, tho' friends, we must part;
> Still fondly our thoughts will return to the spot,
> On the wings of remembrance borne."

I have been informed that the old Academy has long since crumbled to decay, and is numbered with the things that were. No more will be heard within its walls the echo of youthful voices with their mimic speeches, or the joyous laugh of the happy group that there resorted for instruction.

B

Few perhaps are now living who were pupils at the period above alluded to.

> " Some are in the churchyard laid,
>   Some sleep beneath the sod,.
> And few are left of all that school
>   With me to serve their God ;
> But when the time shall come, dear friends,
>   That we are called to go,
> O, may we meet with those we loved
>   Near forty years ago."

Many sad changes have taken place since those happy days of childhood, and sadness oft doth steal o'er my mind

> " When I think of those I loved so well—
>   Those early broken ties."

But I must bid adieu to those fond recollections, and beg pardon of the reader for thus digressing, and return to the point we left in our journal.

We remained in Brownsville but two years, when circumstances over which I had no control compelled me, against my will, to leave the pleasant little village and its interesting school—for which I had formed a strong attachment—to take up my residence in a new and distant part of the State—the county of Tipton. My sister having married a Mr. Sullivan, of Smith county, Middle Tennessee, moved with her husband to Tipton county. I therefore had to go with her.

Yet, in that wilderness region I found several very pleasant and agreeable neighbors, who had daughters near my own age, with whom I spent many pleasant hours. But a home in the woods at that time and in that place was anything but desirable and pleasant. It was infested with bears, wolves, reptiles of all descriptions, and mosquitoes, with every conceivable insect calculated to annoy. We were kept in almost constant dread both night and day. Wolves and bears would prowl about near the house until late in the morning. The nights were made hideous with the howlings of the wolves, and not unfrequently the

unearthly scream of the panther, all in quest of prey. And
through the day we could see the serpentine movements of
almost all kinds of reptiles, from the venomous monster
rattle snake to the more innocent and delicate garter.
Being naturally timid, my mind was kept in dread nearly
all the while. Not unfrequently would they intrude
themselves into our house, producing terror and dismay among the inmates. The mosquitoes were almost
insufferable. One could scarcely perform their daily work
for their tormenting annoyance. A constant smoke would
be kept up near the house, and the children kept
constantly oiled to keep from suffering almost death
from their stings. Stock could feed but a short time ere
they would come bellowing home to enjoy the smoke that
was in constant waiting for them, and not unfrequently
would they die from the sting of the "buffalo gnats," which
were in as great abundance as the mosquitoes. The reader
can judge by the above imperfect sketch whether a residence in that locality was desirable.

When the time came for me to leave that place, I left it
with much pleasure, notwithstanding I had some strong
ties there. At this time my second brother had completed
his apprenticeship, and, according to promise, he made us a
visit. During his stay with us he asked me if I would not
return with him to Nashville, to which proposition I gladly
consented, notwithstanding I thereby had to leave my only
sister and her two sweet little babes; also my youngest
brother. My eldest brother having died sometime prior in
a far distant country, my second brother became my next
natural protector, which place he filled with commendable
brotherly affection and care.

Preparations having been made, we on the 10th of February, 1832, bid adieu to our loved friends in the wilderness, and started for our destination on horseback, amid
the bitter cold and windy weather of that season of the

year. The mode of traveling was uncomfortable, yet my great desire to leave the wilderness, and to once more return to my native home, made the task seem but light, and on the 17th of the same month we arrived safely in the city of Nashville. It was my first visit to that place. I was delighted at it, thinking I would enjoy city life very much.

My brother placed me under the paternal roof and care of Mr. and Mrs. James Thomas of that city—the gentleman with whom my brother had served a part of his apprenticeship. Their kindness and paternal care, together with the pleasure derived from the association of their two little boys, soon filled in a great measure the vacuum caused in my heart by the separation from my sister and her dear little boys. With the exception of the death of my sister, my six years' stay with that kind family was a period of unalloyed pleasure. The death of my sister was a heavy stroke. She had ever done a sister's part towards us all, from the time we lost our loved mother until we were separated. I shall ever remember with gratitude the sympathy and condolence bestowed upon me by my kind benefactors. It was as a balm to my wounded heart. They became to me as my all in all. Language will ever fail to express the boundless love and gratitude I have ever felt for their untold acts of kindness towards me, as a poor orphan, without any claims of consanguinity upon them. The happy times spent in the bosom of that christian family, the effects of which can never be erased from the tablets of my heart, and the retrospect of those days will ever be a sweet reminiscence of the mind. My prayer is that Heaven's choicest blessings may ever be showered upon the entire family.

I did not suspect, when I bid farewell to my sister, it was the last farewell upon earth I would give her, or that the next time I beheld those dear little boys they would be motherless. But such are the changes of human events.

My sister's three boys were very early deprived of a mother's instructions, and a father's counsel, yet I am proud to say they have won for themselves honorable names among men.

The eldest, Wm. T. J. Sullivan, is a zealous minister of the gospel in the Methodist Episcopal church. His brother, I. E., is also an acceptable member of the same denomination. May they be faithful on earth and angels in Heaven. The youngest of them, who lives in Texas, I have never had the pleasure of seeing. May he, too, be an honor to his name.

The terminus of my six years' stay in Nashville, and with that beloved family, ended perhaps the happiest six years of my life. I left them to go with my brother to W. E. Kirby's, Holly Springs, Mississippi. He had recently married, and was repairing to that place to locate— when it was but a small village—in 1836.

My farewell to the above-mentioned place and family was made with deep regret and sadness, but it had to be endured. I felt like I was leaving a father's house. From their kind lips I had ever received the best of counsel, which has had a lasting effect upon the unworthy recipient. Among the many ties thus severed was that of the church, to which I had become attached, and in which I had enjoyed many hours of christian fellowship. Fondly would I have remained always with those people, but duty and sisterly affection prompted me to yield to the strong solicitation of an affectionate and kind brother.

We started for our new home on horseback, that being the usual way of traveling in the days when railroads were not known, and when stages were few and far between. A journey of three or four hundred miles on horseback in those days was considered a "light job," and possessed many interesting attractions to the traveler. Our route led us through many small towns in embryo, such as Dresden, Cambon, Waverly, etc. The houses, as in all the towns of all new countries, were principally log—the public as well as the private; the entertainment at the inns, rude but comfortable, at least to any one who had been all day traveling in the biting cold, and over rough and muddy roads, on horseback.

The fond anticipation of meeting our brother and his lovely family lessened the severity, in some degree, of our tedious journey, and we thereby performed the trip with a good degree of resignation. On the 17th of the same month we arrived safely at our brother's neat little cottage in Holly Springs, Mississippi, and found a cordial welcome by our hostess.

Holly Springs and vicinity at that time was newly settled, and the people were generally Tenesseeans, who had emigrated! to that region on account of the cheapness of the land. As in all new settlements the people are disposed to be sociable and neighborly, so they were there. They continued so until the population become more dense and wealthy, when systems of distinction or grades in society, and assumption of aristocracy, began to be manifested, especially among those who made no pretension to christianity or religion. In fact, at first when a social party was gotten up all were invited, without distinction of grade of high or low, so far as it related to the aboriginee, or Indian of the country; but as the pale face increased, the red skin became uncurrent, and was finally forgotten, or left out. This neglect was sorely felt by the proud Chickasaw, who loved much to be noticed by the whites. They appreciated any attention paid them by the pale face very highly indeed. I have spent some very agreeable moments with some of them, especially the most enlightened and refined.

The two years' residence of my life in that pleasant little village glided by almost as a pleasant dream. Protracted and camp meetings were of frequent occurrence, at which places I enjoyed myself very much. I shall never forget the glorious times we used to have at Coldwater, and other places of worship, where all were invited to partake of the hospitalities furnished by God's people while worshiping Him in the wilderness. Those were days when religion was enjoyed by its professors in its pristine purity, ere pride and the love of the world had usurped the most prominent place in the christian's heart. Days, too, when the seed sown by God's ministers fell upon good ground, took deep root, and brought forth abundant fruit; when wars and rumors of wars were not heard—at least, to exist upon this continent; when brother did not go to war with brother; and when the baser passion of the human heart did not dictate universal devastation over the face of the most beautiful part of God's creation. But the American people had become proud and ostentatious, and had left the old landmarks of their fathers, and had begun to worship mammon, forgetting the injunction of their Creator—"That I am the Lord thy God, and thou shalt have no other gods before me." We had sinned and deserved his chastisement, we therefore should submit with patient resignation all chastisement, for the present seemeth grievous, but in due time it will yield its fruits to profit. It is said in his holy book, "Whom the Lord loveth, He chasteneth." We should, therefore, take courage, and go forward and perform the duties incumbent upon us as citizens and christians with the anticipation of a brighter day in the future.

CHAPTER II.

On the evening of the 31st of December, 1839, I was united in matrimony to J. R. Smith, of Brunswick City,

Virginia, and on the 23d day of January, 1840, we bid a fond farewell to Holly Springs, with all its pleasant associations, and set out for Tipton county, Tennessee, in which, and that of Fayette county, I resided some twenty years. The major part of that time we lived in what is known as the Ebenezer neighborhood — deriving its name from a Cumberland Presbyterian church of that appellation.

With the good people of that locality I spent many agreeable and delightful years, both socially and religiously. In fact, I became thoroughly indentified with them. During my residence in that community I passed through the most trying and heart rending period of my life, in being forced to consign to the dark and silent tomb four of my beloved and lovely children, leaving me with but an only son on whom to expend the fond affection of a mother's heart, and the only star on which to hang my hope of future happiness of maternal love.

Amid all these trying scenes, the good people of Ebenezer came faithfully to my assistance, and gave me all the attention and sympathy that emenates from hearts imbued with pure and undefiled religion and disinterested benevolence, for which they will have a lasting remembrance from a grateful heart. Time can never erase the fond recollections of those kind neighbors, or sever the tie that binds my affection to those people, or to the sacred spot wherein lie the loved ashes of my angel babes. Sad, but fond memory loves to linger near the place, encircled by so many intense recollections, both of a sad and joyous character, covering a space of twenty years.

But I will not tire the reader with comment and detail, however interesting to me, and, perhaps, to some few who may have been participants, but may not be to the general reader.

Time, with his ever moving wheels, found us, on the 6th of June, 1860, bidding a sad farewell to the above friends and scenes, to take up our residence in the city of Memphis, with the intention of trying a city life, hoping that, perchance, a change of locality and scenery might divert our minds from the sad and trying events that God, in His alwise providence had so recently allowed us to pass through.

Thus I have endeavored to give an imperfect and short biographical sketch of my checkered and changing life up to the commencement of the recent war. My object in so doing is, that should a journal of my services in the Southern hospitals ever fall into the hands of my old friends, they may more readily recognize the authoress, whom they perhaps had forgotten for years, and had numbered as with the dead, and through the mercies of the Creator has been spared to pass through one of the most terrible civil wars the pages of history have ever chronicled. The task I have thus taken upon myself of writing a journal of four years of constant hospital life in the Southern army, is not of my own selection, but only a reluctant yielding to the urgent solicitations of friends—made not only by many soldiers who were in the hospitals in which I served, but by many friends since the war has closed.

Without commenting upon, or reverting to, the origin or primary causes of the war, or the unnatural bloody strife we have just passed through, I shall only endeavor to relate some of the scenes and events that fell under my own observation, as far as I am able to recollect them, and should I commit an error, either by commission or omission, I hope the charitable reader will attribute it to the head and not the heart; and also the lack of ability on the part of an aged and feeble woman unused to book or journal writing.

Whatever may have been the cause of the war, or whether the South was justifiable in seceding or rebelling, I will not now discuss. Suffice it to say, that the South thought herself in the right, and therefore justifiable in the course she pursued.   B*

The tocsin of war was sounded, echoing o'er hill and
dale, o'er monntain and valley, and throughout our Sunny
South ! The booming of the big-mouthed cannon at Sumter
fired the hearts of the noble sons of the South, and the cry
"to arms" they promptly responded to. They went forth to
sacrifice upon the altar of their country, if needs be, their
warm heart's blood for what they conceived to be political
and religious liberty. And the women of the South, no
less patriotic than the men, formed themselves into societies
for the purpose of contributing to the wants of the soldiers
in the field. My home being in Memphis, I, with the true,
benevolent and patriotic ladies of that city, entered into
the formation of societies for the above purpose ; and as the
rebels were to be whipped out in ninety days, we found it
necessary to be very prompt in our movements. What we
did—which consisted of a great variety of labors, such as
making all kinds of clothing for the soldiers, scraping lint,
making bandages, etc., with all the paraphernalia pertaining to camp life and a state of war that the ladies were
capable of producing or making—had to be done speedily.

In March, 1861, a young man, Mr. Stewart, of the Bluff
City Greys, One Hundred and Fifty-fourth Tennessee Regiment, requested me to make him a military uniform coat,
which I did. I was afterwards informed that it was the
first rebel coat made in this city by a lady.

Very soon after this, the ladies of the Methodist Episcopal church (Wesley Chapel), called a meeting and organized
an association, calling it the " Ladies' Military Sewing
Society," for the purpose of making up clothing for the
soldiers. A large number met there daily for at least two
months, if not longer, and worked with an energy and
will, impressing one with an idea that they expected to
make clothes enough to last the boys during the entire
war. So it seemed to us ; but we were novices in war
affairs then, and knew not the fearful magnitude of the ap-

proaching war. But soon the ladies were relieved of that
responsibility, for the making of soldiers clothing was
assumed by the Government, and a small sum was paid for
making it to those who chose to do the work for pay,
and those ladies who were willing and anxious to do the
labor and help the brave boys were deprived of that pleasure, not wishing to receive pay for what they could do for
the cause.

But ere long, another opportunity was presented for them
to lend a helping hand, and show their devotion to the
cause of liberty and Southern independence. A hospital
was fitted up as a place of refuge for the sick and wounded
soldiers, and a society or company of ladies, styled "Southern
Mothers," was organized to attend to all the wants and
demands of those who might need their attention, of which
I remember Mrs. M. E. Pope was the projectress, with Mrs.
Law, president. The second of the kind that followed soon
after in this city was gotten up in the "Irving block." The
blessings and benefits of these organizations can be favor-
ably attested by many a sick and weary soldier who found
comfort and relief therein.

On the 26th of March, 1861, my son and only living
child, a youth of seventeen summers, volunteered his services in defense of his country, and became a member of
that old and well-tried regiment, the "One Hundred and
Fifty-fourth Tennessee," which made itself renowned on
many a hard contested battle field during the war. To give
up my only boy, the idol of my heart, and the hope of my
declining years, was a task almost too great for me to endure. I had hoped to see him a ripe scholar, for which he
bid fair, thus rendering him an ornament to, and useful
member of, society. But his books were laid aside and his
teacher dismissed, and in their stead he assumed the imple-
ments of war and the privations incidental to a soldier's
life. None but a mother, placed in similar circumstances,

can understand my feelings, and appreciate the sacrifice. But the love of country and the righteous cause he was about to espouse gave me strength to bid him go, with a mother's warmest blessings and a mother's prayers.

The South believed, she was right; that the hand of the usurper and despot had been raised against her dearest rights and interests; and what true Southern mother, or wife, or sister, would not bid sons and husband or brother go to her country's rescue, and, if need be, sacrifice their precious blood and lives for so noble a cause! With these full convictions impressed upon my mind, I resolved, through the mercies of the God of the oppressed, to let no opportunity pass in which I could give aid and comfort, not only to my son, but to any of his noble comrades in arms, without embracing and improving the occasion to my utmost ability, and that, too, as long as the war should last or opportunities offer—should it embrace the balance of my natural life. I now thank God that my life was vouchsafed to me through the trying ordeal, and that I was permitted, through His mercy, to carry out my resolution to the best of my ability, and to the last moment. Soon after, my son and the regiment to which he was attached went into camp, and were stationed at Fort Pickering. The measles appeared among them, and the surgeon, Dr. Mitchell, conferred upon me the honor of nursing his first patient, who was sent to the city; for an honor I confess I considered it, as well as a coveted privilege, not only from the fact of the patient being a Confederate soldier, but that the surgeon who sent him had been a successful family physician, and one whom I esteemed as a gentleman. He served the army faithfully as a field surgeon during the entire war, and was permitted to return home to greet his remaining friends once more.

The patient's name was Roads. My son accompanied him to my house in a carriage, procured by Dr. Mitchell.

He remained with me two weeks, when he reported for duty and joined his company, which had been transferred to Randolph, or Fort Wright, as it was subsequently called— General Wright being the first to occupy it with troops.

I mention the foregoing incident as a mere introduction to the details that may follow of my experience and observation while connected with the hospitals during the war, which will prove that I was not an idle spectator during the trying events that transpired in that great struggle for Southern rights, religious liberty and national independence.

Our labor began with the commencement of hostilities, and closed after the last patient left the hospital with which we were connected, after the final surrender of Johnson's army.

The regiment to which my son was attached left Memphis sometime in April, 1861. O, with what buoyant spirits and sanguine hopes did they bid farewell to loved ones at home, and march to the battle field, with the foe near at hand. The small remnant that returned home at the close of hostilities well attests the sanguinary and determined struggle the noble and gallant old One Hundred and Fifty-fourth Tennessee passed through.

They had been at Randolph but a short time, ere the ladies of our city visited their camp to examine the fortifications their husbands, fathers and sons were vigorously building at that point. I was among the number of ladies interested in that heroic little band. Four weeks to me seemed a long time to be absent from my soldier boy. I could endure it no longer. I therefore resolved to visit Camp Randolph, and with a lot of starched linen and clothing, I set out for camp, with other ladies with like purposes and aims; but little did we think of the folly of our mission. Very soon white shirts, starched collars and fine clothing became useless, an imcumbrance to soldiers in camp or on the field, and with alacrity and pleasure they were laid aside for the good old fashioned rebel suits of grey, which they wore with commendable pride, until the stern events of war forced them to lay them off and fold them up, to be kept as sad but proud relics of a defeated cause and blasted hopes of a noble people; relics that will be revered by our children's children when the manly forms they once enveloped shall lie mouldering beneath the sod.

On the 20th day of May, 1861, I excused myself to the society I have already referred to, and took passage on the steamer Ingomar, on which fifteen hundred soldiers had also embarked, for the notable little town of Randolph. We had on board, also, Mrs. Melersh, mother of Capt. George Melersh, of the Hickory Rifles, together with Captain Sherwin's lady. We had a very pleasant trip. Arriving at our destination at daybreak the next morning, scaling the rugged hills adjacent thereto, our eyes caught a view of scenes to us then quite novel and interesting. All over the plains and along the slope of hills could be seen the white tents, with soldiers interspersed preparing their morning repast, or standing in groups before their tent doors. We strolled among them until we became tired, when we repaired to Mr. Denis', where we were kindly received, and a warm and palatable breakfast was set before us, to which we did ample justice. The day passed very pleasantly, the soldiers cordially greeting us and frequently inviting us to visit their respective quarters and partake of the bounties of their tables, which were spread with marked neatness and taste, causing everything to appear home-like, and evincing a skill and knowledge in the culinary art. Through the polite and pressing invitation of Capt. Cross, who was then commanding the McNairy company, from Paris, Tennessee, we dined with him and his gallant company. I never received more courteous treatment at any table than at theirs.

I fancied I would feel sad before reaching camp when I

meditated upon its scenes, and that I would find the soldiers uncomfortably situated, and their spirits very much depressed; but what an agreeable surprise. Everything denoted comfort and contentment, and what the soldier needed the most was there in great abundance—that being good and wholesome food. Not a sad face did I look upon during the entire day; all seemed lively, cheerful, and anxious and willing to meet any emergency.

The cordial reception manifested, and the pleasant hours I spent with that brave band of Southern soldiers, left a pleasing and lasting impression upon my mind and heart. When I took my departure from among them, I felt that I was better prepared to appreciate the privations and hardships of a soldier's life, and my sense of duty toward the soldier was more lively, and more firmly determined, through the mercies of God, to do "my duty, and my whole duty" in the soldier's behalf, and that a poor soldier should find in me a friend and not a stranger, for well I felt that they were our country's stay in the day and hour of our trouble and danger.

I had anticipated returning to Memphis the evening of that day by the steamer on which we came; but to my chagrin and mortification, while partaking of the sumptuous repast of Capt. Cross the steamer gave the signal for her departure to Memphis. I therefore was compelled to tarry at that post until another steamer would leave for the same destination.

I was much pleased to find my son well and comfortable, and enjoying himself finely. My curiosity of visiting the camp and rendezvous of soldiers was gratified, and, finding them all right, I felt anxious to return to my post, in order to perform my part of the labor with the sewing society, but I was doomed to remain until another opportunity offered. I therefore tried to make the best use possible of my disappointment; and after the effects, in a great degree, had worn off, I repaired, with several other ladies, to the dress parade ground, and there witnessed, for the first time, soldiers on parade. It was a pleasing and interesting sight to behold such a vast number of stalwart men all simultaneously obeying the commands of the officer, and going through the same maneuverings. I need not disguise the fact that I felt proud to know that my beloved son was among that number who had pledged their lives and sacred honor to defend their homes and country against an invading and merciless enemy. I gazed with wonder and admiration while the maneuvering was going on, and asked myself the question—" How many of these noble souls will survive the war and return to their loved ones at home ?" Reason answered—" But few, very few ! will be left to tell the sad story of those who fell."

By and by, the order was given to break ranks and return to camp, and many a face we then looked upon we shall never see again. Naught remains of the majority perhaps but the good name that follows a faithful and brave soldier who falls at his post in defense of his country. Their names and memory will ever be enshrined in the hearts of a grateful people to the latest posterity.

While we were yet gazing upon the grand scene before us, Col. Preston Smith (who after this was made a brigadier general) approached us, and making inquiry of our names, which were readily given, he remarked to me that he had been informed of my visit to see my son, and that the steamer had left me before I was ready or apprised of its departure, and that I was very anxious to return at the earliest opportunity, and expressed great delight at our visit to camp. He took great pleasure in informing me that the steamer would arrive early next morning, and inasmuch as its officers would be strangers to me, he would not have me go alone, or without a pass, lest I might have some difficulty in getting passage. He therefore handed me a pass, and a furlough for my son to go with me, (which was the first and last he ever received to visit our home in Memphis); and need I say I was not only delighted but surprised at his unsought generosity. Surely such consideration and kindness could only spring from the heart of a true gentleman. I had no token of gratitude to offer him save a beautiful bouquet I held in my hand. Presenting it to him, he received it gracefully, with many wishes for my safe transport home.

The pass received I will insert herein. It may be a curiosity to some who have never seen a pass. The regiment to which the Colonel belonged was on its first organization called the First Tennessee Regiment, but afterward changed to the One Hundred and Fifty-fourth Tennessee. I will now append what was written upon my pass:

"May 21, 1861—Commander Steamboat Mars:—Mrs. Smith, who was in my camp to visit her son, private I. N. Smith, was left by steamer Ingomar this day. You will oblige me by passing her and her said son on your boat.

"Respectfully,
"PRESTON SMITH, Col. Com. Post."

I have many others which were granted at various times during the war, but I deem it unnecessary to insert more. I retain them as precious mementoes of the heroic struggle for Southern liberty and independence. I ever found the officers ready to grant any accommodation asked that was not incompatible with military orders.

I will also here insert the furlough given to my son at the same time:

"Head Quarters First Regiment, Fort Wright, May 21st, 1861.—Private I. N. Smith has furlough to go to Memphis and return on first packet.

"PRESTON SMITH, Col. Com. Post."

We both felt much gratified for the unasked furlough for my son to visit home; and who would not appreciate such a favor after having been absent from home for some time— perhaps for months and years. There may be no time when the charms and sweets of home are more highly appreciated and more vividly enjoyed than when visited by a soldier who has been absent in the cheerless camp. Such were my son's emotions. In anticipation we repaired to the hotel near the river, so we could be in hailing distance of the promised steamer. My son kept vigilant watch all night lest it might pass, and delay us another day.

At day-light the promised craft hove in sight, and in due time the signal was given and a skiff was seen approaching the shore containing two men who informed us that the steamer would stop at a bend three miles below, take on some corn, and wait for us. As I had not been in a skiff for many years, I felt a little timid at first, but on being assured by the oarsmen and soldiers near by that there was no danger, I became composed and confident, thinking I would only be for a short time in so frail a craft, and would soon be set on board the steamer. But to our dismay and utter astonishment, when we came to the bend the boat was gone, the corn having been taken away the day previous by another boat. We had no alternative but to either go back or push forward. The latter we chose to do. So on we went, floating upon the bosom of the "father of waters," although it was sometimes quite rough and boisterous, made so by the wind, and we felt that our journey would be somewhat perilous; yet we continued our course, our speed being much facilitated by the alternate rowing of the two gentlemen and my son, making very near steamboat time. We made the trip in eight hours, arriving in port a few minutes after the steamer, which was just letting off steam as we approached.

Providentially, it was one of those cool days which often visit us in the sweet month of May, or more than likely the result would have been serious, for we found ourselves very near being sun struck. After reaching home, however, we soon rallied and joined the ladies, still plying their needles at the Methodist Episcopal Church, "Wesley Chapel," for the soldiers benefit; but we did not escape some little criticism upon our adventure and the amusing result. "A badly sunburnt face," remarked some one of the ladies; that "certainly I merited the title of the 'heroine of the Mississippi,' for doubtless I was the first, and perhaps would be the only lady who would take so novel and perilous a trip during the war." However, the title did not prompt me to make that perilous journey; yet I enjoyed it finely, and also the good humored jokes of the ladies, and hearty laughs about my sunburnt face.

Nothing of interest or special note transpired during the continuation of the society, but the usual routine of labor until its termination, which took place sometime in June, during which time the "Southern Mothers Home" was organized and ready to receive patients.

On the tenth of June my husband volunteered under Capt. Wm. Jackson, of Jackson, West Tennessee, commanding "Jackson's battery," and on the third of July he took his departure with the company, temporarily commanded by Lieut. Stewart—afterwards Captain on his brother's staff, Major General Stewart.

Thus I was left alone, as were thousands of other ladies, to battle with the world and circumstances as best we could. Many can appreciate my utter loneliness—those who have passed through similar trying ordeals; but I had entire confidence in that God who had ever watched over me in my past checkered life, and that He would not forsake me in this my great need. I continued keeping boarding house, and at the same time rendering every aid to the soldiers that was in my power. I never denied them food or shelter whenever called upon, and I felt blessed in so doing by an approving conscience. Every mark of friendship was shown me by the good people of Memphis. Many soldiers spent weeks in my house while sick, and on their taking leave I realized that comforting feeling spoken of in Holy Writ, "that it is more blessed to give than to receive." I shall ever cherish a kindly remembrance for them for the marked gratitude and reverence they all manifested towards me while under my roof, and the manifest approval of the people of my efforts in behalf of the soldiers.

I learned in July that the regiment to which my son belonged had orders to leave Randolph for a point in Missouri. I felt a great anxiety to see him before he left; and my husband being at the same place, might perhaps go with them. I therefore determined to revisit the camp at Randolph, and on the 24th I took passage on the little steamer Mohawk for the above point, arriving there the same evening, found all well and making ready for the march, which took place on the 27th. I need not say it was one of the saddest days of my life. To bid adieu, perhaps for the last time, to the idol of my heart, my only remaining child, was trying indeed. He was going far out of my reach, where, if he needed my attention when sick or suffering, I could not be present to administer to his wants; but the stern mandates of war had to be complied with. With a heavy heart I bade him farewell. The old adage that "we can get used to anything" was forcibly impressed upon my mind during the protracted war. We thought when loved ones went first into the army, a few weeks absence was a long time, and our hearts yearned to see them; but as time and the exciting events moved rapidly by us, and our minds became engrossed with the care of suffering invalid soldiers, a long separation became less painful. Nevertheless, our hearts turned towards the absent ones as steadily as the needle to the pole. We often felt the force of the language of the christian poet :

> " At home or abroad, on the land or the sea,
> As thy days may demand shall thy strength ever be."

So, God in his great goodness gave me strength to endure all things; and in humbleness of heart, and in deep grati- tude, I submitted to His will, believing my friends were in His care, and the result, whatever it might be, would be right. I was comforted.

How grand was the sight of that magnificent steamer with its thousands of noble souls aboard as she moved off from her moorings, with banners flying to the breeze, with stirring and animating music, vibrating through the air, for the seat of war. All on board seemed to be cheerful and gay, and eager for the conflict, thinking perhaps it would be but a frolic and of short duration; but, noble souls, how they were deceived, both in length of time and result. But God in His wisdom casts a veil over the future, and we press forward with buoyant hopes for happy re- sults when disappointment and disaster await us. Thus it is with all other events of human life. Were it otherwise, our hearts would fail within us, and the great sea of human existence would become a stagnant pool.

I stood on the bluff and gazed with untold admiration at the imposing sight. My heart swelled with gratitude to God, and love for my country.

I shall never forget the sympathy manifested by several of the company, to which my son belonged, when I came to bid him farewell—telling me to be of good cheer, they were as a band of brothers, and should my son fall, they would

take care of him. It was then I learned a true soldier was
a true friend and gentleman, and he did not cast aside his
humanity and finer feelings when he buckled on his armor
to go forth to the field of carnage. From that day the
One Hundred and Fifty-fourth Tennessee Regiment was
endeared to me almost as though they had all been my
own children, notwithstanding my son was subsequently
transferred to the battery to which his father belonged.
Not until life with me shall cease will the chord of affection
for them be severed.

Imposing and grand was the sight to see those magnificent steamers plowing the waters of the majestic Mississi-
sippi, and the boats seemed almost to manifest pride in
having on board so many noble spirits. We watched, in-
tently, the receding boats, giving and receiving farewell
signals from our loved ones, until nothing could be seen
but the outlines of the deck, on which they stood.

Then, with a sad heart, we left the almost deserted
shore, and repaired to the place of our stopping, to await
the departure of the next steamer for Memphis, which did
not take place until the 29th. Bidding my husband a sad
farewell, I took passage on the Grampus, (afterwards
known as the "Dare Devil," on account of the many daring
deeds it performed, between Columbus, Ky., and Cairo,)
which landed us in eight hours after at our lonely home in
Memphis. That loneliness was more deeply felt from the
fact that I had just come from those that alone could make
home happy. The yet sad impressions fresh upon my heart,
of my recent trying separation, weighed me down.

Time past on, and nothing occurred of interest in our
city, until the arrival of some sick soldiers from Madrid,
who were placed at the hospital of the Southern Mothers.
Then we had work enough for all. There was no shrinking
from a duty which God had assigned to the weaker sex—
at least, to those who felt they had a duty to perform in

the great struggle that was pressing upon us, and that in the sick room was the place where the ladies were most needed, and where they could accomplish the most good.

The painful feeling that took possession of me on my first entrance into that place of suffering and distress, will never be erased from my memory, while life may last. As soon as intelligence had been received that patients had arrived, I, with one or two other ladies, hastened to the scene of suffering, with no other intention but to assume at once the work of trying to alleviate the sufferings of any who might need our aid, never reflecting for a moment that my heart would fail me in performing the self-selected work. But on entering, the scenes of distress that met my eyes on every side, caused my heart to sink within me, and my nerves to recoil; but rallying myself, I moved forward. On either side of the long room, on neatly arranged beds, lay suffering soldiers. I hastily passed through the ward on the first floor, for I felt too sick at heart to make a halt, and proceeded up stairs. On entering a small room, I found it contained but one patient—a stranger, in the agonies of death. I approached him, and made some brief inquiries concerning his home, friends and his prospects of a future state. I learned that he was a young married man, from Arkansas, having no means to defray the expense of his young and anxious wife to come and attend him in his dying hour; nor yet to send his body to his native home, where his widowed wife and mourning friends could be permitted to perform the mournful duty of shedding the disconsolate tears over the grave of the true and the brave one of that gallant and heroic band from Arkanses, who made themselves renowned upon many a hard tried battle field during the war.

My sympathy for the noble, intelligent looking being I gazed at, listening to his agonizing groans, and his broken sentences of loved ones at home, and they not aware of his dying. condition, became so great and overpowering that I had to leave the room to suppress my emotions, resolving to return and perform my whole duty, with the help of God, to the suffering soldier, however painful might be the scenes through which I would have to pass.

Just as we stepped out of the door to return to our homes, we met our beloved preceptress, who addressed herself to the numerous ladies present, (who were not idle,) saying, "Ladies, we want help ; come, one and all, and help us. We have undertaken a great work, and we must be aided, or we will fail. All can do something, and, I hope, no one will shrink from the duty before us." We asked her what was most needed. She replied, anything that could be spared—such as beds, bedding, towels and numerous other articles unnecessary to enumerate.

We then started for home, my feelings yet unsuppressed. On my way I hired a dray, which I loaded with bedsteads, beds and bedding, towels, etc., etc., and ordered it to be reported to that dear, patriotic lady, whose name will long be enshrined in the heart of many a true Southerner, for the many benevolent acts she performed for her beloved country's defenders. In the afternoon of the same day, we determined to return to the hospital, and try to have more self-control. On my return, we found the dying soldier still lingering, and was enabled, by the aid of some to whom assistance was applied for, to administer to him in his dying moments ; and while thus engaged, my mind became resolute and composed, so that subsequently we could stand around the bed of a sick or dying soldier any length of time without giving back or flinching. I mention this to merely prove the adage, "that we can get used to anything," however painful or repugnant at first to our feelings.

Day by day as time passed, and new evidences of the heroes of war were presented, we became more familiar

with, and adequate to, the task before us. We could witness the scenes of suffering and distress with less seeming
emotion, nevertheless our sympathies were not in the least
diminished, nor did we grow less determined to do our duty
to those noble souls that were standing, as it were, like a
wall of granite between us and the ruthless enemy. We
could not, nor would we, have witnessed the ten thousand
scenes of untold suffering had we been indifferent to the
calls of mercy, and a sense of our imperative duty. With
the conviction that our feeble efforts might, in some degree,
alleviate the sufferings and distress of the wounded and
mangled soldiers, and as the field of labor became, day by
day, more extended, and our service of greater demand, we
felt that we would incur the displeasure of God, and make
a mockery of patriotism if we left the field uncultivated
and unoccupied.

Such were my convictions; and doubtless they will meet
with the approbation of the intelligent and humane people
who sent their warriors forth to battle for that which they
conceived to be their inherent and constitutional right.
Everything was conducted with the utmost system in that
well remembered home for the invalid soldier. I spent as
much of my time as could be spared with them. I continued to make clothes for them, at intervals between my
services at the hospital and domestic duties at home. In
a few weeks General Pillow returned with his command
from Missouri, and established his headquarters at Columbus, Kentucky.

Feeling a strong desire to see my husband and son again—
for what good mother and wife would not—I, with one or
two other lady friends, made an application for passports
to visit our friends at Columbus, but were positively refused.
A Mrs. Wainsburg, one of the ladies making the application, who had also an only son in the army, stationed at
that point, was therefore, with myself, very anxious to

c

see her son. Each one, in turn, made application with strong appeal to the passport agent, but all to no avail. We then asked if we could not go upon an accommodation boat. The reply was that we would be liable to arrest if we did. We informed him that we would risk that, and go upon our own responsibility, as we believed we had plenty of friends there who would vouch for our "loyalty;" so preparations were made, and on the 29th of September, in company with a young soldier who had been in my house as a patient, we took passage on board the steamer Kentucky, which soon got under way for the seat of war. Our hearts were buoyant with the hope of soon again seeing all that once had been the light of our then desolate homes.

Our trip on that occasion was very pleasant, indeed; more accommodating officers I never before met; and we never spent two days more happily in our lives upon any vessel on which we had traveled. On the evening of the second day we landed upon the shore of that gallant old State of the "bloody ground," from whence many brave volunteers had exiled themselves, and took refuge among strangers in their sister States, in order that they might share the destiny of those who had taken up arms in defense of their homes, and all that a freeman holds sacred—the right of self-government. Oh, how often has my heart bled at the sad and destitute condition of those heroic souls from Kentucky, when sick, wounded and dying, far away from the tender care and sweet caresses of fond mothers and loved sisters, with no fond and affectionate kiss to sooth the last dying pangs of a beloved son or brother, no soft and delicate hand to wipe away the death dews from their marble, but manly, brows. Oft have I imagined what a sweet, but solemn, and sad consolation would it have been to either sisters or mothers of those manly, but dying, youths could they have been present at their last moments, to have pillowed their weary heads upon the bosoms that perhaps first gave them nourishment, or in whose walls beat the tender pulsations of a sister's affections.

But they were like many, very many, of the mothers, sisters and wives of my own loved volunteer State; they could do nothing but weep and pray, and patiently wait for the vague and scattering news that occasionally ran the blockade. I never met a soldier from Kentucky but my heart warmed with admiration for him, and I felt like giving him some kind word of cheer, or doing for him acts of kindness, knowing that naught but pure patriotism could have caused him to leave home and its endearing influences to lead the life of a Southern soldier, with all the attending dangers thereof, and with the uncertainty of the result. Yet they were not alone in their isolation from loved ones at home; the Texans and Louisianians were subsequenly left in the same condition, but not by their own choice. They, too, shared our sympathy and consideration. Home and friends are dear to the absent of all climes, and under all circumstances in life. We honor the true soldiers for their daring deeds and noble acts, and the constant fidelity to the cause they loved better than life. No one can but honor the entire Southern army for its indurance during the four long years of bloody strife.

We were not arrested on our arrival at Columbus, as was predicted on our leaving Memphis; but on the contrary, were kindly welcomed by many of those who had the authority to arrest us, had they chosen so to do. We soon found ourselves ensconced in the Buchannan house, from whence we sent intelligence of our arrival to our friends, who were not long in finding us. I need not say we had a joyful meeting; we passed a few days with our beloved friends with uninterrupted happiness. The extensive fortifications of that place, which became somewhat renowned at the battle of Belmont, Nov. 7th, presented an imposing appearance to us.

We remained with our friends until October 7th, when we took our departure for home. We arrived at home in ten hours, by rail. No events of special character took place in the ladies' department until the battle of Belmont above alluded to, when our labor of mercy was very much increased; not only in the " Mothers' Hospital," but at many other points where the wounded and suffering soldiers were placed. There we all had abundance of work to do. Many died, and were decently buried by the good people of Memphis, in the soldiers' burying ground near the Bluff City, and their places of rest plainly marked.

After the above battle, renewed efforts were made by both sexes, for the comfort and accommodation of the suffering soldiers. The well known Overton Hotel was also thrown open for the reception of patients from the first battle field in our district; in fact every department and place of reception for wounded and sick soldiers was pleasantly fitted up for their comfort. We waited anxiously until the 11th ere any arrived from the battle-field. They found everything provided for their comfort. A warm breakfast, perhaps, was never more highly appreciated, and relished, than by the hungry and wounded soldiers, and especially by those who were able to enjoy it. Great excitement and sensation was manifested by the people on their arrival, as they were the first of that description, and many of the inhabitants had friends among the wounded. Never, perhaps, did a people make greater exertion for the comfort of wounded soldiers than those people at that time.

Every one seemed to vie with the other to see who could do the most for them. All kinds of delicacies were prepared and set before the needy, such as the most delicate

palate could desire. It was an appalling scene to behold
the mangled and disfigured bodies of those brave men, who
had fought the first battle, in this department, for the
rights of the South. It was a new era in our lives, and
our hearts almost failed us on approaching the bedside of
the wounded and bleeding defenders of our country; but
the love of country, and a deep sense of our duty, nerved
us onward to discharge our obligations.

The surgeons in attendance were very successful in re-
storing the wounded patients to their wonted health,
except those who had to suffer amputation. Amputations
prior to that occasion were rare. Hence, the thought of a
man having his leg or arm sawed from his body while living, was horrifying to our hearts; yet we had to get used
to it, as well as all other distressing scenes attending a
state of war. It is remarkable with what fortitude they
generally stood the painful operation, and with what cheer-
fulness they bore up under their great misfortune. Seldom
would you hear a word of regret escape from their lips for
their helpless condition.

Both hospitals were kept up until Christmas, when the
two were consolidated, and the Overton House alone continued. This was in operation until near the time the
Federals occupied the city. Sometimes it was filled to
overflowing. I never shall forget the vast crowd of sufferers who occupied it after the evacuation of Island No. 10
and Fort Pillow. It was heartrending, indeed, to witness
so many hundreds from all parts of the South suffering
and dying, and that, too, so fast that it was a difficult
matter to get them buried in due time.

Those who came from the above named places were
mostly suffering with measles and exposure. On reaching
Memphis, many soon died. There were so many arriving
at once, that it seemed, with all our efforts, we could not
give them comfortable quarters; but in a few days, they

were all pleasantly situated, and receiving due attention.
The oft unpleasant sensations, produced by seeing many a
poor fellow die in a few moments after he was laid upon the
floor in the entry of the hospital, before beds could be procured for them, will never be removed. Unceasing efforts
to relieve and wait upon them, and the urgent calls of
humanity, were so constant that I would become so
fatigued that I could scarcely walk; yet duty urged
me forward, and kept me moving. Sleep was almost a
stranger to me for weeks at a time. Hundreds of these
poor sufferers looked to us as angels of mercy, filling, in
part, the places of their loved sisters and mothers, and
often a beloved wife, far away.

The wounded of Fort Donelson were sent elesewhere to
be cared for, although the people of Memphis would have
taken pleasure in binding up the wounds, and administering to the wants of those heroic and valorous boys, who,
perhaps, had done harder fighting, against greater odds, and
endured greater suffering, than any soldiers in any battle
during the war. The names of the heroes of that eventful,
but disastrous day will ever be held in grateful remembrance
by all true lovers of Southern independence and manhood.
Kentucky should ever be proud of her noble Buckner,
whose name will be held in the highest estimation by the true Southern heart. At the fall of Donelson,
Columbus could not be held any longer by the Sonthern
troops, and it was, therefore, evacuated about the first of
March. On learning they had reached Humbolt, I hastened
to meet my husband and son. Reaching that place on the
7th of March, I remained there until the 12th, and spent
a very pleasant time. My son being eighteen years
old on the tenth, we had a sumptuous dinner to partake of
on the occasion at the well-kept hotel superintended by
Mr. Andrews; but such pleasures, as on former occasions, were short lived, and a sad separation had again to

take place. I could do my loved ones no material service, placed as they were, in camp awaiting marching orders for Corinth, Mississippi, where a great battle was pending.. With fearful apprehensions for the probable result of the anticipated battle at the above place, I bid them adieu, and returned home, leaving them in the hands and care of Him who had ever watched over them and kept them from harm.

On my arrival home, I made a requisition upon the surgeon in charge of the hospital, a Dr. Fenner, to have some of the boys of the Ninth Texas Regiment removed to my house, which was granted. Quite a number remained until they were restored to health—two, however, remained a long time. James Loe and James Roach, being more ill than the rest, (Roach, especially so,) they remained with me six or eight weeks, when they were sent to their command, then at Corinth. The last named gentleman remained until after the battle of Shiloh; but being so anxious to know what became of his company, or what loss it sustained, he could stay no longer. He left for the field of carnage. I never heard from either of them since, though I have made many inquiries. I always felt an increased interest in those to whom I had administered and comforted when suffering, and those two Texas boys I had nursed and cared for many nights and days, as though they had been my own sons. For eight weary days after that bloody battle I labored under the deepest anxiety and solicitude for the fate of my husband and son—both having been in the conflict. At the expiration of that time, I received the joyful intelligence that they both were safe, which removed a mountain from my heart, and begat an unutterable impulse of gratitude to God. However, I relaxed not an effort in behalf of the wounded, which were hourly arriving from the field of blood. The Mother's Home again was fitted up to receive the wounded, and the

Overton hospital was soon crowded. We divided our time between the two houses as best we could. In each I found many of my old acquaintances and neighbors' sons, who desired me to attend them, which gave me great pleasure in being able to do. But many a precious soldier's life ebbed out upon the couch upon which he lay within those hospital walls, and the unconscious sod now covers many a Southern soldier's remains in the Memphis cemetery.

After that battle, many were hopeful that their loved city would not be occupied by the Federals; but about the first of May that delusion was scattered to the four winds, and their dreams of safety fearfully dispelled, with the realization staring them in the face that Memphis, too, must fall, and, as a natural consequence, many began at once to leave the city for different points farther South. I had determined myself to remain until the hospitals were to be removed—an event which was fully anticipated, and when realized, my connection therewith would terminate. With those impressions, I at once broke up house keeping, preparatory to leaving the city, and on the tenth of May, 1862, I set my last table for my boarders, who had been friends to me while struggling for a subsistence. I sold all my surplus effects, boxed up the reserved, and stored them with one of my kind friends, Mrs, A. S., until I could get ready to go to Corinth to look after my husband, who I learned was very sick in camp at that place.

On the 16th of the same month I started for that noted place, in company with Mrs. Rieves, who had learned that her son had been left on the battle field wounded. With tortured and deeply anxious hearts, we moved forward as fast as the (seeming) tardy locomotive would carry us, anticipating in due time to reach the spot around which clustered our greatest solicitude; but to our great dismay and chagrin, on reaching Grand Junction we were informed that we could go no farther—the provost marshal having

that morning received orders to let no one pass unless on
special business. We were at a loss to know what to do
under those discouraging circumstances, and knowing, too,
that military orders had to be strictly obeyed, it was therefore useless to expostulate. I will here state, that during
the entire war I never suffered myself to obtrude upon a
military order or regulation. To retrace our steps, and
return to Memphis, was our only alternative—not knowing
but we were turning our back upon the dead bodies of
some of those we held dearer than life.

After returning to Memphis, I waited several days with
great anxiety and feverish impatience for a letter from my
son; but waited in vain. I then sent a dispatch to the
captain commanding the battery to which my husband was
attached to know if he could be sent home. He replied he
could, if his surgeon said so; but receiving no intelligence
from him, I resolved to make another effort to reach him
in camp. I thereupon applied to Colonel Crowder, commanding the post of Memphis, for a permit to go through.
He said if he had any influence, he would exert it in my
behalf, and at once gave me all the papers he deemed
requisite to pass me through; and with a heart filled with
gratitude to that kind officer, I again on the 27th started
for Corinth, but not without great anxiety and misgiving
lest I should again be unsuccessful. Fortune, however,
that time was more propitious. On entering the cars, I
found my dear neighbor and kind friend, Mr. Minor, who
was passport agent, which fact gave me full confidence of
success. Knowing with the papers I had, all that was then
necessary was a responsible voucher, I at once placed my
case and papers in his hands; and on reaching the Junction again, he at once approached the provost marshal with
my papers, informing him I was the lady he had refused
passage to a few weeks before; that he would vouch for me
without hesitancy, that my business was urgent, and no

c*

harm could grow out of my passing through. On which,
permission was given to pass. On receiving the glad intelligence, my heart overflowed with gratitude to my kind
intercessor. The time spent from thence to Corinth was, by
me, in hope and fear relative to the object of my search.
On reaching my destination, I saw at a glance it was being
evacuated, and one of the most heart-sickening sights my
eyes ever beheld was witnessed there and then. Everything
seemed to be in perfect confusion. Thousands of sick and
dying were scattered, far and near, around the depot for
the purpose of being sent off, with the hot broiling sun
beaming upon them, and they unable to help themselves.
The confusion was so great that but little attention was paid
to them by their comrades. With a few exceptions, they
were suffering much for want of food and water. Soon
after leaving the cars, I saw my friend, Dr. Green, of Memphis, and approaching him, I asked him if he could give
me any intelligence of my husband. He replied that he
could not; but remarked that "Jim" (meaning my son) was
lying in that crowd very sick, pointing to a place where
hundreds lay scattered upon the ground. He advised me
to remain at that point, saying he would go and bring him
to me. He went, but did not return. After waiting with
great anxiety for some time, and the doctor not returning,
and my patience giving out, I started in search of him—
going from group to group of the sufferers. I did not find
him. I then repaired to the verandah of the Tishomingo
House, and there placed myself in a conspicuous position,
hoping that if he were in sight he would discover me, and
give me intelligence of his whereabouts; but it availed
nothing. I employed myself while thus waiting in keeping
flies off of the sick that were thickly strewed around me.
The house was then used as a hospital. But my suspense
becoming so great, I could remain there but a short time.
Returning to my baggage, which I left in care of the guard,

I found there several of my friends, who insisted that I must get upon the train, which would start in a few minutes, and return to Memphis, saying, "the Yankees are advancing, and if we remain, they will soon have us all prisoners." I concluded they were some of the bomb-proofs, and were laboring under a severe fright—so much so, that some of them looked blue. I presumed they were there as spectators, having no special business, and were not posted as to the situation of things as my humble self—especially those who did not have on the soldiers suit of gray.

While standing listening to the expostulations for my leaving, I resolved to remain until I found the object of my search, even if I should be captured in so doing. But to my great joy, while thus standing my sick and emaciated boy came staggering up, presenting more the appearance of a corpse than a living creature. Never shall I forget the mingled feelings of my heart at that moment—joy at finding him, and sorrow and grief at his deplorable condition, being quite delirious at times, but sane enough to inform me that Dr. Green had told him where he left me standing, when he resolved to make an effort to get to me, feeble as he was, believing that he could not live many hours if he remained where he was. With nothing to eat or drink, and no strength to help himself, he felt confident that to remain in that condition, death was his portion. Many were in a like condition, and doubtless perished upon that spot, and filled nameless graves. This, doubtless, would have been my son's case, if I had not come to his relief. I soon learned from him that my husband had been sent to Columbus, Mississippi, on the same day I made my first attempt to meet him at Corinth. I gave my son his choice, to go with me to Columbus, or return to Memphis and recuperate a few days, to better enable him to make so long a journey. He chose the latter, and I immediately applied for permission to put him upon the cars, which were kept constantly locked to keep out citizens, they being reserved for sick soldiers.

As soon as the officer of the guard saw me approaching with my sick charge, he ordered the cars at once to be opened for his admission, and gave all the assistance he could in getting him, with myself and baggage, aboard, and to make him comfortable. Those who assisted me on that occasion of my distress, as well as all similar occasions, have my lasting and heartfelt gratitude.

The cars were soon filled to overflowing with the suffer-ers, and started at seven o'clock that evening for Memphis. They progressed very well for a few miles, when the ina-bility of the engine to complete the trip became manifest, and the train ceased to move, after several attempts to go forward, by backing down and then advancing, failed. About midnight, to our great disappointment, the locomo-tive with part of the foremost cars were detached, and ran on to Grand Junction, leaving that portion of the train on which myself and son were, and there we ramained until seven o'clock the next morning—no light in the cars, and the night intensely dark, and no water for the poor sick soldiers but what little could be gotten from the stagnant ditches on the road side. This was procured by those who were able to get out, but with great difficulty, as the night was pitch dark.

The groans and wails of the sick and dying (for several died that night, as I was informed,) were distressing in the extreme. The piteous cries for something to eat by the hungry, and for water by the thirsty, were constant and agonizing indeed. From my well-filled satchel I distributed to their wants as far as it went. The horrors of that night, language is inadequate to describe; and the unpleasant impression left upon my mind stands out more prominent than any of the effects of the scenes I witnessed during the war. I never had it so forcibly demonstrated, before or since, to what extremes persons will resort when about to perish, as at that time. They would seem to manifest as much satisfaction and pleasure in drinking the muddy and filthy water, as though it was the most pleasant beverage in the world.

At sunrise the engine returned, to the great joy of all, and we were soon at Grand Junction, where we had to change cars; and with some difficulty I got my son and baggage transferred to the cars that were to convey us to Memphis. I procured a seat alone for him, placed his pillow so that he could lie entirely upon the seat,) my lap being the only couch he had since we left Corinth,) which gave us both great relief.

Many inquiries were made by several individuals relative to who he was, where he was from, and what was the matter with him. These were promptly and correctly responded to. In addition, I gave them to understand the condition of my husband, and my great anxiety and suspense about him. This seemed to elicit much sympathy from those around us. At length, a young man stepped up very consequentially, and asked, with great authority, "Who is this you have with you?" "It's my son, sick," I promptly replied. "He has the typhoid fever." "Where did you get him, and where are you taking him?" he again asked. I gave him the desired information—adding that a few days good nursing and quietude would restore him, so I could remove him to Columbus, Mississippi, where my sick husband had been sent. "Well, madam," he abruptly remarked, "you will have to get off of this train, and take some other route; you can't take him to Memphis; no soldiers are allowed to go there now. The Feds. will soon have that place; therefore, you can't proceed any farther." I expostulated with him, telling him "that my son's fever was so great that he was at that time delerious, and it would kill him to lay him out in the hot sun; besides,

there was no chance to get a conveyance to any house or
shelter." At that, he spoke very short to my son, saying
"You must get out here, or I will have you put out."
With that unfeeling remark to one who looked more like
a corpse than a living man, he was about to leave, when
some two or three gentlemen, though strangers, (God bless
them,) rose up, and said, "Sir, who gave you authority to
put off this lady and her son, who is so sick?" "I have
orders," he replied, "to let no soldier go down this road."
They then said, "This lady has told you she was not going
to stop in Memphis but a short time, to recruit her son
sufficiently to travel farther. Therefore, we say you can't
put her off, unless you are stronger than we are. So you
had better pass on, and charge upon some one else, and not
a lone woman, with her son a helpless soldier." A hint to
the wise was sufficient. He did pass on, and I saw him no
more. I have my doubts if that " brave son of Mars "
ever fired a gun in defense of his country. But after this
event, which was trying to a mother's heart, if he had
followed that sick youth, or soldier, whom he wished to
put off so mercilessly, to the bloody battle field of Perryville,
Kentucky, or the great struggle at Stone River, or the
carnival of death at Chickamauga, there he would have
seen this same youth standing alone under a cross-fire of
the enemy, when every one belonging to his battery were
either killed, wounded or missing; and, finally, in trying
to make his own escape, had his horse shot from under him.
If he had been present at Missionary Ridge, from thence
through all the conflicts to Atlanta and its vicinity, and
with Hood through his campaign in Tennessee, and subsequently with Johnston in North Carolina, he would have
seen this same youth ever at his post, both in conflict and
out of.it. And at the last he might have seen him at Salisbury, in the last artillery duel of the war, where, it is said,
he loaded and fired the last rebel gun at the enemy, for

Southern independence and Southern rights, in Johnston's army.

I trust the kind and indulgent reader will pardon me for thus dwelling so long upon the first and last unkind treatment I ever received from a a Southern officer, or soldier' during the war, notwithstanding my lot was cast among them constantly for four long years. I am proud to say, save the case above alluded to, with all my varied intercourse with the army, I met nought but the kindest treatment and greatest respect from the soldiery, from the highest officer to the humble but gentlemanly private— always ready and willing to render me any assistance in their power that I might need. Taking for granted that for the above digression and personal allusions that I am pardoned, I will now proceed with my journal.

At eleven o'clock, May 28th, we reached Memphis, and put up at the Sea House, procured rooms, and soon had my son as comfortable as his sick and prostrate condition would admit of. The next morning, Mrs. A. Street gave me a pressing invitation to accept the hospitalities of her house, which I did not refuse. I at once had my son conveyed to her house, where every comfort and attention was generously extended to him. Her kindness, with others, manifested toward us while under that roof will ever be remembered with pleasing emotions by a grateful heart.

My son improved very rapidly, and in a very short time I deemed him sufficiently recovered to travel and feeling great solicitude about my husband, hastened our departure for Columbus. After preparing a quantity of comforts and delicacies for him, on the 31st of May we bid a sad adieu to Memphis and its attractions, and took the train for the above named place. The journey proved very fatiguing to my sick boy—he being too feeble to sit up more than a few moments at a time.

On changing cars, my only recourse was to make a pallet upon the ground for James to rest upon until I could get my baggage changed; and then, with the assistance of some kind stranger, I would succeed in getting him comfortably placed in the cars again.

I met with but one misfortune on the trip, and that, at the time, (owing to my situation, and the great anxiety I felt about my husband,) gave me but little concern, but subsequently caused me much regret. I allude to missing, at Jackson, through some mistake or mismanagement, one of my trunks, containing the greatest and best portion of my winter clothing, and several valuable books, with other precious relics, which until the present day has never been recovered. It is needles to say the principal articles contained in the trunk were much needed by me before they could be replaced, for in those days of "blockades" goods of every description were very scarce, and enormously dear.

We tarried at Jackson from ten A.M. until six P.M., which greatly refreshed my patient. On entering the cars we found (to me long to be remembered), that christian patriot, the Rev. C. H. Marchall, of Mississippi, who devoted his entire time and attention to the invalids on the train. This endeared him to at least two persons who felt the need of all the sympathy and friendship that, in these trying circumstances could be bestowed by the hand of benevolence.

The morning of June the 2nd found us comfortably quartered in a freight car, at Meridian. With the use of a plank and my trunks I made quite a comfortable bed for my son, who was still improving. This, in combination with other circumstances, made the latter part of our journey much more pleasant and agreeable to us both, inasmuch as he did not have to lay his head in my lap, as heretofore; therefore I could sit in a chair and administer to his wants. He seemed to rest sweetly during the day; and what added greater pleasure to the last days of our travel, we had the company of one of those kind and patriotic ladies of the South we meet so often, Mrs. Sheppard, of Pulaski, Tennessee.

Six o'clock P.M. found us at our destination. Procuring passage in an attending omnibus, we soon found ourselves on the way to the general hospital, where I was informed that my husband had been ordered to report. Parting, at the door of a hotel, with the kind lady above referred to, I was soon ascending the stairway of the hospital, which brought me into the presence of the officer of the department. With an aching heart I soon informed him of the object of my visit. Referring, immediately, to the register, he reported, to my great dismay, and his regret, that he could find no name answering to that of my husband.

My son was soon placed in comfortable quarters, and a warm and palatable supper spread before him, of which he partook with avidity. I was conducted to a remote room, where supper was awaiting me, which I sat down to, through formality, and attempted to eat—but in vain; I had no relish for food, notwithstanding I had not eaten anything but cold lunch since leaving Memphis. I however forced down a few mouthfuls, amid flowing tears, and with an aching heart, unnoticed by the two other ladies who sat at the same board. I soon arose and repaired to the bedside of my sick charge; saw that he was comfortable, and then sought the bedsides of the Shiloh wounded. While mingling with the sufferers my attention was attracted to a gentlemanly looking personage, whose beautiful face, in every lineament, bespoke benevolence and kindness. Approaching me, he said: "May I ask of you, madam, if you are the strange lady, in company with a sick son, who has just arrived from Memphis, in search of

a sick husband?" When he was answered in the affirmative, he replied : "Well, madam, I have heard great interest expressed in your behalf by the surgeons in the office."
He informed me that his name was Wright, and said.that
he was proud to acknowlodge himself a Tennesseean. "I
am," he continued, "ready to render you any service in
my power. Is there anything I can do for you? If so, I
am at your command. You need not hesitate to communicate to me anything you may wish done." My heart at
once filled with gratitude, not only to God, but to the kind
stranger, who, unsolicited, proffered assistance in the hour
of my greatest trouble. As soon as my emotions sub-
sided, I informed him that my great desire was to learn
the whereabouts of my husband, if living; if dead, where
he was buried. He remarked : " Madam, you shall know
before I cease my search ; therefore, content yourself as
best you can ; and I will traverse the streets of this town
until I gain some intelligence of his fate." With these
words he started upon his benevolent, but uncertain, mission. I contented myself as best I could, and passed the
time in conversing with, and assisting, the suffering soldiers.

In about an hour my friend returned, bringing me the
joyful intelligence that my husband was not dead, but
very sick, at Newsom Hospital, distant one mile from
where I was stopping. He wished to know if I desired to
visit him that night. I replied in the affirmative. He then
tendered his services as an escort, advising me to let my
son remain where he was until morning ; then, with my
baggage, he should be sent to me.

We were not long in reaching the place where lay my
sick and emaciated husband. My kind conductor and
friend, wishing me success and happiness in the future,
bade me farewell, and took his departure with the blessings of a grateful heart following him. (I now exceed-

ingly regret that I did not obtain his address, as it would have been a source of great pleasure to me to have corresponded with one who had manifested such a disinterested regard for one whom he had never seen before.)

Early the next morning, according to promise, my son was sent to me, and placed by the side of his father. I was again a happy woman, with a heart overflowing with gratitude to the dispenser of every good thing that we sinful creatures enjoy ; and here I beg the kind reader to excuse a seeming digression in expressing my faith in divine interposition, or supervision of the events of humankind. I believe that God directs all the controling events of human life to our good. Although, at times, we are led to complain at the seeming hard fate, or circumstances, that mark the checkered paths of our existence, yet, when duly understood, in all their various bearings, we are forced to glorify and praise God for final results. To illustrate : Had I succeeded in getting to Corinth in my first attempt, I would have taken my husband home, leaving my son in good health ; therefore I would have had no other call to that place, and my son, when taken sick, in all probability, would not have realized his perilous condition until, perhaps, too late to communicate the fact to me ; and he no doubt, without the careful nursing that none but a mother can bestow, (which he got), would have died, without my knowledge, within twenty-four hours from the time I found him—judging from his condition at that time. He would then have filled, as many others did, an unknown grave, upon the plains of Corinth. Thus, you see, I have a reason for the faith within me. But to my narrative. My husband and son improved rapidly under careful nursing and prompt attention. My son soon becoming convalescent, took charge of a ward until able to return to field duty.

By request of the surgeon in charge, Dr. Brown, of Atlanta, Ga., I took charge of the hospital as matron, the duties of which I endeavored to perform to the best of my ability, under the circumstances. The hospital was generally filled. Many poor soldiers breathed their last inside the walls of old Newsom, and now fill soldiers' graves in its vicinity, owing to their hopeless condition when arriving there, often dying a few minutes after being placed in the hospital.

Through the kindness of a few ladies, who brought in some delicacies, I was enabled to add more comfort to the sick and disabled than I could have done by the ordinary supplies of the hospital.

My son, in a few days was so far recovered as to be able to rejoin his company as it passed through there on its way to Chattanooga, preparatory to the great Kentucky campaign. That was the last hospital my son was ever in, as a patient, during the war. After he left me I felt unusually lonely, having had him near me so long; I therefore resolved to keep as near him as possible at all times.

On the 13th of August my husband and myself bade adieu to Newsom Hospital, and took our course to Chattanooga, arriving there on the 18th of August, two days after the arrival of my son. We found the army in motion, commencing that long and well-remembered campaign. In bidding my son adieu upon that occasion, I felt great solicitude for him on account of his yet enfeebled condition, he not having fully recovered.

On the same day I was assigned position in the hospital established in the Methodist church, Dr. Taylor, of Memphis, being the surgeon in charge. I remained there only three weeks, going thence to Tunnell Hill, Ga., where I was kindly received by the surgeons in attendance in the General Hospital, and also by their patients.

Dr. Wyble, of Louisville, Kentucky, had charge of the same, and being a gentleman, he treated me as though he

knew how to appreciate the services of a lady in such a
place as a hospital. He gave me free access and privilege
to distribute such diet to the patients as I thought best.
Having that liberty granted, it in a great degree, lessened
the duties of a sick room of much that is unpleasant, and
added greatly to the pleasure I found in nursing and taking
care of the poor helpless soldiers, who were sacrificing all
the comforts of home, and jeopardizing their lives, for the
rights of our beloved South and their fathers' land. In
fact, the whole corps of surgeons were gentlemen, and
treated me with a reverence and kindness due a mother,
making my stay of five months pleasant and agreeable.
In the course of time, news arrived that General Bragg
was retreating from Kentucky, which increased my desire
to know the whereabouts and condition of my son. I
daily perused the papers to learn the locality or position
of General Cheatham's division. I thereby learned it was
stationed at Tullahoma, Tennessee. I at once felt a great
anxiety to go there, and endeavor to find my son, if alive,
for I had not received any intelligence of him since we
separated at Chattanooga. I knew not but he had fallen,
with many of his brave comrades, at Perryville. Obtaining
a few days leave of absence from my post, I took the train
on the 20th of November for Chattanooga. On arriving
there, I met Dr. Mitchell, of Memphis, from whom I received the joyful news that my son was not only safe, but
well. While waiting for the train, I met with Captain
Anderson, of the Ninth Tennessee Infantry. After expressing much pleasure at meeting me, he enquired the
place of my abode, and to what point was I bound, and if
I had a proper passport. I handed to him the one I had.
He told me he thought it doubtful, and offered to go with
me to the office and secure a special one—at the same time
addressing a note to General Llewellen, commander at
Bridgeport, asking him to see that I was allowed to pass,

as there was difficulty in a lady passing, owing to the vast
crowds of soldiers that were daily going through. I only
mention this as a pleasant reminiscence of the war, to show
to the world that the true soldier is also the true gentleman; and that he may serve in the army for a term of
years, and be deprived of the society of those whom in
former days felt honored by his presence, yet not become
so demoralized as to forget the endearments of home, and
that his mother also bore an existence among the weaker
sex.   This touching act of kindness, which was a true
mark of a gentleman and a soldier, will ever be enshrined
in memory's casket.

While waiting at the hotel for the train to leave for
Tullahoma, I learned that Mrs. Newson, whose acquaint-
ance I had made at the Overton Hospital, in Memphis, was
at the Ford Hospital, (known as the Crutchfield House).
I immediately repaired to her place of labor, and was
warmly welcomed by that ever true and patriotic lady. I
found her at her post of duty, administering comfort to the
suffering braves, beloved by all for whom she labored. I
spent quite a pleasant night with her.   Rising early next
morning, I made preparations for my departure, which was
to take place at six o'clock—giving me ample time, as I
thought, by leaving the house at five and a half o'clock;
but to my surprise, I was just in time to be too late, and
I within ten yards of the desired conveyance to the spot
where I hoped to meet the object of my search. I must
confess that I was greatly chagrined, and it was some time
before I could be reconciled to my sad disappointment.
However, I returned to the hospital, and made the best of
it I could—passing the day with my old friend, and visiting her patients, and assisting her in the various duties
assigned to her department. I was well assured by the
many kind looks and words of the sick and dying, that
my time was not altagether lost. The lesson of disap-

pointment I so thoroughly learned the previous morning, compelled me to lose no time in being punctual the next morning; and it is unnecessary for me to state that I was at the depot in due time, and soon was speeding away as fast as steam could propel us, over a road which was entirely new to me. It was the first time I had an occasion to travel on the Nashville and Chattanooga railroad, and the first time I had been on my own native soil (Middle Tennesse) for twenty-six years. The many beautiful landscapes and mountain sceneries which the eye is ever feasting upon, it would be occupying time and space unprofitably to describe, as it is too well known to the many who enjoy the pleasure of visiting these places of Nature's most pleasant resorts. At two o'clock, we arrived at Tullahoma. Having learned at Bridgeport that the train ran off the track on the previous day, and detaining the train which I had missed, I found myself just as far ahead, notwithstanding my disappointment. So, as I said before, my time was not lost; and I certainly escaped quite a dilemma, there being no place of entertainment at Bridgeport, and several of the ladies were obliged to take shelter in the soldiers quarters, which were gentlemanly resigned to them. I considered myself fortunate in the event for being five minutes too late.

I soon learned that General Cheatham's division had started that morning for Murfreesboro, Tennessee. So I continued my course, and arrived there at six o'clock the same evening. Having fortunately fallen in company with Rev. Wells and lady, of Greensboro', Tennessee, who were going North, and Captain Lewis, of Knoxville, Tennessee, I accompanied them to their stopping place, (Mrs. Campbell's,) where I received better treatment than elsewhere, and I felt perfectly at home under the kind widow's hospitable roof.

Captain Francis, of Memphis, commanding the Fourth

Tennessee Infantry, whose pleasant company was highly appreciated, as well as that of Captain Bibb, of Tipton county, Tennessee. They being old acquaintances, both took great interest in the object of my mission, and assured me that they would use every effort to ascertain the whereabouts of my son as soon as the army arrived.

On Monday, the 24th, the army made its appearance at about twelve o'clock, and it was late in the evening before the entire column ended their weary march. The most of the command took up quarters on the main street of the city. I had nothing to do but witness the grandeur of those veterans, who had so recently passed through the well remembered Kentucky campaign. It was indeed an imposing sight to behold the many thousands of weary, dusty, yet cheerful and healthy looking veterans, who had cheerfully and happily followed their brave leader to and from that noble old State, and were ever ready to follow him on to other more perilous deeds of valor.

How impatient I was to behold him who had been so long absent, and endured so many hardships. The roll of the canon wheels would startle me ever and anon, and with the anxious hope of recognizing him, my eyes would fly from gun to gun; but not until four o'clock were my hopes realized—to the joy of my heart, which had suffered ten thousand pulsations on his account. I could scarcely realize the fact that he looked so well, after so hard a campaign. Many were the stories he had to relate concerning the numerous trying scenes he had passed through since our separation. Many sad trials he had suffered in seeing his brave comrades fall by his side—some who were children and schoolmates in days of innocence. They now sleep beneath the sod of old Kentucky, and dirges to their memory are sung by her balmy breezes, that sweep through her forests; and, perchance, some of her noble daughters drop a tear as they stand around the graves where sweetly sleep the early fallen veterans of our volunteer State, in reciprocation of the many tears which Tennessee's daughters have shed over Kentucky's exile sons, who nobly fell in our midst. Time fleeted by pleasantly with us for a few days, while we were spending the hours around the pleasant fireside of the already mentioned lady, mending and making as many garments as time allowed me for the soldiers. O, what an inestimable pleasure it afforded me to know that I could contribute to the comfort of one of the well deserving number of those who endured so much for our constituted rights, but blasted hopes.

Having enjoyed myself to the full wish of my heart— that of meeting my long absent boy, finding him in the best of health and spirits, and leaving him a good winter's wardrobe of my own making—I felt it my duty to return to my post, for well did I know that I was needed, and anxiously looked for by those whom I had left on the bed of suffering.

CHAPTER III.

Early on the morning of the 27th, I took leave of my soldier boy, and my ever grateful friend, Mrs. C. May God bless her and her four interesting children, and raise up the kindest of friends for them, will always be the heartfelt wish of her who will never cease to cultivate a debt of gratitude for her disinterested kindness to myself and son. Had every woman in the South possessed the disposition of that charitable lady, the suffering among the soldiers would not have been so great by a thousand fold. Had it not been for that blessed lady, the company to which my son belonged would have suffered intense hunger during the battle at that place, being cut off from their

D

provision wagons. Their only resource for something to
sustain life, and enable them to stand the hardships and fighting of that memorable battle, was from her table. She did
not hesitate to send food from her little store to the battle
field. Who but a true lover of country, and a heart endowed with charity and sympathy for those who were
suffering in a just and righteous cause, would have divided
her scanty supplies, at a time when there was so little
prospect of them being replenished? Doubtless, her faith
was as strong as the widow's on sacred record, who was
assured by Elijah "her cruse of oil would not fail, or her
barrel of meal give out." May it ever be replenished to
the filling of her every want. May her Southern friends
ever stand by her in her every time of need.

I hope this imperfect eulogy will not be considered as
premature, especially of one who so justly merited the
praise and esteem of the great and good. Many a noble
deed of those in humble life are too frequently passed by
unnoticed, where others in more prosperous circumstances
are lauded for far lesser deeds. But God takes notice of
all good deeds, whether rich or poor, and in His own good
time will openly reward them.

I need not say that I was joyfully welcomed back by my
patients at Tunnel Hill. The evidence which will hereafter
be appended, will speak for itself. Time passed on, as was
its wont to do at a place of so much suffering—some recov-
ering and returning to their respective commands, some
dying, while others still lingered with disease. Soon after
my visit to Murfreesboro, the battle, which is recorded in
the hearts, and indellibly stamped upon the memory of
many thousands, was fought. Another period of anxious
suspense with me. My husband was engaged in the same
hospital with me, therefore my mind was at ease in regard
to his safety. But my only child was there in the battle,
and for aught I knew, had fallen a martyr to his suffering
country's cause.

The wounded were sent to us in great numbers, and we were kept very busy attending on them. Each attendant discharged his or her duty faithfully. I shall always revere the surgeons of that hospital for their unremitting services, and for the privilege allowed me of administering to the wants of the patients as I thought best—they relying on me with the utmost confidence for comfort and benefit. Eight days passed before my anxiety was relieved in regard to my son's safety. "Joyful tidings!" were his words. "Mother, I am safe." All the inmates of the hospital rejoiced with me, which greatly endeared them to me. I felt like I could nurse legions, were they with me, so great was my sense of gratitude to God for His protecting care over my only boy. Learning from his letter that he had lost all of his clothes, but those he had on, I hastened to procure some for him; and relieving myself from my patients, on the 20th of January I took a flying trip to Shelbyville in order to furnish him the clothing I had procured. Had I been able safely to send them by the cars, I would not have left at a time when my services were so much needed. However, my patients were all willing to spare me, under the circumstances, saying it was my duty to attend to my own boy in every hour of need.

On arriving at Shelbyville, a little incident occurred, which rather nonplused me for the time; but afterwards, caused no little amusement and criticism, together with much sympathy for my having fallen into such an unrespected and, pardon me for saying, uninvited dilemma. I think it too good to be lost, therefore I will give it as it was, hoping to offend no one by personating one or two who were connected in the affair.

On getting off the cars, I set about looking for my son, hoping to find him in waiting, as he was expecting me. It was now dark, and as I did not meet him, I, with a soldier, (one of my patients who was returning to duty,) started to find a stopping place for the night. Enquiring at the first respectable looking house' from the depot, we were positively refused, with the information "that neither rebels nor their friends were entertained there." On leaving the house, two gentlemen walked up, hearing part of the conversation between us and the landlord and one of them asked if we were looking for a house for the night. I informed him we were; told him who I was, where from, and for what business I had come to Shelbyville. He remarked, in the most gentlemanly and kind manner, "Madam, I procured a room this morning for myself and friends at a genteel looking house, and the family seem to be nice people. If you will go with a stranger to a strange place, I will be happy to coduct you thither, and will vouch for you a comfortable room, if I have to give up my own to you. Nothing gives me more pleasure than to accommodate a lady, and, more especially, one engaged in the glorious work in which you are." Without hesitating, we followed him to Mr. Rumey's. On entering the room, we found the landlady and her daughter by a comfortable fire, while a smoking supper was in waiting. Here allow me to introduce to the reader the two kind gentlemen through whose kindness we were enjoying those comforts. They were Hon. R. Hurst and Mr. Gillespie, of Athens, Tennessee, who introduced us to the kind landlady and her excellent daughter—stating that they had assumed the privilege of conducting us to their comfortable fireside, as I was a stranger in the city, and she seemed to be blessed with plenty of room and provisions. Therefore he hoped he had not incurred her displeasure by so doing. She hardly waited for him to finish his remark, when, "Oh, my!" she burst forth a railing accusation, saying she did not thank him for bringing a crazy rebel on her to eat up her provisions, and she get nothing for it in return. Mr. Hurst politely remarked to her, "that she accused him wrongfully;

that he was able to pay for the crowd, and had not asked charity of her at all, neither did he wish it; that he had engaged a room of her, and insisted on my putting up at her house; and if she would receive me, he would give up his room, and sleep out on the porch on his blanket." I remarked, "Madam, I always travel full handed, and expect to pay my fare. All I ask is to be treated as a lady should be by one professing to be a lady." "Pay, indeed," says she, "what good will the pay do? It's no account when you get it—old Confederate money! who wants any such stuff." We all tried to convince her that, if Confederate money would buy provisions, it was all the same as greenbacks. But not a word could we say that would conciliate our hostess. When my friend saw that argument would do no good, he assured her that I should have shelter that night, he would see to it. That he had advanced for his room, and I should have it. He immediately made a fire, and invited me to take possession, which I gladly accepted, being glad to get away from mine hostess, who had become disgusting to all of us. I have been of the opinion for a number of years that when a lady steps out of her place, and abuses her sphere in society, she becomes one of the most detestable objects in the world, and should be scorned by all her sex. As long as she retains and acts out the dignity which characterizes the true lady, she is worthy of respect wherever she goes. But when she so far forgets herself, and others of her own sex, she deserves the scorn and contempt of all the civilized community.

I retired early, and slept soundly in my comfortable quarters, made so by my then strange, though never to be forgotten, friends, who took their blankets and slept in some other part of the house, without the benefit of a fire, as I learned. I also ascertained, the next morning. that there was plenty of room in the house for twice the number who were there; but for the want of charity to a

stranger, and the knowledge of what is required to constitute a lady, and her hatred toward rebels, we were
thus treated. We all took it in good faith, as we were on
the right side, as we honestly thought, and were willing
to suffer persecution for the same.

At an early hour we were up, and soon a blazing fire
was started ; and I invited my kind friends to seats in the
room so magnanimously given up to us by themselves the
previous night. Breakfast was soon announced by the
old gentleman of the house, who was entirely ignorant of
the kind of reception we had met at the hands of his better half the previous night, and who appeared to be quite
a mild gentleman   He insisted that I should take breakfast ; but I at once declined, telling him that I had a
lunch with me ; and that my desire to have a warm supper the previous evening was because I was wearied from
travel ; and that I regretted very much the annoyance my
presence had caused his wife, and that it should have been
looked upon by her as an intrusion. Mr. H. informed him
that he was responsible, and ready to settle the bill. I
thanked him kindly for what he had already done, and
paid my own bill.

My first move was to learn the whereabouts of General
Frank Cheatham's headquarters, which as soon accomplished, and a courier dispatched for my son, who was not
long in obeying the summons. I immediately informed
him of the treatment received from Mrs. R., and he at
once secured me another place in a good family, by
the members of which I was treated with kindness and
respect, and which soon revived me from the shock of the
previous night. This lady, Mrs. Froquie, had several
interesting daughters, to whom I became much attached
in the short time I remained with them. They were true
Southern ladies, and soldiers of the Confederacy never
failed to receive a hospitable reception at their house.

My time was precious, as I had left many of the brave sufferers of the battle-field of Murfreesboro, and who were in need of all the attention that could be given them.

Finding my son all right, except suffering from fatigue caused by the hard-fought battle and retreat, I took the cars early the second morning, which carried me safe to my post of duty on the following morning. I found everything progressing smoothly, and all the patients improving.

While at Shelbyville I discovered that many of my friends from Memphis were wounded. I endeavored to ascertain their whereabouts, hoping to procure a transfer for them to the hospital in which I was, for I felt anxious to give them my attention. I made inquiries at Chattanooga, Ringgold and Dalton, but could learn nothing definite in reference to any of them; but to my great surprise I discovered that our energetic Doctor Curry, of Overton Hospital, Memphis, Tenn., was at Ringgold, and he soon learned that I was at Tunnel Hill. He sent me a note, requesting my services in his department, Ford's Hospital. As a natural consequence, I felt that I would like to be with one who was, like myself, an exile from home; besides, there was no lady with him to render that assistance which was so much needed, and too much neglected. There were several ladies at Tunnel Hill, so I thought it advisable for me to make Dr. Curry's department my place of duty. I did not imagine that bidding farewell to those with whom I had been so long connected would prove such a severe trial; nor did I know, until the avowal of my intended departure, in what esteem I was held by my patients, and the estimate they placed upon my services; nor was I aware, until that moment, that the faculty appreciated my feeble services so highly—though, during my stay there, I was always treated with the utmost respect, by both physicians and patients, who

acted toward me as though I were their mother. Had I
known it sooner, I should have remained ; but my word
was given, and I could not consistently stay longer at
Tunnel Hill.

On the 22d day of February, 1863, myself and husband
bade a fond and sad adieu to our beloved patients and
kind officers, amid a scene and trial which I hope never to
pass through again. But we may hope, in the flight of
this short life, to escape the sad scenes which so often chill
the very heart's blood ; yet, as a consequence of some of
those sad partings, as time speeds away, we have many
kind greetings, which are made the more sad when again
we must part. Thus it was in the experience of our own
dear soldiers. It was like parting with those of my own
household. I had administered to them in their wants ;
had mingled with them in their most excruciating suffering , had stood by them, and closed the eyes of their most
intimate comrades, who had died on the soldier's couch,
in arm's reach of those who survived them ; had received
the blessings of the dying, and the approbation of the living ; and it was hard to leave them when they assured me
that the services of no one could be appreciated as mine.
Many of them expressed themselves in such pleading
terms that my heart was touched, and tears filled my eyes
at the thought that they would suffer for necessary comforts. "If you leave us," they said, "we will suffer.
One woman is worth a dozen men in a place like this."
Such was the character of their numerous expressions,
which I produce as testimony of the value in which the
services of our sex were held. I often wonder that more
ladies did not lend a helping hand in their behalf when
there was such a wide field for every indispensible usefulness before them. It is true, it was a great sacrifice to
abandon home, comfort, and domestic interest, and go
among strangers, to share the fate and hardships of the

soldier. But did they not do the same, and tenfold more? Did they not leave home, friends, and all who were near and dear to them, for the good of their country? and were not their lives, at all times, risked in addition? Yes; and yet we shrink from the small task of relieving, by our own little attentions, a few of those every-day troubles and sufferings, while they, for us, were risking ten thousand different dangers and perils; and after all, if life was spared, how many thousands of them came home maimed for life from wounds received on the field of battle. Surely, viewing it in this light, we can think it but a very small part of the horrors of war for us to take up our temporary abode with those who were permanently placed within our reach, and do what little we could in the way of administering to their wants. Indeed, no reasonable sacrifice was too great for us to make in reciprocation for their long endurance, perils and hardships, and their noble and heroic bearing, in so many hard fought battles in trying to sustain our lost, though honored, cause.

One hour after leaving our suffering charge at Tunnel Hill, we were making our way from the depot at Ringgold to Dr. Curry's office, where we were kindly met by his affable and courteous self. We soon felt ourselves at home, as the doctor was very kind to us, and there was plenty of material to work on. His hospital was full of the same material we had just left, and no female to speak a word of cheer, or recognize them as friends, brothers, and defenders of their homes.

I soon found, as I always did under similar charges, that I was by no means an intruder in the midst of the patients, and that my services, or those of some attentive person, were greatly needed by the invalid soldiers. My services were gladly accepted, as they were cheerfully tendered. The patients were in the hands of kind and able surgeons, who were always at their posts, and ready

D*

at all times to administer relief when needed while there, as well as at other hospitals with which I was connected. I was frequently compelled to witness many heart-rending scenes. Many noble and brave men fell victims to disease, and wounds received on the field of battle. Many a mother's darling's life ebbed out at Ringgold, Ga., while her name was being written by hands almost paralyzed, as the last breath of life was quickly passing away forever, just when he was leaving some kind message to be trans-mitted to her, if it could possibly be done.

Time passed away with the usual routine of events and incidents which daily transpired at such places. Four months of my time was spent with the patients of Ring-gold, and I trust not to the injury of any one, and I hope beneficial to some.

In the month of June I again made ready to visit my son, who was still at Shelbyville. On the 6th of June, 1863, I took the train for that point, arriving there on the 7th. I stopped with a kind friend, Mrs. Froquie, with whom I had stopped on the previous January. I found her, and her four amiable daughters, the same kind ladies as before ; and, as a natural consequence, the time for a few days, passed off very pleasantly. Captain C., who is not only a soldier every whit, but a perfect gentleman, always ready to make others around him happy, and do justice to his men, released my son from duty, so that he might spend his time with me. Such deeds of kindness were not lightly appreciated by the humble recipient, but are still cherished with the deepest gratitude.

While at Shelbyville I learned that the hospital at that place was without a matron, and that one was greatly needed ; and as one other had joined us at Ringgold, I I thought I would do more good by going where there was none. I therefore returned on the 11th, and informed Dr. Curry of my purpose to make a change. He insisted that I should remain another week, which I did; and by not being too hasty in making a change upon uncertain grounds, I escaped being a participant in the hasty retreat which General Bragg and his army made from that place, which many will never forget.

However, as I had dismissed myself from under Dr. C.'s charge, we repaired to Chattanooga when the army was concentrating there. Applying to Dr. Stewart, who was post surgeon there, for a situation, we were assigned to the direction hospital, conducted by Dr. Lytle, of Nashville. This was a new hospital just fitting up, on the ground formerly occupied as a camp of instruction and direction. There were but few patients assigned it, and only two assistant surgeons—Drs. Burt and Sewel. These were two as perfect gentlemen as ever breathed the breath of life. Always at their post, ready to mingle in social conversation with their patients, as well as to administer medicine and give medical advice. All who knew them, learned to love and respect them. I do not suppose they had an enemy among the inmates of the hospital.

This hospital was not permitted to get under complete operation before it was, with the hasty retreat of the army, removed to Calhoun, Georgia, from the fact that bomb shells were falling too thick in and around Chattanooga, about the 21st of August, 1863, which doubtless many still remember to their sorrow. It being the first time I had been so near the enemy's grounds, I must confess, it to a considerable extent, excited and alarmed me for a short time; but I soon rallied from the shock, and did not mind it. I suppose others besides myself remember that day as a day set apart by President Davis for fasting and prayer. As the hospital was too far from the city for the inmates to attend divine service, a goodly number had met in one of the unfinished wards for the purpose of holding a prayer meeting. And the humble writer was one of them, for I always encouraged the soldiers in holding religious meetings in their wards whenever it was convenient, and was generally present myself, as they at all times seemed to appreciate my attendance and aid. A chapter had been read from the Divine Word by one of the company, a hymn sung, and all were in the humble attitude of prayer, offering up their feeble petitions to the Holy and ever rich Throne of Grace, where we all have divine assurance that we need never come in vain, where all the prayers of the truly humble and sincere are answered in granting protection and christian graces. If we, as a people, ever did need Heavenly aid, it was at that time, and just at that important moment, and in future times we most certainly did. The whole earth seemed shaken by the thundering roar of one of those mighty death dealing siege guns of the enemy. I for one thought it only our boys trying their guns on some new work just erected near the river. But in less time than I have been penning this, on came another, and another, until the whole crowd was excited. Still our service continued so long as prudence dictated, when we were dismissed in good order.

On leaving the house, the spectacle that attracted my attention, language fails me to describe. Every inmate who had not joined in the service was in the greatest state of excitement and confusion imaginable. Some were running in one direction, and some in another—each making such speculation on the times as his own distracted mind suggested. On inquiring the cause of the firing, several cried out "the Yankees are shelling the town, and we will all be captured!" "Are you not going to try to get away?" was a question asked by not a few. I replied that I should remain with them until I had orders to leave. Some rushed into town as fast as their horses could carry them, and hastily returned, bringng various news—all calculated to increase the excitement, which seemed now at

its greatest hight In a short time orders came from head-
quarters to get ready to leave at a moments warning.
Then came the tug of war with us, if I may use the term.
If ever there was haste made in pulling down and packing
up hospital goods, it was then and there—each trying to do
something, yet some effecting nothing in consequence of
not having presence of mind sufficient to settle on what was
necessary to be done, as the firing increased to such an extent
as to create a panic among us. Soon, however, everything
was torn down and packed up. But to our astonishment,
here came a number of wagons loaded with disabled soldiers from the Academy hospital in town, bringing them
out of danger of the shells, which were whizzing over and
around them in their once quiet resting place.

It was painful to us to see the poor, sick, wounded and
emaciated soldiers dragged out in the beaming hot sun, and
laid upon the ground to suffer until beds could be prepared
for them. Doubtless this caused many of them to die, as
the exposure and fatigue was too much for their now exhausted strength. It was impossible for us to make them
comfortable under the circumstances, and, of course, they
suffered untold agonies, though every effort was being made
to prevent it. Poor fellows, they had been hastened off
before getting their dinners, and were hungry. All of our
cooking utensils had been stored away by orders; but your
humble servant, by the aid of some of the good soldiers
who were in attendance, went to work and fried up a nice
lot of ham, procured plenty of bread, and placing it on
some nice pieces of plank served to them with a glad heart,
thankful that we could do that much for them. Though it
was rough, and they had seen better days, and accustomed
to better fare, yet they devoured it with as much alacrity
as if spread in the very best of style, and seemed as thankful for it.

Oh, I never shall forget the seeming fear manifested by

those helpless sufferers. They had the most perfect horror
of falling into the hands of the Federals. I endeavored in
every possible way to quiet their fears, telling them that
General Bragg's boys would protect them; that the
Yankees could not hurt them while the heroes of so many
battles were between them and danger. They, like myself,
soon became accustomed to the boom of the cannon, which
kept up a brisk fire until late in the day. During the excitement our hearts were made sad, occasioned by the death
of one of our patients, whom we had attended with deep
interest for several weeks, and had hoped to see him recover. But that monster, Death, claimed him as his victim,
and the soldier must die in defense of his country's righteous cause, in his adopted home, away from his own native
land, among strangers, with no loved sister or fond mother
to soothe his suffering and dying moments, or imprint a
fond kiss as a last farewell on his lips then cold in death.
It was sad to witness the Norwegian die under such exciting
circumstances as surrounded us then. We closed his eyes,
and dropped a tear of real sympathy for distant friends,
who, perhaps, would never know the fate of their loved
one. The name of this poor fellow was Shafter, and, if I
rightly recollect, he belonged to the Eighteenth Texas.

Notwithstanding we were ordered to be ready to
leave at a moment's notice, we did not receive positive
orders to quit the place until Sunday the 23d, at which
time we took the cars for Calhoun, Georgia, leaving most
of the patients behind us. I need not attempt a description
of my feelings in regard to their welfare, for it would be in
vain. Poor fellows; how many times was my heart made
to bleed at their suffering and want of care and the best of
attention, when it was out of my power to give it to them.
However, they were left in good hands, and received the
best attention that the circumstances would admit of. I
was unable to learn to what point they were removed from

that place, and I do not recollect of having ever met with one of them again.

All was quiet at Chattanooga when we left. No thundering cannon belched forth its death warning to the citizens, and the brave little band, who were standing, as a wall of fire, in defense of their rights. Many families had taken refuge in the woods, and were gathering in groups beneath the shades of the forest. Others had pitched tents, and made for themselves temporary houses to shelter them and their little ones, and in quite a limited and humble way were preparing their scanty repast. They seemed perfectly content with their situation, made so by the advance of the enemy on their once quiet and happy homes. Is it any wonder that there should be a feeling of bitter hatred, for the time, between the invaded and the invaders, from the fact of not following the example of all truly great military men—as Napoleon, for instance, who in all his invasions his orders were peremptory to treat all private citizens and private property with perfect respect, which resulted in his not only succeeding in his enterprises, but in gaining the lasting friendship of the masses ; as did all other noble and successful warriors in prosecuting civilized warfare, only fighting upon honorable principles the governments, and not private individuals and non-combatants. We trace those principles of warfare down through ages to our own noble General Robt. E. Lee, whose order to his subordinates and men were in all cases of invasion to exercise perfect respect for all private citizens and their property, and not to molest, or, in any manner, do any violence to private property or private individuals, under penalty of death. But in this instance, if I mistake not, (as well as in almost all similar cases,) the rules of civilized warfare were entirety disregarded. Without a moments warning, the city was shelled, thereby not only destroying all private property in their reach, but disregarding the lives of women

and children, and all other noncombatants. They not unfrequently inflicted severe wounds on innocent children,
which either resulted fatally or in a life-long disability. In
an instance of this kind, which occurred at Chattanooga,
on that ever memorable event, a little girl was struck by a
piece of shell, causing her to lose a leg. If I mistake not,
others there received similar wounds. I shall never forget
some poor frightened ladies who sought out our hospital for
protection, leaving their aged and invalid mother. They
had secured and erected a tent by which to shelter her from
the scorching sun and rain, when soon came a shell whizzing over their tent, and falling near by, causing a renewed
scene of terror and excitement in their already badly
frightened minds. But a truce to this part of our story, as
there are others much more competent to give a correct and
more interesting history of the frightful events of that, as
well as other events of the war.

Sunday, the 23d, late in the evening, found us at Dalton,
Georgia, where we remained until Sunday, the 25th, when
we left for Calhoun, where we were welcomed by some of
the kind inmates of our hospital, who had preceded us.
They had a warm breakfast in waiting, which we shared
with them, not waiting for a very pressing invitation, as we
had to take the cars at Dalton before the hour of breakfast.
Houses were soon procured, and all hands went to work
fitting up wards to receive patients. Quite a number were
sent to us in a short time, who were placed in comfortable
quarters, and every possible means were used to add to
their comfort and well being. We had hoped to remain
there for a considerable length of time unmolested; but,
Oh, vain hopes, how soon were they blasted. All the hard
labor which had been so cheerfully performed for the benefit
of the wayworn and invalid soldier, must be as a blank,
and the already exhausted sufferers must be hurried from
their beds of comparative ease and comfort, to seek shelter

themselves, with nothing but the canopy of Heaven over them, and a blanketless earth for their couch. The Yankees were near by, and General Forrest in pursuit. Preparations were rapidly made for sending our convalescents to other camps, and those fully able for the field to active service. We were informed that the enemy was advancing. Orders came for us to prepare for another exit from the impending danger. I do not think I ever had my sympathies more keenly aroused than at that time, when not only the convalescents, and others who were not severely wounded or diseased, had to be moved, but, the poor fellows who could not help themselves had to be taken by apparent rough hands and sent off, while others who could not be moved had to be left to the cold mercy of the Federals— who were known by all to be void of feelings for Confederate soldiers, as well as citizens. However, our kind and energetic Dr. Burton, and his assistant, Dr. Williams, remained, from whose hands they recived all the attention they possibly could give them under the circumstances. The remainder of us took our departure for Griffin, Georgia, on the 17th of September, arriving at Atlanta the same day. We remained there until the 20th, awaiting further orders; and at one o'clock the same day we arrived at our place of destination.

We were soon at work preparing for the reception of the sick and wounded from the field of Chickamauga, that ever memorable battle then just opening. It was but a few days before our hastily fitted up wards were filled with those noble braves, who required all the aid that stout hearts and strong arms could possibly give them. And then, with all that the best of surgeons and nurses could do, many of the poor fellows, who had stood the merciless fire of the heavily concentrated forces the enemy brought against them, and now to see them suffering the last pangs of death, after so nobly defending their banners on that bloody field,

was heartrending in the extreme.   If ever men deserved
the elogium of the poets to their memory, and inscribed
on tombs, surely those never to be forgotten heroes did—

> " Who, their liberty to gain,
>   For hours stood the awful fire
> On Chickamauga's plain.
> All honor to the gallant boys,
>   Who nobly warred that day !
> We proudly weave rich garlands
>   To deck their war-scarred brows ;
> And heave a sigh, a tear, for those
>   Now numbered with the slain,
> Who sleep beneath the crimson sod
>   On Chickamauga's plain.
> And we 'll ne'er forget their chieftain
>   Who led the van that day,
> And nobly cheered our Southern boys
>   Thoughout the dreadful fray.
> Long may he live—our gallant Bragg !
>   To hear the cheering strain
> Of victory won by his brave boys,
>   On Chickamauga's plain !"

Many were the victims of that day who were crowned
with unfading wreaths of honor, who, after long weeks of
untold suffering, yielded up their lives nobly, a sacrifice
on the altar of their down-trodden and bleeding country,
and who are now sleeping in soldiers' graves, under the
care of the kind and patriotic citizens of Griffin.   It is due
the ladies of that pleasant little city, and its vicinity
generally, to acknowledge, with grateful heart. their
untiring kindness and undoubted patriotism in rendering
every valuable assistance in behalf of the needy and suffering soldiers placed in their midst to die, or recover from
disease or wounds, as their fates indicated.   It will ever
be a pleasing thought that it was our good fortune to have
our lots cast among those who were so kind to us during
the short time we remained in Griffin.   But a hard fate
decreed that I should not remain there long.   Again I

must bid adieu to my suffering soldier friends. Pardon
me, kind reader, for again repeating what to me was so
sad a remeniscence, or the story of parting with my
patients. Toward them I felt as though they were my
own household; and on me they seemed to depend for
everything that a sick and wounded soldier so much
wanted; and to know that I must leave them, helpless,
and deprived of any effort in me to give them relief, was
indeed hard. Eternity alone could tell the depth of grief
that I felt; and justice will be meted out to those who
were in authority, and who ungratefully, (as was the case
in many instances), to show their power and authority,
deprived one of doing that which duty and love of country
alone prompted, simply because one wished to do justice to
poor suffering heroes, and there was not a sufficient
amount of money placed in their pockets, and their honors
were not in every minor matter consulted. These men held
bomb-proof positions by dishonorable means. If the
soldiers had received one-half the supplies allowed them
by the Government, or if, the kind donations of ladies,
had been found on their tables, some of the luxuries of
diet, that cost the Government of these upstart sub-
officials neither money nor trouble, or if they had received but one-half of the many and very valuable
comforts allowed them, or needed and deserved by them.
notwithstanding those same officials were enjoying at the
same time the very things donated by private citizens, and
appropriated by the Government for the sole use of those
same soldiers, not only of the most desirable provisions,
etc., but fine brandies, wines, and all such articles, four-
fifths of which the persons for whom they were intended
was consumed by those same bloated, spider-like, bomb-
proof officials, while the poor soldiers, who had stood as a
wall of fire in defense of the rights of those same men's
lives and property, while their own dear ones were in dis-

tant States, over-run by the enemy, half starving, insulted, and their property pressed by the Government officials, and the remainder taken by the Federals, the lives of many brave soldiers would have been saved; yet, the few comforts donated to them were used by those in power, who never had been in camp, or in line of battle. If one of the matrons or nurses got possession of a small portion of those comforts, and distributed them among the suffering and half-starved soldiers, they were soon dismissed. I only speak of this for the benefit of those whom it concerns, as none will receive it as their own but those to whom it belongs, for a true soldier in authority knew how to treat his subjects, while the other class either knew not, or would not, give them justice. Even a cloak of religion could not hide the fact that the wolf was there in the guise of the sheep, or good man.

Unfortunately for our country, a great many of the most important offices were filled by that class of men who felt no interest in the welfare of the country, only so far as their own personal interest was concerned; and, as a consequence, everything that could be turned to their own advantage was so managed, regardless of country, or the poor soldiers who were unfortunate enough to be under their management; therefore, thousands, for whom much was donated by private citizens, as well as set apart for their use by the Government, actually suffered for the necessaries of life, to say nothing of the luxuries.

On the 25th of October we bade adieu to our patients, amid their tears, mingled with our own, at the same time receiving their kind wishes for our happiness and welfare, with every assurance of gratitude to us for the little we had done for them.

My thanks are due Doctors Gibson, Richardson and Wright for their kind treatment to us as co-workers with them in a noble and much needed work, a work in which their hearts and hands were faithfully engaged. They will ever have my kind and grateful remembrance, and best wishes for future happiness.

Four o'clock found us at Atlanta, on our way to Ringgold, to join Dr. Burt, who had been sent there from Calhoun to establish a distributing hospital, bearing the name of Hill Hospital, in honor of the intrepid General A. P. Hill, of Virginia. On the morning of the 26th we were welcomed by the doctor and a number of old attendants of Direction Hospital, who were left with him at Calhoun. I felt as though I had just returned home after a long journey, for I was made as welcome by the head of that well-fitted out and faithfully conducted hospital, and its gentlemenly attendants, as if I had been their mother. Everything that was necessary for the comfort of the numerous inmates, and others daily arriving from the battle field, was on hand, of the very best, and in the best of order. As was always the case with Dr. B., we found plenty of places where we could lend our feeble mite of assistance. Having been but a few hours from a place resembling the one we had just entered, I felt, as usual, when among our brave boys, at home, and lost no time in ingratiating myself into their favor by tendering my undivided services, and was delighted at receiving cordial manifestations of their acceptance of them.

I found plenty to do, there being but one other lady in attendance. I was tendered full control of each ward, so far as a matron's authority extended, with full permission to direct and nurse as I saw proper. No limit was put upon me in the way of directing, and I was allowed, for patients, everything that was necessary to their comfort and welfare. Such being the case, I was happy, while at the same time my thoughts would, ever and anon, flit back to those I had so recently left at Griffin, under different circumstances. Sad moments would pass over me in regard to the lonely and unpleasant condition they had been left in; and I prayed that some kind hand would soon succeed the one that had so unkindly denied us the privilege of administering to them

For the short time that Hill Hospital remained at Ringgold, many were the untold scenes of suffering which were daily witnessed. It being a receiving and forwarding hospital, made it the most conspicuous in that respect. Some would be unable to proceed any further, and soon filled honored soldiers' graves, among strangers, in Ringgold Cemetery. Perhaps the green mounds which cover their once manly forms, enclosing hearts that once throbbed with true Southern patriotism, have often been bedewed with tears, shed by some of the inhabitants of that once pleasant little village, and bedecked with clusters of richest flowers. We hope so, at least. They will ever live in the hearts of those who fully appreciated the just and noble cause. Tread lightly, dear stranger, when you approach the sacred spot where sleep noble defenders of Georgia, who fell while endeavoring to keep the enemy from over-running our dear Georgia, as well as the other Southern States. Therefore, dear reader, if you ever pass near the various spots of ground so honored with the good soldiers' graves, halt one moment, and shed a tear for the mother who could not have the privilege of closing their eyes.

Occasionally, one or more of the opposite party, who were captured by our soldiers during battle, would fall into our care, and I am proud to acknowledge that they were well cared for by both surgeons and nurses, as were our own sick and wounded boys; and it was not unfrequently the case that pleasant little parties would be gotten up, and which were attended by both. A recollection of such scenes is still pleasant to memory. The difference of opinion in regard to the origin and ravages of the war, did not at all times alienate the two parties from each other. Circumstances were such that they were often thrown together in a more civil and social way than it was generally the case with those who were engaged in the bloody conflict. And it was then and there that the brave soldier and gentleman was fully tested. As is the case with all really brave gentlemen, they were, when on the field of battle, in full readiness to fight to the death; but as soon as quiet was restored, they could treat their enemies as gentlemen and friends; and in this case both sides were ready to mete out justice to the other; and, permit me to say, that the few who were amongst us, as a general thing, manifested a desire to give us justice, and a disposition to be grateful for the kind care bestowed them, after expressing their surprise at the marked attention given them. Doubtless many of them will always be ready to contradict the many false reports that have been maliciously circulated relative to the cruel treatment received by them at the hands of our Southern authorities while they were prisoners of war.

By way of confirming the truth of the above remark relative to the friendly feeling manifested between the two contending parties, I will relate an incident which occurred while we were at Ringgold. As was my usual custom, after each meal had been distributed, I visited each ward, to see to the general wants of the patients. In one of my rounds, on the occasion relating to the incident, I entered a neat little room in one of the wards, occupied by some new patients. On entering I bade them good evening, and inquired if they had dined, and if they were comfortable; and also if I could do anything for them; and if so, that I was ready to do all I could for their comfort. Each one thanked me kindly, and said that they were comfortable, and highly pleased with the change from the Field Hospital to a good house. Finally, quite a gentlemanly looking man remarked to me : "I am pleased to inform you, kind lady, that we are all doing finely, as well as Rebs and Yanks could, all quartered together, and on the very best of terms." "Excuse me, sir," said I; "are you a Yankee, and seem so cheerful while a wounded prisoner?" "Indeed, madam, I have no cause to feel otherwise than cheerful," he replied. "I have had the kindest of treatment since I have been a prisoner in the Field Hospital; and from every appearance, I think that I will still be treated right. My boys said to me when I left the field that I might bid adieu to kindness since I had to go further South. I said to them that I hoped that they were mistaken; and I believe that my hopes will be fully realized." I said to him that nothing should be wanting on my part, but disability, to make him perfectly comfortable—at least as much so as our own boys; that in war we were enemies, but in peace we should be friends; that I wanted our boys to give them the very best fighting they could in battle, but when they were captives it was my firm desire to see them treated as kindly as friends could be—on both sides. His countenance beamed with delight. He said, "Ah, madam, I would that there were thousands like yourself; then your boys would not be treated amiss, as thousands are, in retaliation, caused by exagerated reports, as I believe, of cruel treatment of Federal Soldiers in southern prisons, especially by the ladies." I assured him that it was a mistake so far as my own observations were concerned; that the ladies of the South were, as a general thing, too noble minded as to so far forget their sphere as to maltreat those in their power any farther than they would be willing to see their own dealt with under similar circumstances. He replied, "Madam, permit me to say, that if any one had told me that I would meet with so kind and motherly an old lady I

should not have believed it from the reports in circulation ; in fact, I do not see how you Southern ladeis can
have the heart to treat us kindly, for we have invaded
your soil ; killed your husbands, sons, brothers and fathers ; and I wonder that any one of them takes any notice
of us only to treat us with scorn. But we fighting men
should not be punished for what we did not bring about.
The fanatics raised the war cry, and we had to obey the
call to arms against our wills. And now your boys have
got us, and our's have got your's ; and here we poor devils
(using his own expression,) may lie and rot for all the fanat-
ical scoundrels care. My leg is broken, and here I may
remain, and not one of them would, if they could, come
near me. If I am spared to get well, I have done my last
fighting. I will go home to my wife and little ones, and
never come here again, or grumble at the hardships of
milking the cow, old Brindle, for her when she asks me
to." This produced quite a laugh among the whole crowd.
Some of the Rebs remarked, " Why our Southern ladies
milk, and do all their domestic work in doors, and the men
the out door work." He said : " The men in our country
do the out and in door work too, to a considerable extent."
One day I saw him smoking an old cob pipe. I asked
him if he would accept a nice new one from an old Reb.
" Certainly, madam ; and thank you, too," said he. I
hastened to my room, and soon returned with a good, new
pipe, filled it with good tobacco, lit it, and presented it
to him, saying : " Now, let us smoke the pipe of peace
together, and say you will fight our boys no more."
That I will, madam," was his frank response ; " and I will
take this pipe home, show it to my wife, and tell her an old
Reb gave it to me." " Yes?" said I, not giving him time
to finish. " Yes," "he responded, "a good old rebel lady,
who is as kind to me as a mother." In this cheerful way
he passed a few days with us under our care ; and was

E

then forwarded to Atlanta. On his taking leave, he bade us a kind farewell, thanking our ever faithful surgeon and his attendants for their unceasing and very kind attentions to him, assuring us all that he was more than satisfied with the treatment he had received at our hands.

Did we not have much pleasanter reflections under those circnmstances than if we had exhibited the same hostile feelings toward them, that, unfortunately for the good name and future to the happiness of both sections, was acted out by the hard hearted on both sides, although we were still on the bloody field of battle? It cost us neither more time, trouble or money to speak and act kindly to the unfortunate prisoners, as to do as so many have (to the disgrace of the North and South) done to them and our own soldiers. Yet, by so doing, if we were not made permanent friends, we did not widen the gulf between us, and we have the consciousness of having done to them as we would wish our own dear lives done by; and if we ever meet them, it cannot be said by them, "there is the surgeon and attendant of that awful hospital where we were treated as beasts, or heathens." If we never meet until the great day of all accounts, we will have nothing wilfully on our conscience of evil towards our enemies, as they were then considered. Oh, that all on both sides had have done as we feel confident we endeavored to do, then we should

> "Speak gently; it is better far,
> To rule by love than fear."

By so doing, it is often the case that we can win a soul from error; when by a rebuke, we only drive it further into the deep that it is just timidly entering, and sink so deep in sin and immorality as to be irretrievably lost, instead of being won to virtue, and hiding a few of the faults already committed. Would that our enemies—who by tenfold numbers overpowered our ever brave little band of heroes, who fought as never men fought before, and fought for their rights honestly and sincerely, and so long, amid so many disheartening circumstances, and so little encouragement, and at last yielded only because their means were exhausted, and, as a consequence, their numbers diminished—would follow the example of the good and great of former days, when the rights of a conquered foe were religiously respected, who claimed no other boon than a full submission to their authorities, instead of continuing to crush them lower and lower, until not only their national rights alone were all taken from them, but every private privilege that could possibly be taken was wrenched from them, putting them lower in the scale than slaves. But with the termination of hostilities all enmity ceased; and the more bravely they had fought, the more respect they received at the hands of their victors. But we must bide our time, having faith to believe in the promises of our Divine Father, "the humble and faithful believer, who does his duty to man and his Creator, will not always suffer." We may yet, in time, be a free and happy people.

In our hospital time sped on, continually changing from one lot of patients to another. All seemed quiet in the camp, and we hoped to remain at Ringgold, for the winter at least; but our hope proved vain and soon blasted. Although all seemed quiet for the time, yet great preparations were being made for the terrible battle of Missionary Ridge.

CHAPTER IV.

On Monday, the 22d of November, all Ringgold was aroused by the report of a few guns from the direction of Chattanooga. There was much speculation concerning the cause. As all anxiety was turned in that direction, and to satisfy curiosity, some of us ascended to the top of the mountain known as Taylor's Ridge, made renowned by the maneuvering and hard fighting of the great General Pat. Cleyburne and his brave followers, who no doubt saved the Southern army from a more disastrous result than that of Missionary Ridge. While we were sitting on a rock far up on the side of the ridge, viewing the magnificent scenery before us, made the more grave and sublime by the noble old Lookout, whose towering peaks loomed up far above all others as far as the eye could see, our attention was suddenly attracted by the flash and report of a cannon, which seemed to be about halfway up the mountain. With anxious hearts we all gazed and waited to see if it would be repeated, and soon there was another flash and report, and still another, when all was quiet again. That was the first time I had witnessed the firing of a gun by the contending parties, and it excited me considerably. The tents of each army were visible, though some ten miles distant. On our return to the hospital, we found several carts already filled with the suffering patients, ready to be moved in case of emergency. Quite early next morning the boom of cannon could be heard at intervals, but things moved on as usual in our department until late in the morning, when suddenly all were aroused by the cry of "The Yankees are coming! Oh dear, what shall I do? Where shall I go to keep them from getting me?" I walked to the door of the ward, which was full of patients, and asked the cause of the panic. "Oh, the Yankees are just down yonder at the mill—only half a mile off; they will come here in a few moments," was the reply of Mrs. E., who was frightened almost out of her wits. I tried to quiet her by saying they could not hurt us if they did come. But what a time I did have with her. She kept screaming out "don't leave me—I shall die!" Well, I must confess I had to laugh at her, although I felt sorry.

Her husband called out, "Rosanna, go over to Mrs. Anderson's and stay with her, and I will take your trunks to the woods." "I shan't do it," she said; I shall not leave Mrs. Smith, and she says she is going to stay here." Poor woman, she would not let me go out of her sight. I was amused at the idea of her clinging to me so closely, just as if I could save her from the Yankees. All was confusion, some running in one direction and some in another. Some couriers loped their horses through the woods, by way of reconnoitering, and returning soon, reporting them to be this way and that; while the post commandant rallied all the convalescents who were available, and forming them in line, marched them off in the direction of the reported Yankees, and, strange to say, I never saw him again. But I suppose he was found in the right place when he was needed, as he was said to be a good soldier, and was a perfect gentleman and a minister of the Gospel. He had been in charge of the circuit of the M. E. church in which I had lived, called Wesley circuit. I refer to Rev. Mr. Poeples. During the excitement, one of the hospital surgeons came running up to me, and said, "Mrs. Smith, I have several hundred dollars of money on my person. Had not I better burn it up, with all of my papers, for fear they get me?" "Oh, no, Doctor," said I; "you had better hold on to all you have until you know they are here, then you can dispose of it in some way; don't burn it up. If you do not need it, give it to me, and I will divide it among these helpless boys, and I will warrant the Yankees will never get it." Another man by me, bidding me good bye, said, "I have got all my papers secured." I looked, and saw he had his knapsack swung around him, and all his dispensary articles in it, and he was making tracks. Things went on at this rate for about two hours, when the joyful news came to the town that it was all a hoax; that it was only three Yankees had captured the guard at the mill;

that Ringgold was safe, and that the enemy had retired. After everything had become quiet, and the frightened ones become calm, then the joking and laughing commenced. Each one had his joke to tell on the other. But the best one was on Dr. H,, who wanted to burn up his money and papers; while Dr. P. had a few passed on him for swinging his knapsack, papers and money around his neck, and so solemnly and affectionately bidding us all good bye, as though he did not expect ever to see us again. Mrs. E., of course, did not escape her share; while her husband was complimented for his gallantry as a scout and for his report, and consequent opinion that he had better run his trunks this way, as the Yanks would come the other.   Finally, it was decided that he (Mr. E., the steward,) had won the day by his intrepidity in keeping out of danger.   After whiling away a short time in jesting and congratulating each other on our safety, a party was formed, and Taylor's ridge again ascended for the purpose of making observations as to the position of the enemy, etc., for there had been an almost incessant firing all day, and it was thought their position could be plainly observed from that point by the smoke from the discharge of the guns.

On reaching the hight of the ridge, oh, what a sublime and awful spectacle met our view.   No one can give the faintest idea how awfully grand a battle is in full blast when viewed from a distance—more especially when the observer is on such a hight as we were, and the two grand armies drawn up on another, but greater hight, and their cannon all in full action.   We can only say to those desiring a description, that the only way to form an idea of its immense grandeur and awful sublimity, is to witness it as we did from our point of observation.   As column after column of Federals ascended the opposite side of the great Missionary Ridge, pouring in volley after volley from small and large guns, and receiving from the Confederates similar volleys, producing an immense volume of smoke, which seemed to blacken immensity of space, and almost obliterate the rays of the sun, while the sound seemed as one continuous roar, deafening those near enough, and at the same time killing by the hundreds our own braves as well as the Federals. All together combined to make the scene in the full sense of the term, awfully sublime. All nature seemed to be draped in deep mourning; and well it might, when of the divinely created beings so many were being rudely murdered to satisfy the malice and hatred of a few leading fanatics, who were not satisfied with having worked for a quarter of a century to ruin one of the most happy people, and one of the best governments, until they had succeeded in both, and now the innocent must be murdered by thousands to satiate those blood thirsty creatures' sanguinary appetite for innocent blood. Oh, who in that awful day to come will account for this unholy slaughter? Will the satanic creatures stand blameless? If volumes were written on this subject, then it would not be exhausted, it is so full of sorrow and never to be forgotten interest. Well might Nature, the parent of those noble forms who stood face to face, dealing death to each other by such immense forces, look down on the wholesale carnage, and, as it were, shed tears of pity for them, and sorrow that man should ever be so corrupted and led on by passion and the influence of black hearted rulers, until they were void of feeling and fellow sympathy. Which party were the real criminals, I will not stop here to say. Our hearts were made to bleed for the fallen sons of the South, who lay weltering in their blood, martyrs to their country's cause. We left the ridge perfectly awed by the terrible grandeur of the scene. Another squad of patients were being sent off, and we hastened to give them their supper. After they were put on the train, assisted by the steward, we gave them rations to last them to Atlanta, bid them farewell, and

again turned our attention to the few left in the wards.
Many questions were asked by the poor sufferers concerning the battle. "Did we think it would be a general engagement? Would our men be able to hold the field? If
defeated, would we leave them to be taken prisoners?"
We assured them they should not be left. Poor, kind fellows, they did not forget my soldier boy, for whom my old
heart was in a perfect agitation, hoping he would come off
safe, admonishing me to be hopeful. No one knows what
a soothing balm it is to an anxious mother under such circumstances to have the sympathy of those of his well-tried
friends and comrades, except the recipients of the kind interest the soldiers ever manifested in my behalf. This is
now as fondly cherished by me as when I was daily in their
midst. As night approached, the firing ceased, and we
hoped all was over, and the day won. But, oh,

> " The few sad hours of shaddow dream
> And valor's task moved slowly by,
> While mute they watched till morning sun
> Should rise and give them light to die."

For at early dawn of the following morning, the 25th
inst., a repetition of the previous day's fighting began with
a renewal of the almost incessant booming of cannon, really
much more vigorous than that of the day before. All hearts
were turned in that direction with a degree of anxiety
which none but those who have witnessed it can feel. The
two parties appeared to go into the engagement determined
to use every possible effort to such an extent that it beggars
description. We were all excited with hope, fear and awful
suspense. During the day, every word of the most meagre
news was caught up, and flew from one inmate to another,
until all were in possession of news which was calculated
to either make us joyful or more sad; and thus passed off
a day of the most intense dread and anxiety that we
ever witnessed.

About the close of the day, the ridge was again ascended by several of the inmates. Among them was our chief surgeon, Dr. B. His anxiety during the day had been very great, fearing that the removal of the hospital would be the result. When he came down, all fears had been banished. From what he could ascertain from his distant view of the position of each army, he hoped General Bragg would be able to hold the field; and he rejoiced very much at the idea of not having to "pull up stakes and git," as the boys would say. He remarked, "I can sleep sound to-night, as I see we are safe."

At six in the evening, a train came up from Chickamauga station. I was near by giving supper to some of the patients who had been put on the cars ready to be sent off at a moment's notice. While there, we were attracted by the conversation of some one on the train and those of the hospital, and heard the remark "that our boys have given the Yanks a good whipping this time." "Have they?" "Oh, they are whipped, scattered and confounded; and it is doubtful if they will ever be reorganized again." Joy was beyond expression in our camp that night. The news flew from one department to another, until all caught it as if it had come by magic; and each had his own comment to make on Bragg and his brave boys. All was joy and gladness among the suffering boys as they speculated on the results of the heroic fighting of their comrades, by whose side they had so recently fought and fell, and left them to press the retreating enemy at Chickamauga. We had supposed that we were settled for the winter, and that the wearied soldiers could rest for a long time. We dreamed not that the words of the immortal Moore, would be so appropriate to our own case that night, that ever to be remembered night, while a few glad hearts were rejoicing over what was thought to be a perfect victory to the Confederate cause:

E*

> " Had closed the conqueror's way,
>   And lightning showed the distant hills,
>   Where those who lost that dreadful day
>   Stood, few and faint, and fearless still,
>   The soldier's hope, the patriot's zeal,
>   Forever dimmed, forever crossed!
>   Oh, who shall say what patriots feel,
>   When all but life and honor's lost ?"

None but those who have given up all that was sacred and dear to them, and offered their lives on the altar of their country's liberty; none but those whose hopes were at one moment full of expected complete success, and were next, by one fell stroke of largely superior numbers forced against, and completely shattered.

The booming of cannon was heard until a late hour, as if both parties were not satisfied, and the Confederates were indeed loth to give it up. Yet not knowing but that all was well with us, we retired to sleep, dreaming of our dear boy, whom we knew was there, but we knew not but he was numbered among the slain. Still our hope was in Him who "directeth all things, and taketh cognizance of the falling sparrow."

> " While the hope within us springing,
>   Heralds of the dreadful strife,
>   We learned too soon, alas, our doom."

For we were not prepared for the startling news which reached us at early dawn of the 26th inst.—"that the day was lost by General Bragg, and he was in full retreat." Our hearts became sick at the thought, for we were not able to realize the fact that all our cheering hopes had been so soon thrown from the full assurance of complete victory to as complete a defeat, and consequent route, which showed us how vain are all our efforts, unless under divine aid, and how uncertain are all our calculations and hopes when built on man's actions and efforts; and more especially, as in this case, based on reports of those who perhaps had never seen the battle field, and were circulating them merely for amusement, and to see the effect they would have. But be that as it may, orders were soon received for us to prepare to leave on the shortest notice. Oh, what a panic there was now—worse than that of the Tuesday previous. If I ever witnessed confusion, it was then. Every patient who could walk, left without ceremony. Those who were unable to walk, crawled out on the verandah, and watched for the Yankees who were reported to be near by. While stewards, ward master, nurses and hands were engaged in packing up and filling the cars, which were waiting for us. If ever there was quick work in tearing down and packing up for a move, it was then. In about three hours we were ready to move off.

About sunrise the straggling soldiers began to come in; and before we left most of the army had passed through, or was halting in and about Ringgold. Poor, wearied and mangled soldiers! It was indeed heart-rending to see the poor fellows fall down on the porch, with the faint words, "Oh, I am so tired and hungry I can't go any farther." I turned my attention from my occupation, and began feeding them and binding up their wounds, and continued until we had to leave. The last we saw of them they were still stretched out on the floor; some asleep, others groaning with their wounds. None but those who are hardened in battle can behold such a spectacle without their very hearts bleeding with agonizing pity.

While we were waiting for the cars to start, a gentleman informed my husband that there was a soldier lying in a little out house on the side of the road, who seemed to be in a dying condition, and wished to see him. He hastened to the spot, and found to his surprise that it was Gus. Flotron, of the One Hundred and Fifty-fourth Tennessee. He soon returned and informed me who it was, and that he thought he would die, and had made some one take him off the cars, rather than die there. I immediately made application to Dr. Bell to take him with us, which he kindly granted. My son, who had come up all right, found some nice straw, placed it on the floor of the box car, while some of our kind attendants brought him on a litter, and placed him on the straw without moving him off the litter, and the train moved off just as he was safe. Poor fellow, he had a severe wound, and none thought he could live to get to Atlanta. But to the surprise of all, he recovered after being confined near four months, and returned to duty, and fought in the battle of Adairsville, Georgia, where he received several shots in his clothing without being hurt. But the brave are found in the thickest of the fight. So it was with him. While making the desperate charges on the breastworks before Atlanta, on the 22d of July, 1864, he received a wound in the head, from which he died on the 27th, at Newman, Georgia; and his remains are sleeping in the grave yard near by, and sprigs of sweet flowers have been placed on his grave by the hands of one of Covington's fair daughters—Miss Mollie Ellis. Doubtless other tokens of esteem and respect have been paid to him, as one of the bravest men that any army could boast of. Long will his name and deeds be cherished by his comrades who fought by his side in so many hard battles, and who so proudly speak of his gallantry. The people of Covington, Georgia, enshrine his name in memory's casket for his intense suffering while among them, and his pleasant society, and patriotic zeal for our lost cause. And those who rescued him by the road side, and watched over him day and night for months, will ever fondly cherish the memory of brave Gus. Flotron.

The cars moved slowly off, passing thousands of our weary soldiers, who had fought bravely to the last, and, after being overpowered, were worn down in the attempt to escape, and made prisoners. More than once I heard them greet me as we passed, but the moving of the train prevented me from recognizing them.

We soon reached Dalton, where part of the army had already arrived, and were preparing fires and other available comforts for the cold night. A heart that is not adamant would have bled at the saddening spectacle. Notwithstanding their suffering and destitute condition, they seemed cheerful and contented. The knowledge of the overpowering defeat they had just met with, where they saw their country's flag lowered in the face of the enemy, and the cause for which they had so bravely and so uncomplainingly fought and suffered so many untold hardships and privations, for the time suffering the consequences of the late defeat, did not seem to utterly discourage these brave soldiers. Though their cause was truly just, yet it was not saved from those awful disasters which are the fortunes of war.

We were detained at Dalton that night for some unknown purpose. It proved the most disagreeable and doleful night I ever experienced. Every box was crowded with sick and wounded soldiers. All were to be attended to by some one. The air was cold, and a heavy wind was blowing, and there was no chance to enjoy the benefits of a fire, and all were without sufficient covering. However, we wrapped them up, and through the kindness of Rev. Mr. Henderson, of Murfreesboro, Tenn., who was chaplain in the army, and had reported to our hospital for medical treatment, we found a cup of hot coffee, and gave to the soldier whom we had found at Ringgold, which was of great benefit to him in his prostrate condition. So, between that venerable soldier of the cross, who was a fit subject for attention himself, and ourselves, we managed to keep him from freezing, as well as many others, who needed all the attention they could get. I was glad when morning came, as we could see better how to manage the poor fellows than during the night; and we soon had them something to eat; and made their situations more comfortable. The car being an open or flat one, it was not as comfortable as a close one, of course; yet, all did the best they could under the circumstances.

Early on the morning of the 27th we renewed our journey, hoping to be in Atlanta by night; but for some cause or other the cars ran very slow, and stopped for hours at one place, which brought us between Marietta and Atlanta at night-fall. There we were again out in the open woods. It was very dark, and the rain falling besides, and no chance for a fire. Of course, the same programme of the preceding night had to be enacted over. The suffering patients taught us wisdom, and how to endure all kinds of suffering; and we profited by the experience of the night before, and were better prepared with food for the boys to eat. Fortunately for us, there was among the attendants of our hospital a young man, Jas. A. Burgess, of the 24th Mississippi, who certainly exceeded all in being extremely kind to the sick. He never seemed more happy than when doing something for his sick comrades. Every time the train would stop he would run to the nearest house, and tell his story about there being some patients on the cars who could not eat such food as we had hastily prepared before leaving Ringgold; and he was sure to come back with his hands full of the very best of that which they so much needed. Long will many a soldier gratefully remember Jimmie Burgess.

We shall never forget two young ladies, Misses Lizzie Greenwood, and Sallie Hampton. While the cars were stopped at Cartersville, those young ladies were busily engaged in bringing and sending bunks to the patients, made and sent them coffee and milk, and every imaginable good thing. How it cheered the soldiers', and our own hearts, to see such kindness from those strange young ladies.

We found the citizens kind at every place at which we stopped, which made the tedious journey appear much lighter than it would have been.

I will here mention a circumstance, which others besides myself know, and which proves the man in his right place and true character, let him be Reb or Yankee in principle, it matters not which. On Tuesday of the battle of Missionary Ridge, Rev. Mr. Henderson, of whom I have already spoken, reported as a patient and was treated as such by Dr. Burt. Just before the cars on which we were going started, Dr. West, who had taken charge a few days before, stepped up to the parson, and addressed him thus: "Who are you, sir?" "I am the Rev. Henderson, sir." "How came you here?" "I am a patient, and here for treatment?" "What right have you to report here? and to whom did you report?" "I have authority from General Bragg, and the colonel of the regiment of which I am chaplain. I have not imposed myself on you. I reported to Dr. Burt, and he turned me over to the ward master, who took charge of my baggage, and assigned me a bunk, etc. Dr. Burt and the attendants have treated me as a gentleman, for which I am under very many obligations." "You should have reported to me, sir; therefore, you can't go on this train." "I did not know there was such a man as yourself to report to. As I did not see you I reported to the one pointed out to me; and I claim the right of other patients. It is my right, and I claim it as such." "Well, I say that General Bragg has no right to send you here; and you shall not go." But, true to his principles, and in obedience to one who ranked a little higher than this shame on the name of surgeon, so far as the good of the Southern soldier was concerned, at least, the parson got on the train, and started with us on the journey. The next day the doctor, was walking by the car in which the old gentleman was; and, as soon as he saw him, he, in great anger, said, "I thought I told you that you should not come on this train." "I know you did; but I consider my right as good as yours; and I am your patient if you are chief surgeon of Hill Hospital, as I reported there; and my name, rank and regiment is registered there, and I therefore claim my right from you as an officer." "Well, I say get off this train, and do not let me have to order you again." That venerable old minister seemed to possess one of the christain virtues, at least—patience, as well as forbearance. He seemed as calm as if he had been holding a pleasant conversation, and said, "Well, doctor, I shall not go unless some of these good boys throw me off, and I don't think they will do it." Well, on we went until night, when we halted as already stated, between Marietta and Atlanta. It was a noted night in my travels, owing to the time, place, and scenes which surrounded us; besides, it was the night on which our gallant General John H. Morgan was so miraculously liberated from his Northern prison, the knowledge of which sent a thrill of joy through the hearts of all true Southerners. On hearing of his escape I wondered if the night appeared as dark and doleful to him as to myself, and those poor soldiers. Perhaps it did not, for he did not even hear the groans of so many of his wounded countrymen, whose sufferings he would gladly have avenged as well as relieved. Peace to his sacred ashes! Long will his name live in the hearts of his Southern friends as one of the greatest men of his time. Our kind old chaplain was still faithful in assisting us in our efforts to aid the poor sufferers. Never will I forget his untiring energy in their behalf; neither will I forget the unkind and uncalled for treatment he received at the hands of Dr. West, which should result in perfect disgust of the so-called surgeon, as it did by all who witnessed it. At Cartersville the doctor came around again, and on seeing the chaplain said, "Now, sir, I have ordered you the last time to get off this train. If I have to repeat it, I will have you put off." No intercession from the old christian man, who was really sick, would suffice; so, off he had to get, not being permitted to get his baggage. He informed the hated tyrant that he thought he, at a suitable time, would report the abuse to General Bragg; and wanted to know why, and by what authority, he retained his baggage. "Simply because you shan't have it," was the impertinent reply. I gave him to understand that I would secure it for him. The cars moved off, and left that aged man standing there, at the depot, a stranger in the place, without where to rest his weary head. My sorrow for him could not be expressed. On arriving at Atlanta I watched my opportunity, and in the absence of this demon in human shape, secured the poor old minister's baggage, put it with my own until he arrived the next morning, and took possession of it, and bid us a kind farewell, perhaps to see his pleasant old face no more on earth. We hope, when the day of final account comes, he will have a resting place in the Heaven of his God, where he will meet no more of the tyranny of such as this untrue man to the noble cause, the motto of which is, "kindness and charity to all." But he, in his treatment of the aged minister, showed a wicked disposition, as well as being disposed to violate the rules laid down by Christ, where he requires us to give drink to the thirsty, meat to the hungry, and administer to the sick. Oh, that those in authority would ever remember, and act out those golden principles in administering to those over whom they are presiding officially, and escape the awful sentence of the blood of their subjects being required at their hands.

It had rained the most of the time we were on the road, and was still raining when we got to Atlanta. In the afternoon it cleared off beautifully, but remained very cold.

The very best quarters that could be procured by Dr.
Burt were given to us; and we soon took possession, and
had good fires made, the first we had enjoyed for two days
and nights. But the house we were in was not plastered,
and fire seemed to do but little good in the way of making
us comfortable. It appeared that we would freeze in spite
of all we could do. Some of the crowd lay down and
covered up head and ears, and some remained up to keep
fires, and in that way we did not suffer so severely, as we
would otherwise have done. I must confess that I never
did suffer so much intense cold without being able to rem-
edy my condition. Mrs. Collins, who was with us, had
her children with her, and sat up all night, poor woman,
to keep them from suffering so severely. She was one of
those unfortunates from the Chickamauga battle-field, and
had to abandon her home and take to the woods during
the fight. When she returned she found her house plun-
dered of everything she possessed, as was the case with
many thousands of the poor Southern women and children,
to the eternal disgrace of the so-called United States, and
republic. There she was, with four helpless children, and
not an article of clothing for any of them but what they
had on, and her husband wounded and no home. She
sought refuge in the Field Hospital, among the wounded,
and remained there several weeks, and then came to Hill
Hospital, where she remained until the break-up. Her
husband was killed in battle afterwards, and the poor,
good woman was left, with thousands of others, to fight
the battle of life for herself and children, a destitute
widow.

As soon as we could get our breakfasts the next morning,
we set out for Empire Hospital, where our soldiers had
been carried from the cars the previous night. The distance was full one mile; yet, the walk in the cold wind
was not half so disagreeable as what we had passed

through the previous night. We found our patients comfortably situated, and doing well; but our one of the roadside was desponding in consequence of all being strangers to him. He had never suffered from a wound before, and he had little patience to bear his suffering; besides, he could not tolerate the idea of our leaving him. I spent the day with him, and then left him, under promise from his surgeon that he would be furloughed and sent on to us, which promise was faithfully fulfilled in a few days.

I had the pleasure of meeting some of my Memphis friends on that day, which reminded me so much of home and its fond endearments. Mr. Cayce, the auctioneer, was amongst the pleasant faces we met that day. He, like thousands of others of Tennessee's down-trodden citizens, had taken refuge among the kind people of Georgia; and, true to his principles, was doing all he could in behalf of the suffering soldiers. His lady and daughter were daily administering to their wants. Many grateful soldiers will long remember the never-ceasing kindness of Mrs. Cayce and her daughter.

On Monday, the 30th, at an early hour, we were on our way to Covington, our place of destination. We were soon there, and quartered at the Female Institute, where we had the pleasure of remaining unmolested eight months; and in this place permit me to say that all praise is due to the noble citizens of that place and vicinity for fidelity and unflinching integrity to the cause. Every available means was used by the ladies to assist us in administering to the wants of the many poor fellows who had fallen in the defense of the country. They gave us a warm welcome, in their midst, and tendered their services in every way possible, and were ever ready to supply the wants of the soldiers. At no time did we call on any of them for the smallest or greatest favors and meet with a

refusal. I say *we*, because I was identified with the soldiers; and when they were favored, I felt grateful to the
donor in their behalf. For them I labored, and for them
I asked aid; and in Covington I received an unlimited
share. In regard to my own personal self, had I been at
home, among my own relatives, I could not have been
treated with more perfect kindness. Every means was
used to contribute to my happiness. Eight months of
more unalloyed happiness I never experienced, excepting
the suffering of our bleeding country, and the troubles consequent upon that. No one knows, but those who have
been exiled from their homes and firesides, how fondly we
appreciate the knowledge that

> 'Tis sweet to think wherever we rove
> We're sure to find something pleasant and dear;
> And when weary, far from the friends we love,
> We're but to make friends of those who are near.
>
> The Heart like a Tendril, accustomed to cling,
> Let it grow where it will, cannot flourish alone,
> But will lean to the nearest, friendliest thing
> It can twine with itself and make closely its own,
>
> Then, oh, what a pleasure, wherever we rove,
> To be sure of the friendship of those who are dear;
> And to know, when far from those whom we love,
> We've made kind friends of those who are near.

Thus it was at Covington, Georgia. I felt as though I
was with my own old friends and fellow-citizens. Every
mark of pure friendship and respect was shown me, which
bound them to me with ties as lasting as time. It is needless to designate any certain one in that fondly cherished
community, for all came forward, in one common cause, as
sisters, and all were diligent to the end. May the debt
of honor and gratitude paid by those patriotic ladies to
the fallen heroes who died in their midst, ever be cherished
in the memories of all who have been witnesses to such
kindness. They decked their graves with all the memen-

toes of the times, and are doubtless still adding flowers to the memory of the sleepers in that consecrated spot.

The lights and shadows of the doom of our country came and went, as day and night passed away. All was quiet in front; and there seemed to reign a dull monotony in military affairs, until the two great generals, Johnston and Sherman, began the campaign which proved so disastrous to the suffering citizens of South Carolina and Georgia; then all minds and interests were turned in that direction with the most intense anxiety, all well knowing that the fate of not only those two States, but the whole Confederacy, depended on the success or defeat of our brave Southern forces then under the command of one of the most efficient strategists, as well as one of the most profound and brave of the Southern Commanders, and, sadly to our shame, not appreciated by the general Government officials, as was afterwards proved in the consequent downfall of the South.

Up to this time we had been receiving only those transferred from other points; consequently, our hospital was not crowded. But as soon as this great contest began, we had plenty to keep all hands busy. Every few days we received more or less of the fallen, shot and cut up in all imaginable forms. A great many of the best men of our country, from each and every State, died, some on the field, and others either on the roads or in the hospitals. At Covington there are graves of those classes of men, representing every State and command.

The surgeon who so unfeelingly treated the aged minister, of whom I previously spoke, was, to the joy of every inmate, removed from our midst, and Dr. Wm. H. Robertson, of Petersburg, Va., sent to fill his place. I suppose there was no surgeon in the whole army who gave more general satisfaction. None knew him but to love him, and admire his devotion to his duty. He was always ready, at all hours of the day or night, to attend the bedsides of his patients, and watch over them as a father would over a beloved son. His patients were always his first and last care; and he saw that they were always supplied with the very best of everything provided for them by the Government, and donated by private citizens. Therefore, everything went on harmoniously, just like clock-work. Such a surgeon was, in every sense of the term—a jewel, more especially at a time when, and in a place where, there was so much suffering, and where all possible means were requisite to stimulate the spirits and nerve of the faint and dying soldier. A gentleman and soldier to the letter, humane in principle, social and pleasant in all his associations, with the general deportment of a perfect gentleman, his name will ever be cherished most sacredly by all those over whom he had charge, and by the community in general, among whom his lot was cast. Happiness and prosperity will surely attend this ever noble gentleman in this world, and immortal bliss in the world of spirits.

Time passed off swiftly, bringing in new scenes as each new day and night rolled by. Daily reports were received from the seat of war; and as is always [the case under similar circumstances, sometimes cheering, at others disheartening. Sherman was moving slowly and surely, acting out the programme of General Johnston, to get them as far into the State as possible, and consequently as far from their base in proportion, as the noble General had planned, when he got him to the point at which he wanted him, and had set down in his plan of operation, he could with perfect ease cut off his supplies, and make his defeat inevitable. But, behold, the edict would soon go out and ruin the whole plan, and defeat the whole scheme; and far more than all, submerege the whole country in inevitable ruin and subjugation, as we all are now to our sorrow. Oh, that the War Department had have seen as General J. E. Johnston did, and saved the country. But it is past, and we are now reaping the reward of bad management by some one.

But to go back to our story. As the Federals were still gaining more and more footing in the noble empire State, and of course destroying everything as they came, leaving the people in a destitute condition. The Confederate general kept his eagle eyes on all his movements, and kept tolling him further and further; yet the people seemd perfectly satisfied that Johnston knew what he was doing in giving up so much of the State. But, oh, the sad change came at last, when he was removed from the command of the army which had unlimited confidence in him in all respects. It is true that he was superceded by a good man in his place; but he was not the man for that place, which was being so perfectly managed by Johnston. Oh, awful mistake! By a few strokes of the pen in the hand of the chief ruler, the whole army was disappointed, discouraged and dissatisfied. From that hour the awful reports of defeat after defeat came to our previous quiet and cheerful little village. Then the formerly unflinching soldier began to desert, making the chance of success less and less. The men who had followed General Johnston so long, and who would have followed him to the Atlantic coast, and jumped off with him, if he had have said the word. But when they saw him superceded by one not half his equal, they could stand it no longer. Just imagine their feelings when we think how we felt ourselves. It appeared like a noble and affectionate father giving the charge of his family unwillingly to some other man, his inferior in every respect, added to the non-relationship. Yet as our sphere of life would not allow us to speculate on such an all-important subject, and one which others who understand it better than any of the weaker sex have never been able to comprehend the unexpected change at such an important period.

We were at ease of mind in regard to the Yankees inter-rupting the quiet little town of Covington, until July, the 21st, 1864, when it was hinted by some few that they were making their way thither, and that we had better prepare ourselves for the worst. Of course I had nothing to do but stand with those to whom I had pledged my fidelity, so long as they offered up their lives upon the altar of their country, and I contemplated myself, or my position, as being one of them, and subject to whatever suffering or hardship that they were. I tried to prepare myself to receive them, if they did get there, as patient as possible. As it had never been my sad lot to meet them in any other manner, I must confess it required all the nerve I could possibly command to be able to submit to being made pris-oner by the enemies of our country. I was determined, at all events, not to attempt to play off Union, or bother with Northern principles, as (to the disgrace of the whole South), so many hundreds did in order to save their property, etc. Yet, if taken captive by them, I expected to be treated badly in consequence of the business in which I was engaged, and was endeavoring to prepare myself for the worst.

Early on the morning of the 22d, the startling report of their advancing soon reached us. Soon after, the alarming cry that Conyer's station, about ten miles above, was on fire; and, as a natural consequence, quite an excitement was the result, for all supposed they would be on us in a few hours. We were not much mistaken, for in less than two hours from the time we had descended from the dome of the house, from which we could see the smoke from the de-structive fire at Conyer's, some one informed me that the Yankees were in town. "Oh," says I, "I guess not." "Yes they are. See yonder; don't you see the blue coats? Look; here they come in full gallop!" I looked a little to the left of where I stood, and sure enough here come some half a dozen dashing up, as though they intended to sweep everything before them. In the mean time, orders had been distributed throughout the hospital for every one to save themselves as best they could; and if ever I saw what is called pell-mell, I saw it there and then. Every one who could walk broke for the pine thicket. Some did not stop under five miles, and some went fifteen. Dinner was being issued to the wards just as they first appeared, and before I was half done, there were not hands sufficient to carry the waiters to the rooms. Some were at the table eating; and you believe me, they did not stop to finish their dinner. Some were crying out, "good bye, grandma; you must do the best you can. We hate to leave you in the hands of those fellows; but if we remain here, we will be taken prisoners by them, and then we can do no one any good." I told them to run with all their speed, and escape if possible. And, sure, they took me at my word, and made good their escape. I hastened to the wards of the sick and wounded to see how the poor helpless boys were standing the excitement. It was indeed a pitiful sight to look on one that would melt the most callous heart to sympathy, to see them unable to help themselves, and of course were at the mercy of those who were not expected to show mercy to any. Nearly the first question, almost simultaneously asked by all, was, if I was going to leave them. I assured them that I had not thought of such a thing as to leave them—more especially as the ward master and the nurses had about all gone; and I would stay and see that they were cared for to the best of my ability, if all the others left, and not to let that trouble them in the least. "Well, we are all right then, if you stay," they said. It was amusing to see the druggist, ward master and nurses fly by the door, and seeking the nearest hiding place, while the other boys were making tracks in all directions. The enemy were now in hot pursuit, catching a few who were

F

unable to run fast, but who afterwards made their escape—
except a few, to whom the Yanks called and asked if they
belonged to the hospital. "Yes, sir," they answered. "Well,
you d—d fools, what are you running for? Stay inside of
your yard, and you will not be troubled." But they be-
trayed a true feature of their deception, for in less than two
hours they called for those same men, and took them off to
Nashville as prisoners. I thought it one of the most hateful
and low down tricks I had ever seen. After assuring them
that they should not be troubled, as they belonged to the
hospital, and getting all of them who heard of it back in
the yard and house, then to take advantage of them, and
easily secure them as prisoners. Yet it is a known fact,
that as the African cannot change his color, or the leopard
his spots, neither can the real Yankee change his principles.
So in this place they were only acting their regular ungen-
tlemanly principles. Poor fellows, we did so much hate to
see them dragged off to prison; especially as they were so
much needed in the hospital. We were then left with no
assistance, as all of the assistants were taken off but one
young man, (who was smart enough to play off as a patient,)
and those who had gone so far off as to escape capture. A
kind negro woman was also left, who said that principle
made her stay with old miss to help take care of the poor
soldiers. She didn't see what made all de fool niggers an'
wimmin run for, no how; de Yanks didn't want dem. She
wan't 'fraid ob dem; she was gwine to stay right dar, and
stand her ground, so she was. And she made good her
word, but not failing at intervals to rail out against "dem
fool nigga's an' wimmin;" saying, that if she was old miss,
"dat dey shouldn't put dar foots back here, after leaving her
and de poor helpless boys to take care ob demselves."

Well, as soon as I could leave my business, I went to the
office to see how our surgeons had stood by their helpless
charges; and to my unspeakable surprise and alarm, I found

Drs. Robertson and Doyle surrounded by some half a dozen Yanks. Dr. Robertson was addressing them with much eloquence, as he was fully competent to do; saying, "You have come and taken me prisoner while performing my duty as surgeon. The men whom you have disabled while contending for their just rights on the battle field, are under my charge. You have gone contrary to military rules in molesting me. I shall, therefore, appeal to General Girard for redress. I could have made my escape, but before I would have forsaken these, my wounded comrades, I would suffer myself to be shot down here in this yard." He then called the attention of the captain, saying, "Let me introduce to you my chief matron. She is in hopes you will not suffer her to be molested. She wishes to be allowed to remain with these, her patients. She is the only one out of five ladies who were willing to run the risk of being captured for their sake; and I ask you to see that she is respected." I was surprised, as well as satisfied, to receive a polite assurance that I should receive all the respect due one engaged in such a charitable work; and should any of his men attempt to molest me, just report to General Girard, and he would have him dealt with. "By the way, madam," he added, "two of our men have been wounded since coming in the place. If I send them here, will you have them taken care of?" "Certainly, I will," said I; "send them on, and they shall be taken care of." But I never saw them. One of them died in a short time, and I never heard what became of the other. I thanked him for his kindness, and begged him to release our surgeon as soon as possible, for his patients needed his services. With the assurance that he would do all in his power to have him released, they then started for the General's headquarters. Oh, how desolate I felt when they left the yard. I felt like my last friend was gone, and I left alone, with no one to look to for protection and assistance. I suppose that out of at least fifty patients, not one was able to give the other a drink of water. Some were almost in a dying condition; and one died about midnight of the same day, with no one to watch over him but the humble writer and the hired young man, named Chris., of the Fifteenth Arkansas Regiment, who played off sick on the approach of the Federals, and saved himself from being captured. Several of the Vandals came shouting into one of the wards, and began displaying their authority and their weapons, as if they were afraid of the poor boys whom they had shot like brutes. At last one of the patients asked, " You are not going to molest us, are you ?" "Oh, no," said they; "we will only parole you now, and when you are able to be moved, we will send you to prison." " Well, you will not trouble grandma, will you ? She stays with us." " Well, I suppose we will have to banish her to the North, or make her take the oath." "Nary time will you do either," said I. "One who ranks a little higher than you requested me to report to General Girard if one of you dared to molest me, and I will do so." They soon sneaked out. It was but a short time until the doctor was released, and back at his post. How relieved I was of a heavy burden. I was in great dread that they might take him off, and one so faithful deserved better treatment. Besides, some of his patients could not live without the very best of medical attention, and his assistants had just all they could do in their own wards. But after the excitement of a few hours, all was well again, with the exception of nurses and cooks. What a time I had, no one could give the most faint idea. Yet it is an old and true saying, that "where there is a will, there is a way" to surmount the most difficult tasks; and I found it true in that instance, to my own experience and profit. I, with the faithful one negress, who still kept abusing "dem dar fool niggers an' wimmin," prepared the supper for all hands, dished it up between us, and our own true soldiers

and friends, with another who came in unexpectedly, ate
our supper as usual. We cleaned up and prepared the
cooking room and fixtures for breakfast; then we took our
rounds through all the wards, dressing wounds and preparing them for as pleasant a night's sleep as circumstances
would admit of. We endeavored to leave nothing undone
that would add in the very least to their comfort. Poor,
dear fellows; how lonely they seemed without their
nurses, and how hard it was that they should be deprived
of their services in the manner in which they were,
for they were worthy nurses. After we were through with
our patients, and I had watched by the bedside of one
whose life was fast ebbing out, until my strength was
almost gone, I retired to my room, but not to sleep, for at
that time, as on many other occasions, sleep appeared to
have deserted me. I could not sleep when I knew one of
our brave fellows was breathing his last, far away from
those who would have watched over him unceasingly, and
smoothed his dying pillow, and shed tears over his departing spirit. Besides, I did not know at what time some
Yankee might make his appearance and frighten us. I
was sitting near my window, which gave me full view of
the ward in which lay the dying soldier. Every groan he
made reached my ears, and went to my heart—as if my
own dear son was in his stead, which made the gloom much
more awful to me under the very unpleasant circumstances, and tried my soul to its utmost capacity. While in
this condition and wondering if my husband and son were
safe, or were they among the slain or wounded of that
awful day's struggle before Atlanta, until I became unconscious of the lapse of time, and had forgotten the fact that
I was a prisoner, cut off from them by the destruction of
the railroads, and thereby all communication cut off by
which I could hear from them. My situation became to
me almost intolerable. No one with whom I could say a

word except the poor, weary soldiers, else I would have
gone into the wards.

There were three ladies with us, who, at the time of the
greatest need, deserted their post, seeming not to care
what became of the helplsss boys to whom they had pledged
their loyalty, only for their own personal interests—as so
very many (to the disgrace of their native land) had done;
and not only ladies, but those in whose hearts should have
been a deep and sacred principle supporting or prompting
noble actions in defense of their country and its rights. I
sat there meditating until I was almost spell-bound. It
seemed that I would have given almost any reasonable sum
had I some one with whom to speak of my troubles. I was,
as it were, in a trance, when, lo, I was startled by a loud
wrap at the door below where I was sitting. As a natural
consequence, Yankees were my first thought. I was at a
complete loss what course to pursue for the best. I thought
if I said nothing, perhaps they would set fire to the house,
for since dark had set in the town had been illuminated by
their hands. But before I could decide what to do to prevent any serious disaster, then came another wrap, more
fierce than the first. Without any further meditation, I
put my head out of the window, and quietly asked, "What
do you want?" "Is that you, Mrs. Smith?" was the quick
reply. "Why, is that you, Dr. Nicol?" said I. "Yes, this
is me, and Dr. Primble. Can we get any coffee? We are
nearly perished," said he. "Yes," I said, "if I have to
make it myself. I never was as glad to see two rebels in
my life as I am to see you two." And down I went, un-
locked the door, and had hot coffee on the stove, though it
was past midnight. While they were partaking of their
repast (the first since breakfast), many questions were asked
and answered, and much speculation relative to the events
of the day. The doctor informed me that they had spent
the night in reconnoitering, and soliciting protection from

the enemy for the good citizens of Covington. That the
Yankees were all gone, except a few pickets who had been
placed at the outskirts of the town, to prevent stragglers
from interrupting any one. They assured me that I might
feel safe, and rest for the remainder of the night, for
Wheeler was too close by for the Yanks to attempt to return, and that they left in double-quick time.

I then gave out burying clothes for the soldier who had
died, and tried to sleep an hour or two, for well I knew
what a heavy task was in store for me when morning came.
How lonesome and how sad everything appeared the next
morning. The busy throng of cheerful boys were not there
as usual, hurrying hither and thither, performing the
duties assigned them, in addition to many voluntary ones,
dictated by kind hearts and sympathy for the poor suffering
Confederate soldiers around them. We did so much miss
them and their very valuable and necessary services, as
did the poor sufferers for whom they had done so much.
It was now almost impossible to supply their places, and,
of course, two or three persons could not do all that was
necessary for their comfort; yet we did the best we could,
and there was not a murmer among them. All appeared
grateful for what was done. In fact, the poor fellows, in
every possible manner, endeavored to aid each other as
well as themselves. In that way they lightened our burdens, and would not ask for aid when they could possibly
do without it. Of course, they knew all was being done
that possibly could be, and really more than would have
been done if it possibly could have been avoided, and they
not suffer. Therefore, this, and the gratitude constantly
manifested by them, fully repaid us a thousand fold for
what we did for them. The ladies who had been in the
habit of visiting and aiding us, still stood by us—continuing their visits, and sent nice articles of food for the boys,
and servants to help us.

Many were the rumors coming from our runaway boys. Some had been shot; others caught and taken off as prisoners, etc. But on Saturday and Sunday the true facts were developed. One by one they began to come in, and by twelve o'clock Sunday they were all in. This was a happy day for the writer, for I did not want those faithful boys to be carried off by the enemy to Northern prisons, to suffer as prisoners were necessarily compelled to; as the most of our boys did while in the hands of those who had no more respect for Confederates than if they were brutes, in violation of all principles of humanity, religion, or civil modes of warfare. I had realized, though in a very limited degree it is true, what were the feelings of prisoners, even when under the most favorable circumstances, while the enemy was there. I am sure I did not think I could have been much more unhappy, shut up where we were, cut off from communication with home and friends, and surrounded by those who I knew were our enemies. But our situation was hardly a foretaste of what some of the prisoners have suffered, when not in a friendly land as we were, shut up and cut off entirely from all that is sacred and dear to them, and insulted and abused in every way their enemies could invent in the way of punishment, and this to last for months, and perhaps years. Now, since the road was cut, we felt like we were confined in a temporary prison. Yet, when our boys, who had deserted from necessity for a time, returned, we felt like ourselves again; and with glad hearts we greeted them, as though we had not seen them for months. All were joyful.

Many were the laughable stories each one had to relate concerning their flying trip in the country. One of them, Frank Hodge, of the Fifth Arkansas Regiment, was minus a leg, and out run others who did not have to go on crutches They collected in squads near houses, and the family damsels supplied them with plenty of good provisions—not forgetting to stand picket ready to give the alarm, should the enemy appear. Some made promises that they would never desert old grandma again; that it was too bad that she should be left all alone. Little did they know how soon their fidelity would be put to the test by another Yankee dash, when they were just becoming quiet from the effects of the former. We had hoped that General Hood would keep them too closely engaged in front for them to have any time for working in the rear of his army, and giving us another scare. Yet we kept a careful lookout; so, if possible, not to be surprised. The patients who could be moved, were sent in wagons to Social Circle, and from there by cars to Greensboro and Augusta. Therefore, we were gradually guarding against another fright, which to some of us who had remained, was somewhat unexpected. Owing to supplies being cut off, evacuation was necessary; but it was being done gradually, as there was some of the patients not in a condition to be moved.

On the morning of the 27th, which was the second hard day's fight before Atlanta, quite a number were sent off—taking advantage of the darkest hours of the night, which is just before day. The sun had just arose in all its magnificent splendor, shedding its cheering rays on all around. Quiet in Covington seemed to reign too supremely to again be under another panic by the early appearance of the blue coats, who were not as civil as the first gang. We were preparing to send breakfast to the patients, when the ward master called out to us from one of the wards, saying, "the Yankees are in town again!" "Oh," says I, "surely you are mistaken." "No, I am not. Just look up the street, yonder, and you will see them yourself." I did look; and sure enough there they came in full tilt close at us. The boys all began saying "Grandma, what shall we do?" " Stay just where you are; run in the cellar and hide; or jump in bed and play off sick, like Chris., and I'll

F*

see that they do not get you." All who had time, did so;
but some were not fast enough. In about two minutes some
four or five dirty, drunken scamps dashed up, almost in
the door, saying, "Oh, you d—d Rebels, come out of there,
and march on the square, where General Stoneman is. We
will show you how to fight against the Union." The boys
gave me an enquiring look. Says I, "Go with them, boys,
like gentlemen and soldiers; they wont keep you long."
In the meantime, Dr. Robertson came and requested me to
see that none escaped, for Dr. Nichol, the post surgeon, had
surrendered the hospital and all the inmates. I then felt
indeed like I was a prisoner; but I knew that our surgeon
would not suffer us to be imposed upon, and I continued
serving up breakfast, with the assistance of the still faithful
negro woman, who did not have quite the same grounds for
abusing "dem dar niggers," for one man stood his ground,
saying "he see 'nuff ob dem Yanks toder time, and he wan't
'fraid ob dem dat he knowed." While I stood gazing at
the two boys who they were taking off, three or four who
had remained in the yard pretending to be sentinels, rode
up to the kitchen window, and demanded, "hand us out
them biscuit there, and that chicken; we are hungry."
The cook gave them a quisical glance. I ordered him to
give it to them, for I saw they were drunk, and I was
afraid of their doing mishief. There they set on their
horses until they devoured the last mouthful that was on
hand, and swore because there was no more. By way
of quieting them, I said, "Gentlemen, I hope you will not
so far forget the dignity of gentlemen, and that your
mothers were women, as to impose on a lone woman because
she is in your power." One of them began to reel, and
spit, and mouth out, "Oh, no, madam, we will not forget
our mother; she was a nice and mighty good woman." I
felt greatly relieved when they were called off. Our poor
boys had to fast until more was cooked for their breakfast.

Our head surgeon was again marched off to head quarters by a motly set, but was soon relieved by the intercession of a Federal surgeon of the same name—Wm. H. Robertson. He showed every mark of a gentleman in his treatment of the faculty, for which they were under many obligations to him.

The sick boys kept their beds during the most of the day. Those who had taken refuge in the cellar, remained there closely hid, while I picketed and supplied them with food. If ever a set of Yanks were cheated out of a trophy, it was Stoneman's set of vagabond depradators that day. Our two boys that were carried off, returned in a short time. Oh, did not my heart leap with joy when I saw them returning. "What did you tell us, grandma?—you said we would not stay long." "How did you get off so soon?" I asked. "Well, just as we presented ourselves to his honor General Stoneman, a courier dashed up, and gave him a paper. On looking at it, he said to us, 'you can go to h—l, for all I care, I have no use for you now.'" "I know why," says I; " I guess General Wheeler and his men are too close on his heels for his good health.' The supposition was correct; for before night the town was as clear of Yanks as if there never had been one there— with the exception of one or two stragglers who pass- ed through at a flying speed, with Wheeler's scouts close at their heels, firing at them as they dashed on and on, until out of sight. If ever I was glad to see a Reb, it was that day. I certainly appreciated our deliverance.

As soon as I had completed the morning repast, I walked up to one of our wards on the square, to see how they were doing after they had been surrounded all morning by their tormenters. I hardly noticed the band of thieves who had been first among us; but I was compelled to notice these, as they made themselves more conspicuous than the first. I thought, as I had to be among, and annoyed by the detestable hords, I would look at them as they were passing. I stood in the door and viewed them to my heart's disgust as they defiled. Here they came dashing through the town pell-mell, while their stars and stripes still floated to the breeze on the square; and if ever the once revered banner of a country was trailed in the dust, it truly was at that time, to the disgrace of those bearing it. The sight which met my eyes there, as displayed by the defenders of this once noble flag, was surely disgusting in the extreme, and one calculated to inspire in the hearts of all honest Southern people the most bitter hatred towards the invaders of their homes under the plea of defending the honor of the stars and stripes. Chickens, eggs, turkeys, ham, and in fact every available article they could possibly find to steal, they had on their horses. From the manner they hastened off, it was very evident that something was in the rear that did not appear very attractive to them.

They had quite a number of stolen horses and mules, on which they had mounted about as many sable riders, social companions, for their forward move. The unfortunate negroes had been gulled off by their equality friends. Some of them could be heard bidding their friends good bye, saying they were free, and were going to fight "de white trash." Poor, deluded creatures. To their sorrow, they soon found who their best friends were. And we heard of many returning to their masters, perfectly satisfied with their pretended friends, who only wanted them as tools to do the meanest part of the most filthy of all work—that of carrying out their treacherous designs of undermining and destroying the rights and property of the former owners of the poor negro. It is to be hoped this deluded race will yet learn who were, and are, their true friends, and what their true interests are, and to whom to look as friends. But, from present appearances, there is not much hope of their learning wisdom until the present generation is almost extinct.

Who are to be blamed in their case? or who are resposible for their suffering and degradation? When the South was first invaded by those professing to be working for the moral, financial, mental and spiritual good of the colored race, the negro was in the hands of, and cared for, by those who were not only legally responsible for their welfare, but who, from interest and principles, treated them almost as well as their own children. As a consequence, the great mass of them were by far the most happy race of people in the world. They were increasing rapidly in numbers, and were taught principles of honor and religion. Now we see them not only the most miserable and destitute of all classes under the sun, and deserting their religious faith, and falling back into all the various heathenish superstitions and paganisms, but see how fast they are diminishing in numbers from starvation and disease. Now, who brought all this on them? Was it not their good friends, the Abolitionists, who freed them? Most assuredly so. Why could they not have been allowed to remain as they were? Then the blood of the thousands of suffering, starving and murdered men, women and children of that race would not have been required at their hands. Oh, I imagine that at the day of final retribution, many who have, in so many instances, acted the wolf in sheep's clothing towards this now fully oppressed race, will wish they had never seen a negro; or that they had have let them remain as they were, instead of being the means of their freedom, and, as a consequence, bring all the evils upon them which they are subjected to now.

While we were standing in the door gazing at the vast crowd of flying foes, our attention was attracted to a very dirty Yankee, who came dashing up and peeped in, and at the same time hurriedly enquired, "How many patients have you here?" I answered three. "You have been sending them off, ha?" "Yes; every one we could," I replied. "Are there any of the Ninth Texas here?" "No; none in your reach." They were too well hid for them to find. I afterwards learned that vengance had been sworn against that intrepid regiment, in retaliation for the way they made the Yankees bite the dust in some previous battle. While he was going on with his indignant speech, a Yank., more thievish looking than the rest, dashed up bareheaded, snatched the hat off of the head of a crippled soldier, saying, "I want this hat," and dashed off at a rapid rate. Says the Rebel, "You have the power now, and can use it; but perhaps it will not always be so." "Never mind, George," said I, "you shall have another one, as soon as I go to my room." It was really laughable to witness the different maneuverings they went through while passing, with their grand equipments. Some of their horses seemed to be corn crib, meat house, kitchen and chamber all in one, or had all these attached to them. Not unfrequently would one cry out, "Howdy, Johnnie Reb. How are you? Our boys gave you a wounded furlough; and they shot your leg off—ah, ha. Well, all right. We are the Yanks that can whip you. Go home, and stay there. What are you fighting for? The negroes won't do you any more good. You and your negroes can both be put out of the cold, if you choose." "Southern independence is the motto under which we fight," said our boys; "and not your black equals. Never mind, Wheeler will make you sing another song in less than twenty-four hours, I'll bet my old hat."

Soon the town was rid of the whole set. And glad were we to see the last one leave; and, as the poet said,

We breathe the air again.

If ever their was a happy and grateful people, it was those of the town of Covington. And well they

might be; for the few hours they had been infested by
Stoneman and his lawless vagabonds, had been hours of as
severe suspense and fear as they had ever witnessed. Most
of the houses had been visited by them. Strong threats
had been made in regard to liberating the prisoners at
Andersonville, and a warning given to the ladies that they
would be sure to visit Covington, and that they would take
vengeance at all places where they went for the cruel treatment they were reported to be receiving in the prison there
at the hands of our men. This threat gave to the citizens, male and female, quite a fright; and many really
feared that it would be put in execution. But, fortunately,
the threat was never, with all their efforts, executed.
There was too watchful an eye kept over their movements
for any such a wholesale murderous plan to be carried out.

Quiet had began to prevail again, dinner was given to
the patients, and the general duties of the evening were in
progress, when suddenly another fright, more fearful than
that of the morning, though it proved a hoax, that ten
thousand Yankee infantry were near town, and would soon be
there, and would sweep everything before them. But this
all soon blew over, and all was cheerful.

Now the hidden boys came out in the fresh air, and all
right. The sick left their beds, delighted at their speedy
recovery. All were ready to join in the changing events
of the day, and many were the merry laughs at the
Yankees being so completely humbugged out of a number
of Rebel prisoners. That night many of them came to the
conclusion that escape was the better part of valor. Having run the risk of being captured more than once within
the last few weeks, they adopted the old adage, that
"a burnt child dreads the fire." Therefore, several left
during the reign of danger. As a matter of course, we
were necessarily compelled to remove elsewhere, as soon as
the nature of the case would admit of. Several patients

were still unable to be removed; and the question was discussed, pro. and con., who should remain with them. Finally, it was left to the humble writer whether I should go out, or stay until Dr. Daniel could get out the patients whose condition compelled them to remain longer.

As the ladies had recovered from their fright, and returned to their posts, with the promise not to leave again so long as the hospital was kept up, I decided to go out, as my anxiety was very great in regard to my husband and son's welfare, whom I knew had been in the battle before Atlanta, and, for aught I knew, had been among the thousands of wounded and slain of that ever memorable day of carnage. In consulting my patients relative to the course I should pursue, they all said that it was my duty to look after my own first; that I had already done more than they could ask, and that justice to my own bade me go. Dr. Daniel was very reluctant to give me up. I referred him to the other ladies, whose homes were in town. They had pledged themselves to stay and do all they could. I said that if I thought by my absence one of the inmates would suffer neglect for one moment, or if, in so doing, I should incur the displeasure of one for whom I had labored, I would still remain and serve them, and trust to others, and to Divine power, to take care of my own, and for their safety. Each one bade me go. I then went to work, fitting up new and clean beds and bedding, and had them all cleanly dressed, and placed in the large, well ventilated ward on the first floor. Dr. Robertson directed one of the attendants to secure a wagon to take me out. By night all things were ready for our departure, and early on Sabbath morning, July 30th, I, with several of the boys, who were on crutches, took our departure from the pleasnt little town of Covington, Georgia. We were accompanied by the Misses Conner, who had seen too much of Yankee rule to be willing to risk their hateful appearance again in their midst. Those industrious and patriotic young ladies had been sufferers by their polluted hands in the destruction of their goods; besides, they had no good feelings for them in any way, and, of course, did not want to see them again.

CHAPTER V.

In taking leave of Covington I felt as though I was leaving home, and dear, kind friends. Yes, some of the best friends I had on earth were there. I was sad at parting from them, and pleased at the prospect of getting out of danger, and where I could hear from my husband and son. I have ever experienced pleasure at the thought of possessing the best wishes of those kind Covington friends wherever my lot should be cast.

The day was exceedingly warm, and we suffered more or less from the burning rays of the mid-summer sun. But the distance being only ten miles, we were not many hours in reaching the place of our destination, Social Circle, where we expected to meet a train of cars very soon, or, at least, early the next morning.

After taking some refreshments, and resting from the toil, as well as from the burning sun, some of our party took a stroll through the little village, where we witnessed the wreck recently made by Yankee invaders. The depot house, a large hotel, and the commissary had been burned to ashes. The railroad was torn up for some distance, and all presented a general scene of desolation. The few citizens who were there seemed very kind. Mrs. Clark, a very kind widow lady, gave us a cordial invitation to take shelter under her hospitable roof for the night. We gladly accepted the invitation, and enjoyed a refreshing night's rest. Arising early the next morning, we took leave of this kind lady, and her two interesting daughters, and were soon at headquarters—or, at least, where our baggage and patients had been sent to. We found them in waiting for us. When our morning repast was over we repaired to the depot, and placed our baggage, consisting of a number of trunks and boxes, containing goods of various kinds, belonging to the hospital, as well as our party, near the track, so that, in case of a rush to get on the train, we would come off second best at least. There was a vast crowd already collected, and the ground was completely strewn with every description of plunder that could be thought of. All were anxious to leave the land of Dixey. Each one seemed to have an eye single to their own individual interest in relation to making good their escape in case a train should arrive, and one was momentarily expected. But hope, which often sheds its rays of promise, withered. The portals of the anxious heart are lighted up by it only to be darkened by a driving cloud of disappointment. As in all our terrestial undertakings, so in this, we were doomed to disappointment.

On the first day of August, 1864, at Social Circle, Georgia, all eyes were fixed in the direction that should bring to our hearts great joy, waiting for the cars to come that would soon take us from danger to the land of liberty, for we felt that we were perfectly surrounded, and as if the walls of a prison encompassed us ; and, to add to our already unhappy state of mind, it was rumored through the crowd that we need not be surprised if, instead of the expected train of relieving cars, the Yankees dashed in upon us, as they were near by. But we were at their mercy at any moment, and we had no way of helping ourselves. So, there we sat, still hoping that the train would venture that far. Soon some one came dashing up, say-

ing " Save yourselves, if you can. The Yanks are within
two miles of the place ! " If you ever saw a flock of
sheep frightened, in a close pen, and no way by which to
get out—or anything else of the same nature, you can
imagine something of the excitement which prevailed
at that time among us; and then imagine a flock of wild
deer, badly frightened, running first one way, then another,
no two going the same way, and you have a faint idea
of what took place in that crowd. Their movements
seemed perfectly aimless, except that the general desire
was to get away from the Yankees; and what became of
the most of them I am unable to say, as I never saw them
afterwards. The depot was minus men, women, children,
and negroes, in the shortest possible time, as if there had
never been one on the ground. The young man who was
conducting us out, Johnnie Davis, of the 154th Tennessee
regiment, and one of the Misses Conner, had gone a short
distance, to see an old friend of her's, where they were
when the startling intelligence reached them. I do not
suppose that they hardly knew how they made their way
to the depot, as they were almost unable to speak from
excitement and running. Almost as quick as thought the
boxes and trunks were thrown into the wagon, and up the
hill we ran, and, without ceremony, took refuge in a side
room of the postoffice, expecting every moment to see a
brigade of Yankees dash in upon us. Every few moments
some one of us would act as scout, or outside sentinel.
In the course of an hour, or perhaps more, the joyful
tidings that it was all a hoax were sent flying through
town; that a few of Stoneman's men had been seen trying to make their escape to parts unknown, General
Wheeler having proved the winner of the day in an
engagement with him, some few miles from Covington,
capturing the raiding general and most of his men, and
leaving the stragglers to the mercy of the wide woods;

and many of them were seen skulking in the outskirts of the neighborhood; and it was reported that some were found not far off, in a starving condition. General Stoneman was carried through Macon, and for a while confined there; and on our head surgeon arriving in Macon, on his way from Covington, strange to say, the first object that attracted his attention was that body of prisoners, and among them the same Federal surgeon (Dr. Robertson), who had so kindly pleaded for him in Covington. Their recognitions were mutual, and simultaneous; and true to his promise, and principles of a perfect gentleman, that if the Federal surgeon ever fell into his power, he would reciprocate his kindness, he lost no time in making good his word, and soon procured his release. In relating the affecting incident, the doctor remarked that he never saw any man manifest more heartfelt gratitude in all his life; that he insisted that, though they belonged to opposite parties, they should be mutual friends; that no service should be too great for him to render should it ever be in his power to do so. Thus, in the very midst of one of the bloodiest wars ever known, was the true gentleman ready to recognize his fellow gentleman and soldier, and lend a helping hand in the way of humanity, which has not unfrequently planted seeds of affection and friendship in each others' hearts, which time will never obliterate.

We slept in our retreat, some keeping watch, while the others, in turn, were indulgiag in a nap.

We were somewhat startled by an incident which transpired just at dark, and which served to put us all on a more vigilant look-out for stragglers than perhaps we would have been. Quite a stalwart looking man, dressed in rebel grey, stepped to the door of our retreat, and, on looking in, exclaimed, in these words, "Lord God!" as if he were frightened. One of the young ladies was sitting in the door. He inquired of her, "Who are those

persons in there?" She replied, "Ladies from Covington." "Have you seen any Yanks pass here this evening?' "No." "Are there any Rebs here?" "Yes;
plenty of them." He immediately turned on his heels,
and was off in so short a time that the young men who
were in the room never got a sight of him. On turning
the corner of the house he met the negro man who had
charge of the wagon, and made particular inquiry who
our party were; where we were going; and whether any
Yanks had passed that day, etc. I think it was one of the
enemy's stragglers. It put us on our guard, fearing he
might repeat his visit; but we saw no more of him.

Tuesday, the 2d, we spent the day in anxious hope,
expectation, and suspense. We received and answered
several letters from our soldier friends. They told of the
dreadful carnage before Atlanta; and of many true and
brave soldiers whom we had known in other days, who
had yielded up their lives on the altar of their country's
cause. And we have the precious boon to know that we
were considered worthy of their dying remembrance, amid
the rain of shot and shell. This can only be more fully
appreciated by those who were daily witnesses to their
untold suffering, as martyrs on the battle-field, and worn
out by sickness and hard service. As one who was in
daily service for those suffering creatures I knew that the
least word of kindness was as a beam of light to the sufferers; and, to be remembered by them, cheered me with
the hope that we did, in some respects, add to their comfort.

We stayed with another kind lady that night, and had
quite a pleasant time; and learned from her how kindly
our patients were cared for by the good ladies of Social
Circle, as they passed through; and how energetic Dr.
Lee had been in providing them with comfortable quarters on the cars, although he was not the surgeon on

detail to transfer them. When he saw that the proper surgeon was not there, he assumed the place for the good of the suffering ; and, like a true gentleman, went forward and saw them safe on the train. All honor is due to the noble and valiant soldier—such as he ; and long will his name be dear in the hearts of many soldiers whom he found suffering for the want of that humane attention which was due them, and which so many failed to receive. The man who would wantonly neglect such objects of charity, and suffering humanity, is not a true soldier, or the soldiers' friend.

Wednesday the 3d, and no train had yet arrived, and there was no prospect of our seeing one soon. Of course, we could not remain where we were. Some plan must be devised, and adopted to enable us to get away ; and as they all looked to your humble servant for advice, and as a guide, I proposed that the wagon should be loaded with our plunder, and I would take two of the crippled soldiers, and the negro man, and go to Rutledge, a station several miles below. We could make two trips that day, and one the next morning ; and we thought that by the next evening we would get a train. All agreed to the plan, and we were soon mounted upon the boxes, and moving off for Rutledge. I wonder if the reader can imagine the amusing spectacle—an old rebel woman, and boys with crutches in hand, perched upon goods boxes, winding their way to, they knew not where ? Surely the venture seemed almost incredible. Several persons stopped us on the roadside, and would invariably inquire, " My good madam, where are you going to ? " On informing them, they would say, " Why, you need not go there ; the Yanks were there yesterday, and tore up things generally. Have you seen any Yanks on your way ? " " No sir ; " or madam, as the case might be. " Why, I wonder you have not. Don't you hear those guns ? " " Yes." " Well, it is them fighting. I wonder they do not get you. You had better turn back." But nary time did we turn back until we reached the place for which we had started.

One lady, a Mrs. Hardins, if I have not forgotten, seemed to marvel greatly at our rashness, and called our attention to the report of guns just in the rear of her field. She said they had been fighting all morning; and that the negroes had left the field, and come to the house for safety. The old lady put up quite a pitiful story, saying the Yanks had taken some of her mules; and our doctors had taken some half-dozen bundles of oats, and spread on the floor of their wagon for their wives to rest upon, and went off and did not pay her one cent for them. I asked her if that was all she had lost since the beginning of the war. She replied, "Why, yes and that's enough. I did not have that to spare." "Well," said I, "if that is the whole amount of your losses in this great struggle for independence, you have been extremely fortunate indeed. Many in your own State have lost everything, and are now penniless; and yet they do not complain, because they know it is the fate of war; and more especially one waged against a people who are merely contending for their own legitimate rights." "Well, I don't want to lose anything by any of them. I think the doctor ought to pay me for my oats." We bade her good by, saying, "We wish you may lose nothing else." We soon reached the depot; and on arriving there who should we see but two of our boys, Bud Carrington and Lieutenant Bean, both belonging to the Virginia army, who had started for that point early the previous morning, before our plan was gotten up. On recognizing us they seemed very much astonished, and called out, "Where in the world are you going, grandma?" "Why, right here," I said. "What is your notion for making this disastrous move?" "In order to get a train." "That you cannot get. There will be no

train here to-day. It is too uncertain, as well as dangerous, for them to venture here. Do go back. The Yanks
are all around us. Do go back if you can. For I am
afraid you will be caught." With that, the railroad agent
came out, and said, "Oh, my dear madam, please don't
put your things off here. The Federals were here yesterday, and burned and destroyed eight thousand dollars
worth for me; and if they should come and find this hospital property here they would not leave anything. I
know they are stragglers from Stoneman's command; but
they are the more to be feared than the main army. I
beseech you to return. The train cannot come up no how;
and we would all be in great danger were you to remain."
As nothing else would satisfy the contending parties, and
my confidence in those two Virginia soldiers admonished
me that to take their advise would be the better part of
discretion, and with a heart too full of sad disappointment for utterance, we turned our course back to Social
Circle, where we knew the rest of our party were in anxious waiting for the empty wagon. Our journey back
was of a more interesting character than the former. We
were halted at almost every turn, and something related
that was calculated to put, or, in other words, keep, us on
our guard. I did not fear for myself, but the two wounded
soldiers I knew would be captured if the enemy came
upon us; but the boys sang, whistled and seemed merry,
chatting away as though there was no danger whatever
from Yanks.

The poor negro was more uneasy than any of us, fearing,
if they came upon us, they would take his team, and make
him join them, leaving the rest of us in the road to finish
our journey as best we could.

Fortunately for us, while also mysterious, not the
glimpse of a Yank did we get in all our route. One man
came running to us, perfectly excited, saying, "Arn't

you afraid to travel this road?" " No; what's up?" said
I. " Why, didn't you see the two Rebel officers dashing
through the woods just now?" " Yes; and what of
that?" " Why, they asked the woman at that house yonder if there were any Yanks in the neighborhood. ' Why,
yes,' she replied, ' plenty of them right over yonder. My
husband is over there, with them. He piloted them, and
carried them to where some Rebs were. Listen, don't you
hear them shooting?'" A mistaken woman that time.
She thought she was giving information to Yankees, and
her information caused the capture of the good Union
husband, and the clan he had piloted, so we were informed,
for, as a natural consequence, the two Rebs made good use
of the opportunity offered them, and the Union woman's
directions.

Many other things transpired on our way, and which
were very amusing to us, notwithstanding our hearts were
filled almost to overflowing by the sad dilemma in which
we were placed.

It is not unfrequently the case that events, which at the
time are painful almost beyond endurance, transpire which
are pleasant to the memory in the future; and there is
generally something soothing in our misfortunes—more
especially if they have overtaken us while we are in the
discharge of our duties. Nature has ordained that all
should be, to some extent, happy; and if we use the
means given us, we need not, at least, be miserable, though
misfortune may meet us at every step in life; though we
may be denied the boon which we were so sanguine of
getting in our dealings and transactions. Yet there is a
pleasing thought in the knowledge that we endeavor to
discharge our duties in trying to attain our objects. Our
unfortunate Confederate soldiers we take as an example.
Just see their cheerful countenances, elastic step, and
the hearty shake of the hand in fond greeting of old

G

friends and comrades when on the bloody field of battle. And why all this? Because they know they have done their duty. Though sad and heartrending misfortunes attended their struggle for liberty and Southern independence; though they were trodden down by the ruthless invader of their loved country—they were cheerful from the fact that they had done their duty, and that all nations will honor them for their undaunted chivalry. Their children's children will remember them with pride, and speak of their sires and grand sires who fought in the Rebel army, and who are no more. The knowledge of these facts nerved them up to go forward in the discharge of their whole duty to their conntry, and in their domestic avocations in rebuilding their broken fortunes, and the institutions of their much injured country, which was once the pride of the civilized world.

It would be vain to describe the sad countenances we met on our return of fourteen miles. We had traveled in the burning sun and dust, and accomplished nothing by the disagreeable and dangerous trip; yet despair had never entered my mind, at least. The word fail had never suggested itself to me. We were to leave our disagreeable situation. But how? or where should we make our next move? "What can we do now, grandma?" was the anxious question. "Well, as it is left to me, I will tell you what I think will work like a charm, provided the first and most important obstacle can be removed." That was to detail two of our party, and send them to the country to press, beg or borrow wagons, or anything to get them fairly, and we would start the next morning for Greensboro, seventy-five miles below, where we could, I knew, get a train. The plan took admirably, and forthwith Mr. Frank Hodge, the soldier who made such good use of his crutches in the Covington stampede, was sent out immediately, with instructions either to bring the

wagons, or make sure that the owner would send them
very early the next morning. Our minds were now more
at ease, as that much of our plan had been put into execution ; and every effort was made to pass the hours off as
pleasantly as possible. Most of the evening was passed in
relating incidents of the morning, frequently being com-
mented on by some of the party, who did not refrain
from laughing heartily when an amusing incident was
related.

Our kind little friend, Lemuel Thomner, of the 4th
Tennessee cavalry regiment, who was one of the boys on
crutches, and who had accompanied us on our morning
expedition, becoming weary and disheartened, concluded
to leave us, and return to Covington, where he imagined
he could soon come up with his company, and rejoin it.
We all felt sad at the idea of parting with this good young
man, and faithful soldier. We had seen so much trouble
together that we felt that to separate from him would
cause regret indeed. Besides, fears were entertained for
his safety on the way. Thus, three of our party had left
us, and perhaps we would see each other no more. But
such is life everywhere. Our kindest friends cannot be
with us always.

Johnnie Davis, and the same young lady had strolled a
a short distance from our humble headquarters, while the
rest of us were standing around the door, not in the least
dreaming of the joyful change that was so near in store
for us, when hark ! a distant rumbling. " Listen ! There
it is again." " What can it be ? " ' Oh, it is a train of
cars ! " " Let us go near the road ; perhaps we can learn
something more definite." Only a few yards had been
gone when, oh, joy too great for expression ! a train was
seen slowly turning a bend in the road. Dear reader, can
you imagine our unutterable joy on beholding the long
looked-for train which was to give us conveyance from a

spot which had been made, from the trying scenes through which we had passed there, indelible on our hearts? Oh! if you have never passed through similar trying ordeals, you can have but a faint idea of how we felt. There were but a few moments spent in hurrying our baggage by our wagon, and others which were standing near by, and were pressed by Johnnie as he came running, having heard the train, and hastened to the scene.

As a consequence, all our goods were run to, and put upon, the train in an almost incredible short space of time. It was " every one for himself," (that day,) as the old adage says.

As usual, people from every direction had flocked to the depot—some to hear the news, and others to get away; but not one citizen was permitted to get on the train.

Our two Virginia soldiers had the luck to reach Greensboro, and reported us as being at Social Circle, without means to get away, and a body of armed men were put on the train—sufficient to protect it from attacks of the enemy, and it was run up for us, without giving a signal on the way for fear of being attacked by scattered bands of Federals who were reported to be near the road. If ever I was happy in my life from any temporal cause, it was surely on that memorable day. The persons composing the party gave full vent to their feelings, manifesting the greatest joy and gratitude for being taken away from so unpleasant a place and situation. Each one had his or her joke on the other. All enjoyed it fully. Some little burdens which they could scarcely have moved at any ordinary time were disposed of in various ways, and we were soon whirling away from Yankeedom as fast as the locomotive could possibly carry us, while our hearts, which had been before so cast down and desponding, were as cheerful for the time being as though the few days of sadness had never been.

While we were enjoying our unexpected exit from Yankeedom, we did not forget poor Frank Hodges, who had gone out in search of wagons. We knew it would be a surprise to him on his return; and we imagined his disappointment and chagrine at finding himself deserted. Transportation was provided for him to follow on the next day, with the promise from our kind young lady friend, Miss Clark, that he should have a home with them that night.

Five o'clock on the morning of the 5th found us safely landed in Augusta.

Poor Frank, on meeting us said he never was so mad in his life as when he returned to Social Circle, and found us all gone; but he reflected on the tedious journey we had escaped, and was then glad we had been so fortunate. The wagons which were to have been at our disposal the following morning were not wanting, as we were safe and snug in Augusta, strolling around the streets of that strange and beautiful city, and wondering where the spot could be found where Mary got so badly frightened at the man with the moustache, when her husband, Major Joseph Jones, was strolling around town with her to see the sights. Ha, ha! we neither found the water-melon cart, or the man with his beard all on his upper lip who frightened Mary so, but thought we found his picture in one of the city galleries; it corresponded pretty accurately with the description the major gave of the man, at least.

We had been directed, on leaving Covington, to report to Dr. Robertson, at the Planters' Hotel, and were disappointed at not meeting him, he having gone to Cuthbert, one hundred miles below Macon. However, we were advised not to proceed any further, until the return of Dr. Nichol, who had gone to Macon to confer with Dr. Stewart, medical director, relative to where he should establish his hospital. We spent a pleasant night with our lady riends, who had come out with us, at Miss Jennie Linus'.

On the morning of the 6th, we stored away our goods, left them in charge of one of our soldier friends, and took the cars for Greensboro, where we had been informed the most of our patients had been quartered after leaving Covington. We were anxious to see how they were situated, and thought we would be of some service to them while they were in jeopardy ; and our time was not altogether thrown away in returning to Greensboro. We found them in excellent quarters, and under the care of an eminent surgeon, Dr. Bell, who was always at his post, ready to render them service.

I need not say that each one seemed glad to see me ; and the general inquiry was, "Are you not going to stay with us?" The kind, lady-like, matrons, Mrs. Reaves and Mrs. Straus, (may Heaven bless them,) gave me a cordial welcome in their sanctum ; and the few days I spent with them were pleasant indeed ; and on taking leave of them I felt as if I were parting with near and dear friends. While there I attended the Baptist church on Saturday, and was pleased to meet with one of my old Ringgold patients, Tip Bledsoe, of the 19th Louisiana regiment, whose whereabouts had not been known to me for several months. Poor Tip ; he is crippled for life.

Thousands of boys have made for themselves names as lasting as time, which they may be proud of.

I also met with Mr. F. Cairman, of the old 154th Tennessee regiment, who had received a serious wound before Atlanta, and was in the very best of hands—Mr. and Mrs. Leach, of Memphis. He was at home with those kind Southern people ; and with the kind attention and winning smiles of Miss Sallie, his hours of confinement passed pleasantly by, indeed.

After spending nearly a week with my old patients, visiting their respective wards each day, adding what little comfort was in my power, Dr. Nichol returned, bringing orders to proceed to Cuthbert, Georgia, where some of the faculty had already gone, as all who belonged to Hill Hospital would be needed, in order to fit up for the reception of all patients who might be sent to us.

I delayed no time in taking my departure from the village of Goldsboro, where I had spent such a pleasant time, and I trust if not profitable, it had proved injurious to no one.

At ten o'clock, on the morning of the 11th, we bade a kind and sad adieu to our suffering patients, and took the train for Augusta, Georgia, and reached that place at five o'clock A. M., on Friday, the 22d. The Waynsboro depot was soon sought for the purpose of starting for Macon. We had to remain there all day, until six o'clock P. M. It was a very pleasant place, where we had to sit, stand, or walk around, in full view of a portion of the city, and the passing of trains.

Our men were transferring prisoners all day. Numbers, in groups, could be seen with guards, going from place to place, bringing back all kinds of eatables in the greatest abundance. I wondered to myself if those same men would not have the audacity to report that the Federal prisoners were starved by our men not supplying them with sufficient food to sustain life. If, from what facts met my own observation, those men were not well furnished with all that was necessary for their comfort, they must have required immense supplies; and if they reported, as so many had falsely done, a want of enough to keep them from starving, I felt confident that it would be just for the purpose of doing us an injury, when they knew it was false. It did seem that I had never seen such a large amount given to any set of the same number— more, I knew, than our men were getting while in the field, in actual service; and, from all the information we can get, much more than our unfortunate men who fell into their hands ever got.

At the appointed hour we found ourselves dashing along at almost lightning speed, on our way to the city of Macon. Sunday morning, at sunrise found us at Ocoee river. There we witnessed one of the ten thousand signs of Yankee depredations, committed on our soil by those merciless invaders. But our train was detained but a short time, as there was a ferryboat instead of the fine bridge that had been recently burned. There were a great many persons to cross, and it seemed that every one tried to be first, I suppose for the purpose of securing seats on the other side. There, in the midst of the push-about, "Take care, and let me pass!" etc., going on, I was left in a confused situation, or dilemma, I might say. Although it all came around right, and sooner than expected at the time, our unfaltering, and ever-faithful, friend, John Davis, urged that I should have permission to cross with our Texas soldier, Thomas Pender, of the 2d Texas regiment, and procure seats while he was getting the baggage. So, over the river we went, and took our seats in a car, expecting every moment to see Johnnie Davis; but no Johnnie came; and in a few minutes off went the train, and no Johnnie. He had been pushed back too often to be enabled to reach the cars in time. For some time we were in great trouble on his account. We knew there was not a house or shanty for him to store his baggage in, or in which he could sleep; and no other train was due that day; and he had no "grub," as the boys called their eatables, for it was all in our possession, and we going directly from him as fast as steam could propel us. Now, was he not in an aggravating predicament more especially since he had not had his breakfast? There was no enjoyment for me that day. I could think of no one else but poor hungry Johnnie. But it was done, and I was compelled to endure it the best I could until he could be relieved.

Eleven o'clock on Saturday, the 13th, found us at the Macon depot, where, in a few moments, we met with Dr. C. Matthews, who had lost no time in making his exit from Covington during the raid. He very kindly conducted me to a nice house, where I enjoyed a few hours' rest, which I very much needed. On arriving at the depot, I met with one of my Memphis friends of the Overton Hospital, D. A. F. Samuels, which certainly was a great treat. As soon as we engaged a lunch, and had a short rest, the next move was to try to find some one who could give me information concerning the fate of my husband and son. Having sent two dispatches from Augusta, and receiving no answer in return, my suspense had become almost intolerable, as is generally the case under such perilous events as had just transpired before Atlanta. We sought Dr. Beamus' office, under whose charge I had been at Tunnel Hill, Georgia, in 1862 and 1863. In meeting with him he gave me the cheering information that my husband had been there a few days since enquiring for me, and that my son was safe. How inexpressibly happy I was in receiving these tidings none can imagine, but those who have experienced similar anxieties in regard to the fate of their only dear ones, from whom they were severed by the awful decree of that monster—War! We soon directed our course to the register's office, for the purpose of learning the whereabouts of the wounded. As we had been unsettled since the time of the great fight at Atlanta, we had failed to learn anything in regard to the destiny of any as yet. The clerk gave me all the information he had received. Many of my old patients had fallen, and were in different hospitals. Oh, how my heart yearned to be with them, for full well I knew they wished me there. As soon as an opportunity offered, I wrote to them, telling them where I was stopping; and

G*

as soon as they could be moved, some of them reached our hospital—others died who were anxious to be with us. What a severe trial those incidents were to me, for, next to my own husband and son, those dear unfortunate soldiers shared my warmest sympathy. One of them died, leaving a blessing for us on his dying lips. Oh, it touched every chord of my heart, and sent a thrill of sadness which left an indelible impression that will never be erased while life lasts. I can never cease to think of the poor fellows, and hope those who died are happy in Heaven; and those who survived are now, and ever will be, in the enjoyment of peace and prosperity. Yet, we deplore the lot of many since our country's liberties were taken away, and we fallen into the hands of those who have proved themselves, in every manner, unworthy of the trust, and have dishonored the name of American freemen. Yet, we should return thanks to God for the preservation of our lives at least, and the lives of so many of those who were near and dear to us; and hope, through his supreme aid, to be enabled to regain the lost honor of our country. And I do feel thankful to Heaven for the protecting care over my own family in bringing them safely through so many dangers; and, also, for the sympathy manifested by the soldiers for me and my dear ones. We visited some of the hospitals, and found many of our wounded braves languishing on their couches—some of them suffering the most intense agony in their mangled bodies. How I longed to stay with them, and smooth their dying pillows, for many appeared to be swiftly passing from time to eternity, with no kind female hand to place the cooling draught to their feverish lips. Under such circumstances, no one who has been deprived of the painful privilege of mingling with them, can form the most distant idea of the looks of deep gratitude beaming from the eye, which is perhaps already dimming with death's approach. They will receive the smallest act of sympathy and kindness from a stranger hand with a "God bless you! That is the way my mother used to nurse me at home. You look like my dear, good old mother. Have you a son in the army?" "Yes—an only child; and my husband," I would answer. "May Heaven spare them to you, as a reward for what you are doing for others." Did our old eyes remain unmoistened while witnessing such scenes? Humanity, the love of God and our country, for which those well-tried veterans who had yielded up their lives among strangers, answer—"No!"

Returning to our lodging place, the doctor and I were talking over old past times at the Overton Hospital, in Memphis, Tennessee; of the many changes and sad events which we had been familiar with, when our attention was attracted by a quick wrap at the door, and an enquiry made for myself. I was soon in the hall in answer to the call; and, to my joyful surprise, there stood our lost friend, Johnnie Davis. Fortunately, an extra train had gone to the bridge, and the opportunity was not lost in making good his escape from the watery ground for his couch, and the open sky his covering. The absence of refreshments made him not altogether unlike poor Frank Hodge, on being left at Social Circle—almost ready to think "cursing words" on being left, but all was right now. "He'd bet he'd be fast enough the next time;" and sure enough, Johnnie's baggage was on the cars Sunday morning, the 14th, in good time, and all parties had seats as soon as the cars were opened to receive them; and I would soon have been on my way to Cuthbert, in Southwestern Georgia, had not a surprising and pleasant incident transpired which kept me from going on until the next morning—the recognition of an old Memphis friend, who had an humble abode in the city. Of course, off I must get, and spend the day with them. "Sallie would never get over it, if I did not. Oh, you must see Sallie. You have been lost to us for the last two years; and now I have found you, my very dear friend." The boys insisted that I should stop, and they would go on with our baggage. I did so; and never had cause to regret it. It was an unexpected and joyful meeting to each of us. I had been acquainted with the gentleman from his infancy, and his amiable wife (formerly Miss Sallie Plott) lived as one of our family for near two years. She was married while with us to S. A. H. Haynes. As a natural consequence, we were devotedly attached to each other. Many had been the anxious though sad regrets at being separated from her who had hitherto filled the place of a devoted daughter to the bereaved mother. The fates of war had severed us for two years, and now we had met again after passing through so many changing events. The day was spent in unalloyed happiness, with the exception of a short interruption from a report that the city was threatened with the near approach of the Yankees. As I had seen enough of Yankee invasion within the last three weeks, and had been fifteen days trying to get out of their reach, every rumor of that nature would dash everything like pleasure to atoms. Finally, all was well; and early the following morning my journey was renewed, having the pleasing thought that another pleasant reminiscence had been added to my weary travels in a strange land. Six o'clock found me at Cuthbert depot, where Dr. R. and most of the good boys were in waiting, ready to convey me to their new home, and give me a warm welcome.

Of course, the many trials and amusing incidents which transpired among us in our various modes and directions of getting from Covington, through all the different points which we passed, and for a time sojourned, were all narrated by each in our own peculiar style. They were all greatly delighted that grandma had got out of harm's way, and was with them again. "And so you are with us again, grandma—ha?" one would say. "I am so glad. I thought

of you so often, and wondered where you were. I hope
you have made your last move during the war." And so
it was our last retreat. But I had a thousand times rather
have moved again and again from place to place for four
more weary and anxious years, could I have seen our war
worn soldiers return with our banner fluttering in the
breeze, with the inscription in bold colors informing the
world that they had accomplished the object for which
they had been battling, and for the success of which they
had not only risked their lives, fortunes, and all else sacred
and dear to them, whose faith in their final success was so
strong. But hidden fate had destined otherwise, which at
the time of our entering our new field of labor was hid
from us; and with the same untiring energy which had all
the time characterized our faculty who had charge of the
Hill Hospital, did they direct and perform their different
offices in organizing and fitting up the renowned old Hill
Hospital, in the large edifice formerly occupied by Rev. Mr.
Dagg, principal of the female institute. It was quite a
pleasant situation, having a beautiful oak grove in front,
and enclosed with a beautiful surrounding grove of pine.
Near by was a magnificent spring, gushing out from
beneath a high bluff, sending its babbling stream far down
into the picturesque forest, which was interwoven with the
tall green bay tree, spotted here and there with its large
white blooms, which were beautiful to look upon, while its
odor was so refreshing to inhale; with here and there the
magnolia and wild honey suckles arrayed in their beautifully
gay dress of spring, which added ten fold to the beauty of
the magnificent scenery of the locality. As we were naturally very fond of flowers, it was often our pleasing privilege to gather wild ones from the woods, and form bouquets
for the invalids, who were unable to look upon them in
their natural beauty as they grew in clusters by the brook side.
Nine months and a few days we spent in the pleasant little

town of Cuthbert—made doubly pleasant by frequent visits from the kind ladies of the place, who followed the patriotic example of other towns and cities, rendering us every possible act of kindness. We shall always feel that we owe a debt of gratitude to our many kind friends in all the different locations at which we were, and more especially to the following named ladies: Mrs. Captain Kiddloo, Mrs. Dagg, Mrs. M. C. Williamson and daughters, Mrs. Lightfoot, and Mrs. Harding, for their kindness to the invalid soldiers; as also to those of us who were placed over them as matrons, etc.

The hospital was soon filled with patients from all points of the South, and from the various commands as was generally the case. The same routine of duties were performed by all with the same unflinching efforts as heretofore, to try to benefit the suffering, and render them as happy as could possibly be done. Of course, all did not recover. Many a heart ceased its pulsations at Cuthbert, Georgia; and, as death was inevitable for them, it was fortunate that they left the world before the news of our cause being lost reached them, as such news would have been sad indeed to all such patients, to know that our sweet Sunny South had lost all but its honor, for whose cause they had so nobly fought. But when the awful, heartrending news was sent over the wires, they were beyond the reach of the effects, and were sleeping their long, last sleep. And, oh, we do hope they are enjoying the bliss of Heaven; and though buried in the far Southwestern part of Georgia, that they and their friends will meet to part no more in the eternal Heaven, where they will not suffer the awful effect of the defeat of their noble cause. And if friends do not visit their distant graves, yet the breeze continues to sing a requiem to their memory as it sweeps over the flowery forrest surrounding their resting places. And perhaps some fair hand in that strange land may be seen decking

their graves with sweet wild flowers, and a noble heart
heaving a sigh to their memory, and fair eyes shedding
tears over the grass grown mound, as a tribute to the
memory of all brave men who fell in defending their
homes and rights.

CHAPTER VI.

It is needless for us to say anything relative to the move‑
ments of the two contending armies, as that is not in our
sphere, only so far as to express the deep interest which
every true Southern man and woman felt in the cause. All
were alike interested, and were ready to grasp at the most
meagre rumors, which were constantly afloat. Atlanta—
that great central city of the Confederacy—had fallen, and
was made almost a Sodom in the way of destruction of
property, and consequent ruin of the citizens. The wives
and children of our brave soldiers, who had stood for
months and years as a wall of fire in the defense of homes
and firesides, and between them and destruction, were left
houseless and homeless, and driven by the march of the
devouring locusts in human shape, whose watch words were
plunder and insult; and from orders from head quarters
they were committing those horrid crimes. Under such
orders the overwhelming host made the last march through
the noble old Empire State, leaving nothing for the poor
citizens to subsist upon, or anything from which subsistence
could be obtained—or, what was worse, nothing from which
they could make subsistence for the future; and by that
means starving them out, which was the only means by
which they could possibly conquer us. They could not
with equal numbers and fair fighting succeed over us. And
we feel thankful to know that we were not whipped, but
overpowered. All nations honor the brave Rebels who
fought no nobly against such overpowering numbers.

Just at this time, General Hood must start his small band of veterans in another direction. With what anxiety did those in the rear watch Hood's movements—while they were trying to restore those who had become disabled, in order that they might rejoin his thin ranks, and increase his forces, who were willing to follow him to the rescue of their bleeding and overrun country, and to redeem the honor of the once proud, but now downtrodden and disheartened old volunteer State of Tennessee, which had so long been in the hands of the merciless invaders; and that her own heroic sons would again plant their feet on their own soil, followed by those of equal merit of her sister States. All were equally anxious to deliver old Tennessee from the galling yoke of tyranny she had so long endured. How we longed to follow them, and be near enough to be able to take care of those who should fall in the mighty struggle, which we felt confident would be the result of the effort to redeem dear old Tennessse, the home of my childhood. But, fortunately, Providence directed otherwise; and we continued at Cuthbert contented with our lot, having plenty of material to work on—for many worn down and emaciated men were coming and going all the time, which kept each heart and hand busily engaged. Yet, notwithstanding all this, our thoughts would daily turn towards the march of General Hood and his noble army, who had reached the capital of our dear old State, or thereabouts. Letter after letter reached me from my son and his comrades. They were full of hope that the shackels of a prolonged tyranny would soon be broken asunder, and the oppressed citizens who had borne the burdens which the usurping foe had heaped upon them, would be cast off, and liberty again be realized.

Anxiety prevailed to its greatest extent in the town of Cuthbert in regard to the result of the approaching battle,

which, in all probability, would seal the fate of our nation.
Hope and fear ebbed and flowed as day and night passed
by. Ere long the news reached us of the terrible battle of
Franklin, on the 30th of November, 1864, and the great
loss of life. Many brave Tennesseeans, whose hearts
throbbed in anxiety at the thought of again throwing off
their exile, and meeting wives and little ones, only reached
the promised land to shed their life's blood on their own
soil, almost at their own threshold, and without being permitted to see the faces of loved ones who were waiting and
watching for the return of husband, son, brother, or father.
Many brave hearts throbbed with pride at the thought of
being allowed the privilege of offering their lives on the
altar of their own native State, in trying to break the
bonds of tyranny which had been woven around them.
Many of the best men that an army could boast of fell in
the battle of Franklin, Tennessee. Where is the army, or
the country, that can boast of braver men than the much
lamented Cleburne, and others who fell at that time?
Nothwithstanding Tennessee was only his home by adop-
tion, yet his heart was fully enlisted in her cause; and
when a call for volunteers was made, none were more
ready to respond than General Pat. Cleburne. His hopes
of the success of the South were sanguine to the last hour
of life. But, oh, the many hopes so fondly cherished are
gone with him, and quenched in the exile hero's grave.

> " And his sword, which had served him so well
> Not to rest near his pillow below,
> By his side it was laid, where he nobly fell,
> With its point still turned to the foe."

Other gallant leaders shed their patriotic blood, and
yielded up their lives in the same great struggle for our
lost cause, whose noble followers made the name of their
brigade renowned by their deeds of valor in many a hard
fought battle. There were many whose names will ever

be enshrined in the hearts of their surviving comrades and all lovers of the Southern cause. They are resting their long sweet rest by the side of the exiled Cleburne, whose name is an honor to the Emerald Isle. Men from all the States had the honor of breathing their last at Franklin with this noble representative of the down-trodden Isle.

> " Fellow-soldiers in life, let them slumber in death,
>   Side by side with the chivalrous brave ;
> That sword which he loved, still unbroken its sheath,
>   And himself still unsubdued in his grave."

For the deeds achieved by his daring generalship, and the unparalleled heroism of his men, he will ever be the Pride of the South. Their names will long live in song and story as time flits by, and other generations spring up to follow their noble and ever memorable example.

The struggle did not end at Franklin. One more bloody battle, and the deed was done. Nashville, the capital of the dear old State, must be contended for. Our boys could see the once glorious, and highly honored by all nations of the civilized world—but now dishonored to the very lowest ebb, and trailing in the dust—stars and stripes waving over the magnificent edifice, which had long since been polluted by the disgraceful set who inhabited its interior, and who are still making laws to suit their own foul purposes. My feelings were indescribable on receiving letters from our soldier friends headed "Nashville, Tenn.," saying strong hopes were entertained of being able to march in and liberate its inhabitants, who were almost wild with joy at once more beholding the boys in gray; while the boys were eager to take a peep at the home of their once happy and peaceful days. How the hearts of those parents and long absent friends would have leaped with untold joy could they have witnessed the march of the Confederate army into their long besieged city; but, oh, the long hoped and prayed for blessing was denied them.

On the 15th day of December the Yankees emerged from their bomb-proofs with a force sufficient to thribble that of General Hood's, and the battle fought, and the day lost to us, forever lost!—though their efforts were great to take possession of the field, they could not. The day following, General Hood saw that he could not stand such tremendous odds, and so concluded to return to the State of Georgia. At the same time, the Yankees confronted him with fresh troops, and double the number of the day before; and Tennessee's most noble sons were obliged to return, as it were, from the very threshold of their homes, to still battle for right and justice, deprived of seeing their kind kindred whose hearts were in the cause, and yet they were not permitted to receive one word of congratulation or encouragement from them. Oh, what a nerve it must have required to endure such a heartrending disappointment! How sad must have been the hearts of those intrepid men! None but the true and the brave could withstand them. But God, in His all wise providence, gave them a heart sufficient to endure such adverse realities. They had fought as never men fought before. They saw thousands of their comrades fall by their sides, leaving their ranks thin beyond a parallel; and with no hope of another engagement with the Tennessee army, they were fighting for their homes and firesides.

Some of the regiments and companies were almost annihilated. Two companies of the One Hundred and Fifty-fourth Tennessee Infantry had only one man each to represent their company, as I have been told. One of those men was my friend, Jno. Davis, of the "Beauregard" company. He visited me after the army reached Corinth, and gave me a history of the terrible carnage; and that he was left alone amidst the dreadful affray. I asked him how he managed to make his escape. "Why," said he, "when I found that all the rest had gone up, I just got up and got, and don't you think, grandma, I had to throw away my knapsack, with all my fine starched shirts, which my sweetheart made for me. But," said he, "I was glad to save my hide, and let the starched shirts go that time."

Does the reader suppose that the minds and the hearts of those of us far in the rear—too ready to grasp at every rumor that was almost hourly reaching us—were idle. No indeed; thay were continually in excitement of hope and fear for the final result of one of the most daring moves that was made during the war. A handful of men marching before a host of well fortified troops ! It was hard to give credit to facts as they stared us in the face, and it was not until the news was confirmed, and a part of the army reached Corinth, we could believe it. While the soulstirring interest was being felt in the heart of every lover of liberty, in regard to General Hood's march into Middle Tennessee, General Lee was not forgotten. Petersburgh, Virginia, was besieged by Grant and his mighty host, who had been contending for the capital of the new born nation for four long years. Sherman, also, was overrunning Georgia with his horse thieves and house burners, laying waste all parts of the country through which he passed, without any serious obstruction. His move reminded us of a destructive whirlwind more than anything that could be imagined. He would not be reported at one place before he would appear at another, stealing, plundering, and striking terror to the very hearts of not only able bodied men, but innocent and helpless women and children.

Soon, part of the Tennessee army was concentrated near Macon Georgia; and it was not many days until I received a letter from my son. Until then I was not certain of his coming off safe in the two late battles near Nashville. On the 7th of February he visited me for the last time during the war.

If I am correctly informed, about this time the news reached us that Fort Sumter had surrendered to the Yankees, and that the same United States flag that General Beauregard captured, and which had been in the fort during the war, was then floating over those proud old walls, and the Confederate flag was laid in the same place that the other had just left, probably to remain for years.

Soon, General Hood took up his line of march for the old North State, to make what many of us did not imagine— a final and last demonstration to determine the fate of our noble cause. The hopes of many were still sanguine, in consequence of our faith in the righteousness of our cause, and the placing at the head of the western army one who was known to be a true soldier, as regards fighting. Though the precarious change in generals was not agreeable to the soldiers, yet they followed him unflinchingly and fought as bravely as if commanded by the never-failing Lee; but General Joseph E. Johnson had been their guiding star in some of the grandest maneuvres ever made, and they all loved him as children love a father. And it was hoped the new life which the change might probably instil into the unflinching ranks, would redound to the completion of the great object which they had in view.

With this hope before us, we toiled on in our field of labor, which was soon filled with new patients, most of whom were afflicted with sore eyes. Some were worn out in the Tennessee campaign, and many were almost blind. In fact, a few were pronounced beyond restoration; and doubtless will have to grope their way through this cold and heartless world deprived of one of the greatest temporal blessings on earth.

I shall never forget how patiently they bore their affliction. One in particular attracted our notice, and how our sympathies were excited for him. He was struck in the eye with a spent ball during the engagement before Nash-

ville, and soon his eye began to inflame, and then the other
one, and he became perfectly blind. He was under the
care of one of the best physicians in the country, (Dr.
Pope), and all was done that could be for him; but this
soldier was doomed to be informed by his physician that
his sight was entirely gone. None can describe his feelings
on being informed of his irreparable misfortune, as language has not power to express the horror felt by one who
knows his last hope of ever seeing light is gone. On going
to his bedside on the morning he received the heartrending
news, he said, "Grandma, I am never again to behold the
beauties of nature, which have always given me so much
happiness. My life is to be dragged out as a burthen to
others, as well as to myself. But," said he, "I could bear
all that without regret, if I only could see my dear old
mother and sweet sister when I get home. It is nearly
killing me to know I cannot see them, after being so long
from them." I endeavored to condole with him as best I
could. Still, I was powerless to cheer one in his condition.
There was, also, Mr. Winter, of the Twenty-fourth Texas
Regiment, who had not seen an object for nine months.
Also, Lieutenant Dice, of Rome, Tennessee, was thought to
be blind. Poor, dear boys; how glad I would be to hear
from them. I hope they are with good and dear friends,
and are kindly cared for.

These, I believe, were the last patients sent to us—something over a hundred in all; who, no doubt, had become
afflicted from hard service in their country's cause. They
represented most of the Confederate States, and were a
noble set of men; and, without doubt, had done their duty
as true soldiers. Some who could get home had been furloughed. Others had been promised discharges, and were
daily expecting them, as they were entirely unfit for
service. But none of us knew how near was the awful
time when a furlough or discharge from the Confederacy
would not be needed. Ah, no!

Hopes of success were still lingering. Commissioners had been sent from Richmond to meet those from Washington, to negotiate terms of peace; and as they could not agree, the word was fight on to the final end as long as men were left to wage the warfare. And as none but those in front and at Richmond knew anything but mere report—and they rumors, all inducing us to hope for final success—of course we expected nothing else. Soon, however, the awful, startling news reached our little town that hostilities had ceased; that an armistice was proclaimed, etc. Every one was almost wild with excitement and speculation. What could it mean? Was the President of the United States preparing to give the South her just rights? It could not be otherwise; anything else would be intolerable. The suspense was almost breathless. Oh! heartrending thought!

The news soon came, like a clap of thunder, that all was lost! that General Lee had surrendered all but the honor of his brave and true band. "It cannot be!" "I cannot believe it!" were the universal expressions. Oh, awful, awful thought! Yes, more than hard was it to believe the thought that not another stroke would be struck, that not one more effort would be made to achieve the stupendous object. But a few more days convinced us all of the truth of of our entire failure, our perfect subjection to the iron yoke of tyranny; that the many hard struggles, and tens of thousands of precious lives lost, had resulted worse than useless; that our noble generals, of whom any nation might be proud, had not been whipped, but overpowered by force of numbers, amounting to at least twenty to one, and surrendered. Their last orders had been given; the last roll called; the last guns stacked; and the last stars and bars—oh, blessed emblems of Southern chivalry—had been furled, no more to be hoisted to the ethereal element, as a token of ground still held, and another battle coming, and to gladden the hearts of the noble soldiers who had followed it into many bloody battles, and to so many victories; and under whose folds they had seen so many of their brave companions fall, urging them on to revenge, and to victory, as a last dying expression. The dear old red white and red will ever be remembered as the most sacred thing next to their honors. The small band of devoted veterans had stood around their noble leaders, and witnessed their last acts in their spheres, that of surrendering themselves, and these brave and good men, as prisoners of war, to the leaders of the victorious army; and tendering their well tried and sanguinary swords. In the case of the commander-in-chief of our army, General Grant (all honor to him if he was the victor for our enemies), refused to receive his sword, and returned it to him as the bravest of the brave chieftains, as a token of the high esteem felt for him; and though an enemy, and fighting in an opposite cause, yet he honored him for having fought so bravely for four long years, and keeping at bay the largest army ever known to have been concentrated at any one point, with but a handful of undiciplined veterans, in comparison to theirs. In returning it he said: "I cannot receive the sword of so brave a man as you are. Keep it. You are not whipped, general, but overpowered." Proud, indeed, should all Southern men and women be of a chieftain who could command such esteem from the chief of their enemies; and we should honor General Grant for his magnanimity towards our commander-in-chief; and, though the 2d of April, 1865, was the signal day of our defeat, yet it should be remembered by us in consequence of that manly act. He showed that he appreciated the efforts we had made, though we had failed, and attributed the failure to the true cause, their superior facilities over ours.

The awful news of our defeat, and the surrender of our

armies, had a horrifying effect on all true Southerners in rear as well as in the army front. All seemed to feel that we were, as a people, ruined for all time to come. Consternation appeared to reign in every breast. After having endured so many hardships and privations, and fought so many desperate battles, and lost so many thousands of our brave and good friends, to lose the all for which they fought, was too much for human endurance. Thus were the exclamations of those who were with us at Hill Hospital. They presented the most heart rending spectacle I ever witnessed in that way. Some who were helpless seemed to prefer death to living in their situations. Others, who were able, would walk the hall for hours, with heads down, looking as if they could never rally from the fell stroke. Many of them would approach the humble writer in tears, saying, " Oh, grandma! grandma! we are ruined—lost, and undone forever! What shall we do? Surely I cannot go home a subjugated man. Honor forbids such a thing. I can never look on my dear mother, my dear wife and children, and know I am a subjugated man after all we have endured. I do not feel as if I could again see their dear faces, to know that they and I are slaves to the tyrant. I will cross the Mississippi river, and join the old chieftain on that side, and fight as long as we can possibly raise men who are as determined as the old chief himself; and at last, if fail we must, I will go to some far land and live and die in exile." I was powerless to console them, as I felt as awful as they. I tried to reason that the best policy would be to choose the least evil in the matter; and, besides I told them we all could obtain a boon of more value than all others if we would seek in the right channel, and that was the consolation of the christian religion, and with the possession of that we could be happy under all circumstances; that our failure was ordained for some wise purpose, and to remain

H

at home where they had achieved honor, and live right-
eously, would insure the most perfect happiness to all.
Quite a number bade us farewell, and started for the
Trans-Mississippi Department, with the full belief that
General Kirby Smith was still operating there. Poor mistaken boys! It was rashness to suppose that so small a
force could hold such an extensive and important point
under the circumstances, when all other portions of the
army had yielded, leaving them with but one star and bar
of the ever noble banner under which to rally—more
especially when the united victorious forces were concentrating against them, determined to possess the last fragment of the old banner. Therefore they found all as desolate on that, as this, side of the Mississippi. As a matter
of course, preparations were being made at the different
points for the soldiers. Quartermasters were busy distributing clothing among those who should have received it
long before; and all who were able to help themselves
did so, whether the officers were willing or not. The
Government tan-yards were inspected, and treated likewise, as also other departments; and the poor fellows prepared to leave for their desolate homes. But one thing
disgraceful occurred relative to the taking of Government
supplies, and that was, citizens, or women, taking what
belonged to the poor soldiers who could not help themselves, and which justly raised the ire of the officers—and,
most assuredly, if they had made a raid on the Old Hill
Hospital they would have met with trouble, as the inmates
were prepared for their reception; but they did not make
the effort, but went to the Distributing Hospital, which
had been run out from Macon, Georgia, on the approach
of the Federals, and literally stripped it of everything
they could find, while some poor patients, who were there,
left to suffer, and the officers and attendants forced to
remain in the woods without bedding or provisions, in

tents, etc., which were afterwards taken from them by those unfeeling wretches, both male and female, who came in wagons and carts, and on foot, from miles around, and took off provisions, clothing, and every other thing available. One filled a fine carriage with articles. This state of affairs continued until the officers had to make a requisition on headquarters for guards to protect them and the country. It was said that one woman was seen taking off with her, some distance into the country, ten sides of bacon on her head; and others, sacks of corn or meal. But, when we consider the great suffering the poor people had undergone, we cannot so much blame them. Unfortunately, however, the most was taken by the other class, who really, did not need them, while the officers would have distributed them among the needy families of soldiers if they could.

One by one our patients left, until about all had gone ; and by way of rest from the heavy labors of mind and body, I accepted a pressing invitation from one of Georgia's noblest daughters, Mrs. O. P. Poeddick, to spend a few days at her pleasant country home.

Soon after reaching the hospital, news reached us that the Federal guard was soon to be at the depot. Knowing that our fate was already sealed, and that we were in their power, we went by to see how they looked, and how they would be received. In a short time they made their appearance, looking as blue and filthy as could be imagined. They came in silence, and were received in the same silent manner. All the demonstrations that I saw were the moistened eyes of the veteran soldiers who were there in grey. Poor fellows ! we could well imagine how deeply they felt the degradation of being guarded by their worst foes. As they stood around our buggy they would give vent to their feelings in the following manner : " Oh, is it not awful ? " " I would rather fight it all over again, or

die in the effort, than to submit to such a thing as this."
" This is the first time they have ever met us without
being sternly resisted. Now we are powerless in their
hands, and must submit the best we can." Dear, brave
men, who had stood as a wall of fire between us and the
merciless, worthless, craven-hearted enemy, who sought
no right, no boon, but plunder and the subjugation of an
inoffensive people. We wept tears of bitter regret with
the poor fellows. It was all we could do, as our hearts
were almost breaking in consequence of the awfully humil-
liating condition we were in, and we felt it so sensibly,
and what our future would be. We sat and looked at
them as they moved around in silence, and it was plain to
be seen that they did not enjoy the victory over us. Not
one would look us in the eye. If they saw us looking at
them, their eyes would fall immediately, as though they
felt how unfairly they had gained the power over us. We
drove off, leaving them in possession of the once quiet,
little town of Cuthbert.

On Saturday, the 10th, I returned to my post, after
spending as pleasant a time with Mrs. R. as I ever spent
in my life, and one to be long remembered in connection
with other very pleasant events during my stay in the
noble old Empire State, feeling that though we had to
drink many very bitter cups, and witness many unpleasant
scenes, that the bitter is often mixed with sweets, as mine
had been for the past few days, and that a spirit of deep
gratitude is, or should always be, prominent in our hearts,
for the very many chances for Divine, as well as temporal,
enjoyments ; and I shall ever feel grateful to that kind
family for the pleasure I enjoyed with them.

We resumed our duties to the remaining few patients,
feeling that it was the last chance we would have to
administer to their comfort. The number became smaller,
and smaller, until, on the 12th of May, 1865, we dealt out

the last meal that we have ever had the pleasure to present to the noble Confederate soldier in Southern hospitals.

And in all probability, we witnessed as much suffering, in all conceivable forms, as any one in the same length of time. Some of the most triumphant death-bed scenes we ever witnessed, were those of Confederate soldiers. We are powerless to even attempt anything like a correct detail of the many heartrending scenes witnessed by us, and which were almost daily passing before and around us. If we had not felt confident that we were doing all in our power to aid a just and glorious cause, and were receiving the universal approval of all with whom we were working, our sensitive nature would have shrunk from beholding the innumerable specimens of suffering of all forms to which humanity is subject, which once were daily presented to us. And but for the fact that all clouds are at times dispelled, and give place to the cheering rays of the summer sun, we would sink under the weight of despondency and gloom. So in this case. Just as it seemed we were shrinking from the pressure of sympathy and responsibility, we would receive the cheering consolation of doing our duty, and relieving the sufferings of those around us; and in this way something cheering would spring up to divert our depressed minds, as well as some word or act of the convalescent who had been in similar situations, and were about recovered, would admonish us that all bitters had their sweets.

Brave, kind soldiers of the South! with you we mingled for four long years in the noble struggle for independence. And to you we shall ever owe a debt of gratitude for the respect, kindness and confidence shown us at all times and under all circumstances.

The last battle has been fought, and the noble cause lost. And we who survive have returned to our homes, and are to the best of our ability endeavoring to follow the quiet

pursuits of life—patiently awaiting the time when the
fruits of our efforts for the independence of our country
will, in spite of all the chilling frosts of the usurping winter
tyrant, fully mature into a plentiful harvest of all the
sweets of national liberty.   Dear soldiers, whatever may
be your fate, we will ever love, honor and respect you as
men, in every way worthy of the cause for which you so
heroically fought.   You are none the less deserving of
respect because you did not obtain the great prize for
which you contended.   The will is as good as the deed; as
no band of patriots could have succeeded in a contest of
twenty to one against you.   Though you did not cross over
into the promised land, yet you achieved honors which
will ever live in the hearts of the good and great of all
countries, and through all ages.   We still hope for scuccess;
and, if disappointed in that, we pray Heaven's best and
purest blessings upon all true Southern soldiers, and all
others who are true to their country and their country's
God.   By constant fidelity to that which is sacred and dear
to all true patriots, and a firm reliance on the Allwise
Ruler of the universe, and an unshaken confidence in him
who has providentially been placed at the head of this now
shattered nation, may we not hope to see in a not far
distant day peace and quiet again restored to our once
idolized country.   Then he would again restore to his
brother patriot the freedom for which our forefathers
fought, and again bring into force the dear old National
Constitution, under whose dictates our country was made
so happy and prosperous—that noble and almost perfect
Constitution, which was the illustrious heritage left us by
our Revolutionary fathers, and which is now by the usurpers by whom we are tyranised over torn into fragments,
and entirely disregarded.   It is no wonder that we all, as
true Southerners, still so fondly love the dear old stars and
bars.   And we are thankful to God that we possess this love ;

and that we have the consciousness of not having been whipped, but overpowered by ten times our number; and that, had we fought none but Northern men, we would have succeeded. We hope ever to love the memory of the old banner, and the cause over which it waved. And until the name of United States of America shall cease to exist, and the continent be in the hands of another and different race of people, will we ever cease to worship, next to Divinity, the banner of the Confederate States; and detest those who are acting the real tyrant over us more fully than ever a nation suffered.

The subject is one worthy of the pen of the most able writer, to express what are the feelings and condition of a race of people who never knew aught but to enjoy the sweets of freemens' liberty. It seems almost presumption in a poor woman to dare assume the privilege of expressing a thought in regard to a subject of such great magnitude— one in which millions of those who (heretofore were free- men) felt an interest paramount to all others of the kind. Who are there on this continent (which for near a century has been considered a home for the oppressed of all coun- tries), who, after enjoying all the political, social and religious blessings possible to be heaped on any people, can turn a deaf ear to the cries of the suffering natives of this, their once glorious country, and not do all in their power to restore to them at least a part of those blessings? Are there any who so far forget the Divine aid given our Revo- lutionary sires, and by them handed down to us in the way of untold blessings, as to hear the suffering cry of the widow and the orphan, and not attempt to alleviate their suffering in some way? The blood of the noble dead, of both rank and file, cries aloud for the retribution which will surely come, in some form or another, in the good time of the Divine Ruler.

Surely, the Southern civil chieftain will not be allowed

to remain from year to year in the filthy, hated prison at Fortress Munroe, denied a fair, honorable, and legal trial, for fear his honest countrymen will give him justice, and end his disgraceful punishment, without a righteous and just retribution. Feeling that our Divine Father has a design in all things, we still earnestly hope and pray that in His own good time He will work out for us something greater than we are able to ask, or worthy to receive, for our and our country's good. We feel that generations yet unborn will rise up and call Jeff Davis blessed. May Heaven grant that he may survive his captivity, and see his noble country for which he and his friends have suffered so much, freed from under the tyrant's yoke, and enjoying the freedom for which all fought and so justly merit.

As an humble participant in the great struggle for Southern independence, in the sphere allowed for my sex, I can say with perfect sincerity of heart, that I have never regretted any sacrifice I made in behalf of our cause. I only am sorry that I was able to do so little, and that little effected so small amount of good for my country. Had I the same field open before me to-day, how gladly would I make every posssible effort to, in all possible ways, further the noble cause, by relieving, as far as I had the power, every pang of suffering of the defenders of our country.

I served in the Hill Hospital for near two years—with the exception of a short absence, caused by the unjust treatment of Dr. Fing, of Mississippi, during the absence of the surgeon in charge; and on his return I was called back to my charge, and remained until the last one left, some for their homes, and the others to Macon to the care of the Federals until able to get home. Mrs. Kiddo, who had been a true friend to all of us from the time of our first arrival at Cuthbert, came to see the last of them leave. Many were the kind wishes and blessings pronounced on us when taking leave of the last of the suffering patriots.

Need I say that we felt most deeply affected when parting with those for whom we had tried to do all in our power for so long. Had the struggle closed favorable for us, the parting would have been different. But now, when we saw that all the hardships, deprivation, suffering, anxiety and hopes of friends and property, instead of proving beneficial, had resulted in our entire ruin, our feelings cannot be described.

Notwithstanding our ever memorable stars and bars worn by our foes torn to fragments, and trampled under their unhallowed feet, yet we still cherish the memory of its motto as a thing sacred indeed, as well as the cause over which it waved; and only mourn over its remains as a memento of our defeat—as the dear soldier mourned that he was necessitated to return to the home for which he had fought, and find it desolated, and he and his dear ones under the power of the most hated foe ever known to any nation of people.

The Southern Rebel will ever be highly honored by all the truly patriotic sons and daughters of not only the Southern section of North America, and the constitutional Conservatives of the North, but their names and the heroism displayed by them in defending their noble cause, will ever be immortal in the estimation of the noble and great of the North, South, East and West of the whole civilized world. Though the noble Spartans did not succeed in their country's defense, yet their names will ever be great. There is not a true Southern heart ncw animate who does not revere the very name of a Rebel soldier who did his duty in his dear country's defense.

Then if the living should be and are so highly honored, surely the noble dead will ever live in our hearts so long as from generation to generation the present race of people exist in the land of flowers. Not only the direct descendants of those patriots, but all who love the South, will ever

H*

remember with pride those who fought, bled and died for her just rights. And all can respond to the sentiments of the poot, Moore, when he says:

> " Oh ! could we from death but recover
>   Those hearts as they were banded before,
> On the face of high Heaven, to fight over
>   That combat for freedom once more !

> " Could the chains for one instant be riven,
>   Which tyranny flung round us then ?
> No ! 'tis not in man, nor in Heaven,
>   To let tyrants bind it again.

> " But 'tis past ! And though blazoned in story
>   The name of our victors may be ;
> Accursed is the march of that glory,
>   Which treads on the hearts of the free.

> " For dearer the grave or the prison,
>   Illumined by one patriot name,
> Than the trophies of all who have ridden
>   On liberty's ruin to fame."

The true patriots of the South, under the awful circumstances surrounding them, will enjoy the happy reflection that they did all in their power to effect success; and still do all that honorable men can to alleviate the mental and physical suffering of the country, and make an honorable mantainance for themselves and dependants. Notwithstanding the laws of the victors are as oppressive as could be imposed on any people, they hold their heads above all depressing circumstances, and strive in the hope of eventually seeing their country victorious over all opposition; yet the victors carry in their hearts a consciousness of having acted unkindly, ungenerously, and, what is worse, wickedly in all they did, and are still doing towards us, which is resulting in the ruin of the whole nation.

But why should one so incompetent to the task attempt to express the feeling of the Southern people now, as they are more oppressed than the subjects of the worst tyrant on the face of the earth.

Let our temporal interests succeed or not, all true patriots and christians may obtain the consolation of honest hearts and christian joys, and in the end obtain a crown of unfading glory where the tyrant's power cannot reach us, and where we may rest from all strife, turmoil and tribulation. And we will ever remember while on this earth with pride and with sadness

The field where so many thousand perished—
  The true, the gallant, the brave!
Though they are gone, and the bright hopes that were cherished
  Gone with them, and quenched in the grave.

Yet the fame of those heroes still lives,
  In the hearts of their comrades who fought
Beside them, that they might achieve
  The freedom of our fair Sunny South.

Their names will long live in story,
  Who fought as did heroes of old,
On many a battle field gory,
  That the rights of the South they might hold.

The graves of those veterans are cherished;
  And light be the steps that we tread,
When we stroll o'er the fields where they perished,
  And a tear to their memory shed.

We'll weave to their honor bright garlands,
  And twine them o'er memory's shrine,
For the deeds of their chief—brave Southman—
  Are resplendent with glories divine.

Brave comrades, we will not forget thee
  Who still live to mourn o'er the lost;
O'er hopes that are blighted and left thee—
  O'er comrades who fell at their post.

An evergreen garland we twine thee,
  To deck thy war scarred brow;
Whatever thy fates, we still love thee
  As ever in bright days of yore.

Since God has deemed that our nation
  Shall not be severed in twain,
Go show thyselves worthy the station
  That freeman should ever maintain.

Submit to God's will, and the laws
  Of a nation wherein thou dost live;
And every rich blessing that flows,
  To His people He surely will give.

For there is life in the old land yet. There is still a spirit of independence and love of liberty existing in the hearts of the Southern people; and we trust it will ever predominate over all other principles, except honor and virtue. The clouds which look so very dark and gloomy will not overspread the once bright canopy, so as to obscure the light of liberty entirely; and we feel confident they will, in time, be dispelled, admitting the bright rays of the sun of liberty in all its noonday splendor. If we continue firm in our fidelity to, and love of our country as true patriots and christians, putting our trust in the God of the victim as well as the victor, we will, in His own good time, see the star of liberty shine forth in all its wonted beauty to illumine the pathway of those who have suffered so much in the effort to free our country from the power of those who are shutting out the beautiful light of Southern liberty—those who are subverting all the pure institutions obtained for us, and handed down to us by our Revolutionary fathers. All will yet be well. The South will be restored to its rights under the constitution at some time. The olive branch of peace will be reached out to her, and the stars and stripes, with all the stars in their place, will again wave over the land once called the home of the free and the brave, as in days when it was idolized by all the American people. With the sincere hope ever prominent in our hearts that these results will at some not far distant day be fully realized, and that we will yet enjoy the fruits of our earnest labor as a nation, and in the final end find a resting place in the home above prepared for all those who did their duty to their country, their fellow men, and their God.

We now bid the kind, noble, generous and brave Southern patriots a kind, affectionate and grateful farewell; and beg the privilege of presenting this imperfect tribute to their memory (which has been gotten up under a great many difficulties—financially, mentally, and in every other way,) in honor of the justly merited and ever memorable names for the noble services done their country, and in compliance with their generous solicitation during our sojourn with many of them in their abodes of suffering. We beg to tender it to them with the most affectionate gratitude for their unabated kindness to us, and their un-flinching fidelity to our great and honored cause.

CHAPTER VII.

For the information of those of our readers whose locality is so far in the interior of the country, that, in all proba-bility, they were deprived of the privilege of visiting any of the hospitals during the late struggle, we consider it due to them to give a brief detail of the manner in which they were fitted up and managed, which, doubtless, will not prove altogether uninteresting, as perhaps many who never saw a hospital have had friends to languish and die in them, leaving those at home in doubt in regard to the proper attention given them. No doubt, some places where the sick and wounded soldiers were deposited, were in too many instances counterfeited; while at the same time, many others can substantially be vouched for in regard to every available means being used to make them com-fortable.

In every city, town, or village where one or more hos-pitals was located, there was a post surgeon, who presided over all the departments. To each hospital, bearing its respective name, there was a surgeon in charge, who pre-sided over his own department—having as many assistant surgeons as was necessary, according to the number of patients. There were, also, stewards, wardmasters, nurses, matrons, cooks and laundresses, whose positions were respectively filled to the letter. As comfortable quarters as could be procured were neatly fitted up, beds or bunks placed in regular rows and numbered, having good mattressess and clean bedding on them. Towels, wash pans and water buckets in abundance were in every ward.

The general wardmaster received and reported the patients as they came in ; assigned them their bunks, gave them a clean change of clothes, which he drew from the linen room, which was kept in perfect order by the linen matron. Their camp clothes were taken to the laundry, put in good order, and deposited for safe keeping by the wardmaster in a room kept for that purpose, and strictly marked, so that each man's knapsack could be identified.

Sometimes there were black men to do the general cleaning in the wards. Soldiers, unable for field duty, attended to the patients, with the assistance of the matrons.

Perhaps some may be ready to ask, "What good, or of service can a woman be in a place where there are so many specimens of suffering humanity, and so many different calls on her for sympathy and aid, and so many different dispositions to please?" We answer, that she can do more than ever can be told, except by those who receive her feeble aid. How is it with you, dear mother, when your darling boy is sick at home ? Do you not try to satisfy his every want ? Just so it is with a matron whose heart is with her country, and whose sympathy is with those at home, whose darling boy has left her fond embrace and the home of his birth, and gone forth to battle for the richest of earthly boons—Liberty ! She can call on the steward for whatever diet his appetite calls for, see that it is prepared ts suit his taste, send or carry it to him, and feed him herself if he is too feeble to do so ; bathe his fevered brow, comb his hair, which perhaps has been matted by the crimson tide which flowed from his wounded head, or from long neglect before

he was brought off the field. She can dress their wounds
in very many cases, which is far more preferable to that of
the male nurses; because, to the credit of our sex be it said,
they can dress wounds more tenderly than men. We have
often heard the remark made by patients, that one woman
in a hospital was worth a dozen men, on account of her
knowledge in regard to their every want, and her tact in
supplying them. There are the various stimulants she can
prepare to suit them; the little pads and pillows to relieve
the wounded parts from the mattress, which naturally becomes hard from several days' using; slings for the broken
arm or foot, to support them when walking around;
crutches can be padded; haversacks made ready, to put
their rations in when they start back to face the enemy—
giving them an extra lunch, if she has it to spare, from the
invalid's safe. Another very essential office she can fill
with propriety, and which will add greatly to the comfort
and health of the inmates—by assisting the wardmaster in
directing and seeing that the wards are in every respect
kept strictly clean; also the beds, bedding and the patients'
linen. And I might go on and enumerate a thousand and
one things that a lady can do in a hospital, and then not be
done; that is, if she is there for the one particular object—
the benefit of the soldier. If, on the contrary, she places
herself there merely for pastime, and to court the favor of
the bomb-proof officials, she had better never go inside of
the walls of a place where hundreds of emaciated objects
of mercy are looking to her for that which will, in a great
degree, change their condition for the better. She will be
a nuisance, a hiss, and a make-game for the whole crowd
whom she serves, in mockery of that which is really necessary to be done in such a place. She can visit their wards
at every spare moment, join in their pleasant conversation.
read to them, sing for them, write to loved ones at home,
encourage their religious inclinations by conversing on the

all important subject, and sitting in their midst during a
sermon from the christian chaplain, which all hospitals
were favored with.   She can easily learn how to approach
them, and in what tone to direct conversation—not hesitating to join in their innocent jests, which are often got up
between them ; and on your entering, more than one voice
will call out for your decision, and you must be careful to
give an opinion suitable to all parties, and you will not be
apt to leave without receiving a pressing invitation to come
back soon ; for some of these bad boys will be sure to impose on me while you are gone.   And last, but not least,
she can stand by the couch of the dying hero, receive his
blessing on herself and loved ones at home, and give him
words of cheer while he is crossing the cold Jordan of
death—not hesitating to leave your own weary couch at
the hour of midnight, or later, and go to such an one after
his spirit has fled from the suffering body, and the lids,
which perhaps his intense suffering forbade their closing
for days and nights, have been sealed in death, and cut a
tress from his war honored brow, and enclose it in a letter
to friends at home.   They will cherish it more than all the
gold of the Indias.   Keep his little relicts until you can
send them safely home.

Some perhaps will be ready to ask, "Can a woman do all
this, and continue for four years in the constant perform-
ance of the same, without body and mind becoming impaired ?"   Experience answers in the affirmative ; and
many other offices too tedious to weary the reader with.
And she will be happy every day of her life, because she
knows others are made happy by her feeble efforts; and
that she has the approval of a righteous God, who has
given her strength sufficient to her every demand.   And
though we did not get our requisite amount of sleep, yet
our health was not in the least impaired.

We would only add, that should there ever be another

call for aid in so great a work, let no one take another's word in regard to filling a place of so much need and great magnitude; but all who can do so, take lessons from experience, and learn thereby whether any good can be accomplished by the weaker sex—hoping that they may be more efficient than was the humble participant in the late struggle for a just and righteous cause, whose hopes are blighted, and its people downtrodden and sorely oppressed.

CHAPTER VIII.

On Monday morning, May the 22d, 1865, my husband and myself, after having all things in readiness, together with a good store of substantial edibles, kindly furnished us for our journey by some of our lady friends, took passage in a wagon (generously furnished to us by our ever true friend, Captain Kiddoo, and his noble lady,) which soon placed us at the depot at Cuthbert, Georgia. There we were without a dollar, except Confederate; and of course, to use the common phrase, that was "played out." Some friend to the financial department having opened my trunk in my absence from my room on Saturday night, and took all the available money we had saved from our earnings before leaving Memphis, we were moneyless. This was a dilemma in which we had never before been placed. Not a dollar!—and we near a thousand miles from home; and all the means of conveyance in the hands of the Federals, who were tyranizing over us in every possible way. Our imaginations were anything but pleasant under such circumstances, as we did not know whether we would be allowed transportation or not. However, as go ahead we must, we intended trying what we could do. My husband being a paroled soldier, was all right. But as a Rebel

woman, according to orders, I was not permitted to go on
Government transportation.   But when the train arrived
for Macon, I went aboard and took my seat, not knowing
but that I should be put off on first sight of the gallant and
loyal guards, or the conductor.   Soon the conductor came
around collecting the fare from the passengers.   On his
approaching me, I presented to him a letter of introduction
which had been given to me at Cuthbert by Colonel Gault,
petitioning him the indulgence of the Federal authorities,
and asking them to pass me, as I had been engaged in
services, etc., and had met with the misfortune of being
robbed on the eve of my departure.   After looking over it
carefully, the conductor politely returned it, saying, "All
right, madam."   I thanked him with a light heart, feeling
all safe to Macon, where I would trust to good fortune to
get on further.

On reaching Macon, and claiming our baggage, we discovered that one of our trunks was missing—the same one
that had been broken open.   We put up for the night
with a kind lady from our own State.   My husband went
back to Cuthbert, found the trunk, and returned on the
evening train.   We took shelter for that night under the
car shed, as it was a long walk from the depot to our
friend's house, and I was wearied from hunting up my
last, and few remaining patients, being anxious to know
how they were quartered before taking my final leave of
them.   I found them comfortably situated in the Ocmulgee Hospital—Federals and Confederates all together, and
also surgeons and nurses of both sides.   They were in fine
spirits, hoping soon to be able to go to their own homes in
Texas and Arkansas.

We lost no time in having everything ready for the
morning train of the 25th, which would take us to Atlanta,
Georgia.   I flattered myself that I would have no trouble
to get passage, as I was on board before the crowd had

gathered; but before the cars were opened there was considerable of a little army there, all eager to get home. When the words, "All aboard!" sounded, of all the rushes I ever witnessed, I think that was the greatest. The old adage, "Everybody for themselves," was strictly adhered to. The car doors were completely clogged, and blocked up, at times, so that none could pass. I began to think that my chance to get on before the words "All right" were given was bad indeed. My husband, having to get our baggage on board, could not help me. But we proved the truth of the saying that "Where there is a will, there is a way;" and just as I was about giving up in despair, who should step up to my assistance but our gallant friend and soldier, Major J. J. Murphy, of Memphis, Tennessee, like ourselves, bound for home. Most assuredly I appreciated his kind assistance in finding a seat for me, which was out of the question for some time, and I was expecting to have to stand, when a gentleman said to me, "Can't you get a seat, madam?" "Not yet," said I. He replied, "Well, if there are any Tennesseeans on the train you will soon get one." I then asked him if he was a Tennesseean, for I felt as though I was lost from all friends at that time. (As yet I did not know whether my husband was on board or not.) "I am," was his reply. "I am glad to know it," said I. He responded, "I can appreciate your feelings, having been from home a long time myself. I have been a chaplain in a Tennessee regiment. My name is Cherry. What is yours?" I gave him my address. "Are you not from Memphis," said he. I told him I was. "Oh, I guess you are the very lady I am looking for. The boys at the Ocmulgee Hospital informed me that Grandmother Smith was on her way to her home in Memphis; and I was anxious to see you that I might send a letter to my sister, Miss Mary C. Cherry. You will find her next door to Asbury Chapel. Please call on her, and deliver it in person. She will be glad to see any person who can bring her reliable information from me." I assured him that I would forward it on the first opportunity, It was a pleasant little episode, in my difficult journey home, to meet with a stranger who seemed so kind. I informed him of my misfortune, and my fears of being detained on my way, for want of means to pay my passage. " I will see to that for you," he said, and immediately went to the conductor and informed him of the fact, and I was soon relieved by the conductor saying my passage was safe to Atlanta ; that he was Mr. Jones, of Memphis, and right on the rebel question. This was a happy day for us ; and I felt that God, in His goodness, had sent these kind friends to me in a way I had least expected.

Six o'clock found us at Atlanta, the Sodom-like city, that once proud and flourishing city, in the very heart of the old Empire State. This city, like much of the good old State, was completely ruined by the ruthless hand of the merciless tyrant chieftain and his band of outlaws. None but those in whose midst, and over whose rights, the band of far worse than savages swept as a tornado, can give the most faint idea, or description, of what this noble Gate City, and its vicinity, suffered, and the great contrast between its former and present appearance. We remained at this place until Tuesday, the 22d, spending a part of our time at the Gate City Hotel, eating our own cold lunch, which was better than we deserved, and slept on a pallet in quite a nice room. The surgeon in charge of the Medical College Hospital finding out our situation invited us to go there, and remain until we could get conveyance through to Kingston by pike. It seemed as though all chances were lost to us. We were more than anxious to proceed on our journey, owing to the fact of having just learned that my son had been taken prisoner

at Salisbury, N. C., in the artillery duel between Johnson's battalions, and Stoneman's Division, and had been
sent we could not learn where, until we met with a soldier
in Atlanta, who informed us that as he was leaving the
Yankee prison, to his surprise he saw my son march in to
finish his experience in hardship and deprivation, at Camp
Chase, Ohio. It gave us great relief to learn his whereabouts; and, as a natural consequence, we wished to reach
a point where we could learn something more definite in
regard to him. Every effort was made to procure transportation of some kind; but all to no purpose for several
days. We called on the mayor of the city, hoping he
would lend us his sympathy, at least, and perhaps devise
some means whereby we could get away; but failed, as in
every other effort. Finally, as already stated, the surgeon
in charge of the Medical College Hospital, on learning of
our being in the city, although he was of the opposite
party, gave us a cordial invitation to stop with him until
a number of transportation wagons should return from
Kingston, and we should have passage with a number of
disabled soldiers who were to be forwarded to the above
named place.

With many thanks, the generous proffer was accepted,
and a nice, comfortable appartment was assigned us. The
stern realities of a cruel war of four years duration, and
the fact that the party to which he belonged had proven
too strong for us, had not diminished all the finer feelings
of humanity existing in his heart, which he shunned not to
manifest, even toward those whom they strove to conquer
in the late cruel strife. We are commanded in Holy Writ
to render unto all with whom we have intercourse in this
life, their just dues, and we cannot pass this kind act by
without giving it a kindly thought, mingled with gratitude—yet he only did his duty.

Several of my old Cuthbert patients were inmates of that

hospital, anxiously awaiting their transportation home, which was promised them. I spent most of my time fixing up the small wardrobe of the patients. I made no new acquaintances there—knowing that they were all Rebs, and I did not want to go through another painful trial of bidding adieu to our brave defenders, who were still languishing on the bed of suffering, unable to proceed homeward.

Our patience had become almost threadbare. My husband did not relax his efforts in trying to get conveyance of some kind—determined not to wait for the promised wagons, if an opportunity was offered before they returned. Every available conveyance was chartered by the Tennessee exiles at the most exorbitant prices, and many a bombproof made a rich thing off of those who were cut off from home. The pile that was in their pockets was sized, and be it large or small, all was required. So it was in our case. Finally, the diligently sought for prize was won, by my husband giving a fine silver watch and five dollars in greenbacks (every dollar he possessed) for passage for myself and trunks in a wagon, which the owner was taking to Dalton for the purpose of laying in goods. With glad hearts we rid ourselves of the last cent of money and the cherished time piece, and we started on the 27th of August for the terminus of the wrecked railway which would bring us to Kingston, where a more speedy way of traveling could be had. My husband walked all the way, and assisted the weary team in ascending the various mountain ridges and hights, which were scarcely out of sight, and were very difficult to surmount with the inefficient team. When we reached Altona hights, our hearts were nearly ready to fail us, knowing the great difficulties which had been encountered in ascending those already passed—which were not a comparison to those of Altona. We made a halt at the foot of the mountain, or pass as it was called during the war, and rested for nearly an hour. After taking some refreshments from our cold but palatable lunch, the kind old widow who lived there accompanied me to the silent resting place of the fallen heroes of the battle fought by General Hood and the Yanks while on his march to Nashville. They had been neatly marked by this kind old lady, and beautifully decorated with various flowers. More than one State was represented in that city of the dead. How I read with solemn awe the names and regiments of the Lone Star State; also, from our own State; others from Mississippi and Arkansas; while there were a few bearing the unfathomable inscription,"Unkown." Who can stand around a soldier's grave marked thus, without feeling a sad emotion and heartrending sympathy for the unwearied awaiting of loved ones at home whose darling is slumbering there? No one, I would suppose, who possess a heart endowed with charity and sympathy. This kind old lady informed us that she had provided for and nursed quite a number of those veterans from her own scanty means, and had bought nice clothes to bury them in, and deprived herself of the last sheet she possessed for those brave defenders who had fallen victims in that disastrous conflict. It is to be hoped that she will reap a rich reward in this life and that which is to come. Those of our Southern martyrs were not all who slept beneath those mounds of Altona hights. On a distant mountain thousands of the fallen foe sleep the same long sleep. Their combat for booty and nigger is over. They are as unconscious of the tyranical shackles their surviving comrades are forging a brave and noble people as is our own sacred dead, who, doubtless, would have preferred a brave soldier's grave, rather than live to see the awful calamity which has befallen their survivors. I noticed in particular a host of the Sixteenth Illinois Regiment. I think it must have been almost annihilated, from the number of graves which were in sight; and we were informed that these

were only a few in comparison to the number buried elsewhere. But let them rest; they can harm us no more.

Finally we resumed our line of march, gradually ascending the hights of Altona, where sleep the Southern hero
and his foe. Such baulking and pushing as was there
encountered beggars description; yet on we went as best
we could at quite a slow gait—often balancing accounts by
the speedy descents as they came in turn. More than once
our lives were in jeopardy in descending those hights. On
reaching the summit, before any one had time to lock the
wheels, down went the mule, rider, driver, wagon and all,
as fast as wheels could roll, bounding over stumps and roots
as they chanced to be in the way, placing us in such an
unpleasant dilemma as to make us think of but little else
than that we would be dashed against a rock, and, in all
probability, be taken up a corpse, while those of our party
who were left far in the rear were making all possible speed
to keep up with us in case we should be thrown out; but
thanks to a protecting providence, we mysteriously reached
the valley in safety, and gave the signal by a waive of the
hand, to the delight of all parties. Being anxious to reach
a spot where some one might chance to live, so that the
dark hours of the night would seem less lonely than those
of the night previous—which was spent in a lonely wreck
of a once magnificent orchard, making our pallet under a
large apple tree, against the trunk of which some one had
placed a large door, which perhaps had been taken from
the dwelling before it was burned—we made as good speed
as possible, which brought us near a farm house at night-
fall, a short distance from Cartersville. Our conductor
being acquainted with the family, of course got shelter;
but as we poor strapped Rebs were minus of greenbacks,
and the charitable (or rather, *vice versa,*) host doubtless had
made plenty off of his bleeding country to make him comfortable, as a natural consequence our shelter was out in a

large shaded lot beneath a grand old oak, whose wide spreading boughs served in some measure to shelter us from the falling dew which was quite chilly. Being worried from our day's journey, we slept soundly, and were satisfied with what some might very justly call hard fare; yet thousands of our brave soldiers had slept less comfortably during the war, and were at that time faring no better while trying to reach their homes, and we were content to share the same fate—as ever was our disposition to do when fate and duty directed it. At the same time, we do not try to disguise the fact that we scorned the person who owned that comfortable dwelling as one void of humanity, and by no means a friend to any one who participated in our lost cause. We made an early start on the following morning, and reached Kingston—the terminus of that part of our wearisome journey—at eleven o'clock, June 1st. Glad were we to have a short recreation, both of body and mind, from the arduous trip and sickening scenes which had been continually presented to us for the last two days, or more, in all of that wide scope of country which, from the wreck left, one would judge was once inhabited by those of wealth and affluence. Nothing but desolation was to be seen   If we remember aright, we passed not more than six farm-houses after leaving Atlanta that were not destroyed. We did not see any live stock or poultry until we reached Cartersville. Not a man, woman or child did we see for miles, only the weary soldier—who had fought his last fight, and honorably surrendered to the victorious foe, and with his humble knapsack, which contained all his wealth, was plodding his way homeward—until on the evening of the second day we overtook a small army of Yankee cavalry wending their way to Chattanooga to receive their honorable discharges for raiding on women and children, burning and pillaging, and slaying our brave citizens when unarmed for the purpose of booty and

I

might—not even having liberty and right (an object) to
justify their ten thousand deeds of unparalleled cruelty.
Thousands of those homeward bound oppressors were passing for more than a day, which only caused a more profound sadness to prevail in our hearts, which were always
moved with regret. However, we diverted our mind as
best we could by looking around to some spot that was
made renowned by our brave heroes, who, at the time they
defended those places, were so sanguine of success. With
what melancholy did our recollection revert back to the
past, but then blasted hopes, when our eyes met for the
first time, and perhaps the last, those majestic Kenesaw
Mountains, and viewed those winding earth works thrown
up on its summit by our once hopeful braves. Here and
there was a little hillock telling to the passing stranger
that somebody's darling sleeps there, unknowing and unknown. More than once the spot where the thundering
guns of the intrepid Carnes of Marshall's Battery (to
which my husband and only child belonged) was pointed
out, and the deeds of him and his braves were related to
us. I felt proud that I once could behold one spot where
those of my own household had endeavored to do their duty
in their country's cause. Here and there the pickets' trench
was visible, and the chain of breastworks were scarcely out
of sight. Many of them were recognized as being the spot
from which many kind letters were written to us by the
soldiers who had erected and bravely defended them.

New Hope Church was not passed by unnoticed. Pine
and Lost mountains were anxiously sought for, but they
were not visible to us. Pine mountain lay far on the left
and it served to refresh our memories with the heroic deeds
of a brave band under as an efficient officer as the Confederacy could boast of. It was there that Leonidas Polk,
Lieutenant General C. S. A., gave his life for his country.
That ground was made sacred by the life blood which it

drank from the veins of that gallant hero. Thrice happy is he to-day, as well as a Stonewall or an A. Sidney Johnson, that he did not live to see the result of the war which proved so disastrous to us. It was really a novel spectacle to see the different sights on the road. All manner of constructions for shelter and sleeping were to be seen; with here and there a lot of decayed baggage. Carcasses of the poor dumb brutes, which had doubtless borne their part in the war, could be seen every few hundred yards, which plainly told of the great mortality among them. Any one not having an occasion to travel that road, could never be able to conceive the destruction done to the railroad—irons torn up, cross-ties heaped up, and fire touched to them, and the rails placed on the fire until they were rendered perfectly useless. Perhaps it was right to do thus in time of war, but it really seemed hard to see so much valuable property destroyed. But why have I wandered from the progress of my journey to speak of what is so familiar to thousands, who are more competent to portray the horrible picture which was before us. Let us proceed further on with our journey homewards.

Well, here we are at Kingston—burnt and devastated Kingston!—the rendezvous of a large part of the Federal army. The post commandant sitting in his post of honor, to render such services to the surrendered Rebs as he deems their respective crimes justly merit from his honor, and I completely at his mercy, as I had not the greenback nor the golden calf to present to him for a passport. However, like the Prodigal Son, I resolved to have my case presented to him. Hoping it would meet his most favorable consideration, my husband carried the complimentary note which Colonel Gault gave me on leaving Cuthbert, and asked his honor to give it a notice; and, oh, did not my heart sink within me when he returned with the intelligence of a stern refusal to our humble petition, for the reason that it gave no evidence of our loyalty to the Government, and he would be doing injustice to his Government if he gave me transportation.   Perhaps I could have bribed his majesty's justice, had I the means.   Most assuredly such treatment from one who had such a fat office did not serve in the least to increase my loyalty to the shattered Government of the United States, which no one prized higher than did the humble writer, so long as we were granted the liberty and rights bequeathed to us by our noble ancestors, and none would rejoice more at the return of the good old times than I; and none desires it more earnestly at this trying hour than I do, when the heart is made sick with unnecessary oppression and tyranny.   So completely were our minds engrossed in the knowledge of our unavoidable situation, that we became almost unconscious of the vast crowd which surrounded us of those with whom we had been unused to mingle; yet we had not despaired of some means of deliverance.   I had resolved to get on the cars when the signal should be given to move off, and, if I was put off, some one would protect me.   I did not believe that every Federal officer would be so inhuman or so far forgot that his mother was a woman as to suffer one of her sex to be maltreated.   I felt relieved at my own determination not to be outdone by this tyrant in human shape.

Soon my distressed heart was made glad by the unexpected meeting with one of my old and highly esteemed patients, James Hartgrous, of Spring Hill, Tennessee. After the usual compliments were passed, he immediately inquired if I had all things right in regard to my passport, I frankly narrated my sad story to him.   "Well," said he, "grandma, don't suffer yourself to be troubled much about the matter.   I believe I can assist you.   The Yankee officers think they are mighty sharp; but sometimes they are caught napping, and get flanked, and maybe they can be flanked in your case.   I have one transportation, and I

believe they will not know me if I go before them again.
I will try it at all events; and, if I succeed in getting
transportation, you shall have it. If I fail, you shall have
the one I now have, and I can go on my parole. When we
get to Chattanooga, I can get what money I want from
friends who live there, and you shall have it." My happiness was better felt than described on that soul trying
occasion at this testimony of the many marks of unsullied
friendship the soldiers had for one so unworthy as myself.
My friend soon returned, bringing with him the treasure,
and presented it, saying, "When the conductor comes
around to collect your fare, tell him that a friend gave it
to you, because you was refused one from head quarters."

In the course of an hour or so, it was announced that a
freight train was soon to leave for Chattanooga, and, of
course, each one made for it in double-quick time, and—as
in one or two other instances—I witnessed the traits of the
true soldier and generous hearted gentleman, though he
had been fighting for the Union (so-called). Sitting on
the platform at the depot, I noticed a tall, portly man in
blue playing with and caressing some children in the crowd,
which gave evidence that he was kind hearted, and had not
forgotten the endearments of home. He had addressed
himself to me several times during the evening in quite a
social way, and inquired to what point we were bound, and
seemed to sympathize with us; which, I must confess, was
appreciated. We are not so embittered against them for
the ten thousand depredations and insults committed by a
large majority, as to cease our regard for those who preserved the traits which constitute the true gentleman. On
seeing my husband lift one of our trunks, and start for the
cars, the soldier in blue asked if there were any other
trunks to go. I pointed out one to him. "Well," says he,
"Uncle Sam's wagon can carry it;" and with this, he
shouldered a large, heavy trunk as if it were but a pin's

weight, and away he went some two or three hundred yards, and was soon back again, making the inquiry "if there were any more?" and was off again with another load equally as heavy as the former, saying, "Uncle Sam's wagon is not yet broken down." After completing this act of kindness, he bade us farewell, saying he hoped if we ever met again, it might be under more pleasant circumstances than the present.

Soon we were on the train, snugly seated on a sack of corn in a box car, speeding away to that eventful place, Chattanooga. It was not long before our fare was called for by one of the shoulder strap followers. I readily gave him the aforesaid passport, but not without some anxiety and doubt as to its acceptance. He perused it carefully, and then inquired, "Is this for yourself, madam?" I replied in the affirmative, saying a friend gave it to me, on my being refused one from head quarters. "Very well, madam," says he, "I will receive it; but every conductor would not. Be careful and say nothing about it, or both of us might be dealt with."

I felt like a bird out of its cage, and rejoiced that the worst part of my journey was accomplished; and through some unforeseen good fortune I would be able to reach Nashville, where, doubtless, I could rest my almost worn out body under the roof of my dear and only brother, whom I had not seen in fifteen years.

Sleep was a stranger to us that night, as was often the case with us when traveling. Scarcely a scene was passed without our notice; and especially was our attention attracted to the wreck of those places where I had spent so many pleasant months, and witnessed so much suffering; where noble hearts were buoyed with the hope of one day enjoying a richer legacy for our perils and hardships than that which fate had assigned us—such as Tunnel Hill, Ringgold, Dalton, Calhoun, etc. With what sad regret did we look upon the desolation and ruin of those once flourishing and pleasant little villages. Scarcely a vestige could be traced of what was once familiar to our eyes. All gone, save here and there a dwelling of some one who had feigned loyalty, and saved a shelter for their heads. But these scenes rapidly passed from view, and the locomotive with its lightning velocity brought us, at an early hour, in sight of the magnificent surroundings of Chattanooga. Old Lookout in all its grandeur loomed up above its sister hights, and quietness reigned as though her towering crags had never been disturbed by the thundering monster of death and destruction sent forth by Marshall and his brave followers, hurling hundreds of the enemy headlong down its rugged precipices, as they were endeavoring to scale its almost insurmountable cliffs. Doubtless, many of their bones still lie there, bleached by the pelting rains and the scorching rays of a summer sun.

As soon as the train stopped my husband immediately set off for the depot to see where our baggage could be safely deposited, leaving me with it on the cars. I was sitting where I had a full view of the city, and was gazing out at the hill where stood the Methodist and Baptist churches, in which I had participated in the friendship of many a noble soldier, and where I had seen more than one breathe out his life, when I was suddenly aroused by the friendly salutation of "Good morning, madam. Glad to know you have arrived safely. How do you feel after your rough journey?" On looking up who should I see standing before me but that same kind Yank, "Uncle Sam's Wagon," as he called himself. "What are you doing here, Yank?" I immediately inquired. "Well, I came on the train last night, and was passing by; once recognizing you, I thought I would stop and see if I could be of any service to you. Do you want your trunks carried away?" I thanked him, saying that my husband

had gone to see where he could put them. " Well," said
he, " ' Uncle Sam's Wagon ' can carry them for you
again ; " and with that he drew one out, and away he
went ; and depositing this, he returned for the second,
which he likewise disposed of, after which he came back,
and extended his hand, saying, " I bid you farewell, kind
lady, hoping we may always remember each other as
friends in peace, if we have not been in war. I have
always found the best of friends among the Southern ladies
since we have been invading their soil ; and I have wondered how they could treat us so kindly under the circumstances. But, madam, let me tell you, in all sincerity, I
am one who never dared to intrude, in the least manner,
whatever, upon the rights or feelings of a lady ; and I am
very sorry that any of our men ever stooped to do so.
Whenever I meet with a Southern lady I am proud to
render her any assistance whatever in my power. Your
boys, also, are a noble set of men, who fought gallantly
for what they believed was right ; and I respect them for
it ; and I hope they will be granted the rights promised
them in the surrender. They have achieved honor on
many a battle-field, though they were finally overpowered,
and lost the cause for which they so nobly and gallantly contended." I thanked him for his kindness to us, and his
honest and frank acknowledgments of what the world will
yet accord them ; and, by way of friendly jest, I remarked,
" Now, Yank, in bidding you, perhaps, a final adieu, let
me make one request of you, and that is — when you get
home, stay there, and never come on our soil again to fight
those brave boys of whom I am proud to know you enter-
tain such high regard. Attend to your own affairs on
your own side of the river, and I will guarantee they will
attend to theirs. But, most assuredly, if you meddle
with theirs, and kick up another muss, they will fight you
again, and perhaps turn the joke on you, for I tell you,

Mr. Yank, the spirit of the South is the same to-day that it was at the beginning of the war which has just closed against them." His frank and respectful reply was, " That's so ; and they have a right to be so ; " and, giving a hearty laugh, he then wished me a long and happy life, and was soon out of sight.

I often wonder if Eugene Dunwoody, of Boonville, Ill., is still living, and if he still remembers the old rebel lady who will never forget his unlooked for kindness at Kingston, Ga., and Chattanooga, Tenn.

My friend, who gave me the transportation, hastened up town for the purpose of trying to get the promised means to secure passage to Nashville. Evening came, and nothing had been seen of him. Fortunately, my husband succeeded in getting transportation without any trouble, the test of loyalty not being required by the authorities, as was the case at Kingston. An officer was sent aboard the train to see that all exiled Tennesseeans were provided with seats. How different were our feelings from those of the previous evening. The true soldier and gentleman was easily recognized in that instant as in many others, contrasting widely with the cowards who gloated over our downfall, and denied us the petty means of returning to our beloved homes. I need not say I was unhappy on that eventful evening. Doubtless there were others on the train bound for Nashville who were in the same straightened circumstances, and who could appreciate our feelings. Notwithstanding our good fortune in procuring transportation, we did not forget our friend, and were anxious to know the cause of his long absence, which cause we remained in ignorance of until the cars were ready to move off, when, to our surprise, we received a message from him, stating that as soon as he had reached the heart of the city he was put under arrest with several of his comrades, the cause of which he did not learn. He was

I*

to be carried to Nashville under guard, and, of course, had failed to accomplish the purpose for which he had left us that morning. I was troubled very much, for he no doubt made a good soldier ; nor did he seem to be a man capable of a crime that would justify such treatment. We had no opportunity of pleading in his behalf, or we would have done so, and used our efforts in having him released. Doubtless the arrest was made by some petty official, who only wished to use his shoulder-strap authority without the knowledge of the post commander, who, in all probability, would have granted his release could we have seen him.

That was not the only instance occurring on the eve of leaving for our home, which wounded our hearts. After we were seated in the train, and were on the eve of moving off, the conductor came in and gave orders for room to be made for a number of commissioned officers, and especially paroled soldiers, meaning, of course, rebels. He went around himself, and picked them out, saying, " You must go ; and you must go," and so on until he reached my husband, when he repeated the order. My husband replied, " This is my wife, and I would like to sit with her, if you please." " It makes no difference, sir ; you can't do it. Yonder is a box car ; you can get in it. A commissioned officer must have this seat." Of course, my husband had to leave me. God forbid that I should ever again be placed under such mortifying circumstances. I saw plenty of vacant seats, which satisfied me that it was done to show shoulder-strap authority over those who were overpowered. I controlled my feelings as best I could, and said nothing, knowing it was best. Soon a genteel looking major was seated by me. Thinks I, well, if this is n't the terms of the surrender to the letter I don't know anything about the definition of the word subjugation. A white man driven from beside his wife, and a

perfect stranger allowed to take his place. I said nothing,
and thought the more. Even the major seemed abashed
for a moment, at the same time asking me to excuse his
seeming intrusion on my right, " For," said he, " I would
have gone in the next car had I been permitted so to
do," which settled the fact in my mind that it was a pre-
meditated thing with the conductor. However, I made
the best of it I could. The major soon entered into a
pleasant conversation, asking me many questions, pointing
out different sceneries; and in fact he tried to make the
time pass off as pleasantly as possible, seeming, in the
meantime, to detect my mortification.

I thought that he mistook me for one of the loyals, and
determined to relieve him of the impression when an
opportunity offered itself. Finally, Bridgeport was
reached. Pointing to the breastworks, he said, " There
are some signs of the war." No sooner said than I asked,
" Did the Yanks or our men throw up these breastworks?"
He looked rather nonplussed, but replied, " Oh, the Federals, madam, threw them up to protect their gunboats."
I replied that this generation would not live to see the
South built up from the wreck and ruin committed by the
Federals. " Oh, yes, madam, they will soon build it up
again. There is a great deal of industry in the South,
and the people will go to work, and it will soon resume its
former beauty and prosperity. Your condition is to be
regretted; but we must make the best we can of it, and
in the end we will be happier than before this calamity
befel us. I hope this war has been useful, and that each
party will profit by their folly in letting fanaticism get the
better part of their judgment, and cause the overthrow of
the best government the world ever saw." I thought his
sentiments were excellent, and came very near asking him
who threw the first stone that caused the overthrow of the
" best government the world ever saw," but I knew it

would bring up an argument that would create hard feelings, and my own were wounded to the very core, and he seeming so particular in avoiding anything that would stir up unkind thoughts, I let the subject drop. I sat in silent meditation, except an occasional pastime with a very interesting little girl, which we accidentally learned was the grand-daughter of the venerable Dr. Ford, of Nashville, who, like ourselves, had been exiled from home by the stern fate of the recent war, but who was now returning to the loved ones, among whom he spent a few short months ere death claimed him as his victim. This little girl was the pet of every weary traveler who chanced to sit near her. She had a witty reply for every question put to her, and sometimes nonplussed her interrogators. One, in particular, attracted our attention, as it showed forth, in unmistakable characters, the bitter hatred which the invaders of the South caused to be instiled, not only into the hearts of the parents, but also in those of their offsprings, by the tyranny they exercised over them in order to carry out their wicked designs. The major seemed to be interested in this little jewel of a girl, remarking that she reminded him of his own little darlings at home, whom he had not seen for many months. My own heart responded in regard to the similarity of dear buried loved ones. Among the curious questions which the major put to the little fairy was, " Don't you love the Yankees, honey ? " Her eyes sparkled as she looked him full in the face, and gave him the frank answer, " No ; I don't love them one bit." " Why, dear, do you not love them ? " was the interrogation. " Because they put my grandpa in the penitentiary because he wouldn't take the oath ; and I don't love them." It is needless to say that the major looked confused, and tried to laugh it off as best he could, saying, " You are a sweet little girl, and the Yankees must not treat your grandpa so again." Again she looked up at him, with a defiant gaze, as she said, " No; they shan't, either."

Soon there was a halt at Stevenson, Ala. My husband asked the conductor's leave to sit with me and eat a cold snack, which was granted, the major politely retiring to a seat that had been vacated. Any charitable man would have supposed that we could be left to occupy the same seat for the remainder of the journey; but we had judged the stern oppressor wrong that time, for we soon found out that he intended to keep good his faith to crush us as low as the deepest pit so long as he ruled that train. Coming to us he sternly asked, " Are you not done eating, sir?" On receiving an answer in the affirmative, he said, " Well, we want this seat, sir." My husband politely asked, " Why can I not sit with my wife ? I see there are plenty of seats, and why do you drive me away while others remain?" "Are you not a paroled prisoner?" was the rigid question. " I am ; and tried to do my duty in what I believed was right." " Well, sir, for that reason I treat you thus. These officers have been fighting for, and you against, the best government the world ever knew, and I say, go and sit where you belong, anywhere at all." Such treatment as this will never win us back to the old land. Mark ! think ! aye, if indeed we have erred from it. If we have, it has been brought on by just such usurpers as yourself. " Have your seat, Major," says he, as my husband retired. The major looked confused, as he remarked, " I hope, madam, you will put no blame on me for your being treated so unjustly ? I wish it could be otherwise, and hope you will not censure all for what a few in authority commit." "Not at all," I answered him; " for, if all are inclined as this man is, surely the burden which is heaped upon us could not be tolerated." On we sped, while our hearts were crushed and bleeding at our down-trodden condition, now and then snatching a gleam of hope as we contemplated a day when perhaps such usurping would cease.

Six o'clock, June 3d, A. M., found us safely landed at the depot of our old Rock City home, after an absence of twenty-eight years. That part of our journey homeward, and we were at its terminus, and glad, indeed, were we to rest from its tedious and weary march, both as it regards body and mind.

Our next thought was to find our relatives—the children of my sainted brother, none of whom it had been my pleasure to see except his son, John L. Kirby, who is now connected with that popular paper the Louisville *Journal*, and his sister, Mrs. Peobler. We were soon making inquiries at the *Gazette* office for my nephew, and were directed to Edgfield, which had been built up since I last saw Nashville. We were not long in crossing the once familiar old Cumberland river; but before we reached the ferry-boat we were again accosted by one of the satraps, in the garb of a guard, who halted my husband, with the command, " You must take off dem ar clothes—you must. You can't wear dem grey clothes—you can't." " Well," says my husband, " I reckon you will wait until I can get where I can procure a change—won't you? Do you wan't me to pull them off right here, in the streets? If you do, you have mistook me, certain." " Well, how long have you been here?" "I have just arrived, and am going across the river." " Well, go 'long, and take dem off, or we will not let you pass so easy next time."

" Merciful Benefactor!" thought I, " will I never be rid of these ignorant pests who know nothing about the oppressor to the oppressed, and care less so they can don the official, and make most use of it that their ignorance may chance to devise?" However, no other difficulty was encountered, and we were soon fondly greeted by my relatives, where we could, in a word, get breath—receiving every mark of kindness from our lamented nephew, W. Raller, and his jewel of a wife. My dear and only brother, whom I had not seen for fifteen years, was soon at my side, presenting the change — oh, the great change — which time had so visibly wrought on his once fresh features and raven locks, now furrowed and frosted by the withering blight and frost of time. Years! Oh, the sad thoughts of each others' features being so wonderfully changed that recognition failed us for a moment. Will time so change us in this life that we will not recognize each other in Heaven? Oh, no; we will know each other there. Thank God we will not be defaced by old age then. Friends will all know each other in that reigon of eternal light and knowledge, for God, who is love, can raise up our bodies which are now morsels of crumbling clay, and will fit us out with a spiritual body, perfect in vigor and beauty. Oh, blessed thought! How transcendently cheering the contemplation that one day these infirm bodies will be raised in immortality.

The cheering news was soon revealed to us that my son had received many kind favors from my connections as he passed through the city on his way to Camp Chase, and left his message to be delivered to us in case we should reach Nashville. I lost no time in dispatching him a letter, which was soon responded to, and on the 20th of June he joined us, having been released according to orders from the President.

It had been our good fortune never to have come in contact with the Federal guards until then, and I must confess that it was repulsive to us, having for the first time to pass through their picket lines going to my brother's, who lived near Lavergn. I was shocked at the idea, and having no pass, I feared the consequence might not be very pleasant. However, my brother had one, and I was not molested. A week of pleasure was spent with him and his interesting family, the joys of which will never be obliterated from memory's table.

On our return we found our other niece, Mrs. Bernal, and family, from Louisville, in waiting for us, which was another addition to our happiness; and to still further add to our already happy pastime, we met several dear old soldier friends. Among them was the kind and generous-hearted soldier, Charles Howard, one of the gallant old 154th Tennessee regiment, of whom I had lost all knowledge since the panic which Jarard's raiders created at Covington, Ga., in 1864. In a few days after meeting Charlie, we were pleasantly surprised at receiving from him an invitation to join his bridal party, and partake of his nuptial dinner, he having led to Hymen's altar, in the presence of the Rev. R. B. C. Thomel, one of Georgia's fairest daughters, Miss Julia Gibbs, daughter of Dr. Gibbs, of the Empire State. A pleasant day indeed did we spend with the happy pair, and their intelligent, noble, christian mother, Mrs. C. R. Gibbs, in whose motherly society we spent many happy days during our stay in Nashville. Finally our attention was directed to Gallatin, Sumner county, or near there, to visit my aged and only uncle, John Kirby. Thirty-seven years, with their many vicissitudes had passed since last we saw our beloved uncle— he a vigorous middle-aged man, and I a little girl of ten summers. What a change had come over us since last we met, since last he sat me on his knee and called me by pet names, placing a silver coin in my hand, which was highly prized by me, as is natural with all children? Now I find him old, and trembling on the verge of the dark abyss of an unknown future, and bordering upon the brink of old age. His locks as white as silver tell the story that all things earthly pass away. Precious old uncle, how sacred is the silver tress which was clipped from off thine honored head to her who, in all human probability, may never see you again, but who hopes to meet you in a happier world than this, when the toils of life are over.

Near by we attended a rebel pic-nic, given by the citizens of Sumner county to the returned rebels for the enjoyment of those who had done their duty in our lost cause, to see who had returned, and who were missing. It was on that pleasant and memorable occasion that we saw Col. Paul Anderson, the once wee babe of whom we spoke at the commencement of our journal. The few hours we spent upon the ground were too pleasant to be forgotten. All was joy and gladness in that vast assembly. Many fond greetings were interchanged among friends who had not met since the close of the war. Of course, some had not returned who once mingled with those who formed that happy group. They had fallen as none but heroes fall—defending their rights, and they were not forgotten by those who survived them. The events of the hour were more pleasant to us from the fact that we met some of our relatives and friends whom we last saw in child-hood's happy days, when our heart was scarcely susceptible to sorrow. Mrs. Barrow and sister were among those of my long absent kindred, the pleasant event of which brought fresh to my delighted mind those appropriate words from the pen of the immortal Moore—with some changes:

"And doth not a meeting like this make amends
　For all the long years I've been wandering away,
To see thus around me my youth's early friends
　As smiling and kind as in that happy day.
Tho' hap'ly, as o'er some of their brows, as o'er mine,
　The snowfall of time had been stealing from them
The fresh bud of youth, yet still in our mind
　We trace the fond smiles of our own youthful friends."

We gazed on their time-worn features, and pondered over the past and the present, and what softened remembrance came over the heart in gazing on those we had been

lost to so long, the joys and sorrows of which were still
around us like the visions of yesterday. Such pleasures
can only be appreciated by those who enjoy them, and not
by imagination.

We must bid adieu to those with whom we could
forever dwell, and repair to Nashville previous to my husband's departure for Memphis, for the purpose of ascer-
taining whether there was aught left of the effects stored
away in care of kind friends on our taking leave in 1862.
A small portion was left, for which we shall ever feel
indebted. Our lasting gratitude to those who secured
them for us, and his visiting our friends in Tipton as a
testimony of their lasting fidelity to us on learning of our
adverse circumstances. They witheld not their generous
mite, but liberally contributed means as they hoped sufficient to bring us to our desired home, Memphis; but transportation being so high, there was not sufficient after paying
his fare to Nashville, and, of course, there was no other
recourse but to remain until we could procure means that
would ensure us transportation. My husband went out to
my brother's, and did such work as was needful at his
country seat until Christmas, thereby obtaining means to
keep house in our humble way with what little household
effects we had left in Memphis, which we had succeeded in
getting to Nashville. My son had obtained employment
with a good firm as an apprentice at $40 00 per month soon
after being released from prison. My husband obtained
employment at $1 50 per day in what some would deem a
hard place—that of laboring on a coal boat in the months
of January and February. Through all the bitter cold
of those two winter months did he toil for that scanty
pittance, while the humble writer did what she could,
keeping as many boarders as that part of the city afforded.
So between us, as a family, we made a comfortable support,
which was more than thousands did who, like ourselves,

were left penniless at the close of the war. How grateful ought we to be to the Giver of every good and perfect gift, that we had health and strength, and that we found means whereby to make a comfortable living. Surely the hand of God has directed us and been our guide through all the trying events of life. Oftimes since returning to our native home we have found ourselves minus of means to secure the forthcoming repast, and yet some unforseen event would spring up that would enable us to replenish our almost exhausted store, and we would have plenty; yes, better than we merit, from the God of the poor, in whom our every hope is placed.

CHAPTER IX.

During our stay in Nashville, we sought and found our beloved benefactors, Mr. and Mrs. Jas. Thomas. A happy day was it to the writer when she beheld once more the faces of those ever dear people, to whom she shall ever owe a debt of gratitude. As my second parents, I was perfectly elated at the thought of being blessed with the privilege of meeting them again this side of eternity, and seeing their noble sons, who had been my pride and the joy of my heart in my youthful days, when every little childish revelry of theirs was a pleasant pastime to us. The joys of those long ago days are yet fresh and pleasant to the aged heart.

We sat once more under the sound of the Gospel in the once frequented sanctuary of God—McKendrie church, the dedicatory sermon of which we heard fall from the lips of one of the ablest ministers of his day, Rev. J. S. Douglass, who has long been enjoying the rich reward which God hath prepared for all the faithful. The old sanctuary looked familiar to us, and we enjoyed the blessing of once more worshipping God within its sacred walls after the lapse of twenty-eight years.

We had been in the city for some months before we could
fully realize the fact to the full satisfaction of our minds
that it looked anyways natural. We even traversed the
streets several times before we could locate any of its former
appearance ; but as time passed, it became more familiar,
and I felt at times as though I had scarcely been away.
Yet we recognized but few faces whom we knew in days of
"Auld Lang Syne." The long lapse of years had changed
them from youth to old age. Like my own self, their features were furrowed, and their heads whitening for the
grave ; and yet there were a few whose features reminded
us of long years ago, though their names had escaped our
memory, with but a few exceptions. Drs. McFerrin, Green
and Thonel were the only ministers we recognized who
once filled the sacred desk in happy days gone by.

My fondly cherished benefactors in the days of my
youth. Mr. and Mrs. Thomas, were diligently sought and
found, which was a bright episode during my sojourn in
the Rock City. The hours I spent with them were too
happy to be described. They will ever be held sacred in
memory's casket. Though their lives have been prolonged
to a good old age, may they yet spend many happy years
with their interesting children before they are called hence
to reap a rich reward in Heaven.

Notwithstanding all those pleasant pastimes, we did not
feel at home. No one would, as a natural consequence.
My heart's richest earthly treasure lay buried in West
Tennessee, and there we longed to be. Yet it was hard to
sever ourselves from our only surviving brother and his
interesting family. And there in the city cemetery sleeps
my sainted brother, to whose grave I oft would repair and
muse for hours over his sacred dust ; and at times we would
imagine we could almost hear him whispering his last dying
message to his far off sister—" Meet me in Heaven." Oh,
precious message ! Thou hast been a guiding star through

all the changing vicissitudes of this life, and are leading thy lonely sister to the crystal portals where thou art basking.

Doubtless, the heart of this soldier in blue would readily respond to the heartfelt sentiments expressed in those unsurpassingly beautiful lines of the magnanimous poet, which were composed on an occasion when the graves of the boys in blue, as well as those in the time-honored gray, were alike remembered by the weeping daughters of the South, whose homes and hearthstones had been made desolate by the ravages of a relentless war; yet when the last tattoo had been sounded, and the last clash of arms had been heard to startle the weary soldier from his broken slumbers, and his sweet visions of home and weeping friends, from whom he had sworn in his dreams never to part; and in reality, a fragment of the Southern braves had hastened to the once pleasant fields traversed so oft, in life's morning march, when their bosoms were young and thoughtless in regard to the desolation which, in a future day, was to be brought upon their childhood's happy home by the miscreant fanatic, and the sacred spot where sleeps their noble comrades was to have homage paid them by the strewing of flowers over their grass grown mounds. Those who sleep there, and fell in the contest for might, not right, are respected as our fallen enemies who can harm us no more.

> " By the flow of the inland river,
>   Whence the fleets of iron have fled,
> Where the blades of the grave grass quiver,
>   Asleep are the ranks of the dead.
>   Under the sod and the dew,
>   Waiting the judgment day;
>   Under the one, the Blue—
>   Under the other, the Gray.

" These in the robings of glory,
　　Those in the gloom of defeat;
All with the battle blood gory,
　　In the dusk of eternity meet.
　　　　Under the sod and the dew,
　　　　　　Waiting the judgment day;
　　　　Under the laurel, the Blue—
　　　　　　Under the willow, the Gray.

" From the silence of sorrowful hours,
　　The desolate mourners go,
Lovingly laden with flowers
　　Alike for the friend and the foe.
　　　　Under the sod and the dew,
　　　　　　Waiting the judgment day;
　　　　Under the roses, the Blue—
　　　　　　Under the lilies, the Gray.

" So with an equal splendor,
　　The morning sun rays fall,
With a touch impartially tender,
　　On the blossoms blooming for all.
　　　　Under the sod and the dew,
　　　　　　Waiting the judgment day;
　　　　Broidered with gold, the Blue—
　　　　　　Mellowed with gold, the Gray.

" So when the Summer calleth,
　　On forest and field of grain,
With an equal murmur falleth
　　The cooling drip of the rain.
　　　　Under the sod and the dew,
　　　　　　Waiting the judgment day;
　　　　Wet with the rain, the Blue—
　　　　　　Wet with the rain, the Gray.

" Sadly, but not with upbraiding,
 The generous deed was done ;
In the storm of the years that are fading,
 No braver battle was won.
  Under the sod and the dew,
   Waiting the judgment day ;
  Under the blossoms, the blue—
  Under the garlands, the Gray.

" No more shall the war cry sever,
 Or the winding rivers be red ;
They banish our anger forever,
 When they laurel the graves of our dead !
  Under the sod and the dew,
   Waiting the judgment day ;
  Love and tears for the Blue,
  Tears and love for the Gray.'

We assume the privilege of appending the above lines,
deeming them worthy of and an honor to the pages of any
work touching on the late war, and they should teach a
lesson to those who hold the reins of our once glorious
and united, but now shattered Government in their hands.
But they are still binding in chains a noble and charitable
people, who are willing to bury the hatchet of strife, and
let the past be forgotten, if the rulers will only give them
the rights for which they struggled—their honorable admission back under the once sacred stars and stripes, with
all their rights and privileges as honorable citizens and
statesmen.　But pardon our seeming digression, kind
reader, and we will leave this weighty subject for a more
able pen, and proceed on our journey homeward.

Every means was used to save a portion of our earnings
for the purpose of which we had never lost sight, and in
the month of August, 1866, we were enabled, with very

scanty means, to put our desires into execution; and on the 20th of the same month we bid a fond, yet sad farewell to all we held dear in the capital city of our once proud, but now downtrodden State; and at six o'clock P. M., August 20th, just three years after the Yankees gave us such a fright at Chattanooga, we reached our long desired home, the city of Memphis, after a lapse of something over four years of exile, amid the many soul-trying events which thousands as well as ourselves are too familiar with for us to deem it necessary to give any further comments.

Thanks to our Divine Protector! His all omnipotent hand has guided us through all the fiery ordeals of the late disastrous conflict for Southern rights, and through His mercy we are all safe at home again, where we have the blessed privilege of again worshipping God within the walls of the fondly cherished sanctuary, Wesley Chapel, and of enjoying the society of many dear old friends, both in the city and those in the country, among whom we lived so long, and where the sacred treasure from whom we had wandered so long lie sweetly sleeping; and where, after our short race has been run, and the work which God has assigned us shall have been accomplished, and He sees fit to call us hence, we expect and desire to be laid beside them, to rest beneath our own native soil, which we love so dearly, until the Morning of the Resurrection.

FINIS.

CORRESPONDENCE.

While the humble writer was engaged in the various duties of hospital life, she was in daily reception of letters from the soldiers in the field, of different States, divisions, brigades, regiments and companies belonging to the Tennessee Army. No clearer evidence of the soldiers grateful remembrance, and appreciation of the feeble services rendered them, while languishing in the hospitals, could be manifested than their own language which is expressed in their letters—a few of which we place before the reader, *ver batim*, claiming them as a most precious legacy of an humble participant in the great struggle for a cause which, though lost, is nevertheless just and honored. With grateful acknowledgement to those who favored us with their interesting and heart cheering correspondence, we take great pleasure in appending as many as we have space for, deeming them a valuable addition to our humble work, and, doubtless, will be satisfactory to many friends, who, while they were at home, mourned their absent boys, and feared they would be neglected in time of need, and perhaps become careless in regard to cultivating the finer feelings taught them while under the parental roof.

We hope we have not incurred the displeasure of any of our kindly remembered correspondents who are spared to share the ills of life with us, and lament the terrible fate which has befallen our once happy and prosperous nation, and mourn the loss of many comrades and friends who fell at their post, and whose letters are mingled with theirs.

J

Buena Vista Post-Office, Ouachita City, Arkansas,
March 16, 1861.

MRS. SMITH:

My Very Dear, though Unknown Friend—I write you these few lines to let you know that should I never see you, that you will ever live in my memory, and have my prayers and well wishes in time and eternity. Thankful am I that my dear son fell in so good hands. I hope that you stood as an angel of mercy, to point him to the Lamb of God that taketh away the sins of the world. In my sore bereavement, I take consolation in knowing how he died, and who stood by him in his affliction. It is true I would not know your face if I were to see you, yet I imagine that I comprehend your soul. You say that you, too, are the mother of one only son; and he, too, a soldier. Should he be sick, and fall in my hands, I would take all the pains and care of him that a fond mother could bestow. And I pray God to provide good friends and christian nurses for him, and all the poor sick soldiers.

I received both of the letters you wrote, with the precious boon you sent, and shall carefully deposit them away; but if they decay and fade away, you shall still live bright in my memory, for well assured am I that the soul will never forget. I will now close my letter, by subscribing myself   Your sincere friend and well wisher,

MARTHA COFFIN.

Tunnel Hill, Ga., General Hospital,
February 23, 1863.

MRS. SMITH:

Madam—I have not the language to express the deep gratitude I feel towards you for your ever memorable kindness to me. While trusting memory breaths a sigh for long departed days, rest assured that you are not to be forgotten by the one who now gives you his most sincere and heart-felt thanks. God grant that not a cloud of sorrow may ever dim the pathway of your future life.

Mrs. Smith, you have been a mother to me. I could not have wished kinder treatment from any one than that which I received from you. You have my best wishes wherever you go.   LIEUT. F. M. ADAMS,

Company H, 154th Reg't Tenn. Vols.

Tunnel Hill, Ga., February 23, 1863.

MRS. SMITH:

In behalf of the patients of this ward, I send you our heartfelt thanks for the untiring efforts you have bestowed on us for our benefit. We greatly regret your departure, and belive your position will not be filled. Be assured, you have our heartfelt thanks and well wishes where ever you go. May your path be strewn with the choicest of flowers; may you be happy in your new situation. Go on in your noble work, for there is many a mother's heart made glad when they receive letters from their absent sons of your kind treatment; besides, there is a reward to be received when our earthly career is ended. We now say farewell, and may blessings crown you wherever you go.

Yours, respectfully,

J. R. BISHOP.

Tunnel Hill, Ga., February 23, 1863.

MRS. SMITH:

We, the undersigned, attendants at General Hospital, Tunnel Hill, Georgia, regret exceedingly to have to bid you adieu, after so many months of pleasant association together. Your kindness to us, and devoted attention to the sick and wounded of this hospital, has been impressed on our minds in characters that time will never obliterate. Rest 'assured, madam, that in departing from this place, you leave behind you many dear friends, who will ever be obligated to you for your unceasing acts of charity and kindness to them. We hope you will be pleased in your new field, and meet with great success. May God bless you in your labor of love, and grant you success in every undertaking. Adieu.

We are, with much respect,

Very truly, your ob't servants,

C. C. SISSIONS, Acting Steward.

C. O. CROCKER, Ward Master.

W. C. SINGLETARY, Apothecary.

Tunnel Hill, Ga., March 4, 1863.

MRS. SMITH:

Dear Friend—It is with feelings of friendship and gratitude that I seat myself this evening to pen you a few lines to let you hear from me. I am improving slowly. I have had some very bad luck since I parted from you. I and Sergeant Garrett got a furlough to go visit his father's, in Mississippi; but was disappointed very badly. We got as far as Selma, Alabama, and had to turn back, on account of the railroad being washed away, and the Yankees being near his father's. We now have a furlough in our pockets, and we can go where we please. Sergeant Garrett speaks of coming up there to see you. I shall pass there in the morning, if nothing happens, on my way to the command, to get some clothing that was sent to me from home, and to draw my money. I expect to return in a short time, and shall stop with you a few days, and I may stay there.

Mr. Clemans received a letter from you last night. We were all truly glad to hear from you. There is nothing that gives me more pleasure than to get a letter from one so much loved and esteemed. I have often thought of you, and wished that I could get to see you. Mrs. Smith, there is no news of importance to write to you.

Mrs. Bell gave us a party last night. We enjoyed ourselves finely. They have about three parties a week here now. Dr. Wileman has got back to the Tunnel. He brought his wife with him. She is going to take charge of a dining room up at Mr. Young's residence for the benefit of this ward and the church. I think she is a fine lady. I hope she will be as kind to the sick as you were; but that will be hard to do, I tell you. Mrs. Smith, we miss you as much as a child would its mother.

Mrs. Smith, I will close for this time, hoping to receive an answer. Write in about a week, for I know not when I may return from my regiment. I will be sure to call as we come back. My kindest regards to Mr. Smith.

From your most unworthy friend,
JESSE D. JENKINS,
6th Arkansas Regiment.

———

Camp near Shelbyville, June 3, 1863.

MRS. SMITH:

Kind Friend—This evening finds me seated, with pen in hand, to answer your welcome letter of May the 22d, which was received in due time; and, believe me, I have thought much over the kind advice you gave me in it, and shall always feel grateful for the interest you take in my welfare—both temporal and spiritual; and although I have not yet followed your kind advice, I hope the day is not far distant when I may be able to rejoice with the people of our Saviour in my soul's salvation. The good work of the Lord still continues in our camp, and many are finding the faith of the faithful. We have but little news in camp at present, as all in front of us is quiet, and we can get but little from Vicksburg. We are having a good deal of rain just now, and the weather is somewhat cool, yet not disagreeable. The crops are looking fine, and I think the rain will be of great benefit to the corn and grass, and I think we have every indication of a bountiful harvest. The boys are all well as usual. Jimmie is camped near us, and is with us most every day, and it seems like days gone by.

Now as I have nothing more to write at this time, I will close, with a prayer for the health and happiness of yourself and all kind friends. I remain,

Truly, your friend,

CHAS. HOWARD.

Camp near Jackson, Miss., June 14, 1863.

RESPECTED FRIEND:

With pleasure I avail myself of a few leisure moments to write you a few lines to let you know that I have not forgotten you and your kindness to me. You, no doubt, think it strange in one not answering your letters, and I acknowledge that it is partly owing to my negligence, but more to the circumstances which surround us. You know that a soldier's duties are hard, and more especially those who are on outpost duty, which we have been doing till we left Tennessee. I have enjoyed excellent health since I left Tunnel Hill, and I am doing first rate here, although the climate does not agree with me. Our trip here was one of the most tiresome I ever experienced. We were constantly on the road both day and night, and got but little rest. When we passed through your town, I saw you, and would have given anything to have stopped and talked over old times, and given you a few items of our life in Tennessee. You have, ere this I expect, heard of the trial drill between Adams' Louisiana Brigade and ours, which the judges say was the finest ever witnessed. The regiment we had to contend with was the Thirteenth Louisiana, which bore off the prize from the Seventeenth Tennesssee; and a splendid drilled body of men they were, but for once they met their superiors in drill; and I am proud to say that General Hardee said that we were the best disciplined regiment he ever saw. I suspect you would like to know why we are here, and turned our backs on our loved homes to help rescue from the hands of an ungenerous enemy this portion of our loved country. It was, for once, left with us whether we would stay in Tennessee, or follow our noble general. Gen. Bragg, in his orders to Gen. Breckinridge, said with his approval he could take our brigade; and with his usual noble generosity, he had our brigade called up, and laid the case before them, and when the vote was taken it was unanimous in our regiment for going with him—not one dissenting voice. Never did a man receive such an evidence of the love they have for him as our general. After all the hardships through which we have passed, and the noble lives lost in defense of the people of the South by our exiled soldiers, General Bragg, in his report, it appears, tries to disgrace them, by not awarding to them credit for their conduct. Our regiment was the first on Friday evening in the fight, and the last out; and our thinned ranks bear evidence of our conduct. I expect in a few days we will again be called to face our enemies, and trusting in the God of battles, we will conquer or their victory will be at a fearful cost.

I have no news that is reliable. Ever since we have been here, there has been a constant cannonading going on at Vicksburg, which is plainly heard here. You have no idea of the immense amount of damage done here. A great portion of the city is in ruins, and the finest hotel (the Bowman House, which the Yanks left,) was burned a few nights ago.

I will have to close, as I fear I will tire your patience with my unconnected and badly written letter. I will try hereafter and write to you every opportunity. You must excuse my negligence, and not attribute it to a lack of love and respect. I shall always think of you, and I hope that at some future day I may have the pleasure of talking over old times. Give my best respects to Mr. Smith, and, if you have an opportunity, to my friends at Tunnel Hill. Write to me as soon as you receive this. No more, but remain

Ever your friend,
DAVID S. HERAN.

P. S. Direct your letter to David S. Heran, Company F, Second Kentucky Regiment, Helm's Brigade, Breckinridge's Division, Jackson, Mississippi.

———

Camp near Shelbyville, Tenn., April 20, 1863.

MRS. SMITH:

Most Kind and Respected Friend—I received your more than welcome letter in due time, and, believe me, I feel grateful for that same, for its perusal carries me back to the happy past, when all was peace and loveliness in our now suffering country. But while we all lament the present, there is, thank God, a lasting hope that none can deprive us of; and when this war is ended, I feel there will be a happy future for those who have been driven from their homes and friends. May the Allwise hasten the day. Those who are high in power seem to think that there are great events soon to transpire, and if we are victorious in the next battle, we may have peace soon after. Our army is in fine spirits, and when the trumpet calls to arms, every arm will be nerved with a freeman's strength, to battle for homes and kindred, so dear to all true Southern hearts. Jimmie and all the boys would like to be engaged in driving the vandal hordes from Memphis, but wherever the battle rages the fiercest, there duty calls us, and then let us strike such a blow for liberty as will make our enemies tremble to think of. I have not written to James, but will do so very soon. All our boys think a great deal of Jimmie Smith. I am afraid that young lady has stolen Johnny's heart entirely; but such things will happen, even to a soldier. You say I must not let Johnny get the start of me, as there is one left. Would I could be so lucky as to attract the kind regards of some patriotic young lady; but I must not presume to so high an honor, while there are so many dashing young heroes to attract their attention. Yet will I be patient, and pray God to bless every one of them, for without them we would be miserable indeed. Now, I must not dwell too long on that subject, for fear I might think myself forgotten. But, no, I will not allow myself to think so. And, now, with a prayer for the health and happiness of yourself and kind friends, I subscribe myself

Your true but humble friend,
CHARLES HOWARD.

Camp 159th Senior Regiment.

MRS. S. E. D. SMITH:

Most Highly and Respected Friend—It is with the liveliest gratifications of pleasure that I address myself to the task of dropping you a few lines to let you know that I am well, and hope you are the same.

Mrs. Smith, I suppose you think that I have forgotten the many kindnesses that I have received at your hands,

J*

but I hope you do not think that I am so ungrateful as that. The many acts kindness you have shown me are indelibly stamped upon my heart, and words cannot express the gratitude I feel toward you, for you are the only one that has ever acted toward me like a mother since I have been away from home. When I think of you it brings to my memory the many happy hours I have spent at home; but now I must think of something else at the present time, for the Yankees are pressing us just now, and I will not have much time to write. They always come on us when we are doing such things as eating or writing. We have had a hard time the last few days, and skirmishing with them all the time; but we have been very fortunate. In our skirmishes we have had but two men wounded, and I suppose you have heard that Mr. Howard and Mr. Wood were the ones. I have received a slight wound on the right shoulder, but it was merely a spent ball, and it bruised my shoulder very much, but it only cut my jacket and not the flesh. Waynesburg was very fortunate, for a ball struck him twice, but not hard enough to enable him to get a furlough on. All the other boys are well and in good spirits, and eager for the fray.

Mrs. Smith, you must excuse me for not writing sooner, for I could not get time; and, another thing, paper is so scarce, that I can hardly get any. Every time I write a letter I beg the paper from the other boys, and I am nearly ashamed of it.

I must bring my epistle to a close, for the Yankees are not more than three or four hundred yards off, and we will soon be where the bullets are flying about us. You must give my kindest regard to the ladies in town. Gus and Willie have just arrived in time to get into the battle, and are well and in good spirits. No more at present.

With sentiments of the highest esteem, I beg leave to remain   Your sincere friend,

F. W. BRINKMEN.

Chattanooga, September 4, 1863.

ESTEEMED FRIEND:

Your kind and welcome letter of the 31st ult. is at hand, and I assure you it was received with great pleasure, and highly appreciated; for I have learned to appreciate the value of a good and true friend, and the knowledge of possessing at least one, is truly soothing to me at all times, but more so in my present exiled state. My dear friend, I doubt whether you was more astonished and taken by surprise at the sudden appearance of the enemy than I was. Notwithstanding that I was aware of their close proximity to Chattanooga, I had no idea that they would be bold enough to pounce down on us in such seemingly small force, especially as they have never been known to do such a thing before. At the time they opened with their artillery I was in town, and, thinking it was our own artillery practicing, I took no notice of it, until a very unwelcome visitor, in the shape of "shell," came whizzing over my head, and fell some distance from me, which was circumstancial evidence enough for me that our friends, the "blue coats," had made their appearance opposite this place. The scene that followed this first proof of their close proximity is easier imagined than described; and even could I describe it to you, I would not, as you have undoubtedly been made to hear it over and over many times. The enemy is still in position on the other side of the river, and has repeatedly assured us of his intention to remain there, through their brazen mouthed cannons—a way of conversing, I assure you, I am not particularly fond of, though it is very convincing—our own batteries only responding at random. Little damage has been done by them so far. The people have almost entirely "evacuated" this place, and are living in the woods and on the mountain, and some of them are being initiated in "camp life" in the full sense of the word.

A great many, I am told, are living in the woods, and some even without tents.

You ask me to let you know all the news, but I hardly venture to do so, as everything we hear is so very uncertain—"Madam Rumor" being quite busy emptying her pockets full of sensation created by herself. The last report is, that the enemy has crossed some forty thousand strong at Bridgeport, and this is the only thing that I place any reliance in. Their advance is reported at Trenton, Georgia, to-day. If so, we will soon hear from them here; and I assure you, dear friend, that theirs will be a warm reception—at least, everything indicates such; and I think that Bragg has concluded to make a stand this time. And if they enter Chattanooga at all, their path will not be "bestrewn with roses," but over the slain sons of our gallant old State, "Tennessee."

To all appearances, General Price has again been victorious in Arkansas, and has given the enemy an excellent thrashing. Huzzah for the "Old Man" say I, and hope that Jeff. Davis will now promote him, as he should have done long ago, instead of some "upstarts" that have never done anything, except received their pay, since the war commenced. But I forget; I must not criticise my superiors, and will therefore drop this theme, by once more saying "Three cheers for old General Price!"

I visited the boys in the company the other day, and found them all enjoying good health. Johnny W. said nothing about having heard from you; though I expect he did receive your letter, as he told me your address. I have not been able to visit your son, as the General keeps me very close, and I scarcely ever have an opportunity to visit my friends. However, I shall see him with the first opportunity. The old One Hundred and Fifty-fourth is encamped at the foot of Lookout Mountain, and are faring tolerably well, and in the best of spirits, awaiting the expected battle. I am getting on finely, as usual, as it must be something very unusual to ruffle my generally good humor; and I assure you, dear friend, that the "Yanks" have not been able to drive my good humor away.

Dear friend, I am truly glad to hear that your hospital has been established in a place that you seem to like, and I hope that you will be pleased with the people, and find me a sweetheart, as I have not been able to find one myself.

But I must close. My paper is about to "secesh." My kind regards to your husband. Accept my sincere thanks for your kind offer, though I hope that I will not find it necessary to pay you a visit under such circumstances. Let me hear from you soon. Until then, I remain

Your true and grateful friend,

FRED. G. GUTHERS.

Excuse the miserable writing. I will try to do better the next time.

———

Atlanta, Ga., October 27, 1863.

MY DEAR FRIEND:

Your welcome favor of the 19th inst. came to hand last Sunday, and I assure you it was highly welcomed, and perused with great pleasure; for you can scarcely have any idea of the pleasure it affords me to read your kind and motherly missives, to which I fear I make but very poor replies, and am not as prompt as I should be, but circumstances too numerous to mention have caused my seeming negligence in replying to them. However, I shall try and be more prompt in the future. I am rejoiced to hear that you have had the pleasure of seeing your son, and judging for yourself of his welfare and good spirits after his deliverance, as it were, from the very jaws of death; and that the Almighty Ruler of the universe and the God of battles has safely delivered him from the bloody carnage uninjured and unharmed, and has heard the many prayers in his behalf sent up to His glorious throne.

Oh, my dear friend, would that I knew that my dear, dear mother was advised of my safety. How sweet would be my rest, and what a fearful burden of anxiety would be relieved from her heart; how many silent and hidden tears would be dried. But why do I dwell on this theme, as you know full well the feelings of a fond mother's heart, and have had your share of anxiety and feelings of dreadful fear mingled with hope—" Hope, the medicine of the miserable."

There is nothing new going on here. It was reported, yesterday, that Cheatham's Division was at Charleston, Tennessee, and there crossing the Tennessee river ; and though I give this merely as a rumor, yet I have every reason to belive the truthfulness of the report. And hope that whatever Bragg's intention may be, that he will be successful in his undertaking, and retake the territory he lost since last summer. General Polk went to Montgomery the other day, where he has been called by the President I hope he will be restored to his command shortly, where he is very much needed ; and, besides, I am getting very tired of this place, and shall not be sorry to be ordered to duty at once. My love to your husband. Hoping soon to hear from you again, I remain, as ever,

Your true friend,

FRED. G. GUTHER.

Foard Hospital, Ringgold, Georgia, ,
January 26, 1863.

MRS. SMITH ɩ

Madam—I heard of your passing this place last evening, and that you are probably staying at Tunnel Hill. I have charge of this hospital, and if you are not pleasantly situated, you would do well to call on me. There are two or three vacancies here, which I wish to fill, if possible, with my old acquaintances.

Yours truly,
G. W. CURRY.

Tunnel Hill, Ga., March 2, 1863.

MRS. S. E. D. SMITH:

Dear Friend—I received your kind letter last evening, and hasten to reply. I am truly glad you have got a pleasant situation. I hope you will be as useful there as you were here. I know you will soon have plenty of friends where you are. I will say so now. I have nothing of a cheerful nature to write as it is very dull with me. "I attended to your request," and Mr. Heart will start up there this evening. Lieutenant Carrol will leave for his regiment soon. Lieutenant Adams is trying to get a transfer. I think he will be up there in a few days. He is mending very fast, and is now sitting out on the piazza sunning himself. Miss Jenkins is here to-day to see him. Mrs. Smith, there is some rejoicing here to-day. Williams has left for his regiment. All seem to be glad of it. Harris and Tumlin have been furloughed from my ward. I lost one last night—George Shortridge, of the Third Florida, died. All the rest are doing well. They all send their best love to you. We miss you very much. We have no other ladies but those who were here when you left. Dr. Bemas left us this morning. He started to Richmond. This is all the news I have at present.

I must tell you that there was a party at Austin's Tavern, last Friday night, and I went. I hope you will excuse me, for you know it is one of my faults.

You said you heard that myself and Williams were going to our regiment to-day. I have heard nothing of it. I am ready at an hour's warning, for there are no charms for me here now whatever, only the girls. Give my best respects to Mr. Smith. Tell him I hope he is all right. Tell him Linch has been turned off already.

I must close, as I am in a great hurry. I want you to write to me soon, and I will promise to do better next time. I will take great pleasure in attending to any business for you here. Write soon. May God be with you in all your undertakings.

Your true friend,
J. R. BISHOP.

Gate City Hospital, Atlanta, Georgia,
September 30, 1863.

MRS. SMITH:

Friend—Yours of the 23d ultimo has just been received. Glad to hear from you. I am sorry to say that I have no information of your son Jimmie as yet. I have made inquiry about him on the arrival of trains containing wounded. I hope that he may escape the wicked ball of the ruthless foe which have been sent to despoil us of our homes and of the rights of a free and independent people. I shall continue to look for him, and make all inquiry that is necessary to know of his whereabouts. I shall write immediately and let you know, should I be fortunate enough to hear from him. My brother Joe was wounded at the battle of Chickamauga in the left hand. He is not with me now, having been sent to Lagrange, Georgia. His wound is not necessarily dangerous, and he is doing very well. I have not as yet heard from my application. I am on duty as officer of guard on the Georgia railroad. Will remain here until I hear from my application, or for further orders. I hope you will excuse this badly written letter. I am in a hurry. Have to go on duty in twenty minutes. I will write again when I have more time. I will close by saying write soon, and let me know if you hear from Jimmie. I remain your friend, as ever,

F. M. ADAMS.

General Hospital, Macon, Georgia.
December 11, 1863.

DEAR MOTHER SMITH:

I was more than surprised the other day when I learned from "Charley" (Captain Carnes' boy) that you had not gone to Memphis. Oh, that I had known it when I passed Ringgold. How much happier I should have been. But as it is, why I shall have to make the best of a bad bargain, and hope for a better day. I have just learned by a letter from the regiment where you are, and that Flotron is in your hands, and I am thankful for that; and I lose not a moment to write to you, for I know you have been wondering where I could have strayed off to. You will see by the heading of this where I am, and a miserable place it is. But thank God, I am not seriously wounded, and have been fortunate enough to find some Memphis friends here. Dear mother, you have no idea what the poor soldiers have to endure here. It would make you feel sad if you were here. But you know me too well to suppose that for a moment I would be imposed upon, or be put out of my way by any one; so I just take things as they come, and make myself as happy as possible. I suppose the reason why I look with so much horror on this place is, that it is so different from old Tunnel Hill. Why, that was a paradise to this, and the doctors there were humane, and had a heart; but here—well, I wont say any more, as I am "all right on the goose," and "don't care for expenses." If

I just had plenty of money, I could enjoy myself hugely here. This is a very nice place—plenty of pretty women. But then as I am "nothing but a soldier," all I can do is to admire them at a distance. I often get disgusted while on the street to see so many men strutting around town in their fine clothes, while so many are in the army enduring so many hardships to keep the enemy from "them." It is enough to make a soldier feel sad; is it not? But I reckon if I had plenty money, I would put on airs, too.

I am truly glad to hear that Flotron is in your hands; for I expect he needs careful nursing. I hope his wound will prove beneficial to him, by turning him from wickedness. Use your best efforts. Oh, if he was religious, I would think so much more of him. He was standing by my side when he was wounded; one of the bravest in the company, always in the front rank, and where the bullets fly thickest.

Mother, you must excuse my brevity, as this is all the paper I have. I will write again soon. Enclosed, I send a few lines for Flotron. I am going to try to get a furlough. If I get it, I will try to come and see you. Let me know why you did not go to Memphis, and all the news generally. Hoping this may find you well, I subscribe myself, Your friend and well wisher.

Affectionately yours,
JNO. W. WAYNESBURG.

Camp near Atlanta, May 28, 1864.

MRS. SUSAN E. SMITH:

My Esteemed Friend—You will doubtless be somewhat surprised to get these lines at this late period. I must offer some apology for my silence. Be assured, you have not been forgotten by me; no—by no means. I shall ever remember your kindness to me and my friends. I had not heard of your whereabouts for a long time, until a few days ago, a Mr. King of our regiment told me you were at Covington, Georgia; that he had been staying there, and was speaking of your kindness towards him. I meet with many who have been recipients of your extreme efforts in administering to the wants of the sick and wounded, and they all speak of you in the highest terms. I believe you have many warm soldier friends. May God bless you for your untiring efforts in behalf of the soldiery. Do you not grow weary? You have been so closely engaged so long. I trust that the Lord will strengthen you and cheer you up, and give you grace sufficient for every trial.

I hope, Mrs. Smith, that you are more comfortably and satisfactorily situated now than you were when I saw you. I hope your task is not so hard. I often have thought of you, and wished that you might get a position less laborious, and one in which you could enjoy yourself better than you have since I knew you. I have had some rough times since I saw you. I was slightly wounded once; and about three months ago I fell from a car, and broke my right arm near my shoulder, (the same arm that was wounded when I was at Tunnel Hill.) I stayed at the Oliver Hospital, at Lagrange, Georgia, about a month. I was not pleased with the place at all. I thought often of Tunnel Hill and Mrs. Smith. Often I would gladly have gone to you if I had known where you were, and could have got there. I suffered a great deal; it was so painful. I grew so tired of the place, I came to the regiment. My arm is not well yet. I was not able to go into this fight, so the colonel placed me in charge of a guard with the wagon train. I have been sick the whole time; can hardly creep about now. The wagons have been moved so much, day and night part of the time. But now we have stopped within seven miles of Atlanta, where, I guess, we will remain until there is some decision about this battle; and I think I will get better, now that we are still. I can't get any medicine; no surgeon near. This is about the twentieth day since we broke up camps at Dalton. Some fighting almost every day. Our army fell back to Etowah river, thirty-five miles from Atlanta. The enemy would not come up and fight; but has endeavored to cut us off from Atlanta, by throwing his columns on our left, which forced us to fall back. Some seem to think that our army was retreating, whipped; but not so. We have whipped him wherever there has been any fight yet; and now that we have his flank movements checked, I feel confident that he will be compelled to fight, or retreat very hurriedly. I am in the rear, sick; can't hear much, and have two brothers exposed, besides many dear friends. I tell you, I am almost miserable. Oh, if I were able to take my gun, and go stand by their sides, how much more profitable. I can't rest here. God grant that this war may soon end! In Virginia it seems to be protracted. I have thought that they will continue at these two points, mass all the forces, and have two mighty battles; and if we be victorious, (which I believe,) the end is not far. I must close now. I have not much news. I want to hear from you. Accept my love and best wishes.

I remain, as ever, your true friend,

W. H. GARRETT,

Sixth Arkansas.

P. S.   I saw Mr. Smith at Dalton the day I left there, but he passed through a crowd before I could go to him, and I did not see him again.

In Line of Battle, near Chattahoochie River,
July 6, 1864.

MRS. SMITH:

After a long silence, I take the pleasure of writing you a few lines to let you know that I am yet alive, and enjoying very good health at the present. I have no news of interest to write, more than I have not heard from you before in a long time. Mr. Heerad, of our regiment, told me where you were, and that you sent your respects to me. I was very glad to hear from you. I think our army has fallen back as far as it will, for I think General Johnston will prevent them from flanking him. Our army is three or four miles north of the Chattahoochie river. We are ten or twelve miles from Atlanta.

Mrs. Smith, I didn't know what had become of you. I have not heard from you before since I left Ringgold, Georgia. I was very proud to hear of you, and of your being well. We have had a heavy siege since we left Dalton. We have only lost one man killed and one wounded. I have come through safe thus far, and I hope it may be my lot to come out of this war safe, and that we may gain our independence. Mrs. Smith, I have nothing to write but war news—except that I received a letter from home in April, and it gave me the glorious intelligence that my wife had professed religion, and that she and the baby were well, and doing well. It gave me great satisfaction to hear that she was well, and trying to live a christian life. I saw John Waynesburg, to-day, and he was well and hearty. I had no time to talk to him. Just said "howdy," and passed on.

I hope you will let me hear from you and the old man, for I am always glad to hear from those who have been friends in time of need. So write and give all the news, and how you are getting along.

Very respectfully, your friend,
LIEUT. D. T. HARRIS.

In Line of Battle, Chatahoochie River,
July 12, 1864.

MRS. S. E. D. SMITH:

Dear Friend—I once more avail myself of the opportunity of writing you a few lines, that leave me well. I guess you have been looking for a letter from me; but as we have been in line of battle for over two months, and it has been almost impossible for me to get paper and envelopes, I beg you to forgive me for my neglect to one I hold ever dear. I saw your husband yesterday, and he told me that he was sutler in Carnes' Battery, so I went immediately to his store and procured some paper and envelopes, and now I have no stamps, so you must excuse me for franking this letter, as it is all the chance I have. No news more than you already know. Our small brigade has lost heavily in this campaign, though it is in fine spirits, and is as determined as it was three years ago. I think that General Johnston is done falling back, and now it comes somebody else's turn to try it. Sherman has got tired of following Johnston, as he did Polk in Mississippi; and I think, or hope at least, that before August he will retrace his steps.

You must not do as I have, and not write to me, for it does me good to hear from you. As they are skirmishing very heavy in front at this time, I will come to a close, Hoping to hear from you soon, I will bid you good bye.

Ever your loving friend,
JAMES R. MATHES.

———

Chattahoochie River, Co. D, 5th Tenn. Reg't.
Strahl's Brigade, July 16, *A. D.* 1864.

MRS. S. E. D. SMITH:

Much Esteemed Friend—I suppose you think I have forgotten you; but you are mistaken. You cannot imagine the great source of pleasure it affords me to address those with whom I have found such kind hospitality. Being so far away from home and relatives, my heart is made glad when I meet with such a friend as you have been to the Tennesseeans. I would have written to you long before this, but we have been on the march and in line of battle nearly all the time since I parted with you at Covington Georgia.

On arriving with my command, I found the boys enjoy-, ing good health and in fine spirits, with a probability of an early engagement with the enemy. But we have since fallen back, and I hope it is for the best; we think so, and I do believe that we will finally destroy the most of Sherman's army. He will get so far down South, and so far from his base of operations, it will give us a chance to concentrate our forces, while it will weaken his army to keep those places we gave up guarded strong enough to hold them. We will attack him at some weak point, and he wont know what to do; he will be like something in hot water. I hope so at least. The boys appear eager for the fray, with a buoyant hope of success, which I humbly hope may be the case; and I do firmly believe that, by a faithful reliance on the Great Ruler of Nations, that our cause will prosper, and our arms eventually be victorious. I hope we will never be compelled to submit to the dictates of our oppressive foe; and that we may secure that freedom of right so justly due us as a people and a nation. The soldiers of our beloved land have undergone many hard trials, privations and exposures, and thousands have sacrificed their lives on the field of battte for the sake of once more enjoying liberty. As they have died faithful soldiers for the cause of their country, so may their never-dying souls ever live to enjoy the freedom that our Saviour has purchased for all who love Him. Their friends and relatives have my deep, heartfelt sympathy.

I received a letter recently from my father, stating that the family and relatives generally were well. Father wrote a lengthy letter, containing an abundance of news. I am always glad to get such letters.

I will close by giving you a sketch of the losses of the Fifth Regiment. It is consolidated with the Fourth Tennessee. I don't remember the exact number of killed or wounded. The boys say that we have lost one hundred. I think I shall go around to each company and get the exact number of casualties by the time I hear from you again. Our Colonel, J. J. Lamb, is numbered with the dead; his wound proved fatal. A good and brave man! His death cast a heavy gloom over the Fourth and Fifth Regiments. Our Lieutenant-Colonel and Major are both wounded. Major Hampton, of General Hardee's staff, now commands our regiment. Two sergeants killed in my company; and one sergeant missing—killed or captured, we don't know which. I close, sending my love to the soldiers generally, to my acquaintances particularly, to my sweetheart especially, and receive a double portion yourself individually.

WM. D. HENDRICKS, Sergt.

Camp 154th Tennessee Regiment, near Tuscumbia,
November 9, 1864.

MRS. S. E. D. SMITH:

Dear Grandma—Kind Providence has again permitted me the pleasure of seating myself, and communicating to one of my best friends. You perhaps think that I have entirely forgotten you, or else have neglected to write; but we have had such a task to undergo that it was rather difficult to write—I being placed under all disadvantages imaginable. Rest assured, whenever I have an opportunity to address my friends, I shall always do so, that they may have all the news, and how I am getting along.

Last night we moved our camp one mile or more north of town. We were wading and sloshing the mud in all directions. There is some talk of our leaving here soon for "Tennessee." Many think we will cross the river here; others think we will go to Corinth, Mississippi, or Jackson, Tennessee. But we can't tell where we will quarter at this winter, as the determination of our generals is to keep things very secret.

I suppose you have not heard of our gallant boy, Johnnie Waynesburg. Poor fellow, he marched with us until he blistered his feet so badly that he had to be sent off with the sick men. Many of our boys wore their shoes out, and had to march barefooted for some distance. I among them; but I bandaged my foot up with rags and cotton, and managed to get through "this side up with care." All that I wish to have is one or two pairs of socks for the winter. I told Willie Fairman to get me some in Covington, but hardly expect he will succeed in so doing. Johnnie wrote me a note stating that he was on his way to Memphis, or in that neighborhood. L. H. Perkins, also, was sent off. I suppose he will go home before returning to camp.

I was surprised the other day on the reception of a letter from my esteemed friend, Lorena Bagby. I had no idea the mail still continued to go through. I answered it, and sent to Cherokee Station to be mailed. It has been some time since I received a letter from any person, and you may know it pleased me on its reception, and I now hope I can always hear from my friends occasionally.

This morning three Yankees passed our camp under guard; two had lost their hats. Since they passed, I learn that they came down in a skiff for the purpose of cutting our pontoons, which are stretched across the Tennessee river, as the night was dark, and they supposed our boys could not see them. It looks reasonable to be supposed

K

that we will cross the river, as the pontoons are on the water; and I have always thought we would cross. If we do, then you may look for another battle this winter; and if we go to Jackson, Tennessee, there is talk of disbanding our brigade, and all go home for once in four years. There is no news that I can relate to you, as everything is quiet here, and nothing but camp rumors afloat. The rain is about to come, and I will have to hustle myself out of this place. Excuse hasty writing and composing. Give all enquiring friends my regards, and accept the love of your correspondent. Write soon.

JIMMY PHIEL,
Company D, 154th Reg't Tenn. Vols.

<hr />

Tuscumbia, Ala., December 12, 1864.
MRS. SUSAN E. SMITH:

Dear Grandma—Having just returned from my visit to West Tennessee among my many kind and dear friends and relations, I was glad to find a letter from you, and pleased to learn that you were still enjoying the same good health, and occupied your same position as when I left. Your kind letters are always hailed with very great pleasure by me—knowing as I do, that they come from one who is my friend, and whose time and attention is so devoted to the sufferings of our soldiers as to merit the praise and admiration of every true and loyal man or woman. Be assured, grandma, that I often think of the high position which you occupy, and the pleasure it always seems to give you to relieve the wants of the suffering. It makes me feel proud that I have such a worthy friend. My visit was indeed a source of very great pleasure to me, as it was the first time I had been home since the commencement of this cruel war. My relations and friends received me with very many blessings, and deeply regretted that my stay with them was so short. I found my father's family all very well, and pa as cheerful and in as fine spirits as I ever saw him. West Tennessee, as you well know, is the garden spot of this little Confed; and the people, although they have been overrun, and had everything taken from them, are to-day more loyal than any other in our poverty-stricken country, and will do more for a soldier. I did not see any of your relatives while there, as I was not in that portion of the State. The people are all doing well, and have plenty to eat and wear, and seem confident of our final success. I think I have given you all the West Tennessee news.

I will now try and interest you for a few moments about our army movements. I suppose you heard of the battle at Franklin, where the enemy was routed and driven from their breastworks, with a supposed loss, as near as we can learn, of four thousand killed and wounded. Preparations have been made here for transporting four thousand prisoners over this road to Corinth. Reports here to-day are that our troops occupy Nashville, the enemy falling back toward Bowling Green. Our loss in generals has been very heavy—two killed and six wounded. The details of the battle have not yet been received here. Our loss is supposed to be about sixteen hundred in killed and wounded. So you see the work goes bravely on, and if continued, our proud old Tennessee will once more be free. God grant it may! We now have possession of Huntsville, Decatur, Athens, Columbia, and are running the captured trains on the other side of the river. West Tennessee is clear of Yanks, with the exception of Memphis. My opinion, which is not worth much, is, that we will soon have peace.

My very kindest regards to my good friend O'Brien, and tell him I will write to him in a day or two. My respects to Mr. Smith. Write soon, and believe me, as ever,

Your true friend and well wisher,

W. B. CHESTER.

————

Forsyth, Ga., September 13, 1864.

MRS. S. E. D. SMITH:

Esteemed Friend—Yours of the 1st inst. came to hand a few days ago. I assure you it was a very welcome visitor. I had lost sight of you entirely since your "skeedaddle" from Covington. I had no idea where you or your hospitals had located. I hope you have found a pleasant and agreeable place, and that you will never more be interrupted by Yankee intrusion. I am in the "rear" yet. I am at present acting adjutant for the post, under Captain Smith, a very excellent Kentucky gentleman. I have been before the Medical Examining Board, and obtained a certificate of disability for field service. I have been suffering a good deal for several days past with a severe cold, but I hope it will soon wear off. Otherwise, I am very well. I am sorry you have lost some of your particular friends in the several engagements since I left you. I, too, have lost some to whom I was very much attached. Lieutenant-Colonel Dossen, of the One Hundred and Fifty-fourth Tennessee, has been here since the 22d of July. He was shot through the face, but is nearly well. This has become quite a business place since the hospitals from Marietta and some from Atlanta came here. There are seven or eight in all. Everybody is amazed at Governor Browns dismissing his militia. The country is full of them—reminding me of Mississippi after the release of the Vicksburg prisoners. I think they are heartily tired of soldiering. Our cause looks gloomy indeed; but as my trust is in Him who doeth all things well, I am not despondent. I wish you much pleasure and real enjoyment in your new field of labor.

Very truly your friend,
J. E. RUFFIN.

Forsyth, Ga., July 16, 1864.

MRS. SMITH:

Esteemed Friend—Your very welcome letter came to hand in due time, but for the want of something to communicate, I deferred writing until the present. Even now, I have nothing at all of any interest. This place is entirely void of anything new or interesting, though it is a pleasant country village of less than one thousand inhabitants, and about a "meeting house full" of pretty ladies, who, by the way, are very kind to our sick and wounded soldiers. The Marietta hospitals, and the Gate City from Atlanta, are here now encamped around the town. A large number of badly wounded men came down with the Marietta hospitals. They were met at the depot by the ladies, and others, and refreshed with an abundance of delicacies and every comfort which kind hearts could suggest. They were furnished with rooms in the Clayton and Hardee until their quarters could be established. As they were brought up from the depot on their beds, I noticed that nearly every soldier had a lady's fan or parasol to protect himself from the sun and flies until he should get to a room. Even such small acts of kindness, from the hands of woman, are very encouraging to the wounded soldier among strangers. A cup of water given in kindness loses not its reward, but gladdens many a friendless patriot's heart, and brings a tear to his eye as he

thinks of mother, sister, wife. What an enviable place
you hold in the hearts of the thousands who bless you for
your motherly care. "Their children will rise up and call
you blessed." But do not be so reckless of your own health
and comfort, as you may thereby impair your usefulness.
Is not the continued buoyancy of our men remarkable? I
regard it as an unfailing omen of success. It is stated that
on the retreat from Kennesaw, there was but one man in
Cheatham's Division who could not be accounted for.
When it is remembered that the enemy's works were only
a few yards from our own, such an example of discipline
and good order will be looked for in vain in any army or
any country.

I have improved some, and I think I will try the front
again before a great while. I received O'Brien's letter the
other day. It was quite a treat. I have never had a line
from Chester. Hoping I may have the pleasure of hearing
from you again soon, I will stop for the present.

Yours, faithfully,
J. E. RUFFIN.

Talladega, Ala., September 7, 1864.

MRS. S. E. D. SMITH:

Esteemed Friend—If you only knew how greatly rejoiced I was on yesterday at the reception of your very
kind and highly appreciated letter, coming as it did from
one who was a true picture of kindness and affection to the
poor sick and wounded of our bleeding country, who were
so fortunate as to be placed under your motherly hand. It
surely was a very great pleasure to me, who was classed
among the few fortunate. I feel that I can never be able
to repay you. You were as kind and attentive as if I had
been your own dear son; and so long as time shall last, I

assure you that I will never forget you, and will ever cherish a warm affection for you. To see your smiling, motherly face approach my room while confined in the hospital, would dispel all sad feelings, and throw a halo of light around the gloomy rooms of the hospital. May God keep you always under the shadow of His wing, is the prayer of your grateful friend.

I arrived here on the seventh day after I left you at Covington. I found all the members of our company here, and looking very anxiously for me, fearing I had been captured, as they had heard of the raid on Covington. I have a very pleasant position, and am associated with some very nice gentlemen, which will, in a great measure, assist in making my time pass off pleasantly. I have received my commission from Richmond as provost marshal.

I hope you will not think hard of my not writing to you sooner. Having your promise to write to me and let me know where you were, I have deferred writing, hoping and expecting every day to hear from you. You write me that poor Gus Flotron was killed, for which I am truly sorry, and I told and warned him about his daring bravery. Poor fellow; I hope he was prepared to meet his God! What has become of our little pet, O'Brien? Hope you have heard from him ere this. If he is with you, tell him I would like to hear from him. Hamner, I hope, has entirely recovered, and is with his regiment. I wrote him sometime since, but have not heard from him yet. I was truly glad to hear that you had met with kind friends and people who can appreciate your true patriotism. May you always meet with kind friends wherever you go. I have no news to write worthy of your notice. With my very best regards to Drs. Robertson, Caldwell, Doyle, Parsons, Flanagan, Dismukes and Blind John, I remain, as ever,

Your true friend,

W. B. CHESTER.

Talladega, Ala., October 4, 1864.

MRS. SMITH:

Dear Grandma—It is with great pleasure that I now embrace this present opportunity to reply to your highly appreciated, very welcome and truly interesting letter of the 21st of September, which came safe to hand this morning. The interesting intelligence which it gave in relation to my friends—who still, unfortunately, are confined to the hospital—but, fortunately for them, they are committed to your kind and motherly hands, and will be well cared for—is very gratifying. My friend, O'Brien, I was glad to hear from him, and learn his whereabouts. Poor fellow; he has suffered so much since he was wounded; and I hope since he has had his leg operated upon, that he will soon get well. Present my very best and kindest regards to him, and tell him I think he might honor me with a letter, for there is nothing that would afford me greater pleasure. I have often thought of him since we were separated, and anxiously expected a letter from him. He knew where I was, but I did not know where to address a letter to him, consequently I could not write. I was truly glad to learn that you are now situated where you have many kind and pleasant friends, who are ready and willing to lend an assisting hand to the patriotic labor in which you are engaged. May your life be one of sunshine, and may you always meet with kind friends. If any one deserves to be praised for their devotion to our cause, the sympathy for the poor wounded and dying soldiers of our bleeding Confederacy, the motherly kindness to sick, administering to their every want as far as it is in your power, you should and will be beloved and blessed by every one who is so fortunate as to be placed under your kind and benevolent hands. I feel that I, for one, can never repay you for your kindness towards me, and I look back to the time when I was with you with great pleasure, hoping that the time may come when I can show my gratitude for past kindness shown to me.

We are having glorious news from our old Tennessee war horse, Forrest. He is driving the Yanks before him like chaff before the wind. He has already sent to Meridian 2,200 prisoners—eight hundred are negroes, whom he captured at Athens, Alabama. He said upon going into Tennessee that he did not intend to come out, but that he would clear Middle Tennessee, as he had done West Tennessee. The Tennesseeans are flocking to him by hundreds and thousands, and still continue to come. I hope he may be the saving of our poor downtrodden State. I have no news of interest to write. My general health is very good, but I am still lame, and not improving very fast. Our courts will leave here on Thursday for Roddy's command, which is now at Tuscumbia, Alabama. we having gotten through with all the business here. With my kindest regards to Mr. Smith, and O'Brien, and other friends, I remain, as ever,

Your true and everlasting friend,
Lieut. W. B. CHESTER.

Near Atlanta, Ga., July 26, 1864.

MRS. S. E. D. SMITH:

Worthy Mother—Yours of the 17th inst. was handed to me half an hour ago. I was highly gratified to hear from you once more, and especially to learn that you are still in good health, and at your old stand administering to the many wants of our suffering veterans. God, in His providence, has placed you there as a ministering angel to alleviate the wants of suffering humanity. I have been in two very severe fights since writing to you last; but through God's kind providence, I am yet spared, unhurt. We have

K*

lost many of our brave boys. In the two engagements our brigade lost three hundred out of seven hundred and fifty—forty killed, and the remainder wounded. Our regiment lost seven killed and forty wounded—none of whom, I suppose, you are acquainted with, unless it be Lieutenant Wm. Miller, of company C, the widow Miller's son, of Shelby county, Tennessee.

The first day's fight, we charged the Yankee works, and failed to take them; the second day we flanked their works came up in their rear, completely surprising and routing them. We drove them about one and a half miles. The fight at places was hot. We lost more men the last day than the first. Only Hardee's corps was engaged. You have ere this learned more about the total loss and gain from the papers than I can tell you, owing to my limited opportunities of learning. The field was the richest one of booty that I have ever seen—a little of almost everything was there, I suppose owing to their surprise. I will take pleasure in sending your letter to Mr. Sullivan the first opportunity. I very much regret not getting your letters written since leaving Dalton. The Fifty-first donated their to-day's rations to the destitute women and children of Atlanta. Please continue to write often. Lizzie was well a few days ago.   Yours, as ever,

LIEUT. J. R. FAULK,
Comp. B, 51st Tenn.

Wednesday Night—Depot Hospital,
Macon, Ga., Sept. 28, 1864.

DEAR MOTHER SMITH:

My Dear Friend—Excuse me for not answering your note sooner. My reasons for not doing so I hope will be satisfactory. Lieutenant McGrath was very low when I got the letter for him. I saw a lady friend of his who visited him daily, and carried him proper nourishment. I asked her to carry the letter to him, and read it for him if he was too low to read it himself. She told me she would. I know the lady. I am sure he suffered for nothing that they could do for him, for they seemed very much attached to him. I have been wanting to get the particulars of his death, so that I might give you some satisfaction, but I have failed up to the present moment; but will not close my letter to-night, so that I may get news in regard to his case to write you in the morning.

My cravat is very nice. Receive my sincere thanks for the present. I am quite worried to-night with this evening's labor, so I beg to be let off with a short letter. I am going to try to come to Cuthbert again soon. I will come to see you if I have time. I humbly ask to be remembered in your prayers. I will write you more in the morning. Good night.

FLEMING J. MATHEWS.

Thursday Morning.

I have no news to write you this morning in regard to Lieutenant McGrath's death. I have this much to tell you—I saw him when he arrived here; he was quite low then; the ladies that I have spoken to you of came with him to this place.

You seem to cherish me as a warm friend in time of need. May you never have cause to think otherwise. May you persevere in your good mission, and be much blessed, is my humble desire. My kindest respects to enquiring friends. Very sincerely, your friend,

F. J. MATHEWS.

Eighteenth Tennessee Regiment,
Near Etowah River, May 24, '64.

KIND FRIEND:

With much pleasure I take my pen in hand to answer your most kind letter, which came to hand in due time. I received your letter while in line of battle, and have not had the opportunity of answering it until now. You are aware ere this that we have retreated from Dalton; not because we were whipped, but because we were being flanked. We first fell back to Resacca, and there we gave the enemy battle, and we punished him very badly. Our corps (Hood's) did the most of the fighting. Brown's Brigade of Tennesseeans engaged the enemy on Saturday, 14th, and turned their right wing two miles. Our loss was very small, considering the amount of fighting we did. Saturday night we fell back to a more desirable position, and threw up some temporary parapets out of fence rails. On Sunday, 15th, the enemy made eleven assaults on our brigade (Brown's), and were eleven times repulsed, with great slaughter. As far as you could see they lay so thick in front of our works that you could walk upon them. Our loss was very small. On Sunday night the enemy undertook to go around again, and we had to fall back again. We are now on the south side of the Etowah river. They have stopped pursuit. I cannot tell what General Johnston will do, I have the greatest confidence in him. Our boys are in the best of spirits, especially the Tennessee soldiers. I believe I will quit, as I have no more news to write. Be certain to write soon, and I will write every opportunity.

Ever your true friend,
JAMES ROBERT MATHES.

Gamp Company A, 154th Regiment,
April 24, 1864.

MRS. SMITH:

Kind Friend—I received your kind letter of the 7th sometime ago. I would have answered it sooner, but I have been busy every day drilling, and working on the fortifications. I am very thankful for that beautiful tobacco pouch Miss Conners sent me, also for the nice way in which my clothes were done up. I feel now as if I had a kind mother in you, and if I am so unfortunate as to be wounded in this coming fight, I will surely try to get near you, where I am certain I will have a friend. John Waynsburgh tells me that his mother is coming out from Memphis. I am really glad of it; it will be a great pleasure for her to see John. I hope when she does come that John will get a furlough.

Everything looks as though we were going to have a fight here. All the extra baggage is to be sent to the rear immediately. The Yankees are maneuvering in our front, and I expect will be down on us in a short time. I have every confidence in our army doing their duty when the time comes. They are anxious to meet the Yankees and wipe out the stain of "Missionary Ridge." God has given us the victory at every point this spring, and I trust He will continue His blessing. I firmly believe that the war will end this year if we are successful in the next two battles. They will be severe. The Yankees trust in nothing but superior numbers; we trust in God, knowing that we are fighting for freedom. It is believed that the enemy have seventy thousand men in our front. Acting on the defensive, I feel certain that we can whip them.

All your friends in camp are well, and send their kind regards to you. Write whenever you feel inclined. I will be more punctual in replying hereafter. Remember me to all my friends in and around Covington. Hoping that you will excuse my negligence in answering your letter, I remain, as ever,   Your friend,

A. McGRATH.

Camp Company A, 154th Sr. Reg't Tenn. Vols.

MRS. SMITH:

Kind Friend—No doubt you think I treated you rather shabbily the day I left the hospital, in not calling to see you before my departure. My reasons for not doing so were these : I heard, while up in town, that Mr. Ellis had notified several persons that were in the habit of visiting the hospitals that it was contrary to orders for persons to visit any one about a hospital without permission, and not wishing to create any ill feeling, I kept away. I enjoyed myself very well that night at "Social Circle." I left the next morning for Atlanta.

I can never forget the kind manner in which you treated me—a perfect stranger, at least one whom you had never seen before, and scarcely heard of. I shall always look back with pleasure to the quiet, happy days I passed in your company. It reminds me of days gone by; "when our land was blessed with peace and plenty." It could not but make an impression on one who has been excluded from the society of ladies for three years. My stay in Covington is almost the only bright spot in my life as a soldier. I shall always be thankful to Mr. Starr and his family for their great kindness. Give him my best respects, and tell him to give my kindest regards to all the members of his family. I have not had time to visit his son since I got back to the regiment. We are to have a sham battle to-morrow if the weather is fair. I wish you were here to see it. There is nothing of interest transpiring at the front. A great many are of the opinion that we will go to Virginia this summer. I should like to very well, for I have always had a desire to visit the "Old Dominion." How is Mr. Hodge? Give him my kind regards. Remember me to Messrs. Harris and Crumpton. Will Fairman has got a furlough of forty days, on a recruit. How does Gus and Freddy get along? I suppose they are having a nice time. Tell Fred to be sure and bring up my jacket and pants when he comes. John Waynesburg, Thirl and all your friends in camp are well, and send their best respects to you. It would be a pleasure to me to hear from you as often as you have time. Remember me to all enquiring friends, and believe me

Your friend,

A. McGRATH,

Company A, 154th Reg't Tenn. Volls.

Camp near Dalton, March 22, 1864.

MRS. SMITH:

Dear Friend—I received your very kind and interesting letter of the 15th, and was truly glad to know that you were well. My health is excellent—better than I ever enjoyed at home. There is but littly army news floating around. It was rumored that the Yanks were advancing, but it was a false alarm. It appears like winter is going to remain with us longer than is agreeable; it has been snowing since midnight, and I doubt whether "the oldest inhabitant" ever witnessed the snow so deep as it is now. We have been fighting all day. This morning our brigade opened the fight by attacking Bate's old brigade, and after a heavy skirmish, they agreed to storm the camp of the Florida brigade, which was done in gallant style. You have seen schoolboys snowballing, and can form some idea of the sport, only it was on a larger scale; it was a continuous storm of snowballs. Finally, we come to terms, and agreed that all three brigades should attack Stewart's Division. Bugles were sounded, regiments formed, their colors proudly floating to the breeze, our field officers in command, the charge was sounded, and away we went with a yell, and soon drove them out of their quarters, captured several stands of colors, and returned with our spoils to our camp. We had scarcely got back when a courier arrived with the news that Stewart's Division was preparing for battle, their intention was to capture our camps in retaliation for what we had done early in the morning. Again the bugle sounded, and we moved out in line of battle beyond Bate's old camp. When we arrived on the field, we found them (Stewart's Division) formed in line ready to attack the Florida brigade. We were soon ready for action, skirmishers thrown out, and in a few minutes the action commenced. It was a grand sight to behold two divisions throwing snow with perfect fury, the balls flying as thick as hail. They charged us, and the battle raged with fury along the whole line. Finally they flanked us, and we had to retreat double-quick. They run us clear through the Florida and Tennessee camps, and nearly back to the Fourth Kentucky, when we rallied, charged them, and saved our camp. I will add, though I don't like to, they captured two stands of colors from us; but we have enough to exchange with them. So ended the greatest battle ever fought on this continent with snowballs. I know that you would like to have witnessed it. Of all the rolling and tumbling in snow, it beat any I ever saw. I could relate several personal adventures in which I was engaged, sometimes coming out all right, and only second best at others. In the muss I pitched into a captain, and was in a good way to capture his sword, when he received re-enforcements, and I had to retreat, though not till I wallowed him pretty severely in the snow. It was an exciting scene, and was engaged in by both officers and privates finely, and, I am happy to say, ended in the kindest feeling. I don't know what name they will give the field. I expect you will see an account of it in the papers soon. With all the hardships of a soldier's life, the boys are getting on fine. Some of the boys are taking to themselves partners for life. One of my company was married a few days ago. Last night there were two more weddings; one of the boys was of my regiment, the other from the Seventh ; they married sisters.

I have met with several of my old friends of Tunnel Hill—Mr. Boggs, and my particular friend, Wm. Dillyhunt, also his wife, (Miss Freeman, she used to be.) He is well, and would like to hear from you. I have not seen or heard from Mrs. Bell and family since we came through there. I heard that Sowders was taken prisoner at Chickamauga. I have just received a letter from home by flag of truce. You have no idea how glad I was to hear from my loved friends. All are well, and doing first rate. Oh, how glad I would be to see my dear old home once more. I could have that pleasure by deserting, but if that is the only way, I never will see it again, for as well as I love my friends, I love my honor and my adopted country too much to leave them now, when every man should be at his post. Our army is in fine spirits, and whenever the Yanks are ready to try their "on to Atlanta " again, we will be ready for them. General Grant is now in command, and will try the "on to Richmond," in which so many have failed. I will just say for their edification that the Lee side of any shore is unhealthy; and will go old Grant, and down will go Abe Lincoln, then will come peace, and once more we will breathe the air of freedom. Well, I will quit my nonsense till some other time. Excuse all mistakes. If the battle takes place, I will let you know. No more at present, but remain— Very truly, D. S. HERAN.

Monticello, Ga., July 15, 1864.

ESTEEMED FRIEND:

It is with the greatest of pleasure that I seat myself this evening to drop you a few lines to let you know that I am getting along as well as could be expected. I went to Mrs. Pope's; found Mr. McCrocklin there; she had two or three there. I came on to this little town, and am now staying with a family by the name of Gooseby—a fine old gentleman and lady, with three grand daughters, and they are all as nice as red shoes with blue ribbon in them. I want you to tell Hoopper that he was laughing at me, and wanted to know how I fared in the country. Tell him if he was here I could tell him. Now I am setting back in town with a pocket full of rocks, eating berry pies, chickens, biscuits, waffles, good milk and butter, and eggs, all kinds of preserves—eating all the time out of two or three sets of dishes, all at the same meal. Tell him that I can tell him "what's the matter." I have got plenty to eat, and every now and then upset a glass of wine; and then to set the thing off, just walk into the parlor and hear the ladies sing, and play on the piano.

Grandma, you must excuse my bad writing and all mistakes, for I am in a hurry to get this mailed. I thought I would drop you a few lines to let you know where I was, as I think you would like to know. Give my respects to Sykes and others if they are there, and tell them to leave. So I will close at present.

S. F. BUNCH.

Camp near Dalton, Ga., January 10, 1864.

RESPECTED FRIEND:

I received your kind and welcome letter dated the 5th of January. I was truly glad to hear from you. I had begun to think that you had forgotten me; but, how-somever, I see it is not the case. I read your letter with great pleasure, for it brought me news of Gus, and also news from you. I am glad to hear that Gus is improving, both morally and physically. I am glad to hear that he is going to forsake his bad ways, and lead a better life, and be a christian—although, I am as bad a boy as he is. I would be truly glad to hear of Gus being converted to Christ. It is out of my place to be talking this way to Gus, or to anybody else, for the Scriptures say, "And why beholdest thou the mote that is in thy brother's eye, but considerest not the beam that is in thine own eye: first cast out the beam out of thine own eye, and then shalt thou see clearly to cast out the mote out of thy brother's eye." And, therefore, I will leave that matter in your hands, for I think you are more capable of converting him than I am. I see a great deal more pleasure in reading the Testament than in idling away my time and spending it foolishly. I find that there is a great deal more of knowledge found out by reading the Scriptures than any other employment I could engage in. I think by the motherly advice you have given me on several occasions, it may have a tendency to change my mode of life, and be the means of converting me also; for a boy like me, away off in a strange land, far from home, kindred and friends, has need of all the symp-athy he can get. I have no fond mother now to watch over me and guide my footsteps in the way to righteousness, or give me that advice which I stand so much in need of, for this world is full of temptations to lure the young men from the paths of virtue and rectitude. I hope the time may soon come when I shall be able to meet my dear mother once more, and there shall be peace once more in our country.

There is cheering news now in circulation in our regi-ment about a petition from General Forrest being sent to

Richmond with the request that the old One Hundred and Fifty-fourth would be allowed to go with him for the war. It was signed by every officer in our regiment, and a man from Memphis by the name of Ganaway has taken it on to Richmond, and our Congressmen are going to put it through as quick as possible. Foote, Curran, John V. Wright and Governor Harris have taken it in charge, and I think that if such able statesmen as they are should fail, there is no possible hope for us. I do hope that they may prove successful, so that when Gus is able to get up, he will just have to get on his horse and ride off. Then we will start for our adopted home, Memphis, and try and redeem it from the Vandals who now hold it.

You can tell Gus that Freddie Brinkman has got back, and also John Baker, of the Light Guards, who was wounded at the battle of Chickamauga. They are to be sent back to the hospital, as they are not fit for field service. John Waynsburg is well, and in good health, and also Jimmy Thirl, and the rest of his company. I would like very much to know whether Gus has ever received a letter from that young sweetheart of his at the Empire hospital. I would give anything to have Gus up here again as well as he was at Missionary Ridge, for he is the liveliest comrade I ever met with. I think my furlough will prove a failure, as there is no prospect of me getting one now. I am on detached service now, and have to build bridges for the division. It seems to me that everybody can get a furlough but me; I am the unlucky one always; but I hope my time will come before long. I cannot get sick, for I never had better health in my life. Sometimes I wish I could get sick for a few days, and then I would be able to go down and relieve you a little by waiting on Gus; but I am very thankful that I have such good health. There is no news stirring as regards the army—both sides are still. There is always a calm before a storm. I see

Congress is doing something very sensible now—that is by putting those in the army who have got substitutes there to escape death themselves. Why do not they come out and risk their lives like the balance of us; it is because they are too cowardly. Why, if they would come out like men, our army would be increased to twice the number it now is, and then we would be invincible in the coming campaign. We have need of every able bodied man in the Confederacy at the present time to hurl back the invaders of our country, so that we may be able to regain Tennessee and Kentucky, for those two States have done more to support the army than any other two in our young Confederacy. I shall make application to the officers until they do give me a furlough. My lieutenant has gone to Covington on furlough, and if you see him, you must request him to give me a furlough, so that I can go down there. Give my love and best respects to Gus and all enquiring friends, and answer this letter immediately. With my well wishes for your welfare, I am

Your sincere friend,
WILLIAM FAIRMAN,
Company H, 154th Reg't Tenn. Vols.

De Soto Station, Ala., August 1, 1864.

MRS. SMITH :

Dear Grandma—I have at last arrived at my Mississippi home. Our trip was a long one, and very fatiguing. We were just eleven days from the time we left the hospital until we arrived at De Soto. In our travels I got to see nearly all of Georgia, and most all the ladies, too. At every station it was—"Is you'uns come from Atlanty?— Do you'uns know my son Bill in Johnston's company," etc. We could not give them any of the desired information.

The ladies of Georgia gave us every attention; but when we struck Alabama the cars were crowded with ladies, and they had everything that was nice to eat, and plenty of apples and watermelons. When we got to Union Springs, Alabama, the old citizens came to the cars and took us to their houses, and they seemed like they could not do enough. They then put us in their wagons and sent us to Chehaw Station, distance twenty-five miles, and never charged us anything. The ladies of Tuskegee, Alabama, stopped us, and made us stay all night, and next morning sent us on down to the cars; and they gave us everything that was good to eat, and took our clothes and had them washed, and then in the morning gave us a nice lunch to take with us. The world never saw so many pretty young ladies. But, thank the Lord, I never will forget some of the ladies of Covington. May their lives be as happy as the angels. Those ladies were both mother and sister to me while there, and I hope that the time may soon come that this poor soldier may be able to return the favor and kindness in a two fold ratio. Long will a Texan soldier remember Grandma Smith; and when peace is made, may her lot be cast among some of the Sixth Regiment. With them she will find a home, and the hairs of her head will be held as precious relics, when her soul rests in peace with God in Heaven. Long will they remember Mrs. Levey. Her mind seemed to be on the welfare of the soldier and her country. I will long remember her parental care. And here to Misses Harper and Conner— May their lives be one of peace and happiness, and when peace is once more restored to our country, may they find their way to the beautiful prairies of the Lone Star State, and then may some one of the Texan heroes be so fortunate as to win their favor.

Gustine and myself have been improving ever since our departure from the hospital. I am very much pleased with my new home, and there are more pretty girls than I ever saw, so I will have a fine time. Give my compliments to Mr. Wolley, Arkansas and Betts. I heard that Hogan died after we left. Mrs. Gustine and Amos join me in love and good wishes to you, and Mrs. Levey, and Miss Harper. God bless all the pretty girls of Covington is the prayer of a Rebel soldier.

Very respectfully,

B. F. WILKS,

Sixth Texas Regiment.

Head-Quarters Polk's Wing,

En route for Chattanooga, Sept. 22, 1863.

GRANDMA:

My Dear Friend—Your letter reached me on the 20th, about five o'clock P. M., just as we were preparing to make the last attack on the enemy's works, and which surpassed our most sanguine expectations, for we completely routed them, and the cover of night only saved old Rosecrans' army from entire annihilation. But I have neither time nor paper to give you an account of the two days' hard fighting, and my object in writing this is only to let you know that your son James is well and hearty, and that he was the last man to leave the battery when it was taken by the Yankees. The enemy took Carnes' Battery early in the action, but it was retaken late in the day. Waynsburg is all right. The old company had twelve men wounded—among whom was Howard, Botts, Beazly, Leach, Williams, John Jones, Anderson, and I forget who else. I am all safe, as you see, thanks to the protecting wing of the Almighty Father above. Colonel Richmond, of our staff, was killed. Our loss is heavy in wounded, but very small in killed. We have every reason to thank the Almighty for this new victory, and I hope everybody will do so. When we get to Chattanooga, I will let you hear from me again.   Your friend,

                                                         FRED.

———

                              Hill, Hospital, April 18, 1864.
MRS. SMITH:

My more than Mother—To you I owe my life. Pardon my seeming coldness toward you for the last three or four days. It was foreign to my mind to treat a lady who has been so kind and indulgent to me with disrespect. As far back as I can remember I have been attacked with these dark and gloomy spells. Pardon me if you can.

                    Your obedient servant,
                         LIEUT. J. B. O'BRIEN.

———

MRS. S. E. D. SMITH:

My Very Dear Friend—Circumstances suddenly sever my connection with the hospital. I may not be able to see you before leaving, but the friendship I bear to you, born of your kindness, will never abate by the stretch of distance, or the lapse of time. Remember me kindly to Hobson, Texas and Mississippi. Lieutenant Lewellen will return the book; many thanks for the use of it. I leave in haste.   Your friend,

                         CAPT. W. G. STARR.

———

                    City Hall Hospital, Macon, Ga.,
                              October 22, 1864.
DEAR GRANDMA:

It is with unfeigned pleasure that I now resume my pen to drop you a few lines informing you of my increasing

good fortune. Day before yesterday I received orders from Dr. Stout to report for duty at this post. I left Opelika yesterday, and arrived here this morning, when I proceeded to report to the surgeon of the post, who assigned me to duty as druggist. I have an old physician for my assistant, a negro boy to wait upon me, a good room well furnished, gas light to read and write by, and good fare. Imagine my surprise to find little Wood, of our company, nursing here. He did not know me until I told him my name and where I belonged. Grandma, I believe that it is owing to yours and my mother's prayers that I am thus fortunate. Will you continue to pray for my success? It is useless to ask that question, for I feel assured that you will; and, dear grandma, will you pray that I may live to cheer my mother's declining years? You cannot imagine how dear she has become to me since I have lost her. It is now nearly three years since I have seen her, and almost a year since I have heard from her. My heart misgives me when I think that I no longer have a mother; but God grant that my fears may prove groundless. I have written letter after letter to Memphis, and still no answer comes. Surely, they cannot all be dead. This is all that mars my happiness. If I could feel assured of their safety and well-doing, I would be as happy as the day is long. I would be content to suffer all that man may suffer, provided they could be spared all unhappiness. How few of us know the true value of a mother until we have lost her, and then every gentle smile and kind word that she ever gave us comes up like a reproachful spirit, censuring us for not lavishing all the kindness and devotion in our power upon her while she was spared to us. If God only spares my mother to me, a lifetime of devotion and care would hardly repay her for her tender care of me in bygone days. Write to me soon, dear grandma. May God bless you, is the sincere prayer of
Your loving friend,

L ALEXANDER F. S.

Hill Hospital, January 26, 1864.

MRS. SMITH:

I fell grateful to you for a fine pair of socks left under my pillow. I have learned to appreciate the kind work of our noble spirited women. I hope you will accept my sincere thanks in return.

Respectfully, your friend,

TIMOTHY CONWAY.

Camp 154*th Senior Tennessee Regiment,*
Near Dalton, Ga., May 2, 1864.

MRS. S. E. D. SMITH:

Highly Esteemed Friend—It is with unfeigned pleasure that I address myself to the pleasing task of writing you a few lines. I should have written before this, but have been waiting for you to write. You must excuse my short and imperfect letter, as I am so unused to writing that it is quite a task for me to write, particularly a letter to one of your sex; but let it be ever so lame, I know you will appreciate it, and pass all my imperfections by. Since you last heard from me I have had quite a pleasant time. I went within seven miles of Memphis, and could have gone into the Federal lines, but was afraid to risk the Yanks. I spent the greater part of my furlough in Mississippi and Alabama. All along my route I enquired for you, but could learn nothing of your whereabouts until I returned to the regiment. When I learned that you were at Covington, I regretted it very much, as I was within sixteen miles of you, and would have been very happy to have paid you a visit. I learn from the boys that you have a very nice place, with some very fine young ladies staying with you. You may rest assured that if I am so fortunate as to get a furlough this summer, I shall be more than happy to call upon you. We are all in momentary expectation of being called out to the front. The Yankees advanced to Tunnel Hill this morning, and there was some skirmishing; but I learn that they have gone back. We have no news of a definite character in regard to the movements of the Federals; but this much I am sure of, we are prepared to give them a warm reception whenever they may choose to come. I do not think there is any army in the Confederacy in a better fighting condition than this. Dr. Samuels, one of your Overton Hospital friends, joined this company about a month ago, and is now with us.

I have told you all I know, and must now close for want of something else to write. Hoping soon to hear from you, I beg leave to remain, as ever,

Your devoted friend,
CHAS. HOWARD,
Company D, 154th Senior Reg't Tenn. Vols.

Head-Quarters Army of Mississippi,
Camp near New Hope Church, June 2, 1864.

MRS. SMITH:

My Dear Friend—Your welcome letter reached me at Tuscumbia where everything was bustle and confusion, owing to orders we received to join the General in the field at Dalton, and consequently I found no time to answer it up to the present moment; but now I believe I will succeed, having obtained (no matter how) a sheet of paper, pen and ink, and also a few moments of leisure, which I now devote to you. I left Tuscaloosa on the 17th, went through Demopolis like a streak of lightning, and placed our horses on the train at Monticello and proceeded to Blue Mountain, thence on horseback towards Rome. After we came within a few miles of Rome, news reached us that it had fallen, and, of course, changed our front; and after

two days hard riding, we managed to come up with the
army just as it was falling back from Cassville south of the
Etowah river. Since then I have been in the saddle nearly
all the time—now in front and now in rear, surveying
roads, etc.; but as has ever been my fortune, am still in
good health and fine spirits. I had the pleasure of meeting
your son and husband the other day, and was very glad to
see them looking so well and hearty. Jim had command
of one gun, and I am told that he managed it very hand-
somely through the innumerable skirmishes we have been
having with the enemy. But while I am speaking of
skirmishing, I must give you a little sketch of a field after
one of those little skirmishes, as they call them, viz: Riding
along our front line of battle, I was told that Cleburne had
a fight the evening previous, and as he is, or was then, on
our (General Polk's) right, I thought I would go and see
the battle field. I soon came up with the "Wild Division,"
(as they call Cleburne's,) and there in the immediate front
of Granbury's Brigade a spectacle presented itself to my
astonished sight that was almost startling, and would have
made a braver man's cheek than mine turn pale, for there
within the small space of about one acre lay over seven
hundred dead men, all Yanks, and the most of them within
ten or fifteen yards of our line. Our men, as it seems, reserved their fire until they came within such deadly range
that every shot took effect. I have never witnessed anything equal to that in its dreadful aspect. I shudder as I
think of the mutilated forms lying, as it were, piled on one
another, and their ghastly wounds are even now haunting
me and chilling me to the heart, enemy as they are.

I saw Johnnie Waynsburg the other day; and, in fact,
all the boys. The company had two killed and six wounded.
Parsons is one of the killed. Everything goes on as usual
here; skirmishing is the order of the day, and I have become perfectly indifferent to the rattling of musketry, now

and then echoed by the heavy boom of cannons. But enough of this. I must close. Let me hear from you soon, and think often of your

True friend,

FRED.

Camp 154th Senior Regiment Tennesece Volunteers,
Near Dalton, Ga., June 27, 1864.

MRS. SMITH:

Dear Old Friend—Your kind and highly appreciated letter of the 21st has just reached me, and now that all around me is still, I take my seat to try, in my feeble manner, to reply; but were I to write for months I would be unable to do justice to your heart-cheering missive; but let it be ever so imperfect, I feel that you could not find it in your kind heart to criticise my humble reply; and I feel thankful to my Heavenly Father that I am so blessed with such a one as you to be called by the endearing name of "friend." Oh, how much happiness is combined in the simple name of friend—and such a one as you. I will not weary you by again offering you my sincere and heartfelt thanks, for words alone cannot repay the great debt of gratitude I owe you. You little know how your motherly counsel has helped to cheer me on in my duty toward God and man. Oh, I have need of it indeed at this time! You would be shocked could you see the way in which the warning of God is set aside by men in the army; and, worst of all, by some who have openly professed their determination to serve God, let others do as they may; and now in this trying time when the spirit of God has been so freely poured out upon us, oh, how it hurts me to see those whom I have loved, those who I have taken such a delight in conversing with, boldly assert their independence of God, and cast aside His love, and again launch themselves upon the broad ocean of sin and folly! Let me assure you, my blessed old friend, that I am stirred up to a greater will to live a christian, God being my helper. Oh, to think that those who should have set a bright, christian example to their sinful companions are again mingling in sin! Oh, I thank God for so blessing me with health, strength and understranding, and for the blessed comforts of religion. Oh, I would I were worthy the many mercies of the Almighty! Let me ask your kind supplications at the Throne of Grace in my behalf, that I may stem the current of all opposition to the laws of God; that while others are falling off, that I may still hold on to the precious promises of my dear Redeemer.

I am rejoiced to hear of the rapid recovery of Gus. Present my kindest regards to him, and tell him not to forget me among the ladies. I sent him some money that I raised among the boys, but up to the present have received no receipt of it from him. I sent it by express. Let me know if he gets it. If not, I will send the receipt I got from the agent. I shall make my letter short this time, as I am one ahead of you already. I have no news worth communicating. We are having some of the most beautiful weather, almost like spring. We are having a nice time. I have my little cabin fixed up in style. I wish you could see it. I think I would elicit some praise for my housekeeping from you, as I am the "old woman" of the house, and always keep a good "hickory" in the crack to keep the "young 'uns" straight. Two of our wounded boys from Chickamauga have returned—Freddy Brinkman and Tom Anderson—and having no place, I had to take them in. The battery has gone somewhere; I don't know where. The bugle has blown for dress parade, so I must close. My regards to Mrs. Ellis and all friends. Write soon to your   Devoted friend,

JOHNNY.

In Line of Battle, near Marietta,
Head-Quarters 154th, June 29.

KIND FRIEND:

Again am I permitted, through God's providence, to pencil you a few lines informing you that we are all well and in fine spirits. We have had quite a lively time of it the last few days. On the 22d the enemy charged our works, and thought they would drive us out of them; but in that they were sadly mistaken, and paid dearly for it. There were some ten or eleven that got within a few steps of our works, but they never returned, for they lost their lives in the attempt. To-day everything is quiet along our lines, as there is a flag of truce established, so that the enemy can get their wounded and dead out of the way. I have just been over to see how many we killed of them. I was astonished when I saw so many of them lying dead at our works. I will not attempt to describe the terrible slaughter, as I am wholly unable.

Early this morning, a little after sunrise, we spied a Yankee waving a paper, and all eyes were at once turned in that direction, and in a few minutes one of our men did the same, and directly they advanced, paper in hand, to indicate that they wished to exchange with us; we met them half way, in an open field, and there the merchandizing commenced. I, of course, was not backward in going; and having some of the "chicken pie" (as we term it), I got as much coffee as I wanted, and two papers. While with them, we talked and laughed at one another as if there was no war at all, and no animosity existed. How strange it is that men will talk so friendly in one moment, and then in the next do their best to kill each other. While making the exchange (tobacco for coffee), I procured a paper for you. I will send it with my letter, and I hope you will write to me on their reception, so that I may be assured you have them.

Grandma, I must close my letter now, for the truce is out, and we are ordered in the ditches, in case the enemy should make another attack. I wish you would let my lady acquaintances read the papers when you get through with them, and whenever I have an opportunity to procure more, I will send them to you. Jimmie and Johnnie join me in sending their best respects to .you. No more at present, but remain, as ever,

Your faithful and devoted friend,
FREDDY W. BRINKMAN.

Camp 154th Senior Reg't Tenn. Vols.,
In Line of Battle, near Atlanta, July 25, 1864.

DEAR GRANDMA:

Through the mercy of God I have been spared through two dreadful conflicts, where the leaden messengers of death came thick and fast around me, and where death was stared in the face by thousands of those gallant souls of Hardee's Corps. It is with a heart beating with thanks to His holy name that I attempt to write you a few lines this morning in answer to yours of the 20th, which was handed to me by Mr. Midlebrook, who arrived last evening. Oh, dear grandma, would I were with you, where I could express myself as I wish; but it is impossible, so I shall content myself with writing you a few lines. You have, perhaps, ere this heard of the last battle we have had, but I fear have not heard the worst that is to come—that is the loss (I fear) of my two companions, Gus and Freddy, and the wounding of Jimmie and Willie. Thus you see I am left alone with but one with whom I love to associate, Tett Perkins. Willie was wounded on the 20th, when we so recklessly charged the enemy's works. He was taking a wounded man from the field when he was wounded in two places, shoulder and leg. Gus, Freddy and Jimmie on the 22d, where we gained such a victory. We had driven the enemy from his first works, and were firing from them ourselves, when Gus came running by me, calling me to come on, saying "there they go." I called him to me, and made him stay, as he was rushing heedlessly on to death. My attention was called away for a moment, when one of the boys called me, and there lay Gus weltering in his own blood, shot through the head, the ball entering the right eye, coming out in front of the ear, and tearing away half of it. Oh! you cannot imagine my feelings to see my old messmate the second time thus struck down by the enemy. I never left him until I got him started back to the division hospital, which I was a long time in doing, as I could get no litter to carry him from the field to the brigade hospital. I got some of the boys to help me, and with two or three blankets I got him off. Almost his first words were, "Wesley, write to mother Smith and Mrs. Neal." Jimmie Thirl assisted me in getting him off the field, and then went back to the command, and in a short time came back slightly wounded. I was going for some water, when some one called me; I looked, and saw little Freddy sitting up, leaning against a tree, and oh! what a different person from what he formerly was. I did all I could for all the boys, and then went back to the command. I went over the portion of the field we had fought over, and I am glad to know that Gus and Freddy are revenged. I have not heard from the boys to-day. Yesterday evening Midlebrook told me Freddy was dying; Gus had been sent off. I have strong hopes that Gus will recover. Freddy I did not think from the first would get over it; the ball entered just below the nipple of the right breast, coming out below the ribs on the same side. I believe he is resigned to the will of God, and if he should die, I earnestly hope he may go to a better land. I conversed with him sometime after

L*

he was wounded, but he had taken so much opium he was almost asleep. Oh, have I not cause to be thankful to God for thus sparing me, while there were many, perhaps better than I, called "to that bourne from whence no traveller returns?"

Grandma, I must bring my letter to a close. I wish I had time, I would write all the evening. I am going to hunt for Jimmie, and give him the tobacco pouch. I have some trophies of the battle I want to send down by uncle Jim, if I can see him. You see what fine paper and envelopes I have, besides a fine gold pen and pencil, with a pocket inkstand. I will write again as soon as I find where you are. There is no mail to the army now, therefore it will be sometime before you get this. I wrote to Mrs. Neal, and told her to let you know the contents of her letter, provided you were in Covington. No more. May God bless and ultimately save us in Heaven, is the prayer of   Your affectionate friend,

JOHNNY.

In Line of Battle, near Marietta, June 7, 1864.

MRS. SMITH:

Your kind and welcome letter has just reached me, and found me enjoying the best of health. We are all safe yet. I think, dear grandma, that I feel a great deal better since I have been instructed by you. I hope and trust that my heart is right in the sight of God. I know that I am a great sinner yet, but I hope, through God's mercy, to reach Heaven in safety. I do not neglect to say my prayers, and supplicate before the mercy seat of God every night. I feel a great deal better when I arise from my knees after saying my prayers. I am glad to hear that little Bob arrived down there; but am very sorry that he is so low. I am afraid he will be cut off in his sins before he will have time to repent; he said he was going to be a better boy and read his Testament. I told Bob to go down and place himself under your care, and give heed to your advice, and then he surely would be a better boy. I do hope the poor little fellow will get well. I informed Johnnie and Freddy that you would be glad to write to them on the first opportunity. I was completely surprised when I heard of little Bob being so low. Some reports come here that he was walking around in Covington as lively as ever, doing well. The doctors here said that he would get over it, as they did not seem to think it was a very dangerous wound. Have any of his family been to see him, and what did they say about him? I suppose they were very angry with me, but I could not help it. I am sure if I had it to do over again, I would never let him join my company. I thought that every one capable of bearing arms should be in the army. Well, I am sorry that it occurred. Our company is now on picket duty; the skirmishers are "banging" away at each other without doing any material harm. The boys were glad to hear that Lieutenant McCullong is able to be around on crutches; hope it will not be long before he is entirely well. I wish you would ascertain who those boys are at the Lumpkin Hospital, and I will inform their officers where they are.

Johnnie and myself were called on this morning by General Vaughan to go out as far as we could. We left without our breakfast, we were so eager to get a sight of the blue coats. We went about three-quarters of a mile, till we came to a large open field, and behold yon sight on the skirt of the woods! We came across a large wagon train, and a large encampment of tents, belonging to the Yankees. Johnnie climbed a large tree and surveyed them, while I stood guard at the foot of it. When he came down, we wandered about in the woods a little while looking at the Yankee skirmishers, when we concluded to go back and report to the General. We then went back to the breast-works, and I was just beginning to eat my breakfast, when our company was ordered on picket.

The people are abandoning their houses between the lines as the Yankees approach. They will not come much further before a terrible retribution will overtake them, and they will be sorry for the misery they have caused our people. I would write more, but as paper is a very scarce article, and hard to get, I will endeavor to do the best I can. Johnnie, Freddy and Jimmie all join me in sending you our kind regards and well wishes. As I have not received any money for some time, I will have to frank this letter; I do not like to do it, but situated as we now are, I am compelled to. While I am writing I can hear the Yankees discoursing pleasant and beautiful music. If you see Gus Flotron, tell him to answer my letter, as I answered his immediately. Remember me to all the ladies of Covington. Hoping you will answer immediately on receipt, I remain, as ever,

Your true and devoted friend,

WILLIAM FAIRMAN.

Franklin, Tenn., May 2.

MRS. SMITH:

I received the sad news of the death of my son, Willie T. Bailey, company D, First Tennessee Regiment, who died at Hill Hospital, 28th of February. Will you be so kind as to have his grave marked, and keep the lock of hair for me till I send for his remains? Please to write me the disease he died with, and everything in regard to his death. Please to have his grave marked, and you will be remembered by an unhappy mother. It may be years before I can send. Have something substantial, so there will be no mistake, and you will be remembered. My kindest regards to the chaplain.

Yours truly,
LOUISA A. CRUMP.

Greensboro, Georgia, May 29, 1864.

ESTEEMED FRIEND:

Allow me to give you my thanks for your kind treatment to me while in Hill Hospital. I suppose you have often thought of me since I left your kind care. I never can forget your kind treatment. You may have forgotten the poor boy who had his left knee shattered to pieces, and who was under your kind care so long, but he will ever remember Mrs. Smith. We had a hard time going to Atlanta; we did not get anything to eat after we left you until we reached there, and we were nearly two days on the way. I suppose you have heard of poor Vick's death. I did not see him after we got to Atlanta, as I was put in one ward and he in another. I heard from him every day or two. He died about Christmas. I was furloughed on the 13th of January, and came here to my uncle's. I could not walk for several weeks after I came down here. I went up to Atlanta, and then down to Talbot. About six weeks ago, while on the cars, I heard from you. I came back a short time since, and I heard from you again in the same way. Nothing would afford me more pleasure than to read a letter from you. I will be glad to hear from you at any time that it would suit your convenience. If Peter Lolis is still with you, give him my best respects. Tell him I hear from the boys occasionally, but I will never be able to join them. I am crippled for life; but I will not murmur, for it is God's holy will.

If I ever get the chance while traveling on that road, I expect to stop and see you. Let me hear from you, my dear friend, as soon as possible. You have been my friend in affliction, and may a just God reward you.

Your true friend,

TIP. BLEDSOE.

Savannah, October, 1864.

RESPECTED FRIEND:

Having been permitted to look once more upon the face of an only and much loved brother, and to hear from his own lips of your many kindnesses to him, I embrace the opportunity to return to you my mother's and my own most sincere and heartfelt thanks. You who know a mother's love, and perhaps a sister's fond affection, must also know how profound the gratitude, and how weighty the obligation felt towards those who, in any way, benefit the objects of our heart's warmest feelings; but in this instance love has taken the place of gratitude, and I cannot feel that we are strangers.

Deprived by death of a father when but little more than a child, and left the sole protector of myself and invalid mother, he soon felt the responsibility, and became a man in all but years. Our whole affection centered on him; we indulged in fond anticipations, and knew that in all our trouble we had still much to be thankful for. Soon, however, we were called upon to yield our heart's best treasure to our country. We did so; and with agony indescribable we bade him go, and prayed that God would nerve his arm to assist in repelling the hostile force, that He would shield him in the day of battle, and raise up friends for him in the hour of need. Our prayer has been answered. You— a sister of mercy!—have been all that we could desire or deserve. Your hand it was which ministered to his every want : you have been friend, sister, mother—all. Sincerely I hope that the time may not be far distant when we may be able to prove the depth of our feelings; and though poor indeed the thanks that *we* can give, there is One above who will reward you. May God protect and defend you ; may your declining years be soothed and comforted by loving hearts and hands; and when your sun of life shall set, and your spirit wing its flight above this vale of tears, may descending angels meet and bear you to the throne of Him where all is joy and peace, is the prayer of

JOHNNIE'S MOTHER AND SISTER.

P. S. Please return our thanks, also, to Dr. Robertson for his kindness in allowing Johnnie to come home in this the hour of bereavement.

SALLIE.

———

City Hall Hospital, Macon, Georgia.
November 7, 1864.

MRS. SMITH :

Your kind and cheering epistle of the 3d ult. reached me this afternoon, and I hasten to reply, thus giving you repeated assurance of my deep regard and remembrance. I am sorry that I did not receive your first letter, thus missing a great treat; for I assure you it always gives me great pleasure to read your kind and pleasant letters. I am very pleasantly situated here; and among other privileges, I enjoy that of attending divine worship, and listening to sacred music. Sacred music, however, has a very depressing influence upon my spirits now, invariably moving me to tears; but I cannot help it, although I know it to be unmanly. Our little friend, M. L. Wood, of company D, One Hundred and Fifty-fourth Senior Tennessee Regiment, is here with me, acting as nurse in ward 2. He

sends you his kindest regards, and wishes to be remembered
in your next letter to me. He says he will write to you
next Tuesday or Wednesday and let you know all the
news. He is greatly improved in health, and is still suffering from the effects of his wound, but is able to be around,
and be of some service to himself and his country. I have
no news to send you now; everything is very quiet at
present. I heard to-day that our army was at Lebanon,
Tennessee, but I can't help treating it as a mere rumor,
although I receive it from very good authority. I have
not become acquainted with any ladies of this place yet,
but confine myself very closely to my duties, and my
leisure time I pass in reading surgery and my Bible. I
have just finished the Phædon of Plato. It is an admira-
ble work, and treats of the immortality of the soul. If
you have never read it, I would advise you by all means
to procure it, and read its splendid truths. Plato was a
sublime writer, and Addison in his Cato thus speaks of
him :

> Plato, thou reasonest well !
> Else, whence this pleasing hope, this fond desire,
> This longing after immortality ?
> Or whence this secret dread, and inward horror
> Of falling into nought ? Why shrinks the soul
> Back on herself and startles at destruction ?
> 'Tis the divinity that stirs within us ;
> 'Tis Heaven itself that points out an hereafter,
> And intimates eternity to man.

Dear grandma, there is some talk of either breaking up
this hospital or moving it further west. I don't know
which they will do, or how soon, and therefore I would
advise you, by all means, to write to me immediately on
receipt of this. Write me a long letter this time, and tell
me all your troubles, and probably I can assist you in finding consolation for them ; at any rate, the burden will be
lessened by sharing it with me. You know, dear grandma,
that I take a lively interest in your welfare and comfort,

and desire your happiness above all things, and why not make me the recipient of your troubles? If I can give you any consolation, I certainly will do so with pleasure. Be sure and write immediately, and tell me all.

"Blessed are they that mourn, for they shall be comforted." "Pray for us; for we trust we have a good conscience: in all things willing to live honestly." "That the trial of your faith, being much more precious than of gold that perisheth, though it be tried with fire, might be found unto praise, and honor, and glory, at the appearing of Jesus Christ."

I would write you much more, but I am writing this at night, and the gaslight hurts my eyes. I will now close, by wishing you all manner of happiness and peace.

Your devoted friend,
A. F. SAMUELS.

I open this letter to inform you that the hospital is to be broken up and the attendants disbanded. I do not know what disposition they will make of me. Wait until you hear from me again, before you write.

A. F. S.

Camp 18th Tennessee Regiment, near Dalton, Ga.,
March 8, 1864.

DEAR MOTHER SMITH:

Ever Kind and Respected Friend—I seat myself to write you a few lines. You wrote to me before I left Griffin, and as you have not written since, I suppose you did not receive my answer. I would have written again ere this, but I had come to the conclusion that you had moved elsewhere, as I never could hear from you. However, I will write again. I am in as fine health as I ever was in my life, and in fine spirits, for I think we will move before long to Middle Tennessee. If the Yanks don't make a better stand than they did at Tunnel Hill, I know we will. Our army is in the finest spirits I ever saw it in my life. Our Tennessee boys have all enlisted for the war, or lifetime—let it be long or short; and I believe the majority of the other States are doing the same thing. My kindest and best friend, you don't know how bad I want to see you. You are like a mother to me instead of a stranger, although I have not treated you as such; though if you will excuse me this time, I will promise to do better in the future. If I was only with you I could tell you a great many things that have transpired since I saw you, and you could interest me very much. You must write long letters, and often. I would write more, but I am certain I cannot interest you. If this letter reaches you, you must answer it immediately. As I can think of nothing of interest, I will close. Excuse my bad pen, bad spelled, bad written, and worse composed letter. Write soon, and remember one of your best friends.

JAMES R. MATHES.

Tuscumbia, Ala., November 12, 1864.

MRS. SMITH:

I received your last just before I left Decatur, and was very glad to hear from you, and to know that the Yankees did not hurt you. I saw Dr. Lee in Selma, Alabama, and he gave me an adiea how the blue coats behaved when they were in Covington. He did not tell me what became of Miss Conners and Miss Harper. I would like to know. Also, Mr. Norley, Betto and Josh, and what has become of that vagabond, Pete. He went off with the Yankees, I suspect. I forgot Mrs. Levey and Duncan. Grandma, I have seen some hard times since I returned to my com-

mand in trying to keep up with it. I find my leg is very
weak, and in marching all day it pains me very much; but
I cannot think of turning back, and miss going to Tennessee. The army is again in motion, after a rest of some
days; and probably by the time this is in your hands, we
will be near Nashville. Oh, I know that will make your
heart leap for joy, as well as the soldiers. I never saw an
army in better spirits—no grumbling, straggling, or anything of the kind. Our rations have been short, once, for
twenty-four hours, on account of bad, muddy roads. Our
clothes are good, and our teams in good order for the time
of year, and we have all the advantage of Sherman now.
He has not been able to give us any trouble since our army
left Atlanta. Thomas Phorris and Vaughan are with the
brigade, and join me in best wishes and love to you.
This leaves me in good health. Mrs. Gustine and Amos
wish to be remembered to you.

I am, as ever, your friend,

B. F. WILKS.

[Written for MRS. S. E. D. SMITH.]

GRANDMA:

May thou have health—and fortune, too—
And live to see this long war through.
Thou art so kind, and friendly, too,
That all the praise to thee is due.
Thou wilt thineself no doubt deny
The soldiers' wants to supply.
To comfort soldiers is thine heart's delight,
So on memory's page thou wilt shine so bright
That all who knew thee, while in pain
Will cast a smile to hear thy name.

JAMES LEVI PFLUGER,

Co. A, 5th Reg't Tenn. Vols.

In Line of Battle, near Chattahoochie River,
July 7, 1864.

MRS. SMITH:

Dear Friend—With pleasure I write you a few lines to inform you that I am well, and, thanks to kind Providence, been permitted to pass through this campaign, so far, with only a slight bruise. This is sixty-one days since we left Dalton and formed our line of battle, and since that there has not been a day that we have been out of hearing of small arms, and only about two days that we were not exposed to fire. You have long since heard of our fight at Dalton, and the heavy loss we sustained there. My company has suffered severely. We have had four killed and twelve wounded; every officer lost—two killed and one wounded. We have eleven men for duty out of thirty-one who left Dalton; some of them are prisoners of war. I wrote to you about three weeks ago. I received the articles you sent me by Sergeant Smith, and I assure you they were very acceptable, and I am under many obligations to you for them. Your kindness will never be forgotten. I hope that at some future time I will be permitted to thank you for the kindness you have always shown me. All is quiet along the line, with the exception of the usual picket firing. We have a splended position, well fortified, and feel confident that we can hold it. The spirits of the army are fine, the discipline good, and all are ready for fight. I would like, if I had the material, to write you a full account of our operations since we left Dalton; probably it would interest you. Write soon, and give me all the news. Excuse all mistakes, and I will try to do better next time.

Your friend,

D. S. HERAN.

Greensboro, Ga., August 20, 1864.

MRS. SMITH :

Dear Friend—Your letter, be assured, was a welcome visitor to me. Any demonstration of kind remembrance is cheering to the wounded, suffering soldier—particularly to one cut off from his home ; consequently, yours was to me peculiarly so. In some respects my health is somewhat improved to what it was while you were here—*i. e.*, I have not had a chill in a week, and I am clear of fever. I hope the gangrene is entirely killed, for it has progressed until the artery is exposed, and a very little more will endanger my leg. The doctor, however, says that all I lack now is an appetite, which it seems hard to regain. Miss Conner has not been here since you left. She promised to come and bring me something that I could eat. I have written her this morning, and hope that ere long she will fulfill her promise. I would like very much to be with you, and unless some unforeseen trouble, I hope to be able to travel in the course of three or four weeks, and intend coming to you. Ask Dr. Robertson to please have a tent erected for my special benefit. I am sorry, grandma, that I am not a christian, and I would be one if I knew how. Since my late afflictions, I have thought more seriously and felt more earnestly on the importance of the subject than I have since the days of my childhood and youth, and I feel no disposition to resist those impressions as heretofore.

You will be very busy I know, but I should be glad if you could steal a few moments and write to me occasionally. Mr. Wells sends his respects to you. I shall always be happy to hear from you. Write whenever you can.

Affectionately, your friend,

B. P. NANCE.

MRS. S. E. D. SMITH:

Though youth and beauty are blighted, and though old age is creeping over thy honored brow, yet there is a strong attraction of filial affection for thy parental love and care impressed on my heart that time and change cannot efface.   JOE F. HARPER,
                    Company H, 9th Tennessee Regiment.

———

Near Atlanta, July 23, 1864.

MRS. S. E. D. SMITH:

Highly Honored Friend—Your kind and highly interesting letter of the 13th ultimo was handed to me this morning by one of our boys who was wounded in the charge yesterday. I have been very busy dressing the wounded, and have not had time to answer it before now; and as it is almost dark, I cannot promise to write you a long letter this time. Our regiment was badly cut up, a great many of the boys were killed and wounded. Gus Flotron and Freddy Brinkman were seriously wounded, and I greatly fear that Gus will die. They were wounded in the charge made yesterday. I suppose that you have heard that I am now staying at the Division Hospital, where I can do a great deal more good than in charging Yankee breastworks. I could not stand the hardships of the campaign, and my health is completely prostrated. I expect to be ordered on duty in some of the hospitals shortly, and I should be only too happy to come to you, and remain with you until the termination of this unholy war. I feel that my proper sphere is not to inflict, but to relieve human suffering, and I long to be in a position where I can exercise my vocation to good purpose. It is getting too dark to write any more, and I will now close, by bidding you God speed.   Your devoted friend,
                    A. F. SAMUELS.

One and a half Miles from Atlanta, Ga.,
July 24, 1864.

Dear Friend—I resume my pen this morning, if for no other reason than to avoid sending you a blank sheet. I always dislike receiving a blank sheet, it looks to me unfriendly. Freddy Brinkman and Gus Flotron were both dying when I saw them last. This makes two more brave and noble spirits that our company have to mourn. We left Dalton with thirty-six; thirteen of those have been wounded, and eight killed—twenty-one in all. But I hope they have taken their flight to a better world, "where the wicked cease from troubling, and the weary are at rest." I am fearful that the sad scenes which I have passed through in this war will leave a cloud upon my spirits for the rest of my life; but I hope that it has been the means of bringing me into the ark of safety. It has taught me to place my trust in God alone, and to read and love His Holy Word. Who then can say that it has not been a real blessing to me? You have doubtless heard of poor Conner's death. I was with him when he breathed his last. We conversed earnestly for a long time, and I cannot help remarking one expression that fell from his lips a short time before he died. Taking hold of my hand, he uttered in a very peculiar and solemn tone, "Doc, this is the last campaign." God grant his words may prove true.

The roar of cannon and rattle of musketry are dinning in my ears as I write, and from my very heart I utter a fervent prayer to God to spare the few friends that I have left. Alas, how few in number! I almost feel desolate.

Your earnest friend,
A. F. SAMUELS.

On Picket Duty, seven miles from Marietta, Ga.,
June 7, 1864.

MRS. SUSAN E. SMITH:

My valued Friend—Your kind and cheering missive
of the 4th ult. has come duly to hand, and the contents
were eagerly perused, being the first letter I had received
from any of my friends since leaving Dalton. For the
kind wishes expressed therein I return my earnest and
heartfelt thanks; for the good opinion you have of the
regiment, I return you thanks in the name of the regiment. We removed from our position near New Hope
Church a few days since, and marched all night, through
mud actually knee-deep, as the appearance of the company will bear witness. We arrived at our position in
line about ten o'clock A. M. yesterday, and after resting a
few hours, girded on our armor and took our line of march
for the picket post, where we arrived yesterday afternoon
We are still here, and our videttes are thrown out in front,
and we are calmly awaiting the approach of Mr. Lincoln's
"army people." They, however, seem to be in no particular hurry to advance, as no one here has seen or heard of a
Yankee since we've been here. There is plenty of fresh
pork running about here, and the boys are eating it to keep
it from the Yankees. I think they are perfectly right in
doing so. The rations that we draw are just sufficient to
keep us from starving, but I assure you they never appease
our appetite, and the sight of a full meal, such as we used
to have at home, would astonish us out of our boots (or
shoes). We have some faint recollection of eating good
things in times past, but we have almost forgotten how
they looked or tasted. I should like above all things to pay
a visit to Covington, and mingle in the interesting society
that you mention; but I am afraid (unless I should get
wounded) that it will be a long time before I am permitted

to enjoy that blessing. I am enjoying excellent health, and so far have escaped without a scratch, for which blessing I return my humble thanks to Almighty God, and pray that He may still continue to guard and protect me as He has done through my whole life. Write me soon. You can't imagine what a boon it is to receive a letter from a friend, surrounded as I am by the insipid dullness of a camp life. Hoping soon to write you more interesting news, I remain

Your true friend,

A. F. SAMUELS,

Company D, 154th Senior Tenn.

Department Head-Quarters,

Demopolis, Ala., March 17, 1864.

MRS. SMITH:

My Dear Friend — It is now more than six weeks since I addressed my last missive to you; but, as yet, I have not received any answer, and that, through the irregularity of the mails, you have never received my message, I thought I had better write again, especially as I have a few moments to spare, which I could not spend more pleasantly than in communion with such a kind friend as you have always been to me, and to the Southern soldiers generally. Yes, my dear friend, I am only one among the many who have cause to invoke God's manifold blessings upon you and yours; and I am convinced that you are the theme of many conversations around the camp-fires of our braves in the field; and many a heart that beats for our cause, beats also in gratitude for the kindness you have done its possessor when wounded or sick, and in need of such a ministering angel as you have proved yourself. Poor Gus Flotron, I am sure, owes his life to your care and nursing—one out of many

M

other similar cases. How is he getting on? I hope he has recovered from his last wound. Remember me kindly to him, and ask him to let me hear from him some time.

I had the pleasure of seeing all the boys of the 154th, not long ago. John W., and all of the Zouaves, looked well, and were in excellent spirits. The whole of Cheatham's Division came up and serenaded the General, who made them a little speech. The boys went away very much pleased, but sorry that they could not remain with us longer. They had a dinner given them at Selma by Captain Shirley, and were treated well everywhere. They have made quite a name for themselves by their gallantry at Missionary Ridge, and setting the example of re-enlisting. Tennesseeans stand high among the patriotic citizens of the Confederacy, and I hope the people will not run them down again, and endeavor to make a stain on her fair escutcheon, as they did not long ago.

I have not heard from Memphis since I last wrote to you, and am anxiously awaiting some news from home. God grant that it may be good when it does come. I have written several letters to Memphis, and among them I am sure several reached their destination. When I hear from home I shall inform you, as you have taken so kind an interest in me and mine.

The weather has been very disagreeable of late, and I have kept close to the fire. The prospect for to-morrow, however, seems better, and I hope I am not mistaken.

My love to Mr. Smith—and to James when you next write to him, and accept the same for yourself, from

Your true friend,

FRED G. GUTHERS.

P. S. Excuse this badly written epistle. I will try and do better the next time. "Writ it is;" would it were worthier.   F. G. G.

Talladega, Ala., April 6, 1864.

MRS. S. E. D. SMITH:

My Dear Friend—Here I am, in a very much out of the way place, on duty as an engineer. I think I told you, in my last from Demopolis, that I had been transferred to the Engineer Department; and, as you see, they have already placed me in active service, in this, my new capacity, and I must say that I like it very much, and hope to give full satisfaction to my commanding officer; and if I should fail in that, I shall be sure that it will not be because I was unwilling, and did not do everything to the best of my knowledge and ability.

I have been in this place several days, awaiting further orders from Captain Morris, my new Chief, and must confess that I am getting anxious to hear from him, as he left me here entirely by myself; but I can only obey, and await further instructions in the intervening time. I pass my time looking at the "fair and fascinating sex" who pass to and fro on the streets of Talladega, the "Classic City," and bloody ground of some Indian battle, as I am told.

I had the pleasure of meeting Mr. Barbier, now Major Barbier, of Memphis. He commands the Post, and is enrolling officer of conscripts in the District. He is a very clever gentleman. Probably you remember him in Memphis. He was connected with a newspaper there. A few months ago he was up near Memphis, and brought his sister out with him. She is now here, with the balance of his family, adding one more to the innumerable names of exiles and refugees from our gallant old Tennessee.

When I last wrote to you I promised to write you a long letter, but I am afraid that I cannot be good to my promise, as I am really at a loss what to write, there being nothing new here, excepting the good weather we are having to-day, and I must confess that I have not seen such a beautiful day for a long time, and I would say that Spring has set in in good earnest were I not afraid of committing myself for the twentieth time; however, it has not set in this time. I am sure the day is not far distant when everything will bloom, and the earth will be again robed in the mantle of green, spring birds rejoicing, bees storing away their sweet subsistence, and everything cheerful and happy. No! I take that back; for how can a mother be happy when this fair young Spring will only reopen new operations, and the flowers and grass be trodden down by the step of armed men and hostile armies, their beautiful colors soiled by the blood of a much beloved son or husband? How can there be happiness when the destroying angel is hovering over the land, devastating everything that lies in his path—here driving the aged and young innocence from their burning homes—there destroying beautiful fields of grain, etc., that hitherto yielded abundance and plenty, and supplied the boards of many happy homes? How can there be the smallest spark of happiness with all these sad truths staring us in the face at every turn of the road—at every single thought and glance? But I have dwelled sufficiently long upon these things. Would to God every one would look about him, and think of these things, and relieve where they are able; how much misery, how much anguish, would be saved and relieved. God grant that the hearts of those people who have not suffered as much may be opened to the charity that is even knocking at their more tender feelings.

I expect to be ordered to proceed to Dalton and Rome, Ga., and then I will see all the boys again. I should like to see them very much; and, if possible, I will pay you a visit, which would be the greatest of pleasure I know of at present; but I am again at my castle building, which I have long since found not to be the most profitable business, and you must not expect me until you see me stepping into the door.

I have not heard from home since I last wrote to you, but hope that everything is all right. I have never seen your son, and expect that he did not come by Demopolis, or I should have seen him on his return.

My kindest regards to your husband and Gus Flotron. I should like very much to see Gus. You may tell him that I say he had better be careful how he is flirting with the girls, as this is leap year, and the first thing he knows he will have his heart gone—who knows where? Tell him to find me a nice sweetheart, as I believe I will not be able to find one myself, having failed thus far in all of my efforts.

Farewell, old friend! I have succeeded in drawing out my letter so as to make it appear " some pumpkins," but, alas, it is nothing. Would it were worthier. Let me hear from you soon, and think kindly of

Your true friend.
FRED G. GUTHERS.

P. S. Address my letters to Demopolis.

———

Stout Hospital,
Milledgeville, Ga., Feb. 24, 1865.

My Dear Grandma—Once more am I permitted, by the kind hand of Providence, to pen you a few lines to let you hear from me.

On the 4th of this month, coming to this place, the cars ran off the track, and I was made one of the sufferers among many others of the Texas boys. Uncle Jimmey Rainey's son was so badly bruised that he died on the 21st of this month, and two others have died, and several are

M*

in their beds from injuries received.   One lost his leg, and
is maimed for life.   As to myself, I can get around the
house, though I am badly bruised.   I would have written
to you long before this, but Mr. Burrill told me that the
Grampkin Hospital was broken up, and that he did not
know what had become of you.   I met with a little Ken-
tuckian here, by the name of Mills, who told me that you
was at the Hill, so I concluded to drop you a few lines to
let you know that I had not forgotten you, nor will I ever
do so as long as I live.

I wrote from Natasralga, Ala., and sent you a letter
from my dear sister ; and in the letter I made a request
of you, but was compelled to leave in a few days, so I did
not get your answer.   Let me know if you receive this
letter.   I have only received the note by Mr. Burrill since
I left the hospital.   I am very anxious to hear from you :
and if you can comply with my request, you will oblige
your Texas friend, Bobbie.

One of my brigade, who was left at the hospital when I
left, said that several letters came for me, and were sent
on to my command, while it was in Tennessee, and that
all of the mails that were sent to us, while we were up
there, were lost ; the Yanks got one, and the bushwhackers
got the other ; so, if you wrote, that was the way they
went.

I went all through the Tennessee campaign, and I tell
you that I saw some hard times, and then to get nearly
killed on an old car, is rather disheartening.   I could tell
you a great deal if I could see you.   I am very weak, and
can write but little.

I asked the doctor for a furlough to go and see you and
the Misses Conners, and he said that there was no chance
for a Texian to get a furlough.   So, if I can get a blank,
I will go and see the Misses Conners anyhow, as I want
to get my clothes.   I have been without socks all this

winter, and while I was in Tennessee I suffered very much.

Oh, Grandma! I do wish that I could get a furlough, so that I could visit you, for you have been like a mother to me; and when I write to my dear sister I always tell her that I have a friend and a mother here; and sister wrote you a nice letter, tendering you many thanks, indeed; and if you did not get the letter, I am very sorry.

When I got here, the first thing I tried to get was a transfer, and the surgeon in charge told me that he would not transfer any patients, as it was against orders.

Poor Ogle Love was killed at the battle of Franklin, and McHenry was taken prisoner, so I believe that I am the only one of the old rats who is left.

Dr. Doyle is at this hospital; and Mr. Lane is also here. This is a poor place. I have seen the matron some four or five times since I have been here, and think she is of the Mrs. Ellis stripe—only for the doctors to play with. She does not do like old Grandma.

No news worth writing. Doyle is very friendly with me. I was not in his ward. I was under the treatment of Dr. Gockhart.

Hoping to hear from you soon, I will close. Let me know if the Misses Conners are at Warrington or at Covington.

My love to your husband, and remember me in your prayers, is my honest request.

Your true friend until death,

R. D. COMPTON.

Hill Hospital, Feb. 26, 1865.

Many thanks to Mrs. Smith for the nice present sent me, with many assurances of the highest esteem; and also my best wishes for her happiness and prosperity. I shall keep it as a memento of my true, tried and constant, friend; and when I smoke the pipe of peace over a redeemed and disenthralled nation, I promise to remember kindly one who assisted me so faithfully in administering to the wants of the suffering, but gallant soldiers who have been under my care whilst in charge of Hill Hospital. With sincere regard, I am, as ever,

Your true friend,

W. H. ROBERTSON,
Surgeon P. A. C. S.

———

Nottaway County, Va., January 7, 1866.

My Dear Old Friend—You have no idea how gratifying your kind letter was to me, and how I appreciate the kind feeling you have for me. You are well aware that it is fully reciprocated, as I esteem you always for your generous heart, your true patriotism, your high sense of honor, and last, though not least, for your indefatigable efforts in behalf of the suffering soldiers. Your assistance in the arduous duties of the hospital was a source of very great sasisfaction, and I shall always remember you, and feel grateful to think that I merited your friendship. I am now living two miles from the junction of the Richmond and Danville railroad with the South Side. This point is fifty miles south of Petersburg and Richmond. In consequence of the liberation of the slaves, and the losses I sustained from the destruction of Confederate notes, I am unable to live in Petersburg for the present; but hope to move to some city before very long, as the country practice is both laborious and unprofitable. You must have encountered many difficulties in reaching your home, and I congratulate you on your safe arrival and the safety of your son. I sm sure Mrs. Mughs made the hospital pay her for the disappointment she suffered at not getting your place. I found great difficulty in getting to Virginia, and remained sometime at Gov. Pickens' after the surrender. I found my dear family quite well, though they suffered very severe losses. My five little ones are very fair specimens, in fine health, and a great help to us in these troublous times. I have heard from none of our Georgia friends, with the exception of Mrs. Luckie, who asked me to see after her husband's grave, which I did, and have written to her to-day. I wrote to Nichol a few days since, which makes the second letter without receiving any reply. I do not know what has become of Clay, not hearing from him since leaving Cuthbert. I would like to meet all of my old friends again; but, alas, we can never meet again on earth. I need not tell you anything of the times, for we are all sufferers together. Give my kind regards to Mr. Smith and your son. Beck, my wife, desires to be remembered to you. If you ever visit Virginia, be assured you will always find a cordial welcome at my house. I would like so much to have a social chat with you to-night, and fancy I can see you sitting near your fire in your neatly kept rooms with your pipe, and your friends around you; or, else I can picture you going from tent to tent dispensing charity to the poor wounded soldiers. God will reward you for this, and many a noble spirit will bless you through all time. Write soon. May your life be prosperous and happy, and God bless you, is the sincere wish of

Your friend,
WM. H. ROBERTSON.

Nottaway, May 4, 1866.

My Dear Old Friend—Your favor of the 25th of April reached me safely, and, as usual, gave me unfeigned pleas-

ure, for I feel a very deep interest in your future welfare
and happiness, and can always remember your generous
ovations in contributing so cheerfully, and with such untiring energy, to the comfort of the poor wounded soldiers;
and I myself can never forget your kindness to me when
a soldier, and far away from friends and home. If I cheered
you on in the discharge of your laborious duties when
matron chief of Hill Hospital, I was fully compensated
by your assiduity and tender, motherly concern for the
poor wounded soldiers while I was surgeon in charge.
And though our section is downtrodden and oppressed,
though poverty with its thousand thorns pricks us, even in
this dark hour of Southern degradation and Southern
ruin, it is consolatory to us all to feel that we have discharged our duty. My youngest child has been very ill
with pneumonia, but I am thankful to say is much better.
We are getting on, but have suffered many privations. My
practice is extensive, but the people have no money. I am
pleased to hear that you are succeeding, and hope that you
may yet reap a golden harvest for your kindness in this
life, and reap a richer reward in that far off but happy
land, where the faithful are beatified. I would like so
much to see you and hear you talk to night, and see you
enjoying your pipe after the arduous duties of the day.
But hope ere long, when I make a big fortune again, to
visit Nashville, and of course I will be your guest. Nichol
is a lazy fellow, and has never written me a line in response
to my letters, save in a business way. I wish him great
success in life, and always esteemed him as a kind friend.
I received a letter from Clay. Some two months ago he
was in Cuthbert, and loving Miss Smith very much indeed.
He told me he had made a profession of religion, and was
rejoicing in the hope of a brighter and happier home beyond
the skies. You mentioned in a former communication that
you intended writing a journal, or a brief history of your

four years' service in the army. I think it would be interesting, as well as instructive. If I can be of any service
to you, I need not tell you that it will be a source of gratifi-
cation to contribute in any way. I read the extract sent
by you in regard to the ruin of a poor, unfortunate woman
from Virginia. I have no idea who she can be, as nothing
in regard to it has appeared in the Virginia newspapers.
She is said to be (as I see from the statement forwarded)
from the county of B. It must be either Bedford, Belle-
wood, or Buckley—the latter in Northwestern Virginia,
the two former in the Southwestern portion of the State. I
pity her, and contemn the wretch who effected her ruin.
My wife unites with me in kind regards. Remember me
kindly to Smith and your son; also, to Nichol and family.
Write soon. May God bless you, is the sincere wish of

> Your friend,
> WM. H. ROBERTSON.

Department Head-Quarters,
Meridian, Miss., Feb. 3, 1864.

MRS. S. E. D. SMITH:

My Dear Friend—Your highly welcome and interesting
missive of the 26th ult., was received last night, and I
now hasten to answer it.

You write truly, my dear friend, when you say that I may
be thankful to the Almighty Father on high for granting
me the great pleasure of seeing my dear old mother
again; and I really feel that his kindness towards me so
far can never be fully repaid. I am also very glad to hear
of the conduct of the old 154th, and I assure you my
heart leaped within me when the news reached me that
they had taken the lead, and set the example to all other
States, who, I am gratified to see, are now following suit.

Old Tennessee is still the old Volunteer State, and can hold its head high among its sister States. I have also heard of the gallant conduct of the Old Division, (Cheatham's,) at the disastrous battle of Missionary Ridge, and I may well be proud to count myself as belonging to it. Though detached at present, yet I have never refused to comply with the calls of duty, and have endeavored to do it to the best of my ability and knowledge wherever I was placed ; but this sounds too much like self praise, and I must drop the subject.

I am glad to hear that Gus Flotron is getting on so well. I should like to see him very much. He is a gallant soldier, and a good-hearted fellow. Please give him my very best regards, and also to your son James, and Johnny Waynsburg, when you next write to them.

This is a very dull place, nothing going on.

General Forrest, I think, is up in West Tennessee again. The Yankees, I believe, will soon make a demonstration on this part of the country via Vicksburg ; but old General Polk is not asleep, but ready for them.

I am going to Mobile with the General to-night, and may stay there a few days. Do you not think that I have a fine time of it ? I am satisfied and content. My love to your husband ; and hoping to hear from you soon, I remain, as ever,

Your true friend,

FRED G. GUTHERS.

www.ingramcontent.com/pod-product-compliance
Lightning Source LLC
Chambersburg PA
CBHW021038030726
47496CB00006B/1587